Follow My Lead

KATE NOBLE

BERKLEY SENSATION, NEW YORK

THE BERKLEY PUBLISHING GROUP
Published by the Penguin Group
Penguin Group (USA) Inc.
375 Hudson Street, New York, New York 10014, USA
Penguin Group (Canada), 90 Eglinton Avenue East, Suite 700, Toronto, Ontario M4P 2Y3, Canada
(a division of Pearson Penguin Canada Inc.)
Penguin Books Ltd., 80 Strand, London WC2R 0RL, England
Penguin Group Ireland, 25 St. Stephen's Green, Dublin 2, Ireland (a division of Penguin Books Ltd.)
Penguin Group (Australia), 250 Camberwell Road, Camberwell, Victoria 3124, Australia
(a division of Pearson Australia Group Pty. Ltd.)
Penguin Books India Pvt. Ltd., 11 Community Centre, Panchsheel Park, New Delhi—110 017, India
Penguin Group (NZ), 67 Apollo Drive, Rosedale, Auckland 0632, New Zealand
(a division of Pearson New Zealand Ltd.)
Penguin Books (South Africa) (Pty.) Ltd., 24 Sturdee Avenue, Rosebank, Johannesburg 2196,
South Africa

Penguin Books Ltd., Registered Offices: 80 Strand, London WC2R 0RL, England

FOLLOW MY LEAD

A Berkley Sensation Book / published by arrangement with the author

PRINTING HISTORY
Berkley Sensation mass-market edition / May 2011

Copyright © 2011 by Kate Noble.
Excerpt from *If I Fall* by Kate Noble copyright © by Kate Noble.
Front cover art by Aleta Rafton.
Back cover photograph by Shutterstock.
Cover design by George Long.
Interior text design by Kristin del Rosario.

ISBN: 978-0-425-24151-6

BERKLEY® SENSATION
Berkley Sensation Books are published by The Berkley Publishing Group,
a division of Penguin Group (USA) Inc.,
375 Hudson Street, New York, New York 10014.
BERKLEY® SENSATION and the "B" design are trademarks of Penguin Group (USA) Inc.

PRINTED IN THE UNITED STATES OF AMERICA

10 9 8 7 6 5 4 3 2 1

To Harrison,
for Super Adventure Time.

Prologue

A Letter from a Sister to Her Brother:

April 25, 1821

Dear Jason—

I am afraid I have to disappoint you yet again, and break my promise. I cannot come to London this year. And as you are likely able to guess, the reason is much the same as last year when I could not travel south and join you in town: I find myself expecting again. You have probably thrown your hands in the air at this juncture and exclaimed, "Again?!? Little Anna is not even a year old!" My reaction was similar. Byrne, of course, accepts his culpability in this unfortunate state of affairs—however, without any sign of remorse I could decipher.

If you decide to postpone until I can join you next year, no one will think the worse of you. Men are given far more leeway in this area than we of the fairer sex. Consider, Father did not marry Mother until he was nearly forty! Surely you are too young. Besides, I would feel much better knowing you were not to face the hordes of marriageable women without some guidance. They can be vultures, and you—baby-faced, not yet thirty, titled—are prime meat. I know, because I was once one of them. Perhaps you should come up to the lake this summer. I'm certain Anna would love a visit from her favorite uncle (being as you are the uncle who introduced her to marzipan, you absolute rotter). And Byrne says Mr. Johnston at the Oddsfellow Arms keeps a bar stool open for you . . . and a spot in the mud out front for when you decide to fall flat on your face.

Yours, etc.
Jane

☙

A Letter in Response from a Brother to His Sister:

May 1, 1821

Dear Jane—

I object to a number of items in your last letter, in the following order:

1. *Twenty-nine is an excellent age for a man to marry.*
2. *I am not baby-faced. Red hair simply doesn't grow as visibly on the chin as dark. (As you should know— didn't you have a slight mustache in your formative years?) I promise you, my valet grumbles every morning when he takes a blade to my jaw.*
3. *I am not a piece of meat, meant to be weighed, mea-*

sured, and purchased. I believe in the horrific, cut-throat world of metropolitan marriage machinations that you have concocted in your head, the young ladies in question would be the meat for choosing, not I.

4. *I believe I will be able to handle what is bound to be a fairly easy decision. I'll be fine without you.*

5. *So I bribed your daughter with sweets to like me. It was not difficult; she was far too innocent and susceptible. I merely succeeded as an uncle, whereas you have failed as a parent. I win.*

As for Mr. Johnston and his bar stool—FOR GOD'S SAKE, THAT WAS FIVE YEARS AGO.

Yours, etc.
Jason

❧

A Letter in Response to the Response to the Letter from a Sister to Her Brother:

May 17, 1821

Dear Jason—

You may think that I am callous and cruel, and that I do not know that you are very much your own man, allergic to coddling. I know you well enough to realize that since you have set your mind on this path, you will not alter. And of course I admire your determination to do this on your own (something you attempt all too rarely). But since you have long avoided the Season and its high-minded trappings, you must be forewarned: You are not seeking these women. You are the prey. Hunted. Stalked. Soft flesh to be pulled from the bone in easy strips, marinated, roasted, and served up in golden foils. (You must forgive me the imagery in the preceding sentence. Byrne remarks that my condition makes me terribly carnivorous.) That said, the invitation to the lake is always open, should you change your mind. I will even refrain from saying "I told you so," should occasion call for it.

Yours, etc.
Jane

P.S. I did not and do not have a mustache. But if you can compare your beard to a clean-faced woman, I doubt your valet grumbles about the hard work—more, its lack of necessity.

A Letter from a Brother to His Sister, in Angry, Protesting Tones:

May 24, 1821

Jane—

I am purposely ignoring your jab at my rare attempts at responsibility (and my beard, which I may grow out just to spite you) if only because I have to meet with the estate stewards, who wish me to sign off on many ducal things, which you would simply not understand. But only after this morning's session of the House of Lords. My secretaries tell me it is a terribly important vote. (Although how corn can constitute legislation, I have no idea.) So, as you see, if I am able to manage the rigors of a dukedom, surely I can manage to pluck a bride from the petticoated masses.

Yours, etc.
Jason

๛

**A Piece of News Taken from the Pages of a
Particularly Well-Read and Influential Scandal
Sheet:**

May 25, 1821

An uproarious fracas occurred last night at the home
of Mr. and Mrs. R— as they presented their youngest
daughter to society in a tragically average fete . . . average, that is, except for the Locking of the Duke.

Lord C—, Duke of an ancient estate and impeccable
lineage, and undisputedly the most sought-after potential husband in England, was found locked in a storage
room in the cellar of Mr. R—'s house in St. James, with
not one, not two, but three young debutantes!

Upon their rescue, the Duke's countenance vacil-
lated between blanched horror and utter relief as each
of the three girls claimed the Duke had been caught in
a compromising situation with her, and therefore they
must marry. Luckily, logic was provided by one of the
assembled bystanders: a young Miss F—, whose debutante status belies a sound and reasoning mind. She
deftly pointed out that Lord C—had compromised none
of them, as they each had provided chaperonage for the
others, and unless two of the girls were willing to testify
that something inappropriate had occurred with the remaining miss, no impropriety could be claimed beyond
the discovery of sadly rusted and sticky doorknobs. As
the grasping girls squabbled over which of them would
claim compromise, and claim the Duke (and his enormous fortune) in turn, their story fell apart, and the
lucky man was afforded the narrowest of all possible
social escapes.

Unsurprisingly, the Duke's carriage was spied on the
north road out of town early this morning. The author

cannot blame him. Three shrill debutantes are enough to drive your average man insane—let us be thankful that our Duke merely drives to the country.

A Letter from a Brother to His Sister:

May 26, 1821

Dear Jane—

I feel I may have acted rashly in refusing your invitation to visit, and as such, have decided to remedy my mistake. Immediately . . .
And don't you dare say, "I told you so."

A Letter from a Sister to Her Brother:

Jase—

Never fear. I shan't say, "I told you so." I'll let Byrne do it.

Jane

One

*Wherein our hero must
confront his truest fear.*

May 1822

THIRTY is an excellent age for a man to marry. It is a nice round number. A number that, when read in the papers in a wedding announcement, seems neither too old nor too young, and yet at the same time, a declaration of adulthood and intelligence. Thus, Lord Jason Cummings, Marquis of Vessey, and more recently, the Duke of Rayne, was determined to do it. Marry, that is. At the round, sensible age of thirty.

Granted, he had determined something similar last year, at the not round, but prime and robust, nine and twenty. A mature age—an age at which men slough off the last of their youth and embrace their futures. And marriage is a strong way to declare that intention. After all, most of his friends had already gotten married. His best friend from school, Nevill Quincy-Frosham, was the last person he ever expected to fall into the parson's trap, being as Nevill was without a doubt the most irresponsible human being in all of Britain, second only perhaps to his brother Charles. But, somehow, Nevill had been hitched to a smart little heiress since the previous winter. She controlled the purse strings and allotted the brandy, and Nevill, confoundingly, couldn't be happier. Charles, too, had managed to find a young lady willing to look past his puppyish demeanor and marry him. So, last year, Jason had determined to find a bride in that annual exercise in buying, selling, and trading known as the Season.

Oh, that wasn't fair. Jason was not that cynical. At least, he hadn't been until last Season, when at the still far-too-young-to-be-married age of nine and twenty he had been hunted, stalked, giggled at, and swooned over by the far too eager baby-faced debutantes with claws like steel and mothers with the beady eyes of vultures.

Jason was aware enough of his own attributes, good and bad, to know he was not the type that women swooned over.

Then again, he was a Duke. A young Duke, and perhaps, a manageably good-looking one—despite the curse of his red hair. And as a Duke, he knew the lack of marriageable Dukes in England made him a rare breed, red hair and lack of swoonable attributes or no. He'd fully expected his entrance on the marriage mart to be met with a certain amount of interest.

Interest. That was an understatement.

Jason had spent years avoiding the tepid affairs of Almack's, coming-out balls, tea and cards, and droning musicales that made up "good" society. He'd expected to be bored. And he was. But he had not expected to be bored and, simultaneously, scared out of his wits.

The plan to marry at twenty-nine died a quick death when he found himself locked in a cellar with three of the most frightening creatures he had ever encountered: Miss Rollins, Miss Quigley, and Miss Halloway.

And now, he found himself seriously questioning the wisdom to marry at the age of thirty, seeing as he was cornered by the same Miss Rollins, Miss Quigley, and Miss Halloway at Phillippa Worth's garden party.

"Ladies, please!" he exclaimed, stopping their overlapping dialogue—that seemed to be aimed at him, but damned if he could tell what they were talking about. "It's so . . . *interesting* to see you all again."

All three smiled at that, blushing and waving their fans in what he supposed was meant to be alluring fashion, but Miss Rollins employed hers a little too vigorously, smacking Miss Quigley's rather too languid fan into a nearby shrub. While a horrified Miss Quigley gave up her position to root around the shrubbery for the missing fan, Misses Rollins and Halloway closed ranks.

"And we were so pleasantly surprised to see you again, Your Grace!" Miss Rollins said, while Miss Halloway nodded brightly. Miss Rollins eyed her friend and competition, and took a predatory half step nearer to Jason. "It must be fate, Your Grace. Destiny. To think, my father did not even think I should have a season this year, and yet we run into you at our first garden party!"

Just breathe, Jason thought to himself. He was, at least, in a better position than the last time Miss Rollins and her friends had cornered him. First of all, they were outside. In daylight. In full view of dozens of other garden party attendees. They couldn't possibly lock him in anywhere.

But on the other hand, Phillippa Worth's garden did boast a number of scenic alcoves and trees with low-hanging branches. And an even larger number of zoologically trimmed topiary that could shield one from the eyes of other party-goers. In fact, if Jason wasn't mistaken, Miss Rollins was angling him toward an oversized rabbit-shaped shrub now. Each inching step of hers, causing an inching back of his. By now, Miss Quigley had rejoined the group, flanking Miss Halloway, the three of them looking for all the world like a brigade of troops rounding up the last resister.

"Ladies," Jason said, thinking quickly, "have any of you partaken of the refreshments yet?" He eyed the refreshments table, surrounded by other people, *sane* people, shrinking into the distance with every minced step backward. "I would be more than happy to fetch a cup of tea or punch . . ."

"Oh!" Miss Halloway fluttered. "I would love a—" But she was cut off by Miss Rollins's elbow to her solar plexus. "But Sissy—a *Duke* was going to fetch me punch!"

One sharp look from Miss Rollins told Miss Halloway to hold her tongue. Then she turned her intense stare back to Jason, the feigned sweetness doing nothing to mask that young lady's intensity. "Now, now, Clarissa—we wouldn't want the Duke to overly exert himself. After all, he's so very popular, if he wandered away, he'd likely be held up, dare I say assaulted, by any number of other people."

Well there goes that idea, Jason thought ruefully.

"Never fear, Your Grace," Miss Rollins ventured, being so forward as to put her hand on his arm and pat it reassuringly. "We will keep you safe."

So. This is hell, Jason thought. A garden party, being backed into a corner by three of the most baldly opportunistic furies to have been formed in the British system of wealth and aristocracy. Who knew?

Just as Jason was panicking his way to an escape plan, and judging that his best bet would be jumping the low hedge by the south wall, he was rescued.

By someone who would never let him live this down.

"Miss Rollins, Miss Halloway, Miss Quigley," Jane, Jason's sister, cried brightly as she swept to his side, practically knocking him over as she attached herself to his arm—and gracefully removing said arm from the claws of Miss Rollins at the same time.

"Lady Jane," the three misses mumbled as they dipped into curtsies.

"So . . . interesting to see you here!" Jane smiled through her teeth. Jason thought that perhaps Jane was in some danger of amputating his arm, she squeezed it so hard as she forced herself to maintain a pleasant expression. "Jason, I've been searching all over for you!" Then, to the girls, "I'm so sorry, but my brother is required elsewhere."

"Where is this elsewhere?" Miss Rollins boldly asked, making one last attempt to hold on to her quarry.

But Jane just lifted an eyebrow. "Anywhere else."

And with that, Jason was steered away from the three misses, their disappointment as palatable as his relief.

"Well?" Jason asked, once he and Jane had gained enough distance.

"Well what?" Jane replied, her gait remaining fast and her attention focused on their destination.

"Aren't you going to say 'I told you so'?" Jason asked, quickening his pace to keep up with her. "Or, 'you'd be lost without me,' or perhaps, 'you can thank me later'?"

"I did, you would be, and you can," she countered, "but right now I'm far too angry to say any of those things." Jane shot a look over her shoulder. Jason followed suit and saw the three misses lamenting his departure—or more specifically, Miss Rollins roundly abusing the other two with her fan, her frustration breaking through anything that might be considered polite behavior.

"How on earth did those three manage to get into this garden party?" Jane hissed.

"I thought Phillippa invited everyone who was anyone to these things."

"She did!" Jane exclaimed. "Everyone except them!"

Jane cut through the milling guests, the casual acquaintances of good name. She cut through the well-raised and demure young ladies and their mothers, the lords of state who had an idle afternoon, willing to respond to a beck and call from Phillippa Worth—and to own the truth, they all did. No one could or ever would go against Phillippa Worth.

Which made Jane's words to Phillippa once she reached her side all the more surprising to those within earshot.

"Have you lost your mind?" Jane cried, going up on her toes in order to stare into Phillippa's eyes.

Phillippa looked at her queerly. "Only for that sparest moment when I agreed to throw a garden party for your brother. But I have been in the pink of health ever since."

"I'm afraid I have to disagree with you," Jane replied. "I sincerely doubt your health's pinkish hue, and your sanity. I think you might have had a relapse when you invited those three!"

Phillippa looked in the direction toward which Jane gesticulated wildly, and her eyes finally fell on the three offending young ladies. Miss Rollins had regained some of her composure and stopped hitting the other two—now she was regrouping, and pointing at and directing her friends. Jason could not hear from this distance what was being said, but he had a feeling a second assault was being planned.

"But I didn't!" Phillippa replied. "Marcus!" she called, and her husband, Sir Marcus Worth, was at her side in an instant. Jason knew the man a little, but he better knew Marcus's brother (and Jane's husband) Sir Byrne Worth. Byrne had obviously been with his brother when Phillippa called for him, because he too materialized next to his wife.

"What is it?" Marcus asked, and threw his spectacles on when his wife pointed to the three misses in the distance. A few whispered words between husband and wife, and Marcus was headed toward the young ladies. A quick glance at Byrne had him following.

"They'll sort it," Phillippa said to Jane and Jason's unasked questions.

"What are they going to do? Throw them out?" Jane asked. "Can you do *nothing* without causing a scandal?"

It was at this point that Jason thought he might be safer with the three misses, and almost suggested he follow the Worth brothers—such was the murderous look in Phillippa's eye. But wiser men than he had fallen into that trap, and Jason decided to just keep silent and let them fight it out.

Besides, since Jane and Phillippa—notorious enemies in their youth—had married a pair of brothers, they were all connected on the Worth family tree. So no matter how often they might spar, the two had no final recourse other than friendship.

"Your husband might use such uncouth methods," Phillippa replied coolly, her eyes sparkling like ice. "But mine prefers charm to brutishness."

Jason chanced a look over his shoulder. Indeed, Marcus Worth was bowing low (any bow was low for him, as he was exceptionally tall) over the hand of Miss Rollins, who seemed to be giggling. Meanwhile, Byrne was walking with the other two young ladies. Whether or not his objective was to pitch them over the low hedge to the south was open to debate.

"But I don't understand how they got *in* in the first place." Jane stamped her foot, a gesture not often seen by a lady old enough to have borne two children.

"Neither do I—no one was admitted without an invitation. I made certain my butler collected them at the door."

"So how did they get the invitation?"

"I. Do. Not. Know. There were no regrets. Everyone who was invited came," Phillippa replied evenly. Then, like a child caught in a puzzle, tapped her fingernail against her tooth for a moment. "Except . . ."

"Here it comes." Jane rolled her eyes.

"Totty told me before we sent out the invitations that she couldn't come—her friend Miss Crane had some big event she absolutely had to attend today, although what is more important I cannot imagine—so Mariah suggested I allow her to invite one of the ladies from her charitable group."

Jason quickly ran through his memory to decipher who all these names belonged to. He didn't recall a Miss Crane, but he knew Totty was Mrs. Tottendale, Phillippa's old companion who had moved to her own residence when Phillippa and Marcus began a family—small children made wine less enjoyable, she said. And Mariah was the other Lady Worth—wife of the eldest Worth brother, Graham. (With Graham having inherited his baronetcy, and both Marcus and Byrne having been knighted for their services to the crown, that made three Sirs and three Ladies Worth—remarkably confusing for anyone trying to assign seating at a dinner party, or so his friend

Nevill said.) Mariah was somewhere in the midst of the party, likely lecturing some poor soul on the needs of foundling children in their country.

"Which friend?" Jane asked impatiently.

"Mrs. Pritchard . . ." and Phillippa sighed, as all the pieces fell into place, "who is cousins with Miss Rollins's mother."

"And you thought you had control over this party!" Jane crowed.

"I cannot believe any duplicity on Mariah's part—perhaps Miss Rollins stole the invitation from her mother's cousin . . ."

As the conversation escalated, Jason was faced with that eternal question: Should he stay or should he go? The quarrel had gotten to the point where staying might mean he would have to interject. Or God forbid, get dragged in by one of them asking for his opinion.

On the other hand . . . he had promised Jane that he would not run. He had promised himself he would make the effort with this party and do as he set out to do, find himself a mate for life. Even though running away was the most appealing option right now.

"Don't bother," Byrne's voice came from behind him, low enough so it went unnoticed by Phillippa and Jane. "She will see it the moment you take one step back."

Byrne came to stand beside Jason; having disposed of the three misses somewhere, he began to watch the conversational volleys with the attentiveness of a crowd at a tennis match.

"How did you know?" Jason asked.

"We're in a garden party in London. Escape is all I've been thinking about, as well."

"I cannot run. I set myself up for this." Jason shook his head. "I have to see it through."

"Remind me why you are so determined to marry at the age of thirty?" Byrne drawled.

Jason paused for a moment, then shrugged. "Because it's what comes next."

Not a terribly incisive answer, but there was no simpler

explanation. It had taken him awhile, but he had mastered all the duties of being the Duke of Rayne. And Jason was smart enough to know he didn't know everything—so if there were some details that went over his head, he had certainly found trustworthy employees who would make certain nothing went awry. He had no concerns on that score—and neither did his family. Marcus and Byrne had undertaken the task of thoroughly investigating any of his hires. Jane hadn't even had to insist; Jason had asked the Worth brothers himself.

Indeed, the ancient and noble name of Rayne was strong and secure. Jason Cummings had stepped fully and completely into the role of his lifetime. He was content. Comfortable. Marriage was what came next on the list. Besides, all his friends were married. So it couldn't be so bad. Could it?

But at Jason's declaration, Byrne just slipped him a half smile, and replied, "If you say so."

"It's just . . . it's less straightforward of a process than I had imagined," Jason said, surprising even himself with his honesty.

Byrne thought for a moment, then fixed his gaze on his wife, who was requesting that Phillippa provide her with a family tree for every party attendee, even those that she herself had known for dozens of years.

"Well, we could just ask the eligible ladies to line up in a neat row and you point at the one you like best." Byrne smiled. "But I doubt that would provided you with a loving mate." He caught Jane's eye and winked. "Think of this as a battle."

"A battle?" Jason raised an eyebrow.

"Yes, there are strategies and traditions. But more important, there are rules. Make use of cover. Never fire until you are sure of your shot. If a solider lays down his arms, you are to treat him with kindness, all that sort of thing. To survive, you simply have to learn the rules and be a better soldier than anyone else on the field."

Jason's other eyebrow joined his first. "And you followed all these rules when courting my sister, did you?"

Byrne had to laugh at that. "No. But I knew the rules well enough to break them with impunity." But then he met Jason's eye dead on. "Unfortunately, you are not I, *Your Grace*."

"Are you implying that it is my title that will separate us in courting styles?" Jason asked sardonically. "I assure you, I'm well aware."

"That, and many, many other things," Byrne replied drily. "But yes, you will be limited by it. Girls will fawn over you, fall into you."

Jason rolled his eyes. He knew that, too.

"You have to maintain the strictest posture possible," Byrne continued. "Really, you'd almost do better to simply choose a girl, hand her over to Jane, and let her do the courting."

"If only it were that simple," Jason murmured. "If only I could convince Jane to do it."

"Are you certain?" Jane's voice broke into their conversation. "Absolutely and completely?"

"For the last time, yes." Phillippa sighed.

"Excellent. Jason," Jane called, bringing both men to attention. "I am assured that there will be no more unexpected guests at this party."

"See if I offer my hostessing services again," Phillippa muttered under her breath.

"What was that?" Jane asked sharply.

"Nothing," Phillippa replied brightly.

"Good. As I was saying," Jane continued, turning back to Jason, "shall we introduce you to some lovely *sane* young ladies?"

Two

*Wherein our hero meets someone new,
and with some force.*

As the carriage rolled away from the Worth mansion on Grosvenor Square, Jason could not contain his relief. After being properly introduced to the most eligible of the Upper Ten Thousand's daughters, he needed to escape as far away as possible. To Timbuktu or the wilds of India. To the Americas or the moon. Or at the very least, across town.

And a drink. He could use a drink.

The tea had to have been the worst of it. Too sweet hot tea served on a very warm May day, and he must have drunk a large pond's worth, while chatting with the Earl of Whomever's daughter and Viscount Something's niece. All he had wanted to do was run. His preference for flight at full alert, Jane had moved him from one group of young ladies to the next, thankfully everyone on their very best behavior, no one trying to corner him behind shrubbery or tackle him in a locked cellar.

He shuddered at the memory. Really, the three misses were enough to put a man off women altogether.

Not that the afternoon had been wholly terrible. Indeed, Jane introduced him to a number of young ladies who managed to flush and flutter at all the right moments, but also didn't stammer or threaten to faint—hell, a few managed to hold an easy conversation. One young lady—Miss Sarah Forrester, if he recalled correctly—had even managed to tease him.

"The south hedge."

"Hmm?" His head had come up at her words.

"I think it's likely the easiest means of escape." Miss Forrester had raised her eyes to his, shy and laughing. She continued when he only blinked in reply. "I can make a small distraction if you need. Then you can run for it."

At that, Jason was the one left blushing and stuttering. "Is my discomfort that obvious?" he had said.

"No. Maybe. Maybe I scouted the south hedge for my own escape." Miss Forrester laughed a little to herself. Just then, her mother's voice had interrupted their thoughts.

"And you should see my daughter's screen painting, Lady Jane, there is simply nothing like it!" she had been crowing to his sister.

"But alas, I fear I would be caught," Miss Forrester had whispered.

"Me, too," Jason whispered back mock-ruefully, and then had his attention brought around to the other ladies of the circle.

The memory of that moment gave him comfort—if for no other reason than it was the one small success in a sea of bare survival. The question that Byrne had asked—and his own answer to it—haunted him as the carriage racketed down the cobblestone streets toward the Thames and Somerset House.

Why are you doing this?

Because it's what comes next.

Because it's what comes next. Such a broad, empty answer. Yes, getting married was next on the list of his life. He had taken up the role of Duke of Rayne. Had learned to manage the estates. And if he hadn't found fulfillment, per se, at least he had a sense of accomplishment at the end of most days. Marriage was what came next. It would not be the death knell that all his (married) friends took unremitting joy in telling him it would be. Certainly not. It would, instead, cure this vague loneliness that had begun threatening the edges of his life. It would be a beginning. It would be what came next.

So why could he not quell that old, familiar urge to run and hide?

When that urge overcame him, at least he didn't have to run far. His driver lurched to a familiar stop, and his footman opened the carriage in front of Somerset House, a grand neoclassical structure that sat along the Thames, housing the great learned fraternities of the day: the Royal Society (known far and wide as the Royal), the London Society of Antiquaries, and Jason's personal refuge, the Society of Historical Art and Architecture of the Known World—or the Historical Society for short. Somehow, in the past few years of overseeing his estates, and oh, just being ducal, Jason had actually managed to complete his long overdue academic paper on the "Damage to Medieval Architecture in European Cities after the Napoleonic Wars." Mostly from notes he had made when he had gone on his grand tour after graduating from Oxford. Maybe not with a First, but he had graduated, thank you very much. Dukes, he had been informed, had no use for Firsts.

And, once he had that pamphlet published (using his own printing establishment, which he had acquired the controlling interest in just the week before, but published nonetheless), he had petitioned for and been granted membership to the Historical Society. And now, he was free to use the Society's offices and rooms at his leisure. It was essentially his club, but different from White's or Brooks's or the other gentlemen's establishments that lined St. James. This club hosted some of the best minds in the country and held some of its most interesting treasures, and best of all—absolutely no one there would dream of an offer of marriage from him.

He disembarked from the carriage, nodding to his driver. "This little adventure may take longer than anticipated," he said, earning a cackle of good humor from Bones, his driver.

"I know what that means," Bones replied. "It means head on home for supper, and maybe you'll wander back around three in the morn."

"That happened *once*," Jason countered, but with a smile. Bones had been with him for years, through more than one misadventure, so his informality with his master was easily forgiven. "Go have supper," Jason conceded. "But I expect you back here within two hours to collect me!"

Bones, not one to waste his master's generosity, tipped his hat to Jason and put the horses into trot before the Duke could change his mind.

Jason sighed the deep sigh of the utterly free. Finally. For the first time all day, he felt free of the exhausting task of trying to find a mate, free of the weight of being the Duke of Rayne—he could enter this columned and storied establishment a clean man, one whose only purpose was to improve and amuse his mind via other men of interest.

Ah, freedom.

Of course, that was when—as Jason turned left in the courtyard toward the Historical Society's wing—he ran directly into the outstretched hand of the tawny-haired lady who would turn out to be the cause of the greatest tangle of his life.

❧

Miss Winnifred Crane did not intend to smack the young gentleman. Truly, she didn't. He simply, sort of *ran* into her hand. And really she shouldn't be blamed for her hand being as outstretched as it had been.

George should.

It had begun when she had rounded the corner from Aldwych onto Strand, some minutes before the stately carriage bearing the poor soul whom she accidentally smacked appeared. She had been so startled to come upon Somerset House so suddenly, the building that held all her hopes and aspirations, that for the barest of seconds, she lost her nerve.

She made it as far as the courtyard before she had to stop, had to take a moment to gather her strength.

"Do not become overwhelmed," Winnifred whispered to herself, clutching her folio of papers to her chest. She wished briefly that she had worn her thick coat, as a chill ran down her spine. But the coat was unfashionable, and she at least had to try for what fashion she could afford in London. Besides, it was a warm day, and the chill could easily be ascribed to other sources than the weather. "You are not doing anything against their rules, nor against the law. You were invited. You even have a letter of introduction."

As gentlemen in top hats and coats walked past her up and down the steps, more than a few giving a curious glance to the small woman paused at the central fountain, she hesitantly took the first few steps.

Somerset House was a large columned structure, one side lining the Thames, the other folding itself along a courtyard of some impressive acreage. It was home to numerous endowed learned societies and government agencies, and as such, it was almost impossible for Winn to know precisely where she needed to go.

The naval offices were straight ahead, she knew, marked easily by the building's central dome. But after that it became a bit hazy. She thought back to her father's descriptions of the building. The Royal Society was . . . to the left? No, the right. It had a lovely exhibition hall, for those men who wished to see the progress of the world. The London Society of Antiquaries was its younger cousin, relegated to a few rooms in the attic and basement. So that must mean the Historical Society's rooms were to the left of the courtyard.

She turned and, with the conviction of purpose, moved toward her destination.

Until an oversized, strong hand grabbed her by the arm.

"Not so fast," George Bambridge, her cousin, said in her ear, his breath coming in heavy gulps. He must have run very fast to catch up with her. Damn it all. If only she had not paused by the fountain! She would have been in the building, at her audience with Lord Forrester, and George would have had to vent his spleen in the street alone.

"You left me sitting in the park with bloody Mrs. Tottendale," George said once he finally managed to catch his breath.

"And she was supposed to keep you from following me." Winn rolled her eyes. "How did you know?"

"That you'd come here? Winnifred, it's been the only thing you've spoken of since coming to London," George replied, smirking superiorly. "Nor are you that difficult to spot. Would you like to know why?"

"Because I'm the only one here in a skirt?" she guessed drily.

"Because you're the only one here in a skirt!" George cried. "And that's because there are no women allowed into the Historical Society!"

"Yes they are," she replied calmly. "For exhibitions and lectures, women often attend."

"Those are public functions." The wispy dark hair that fell over George's brow shook precariously. If he was not careful with his temper, he would reveal to the world his carefully hidden receding hairline. "Women are not granted entrance to the Society's main rooms as they are not granted membership. And I should know, because of the two of us, *I'm* the one being considered for such."

"There is absolutely nothing in their charter that forbids women," Winn countered rationally.

"And how do you know so much about the Historical Society's charter?"

"Because my father helped write it. And he told me."

That flummoxed George, causing him to gape like a fish for some moments.

"Winnifred," he began calmly, though he did not loosen his grip on her arm. "I feel responsible for you, not just as your only living relative but, I would hope, as something more. So please believe me when I say this is not a good idea. If you so ardently desire to be introduced to Lord Forrester, I will endeavor to have him invited to dine, and I'm sure he will find you and your infatuation with art history extremely diverting. But not here." His voice lowered to a desperate whisper. "And not now!"

As Winn's reaction ratcheted from a weak queasiness to annoyance to utter lividity at George's impassioned speech, she clutched her small folio of papers all the tighter to her chest. When he was finished, she spoke in a very low, very clear voice.

"George, if you want me to leave this establishment, you will have to physically drag me away, kicking and screaming." Her gaze bore into his, so sharp it could cut diamonds. "In front of all these people you are *dying* to impress. Now, you may be a foot and a half taller and five stone heavier than me, but do you really think imposing yourself on a tiny female in such a manner is something you should do?"

George paused. For the first time, he seemed to recognize the potential they had for making a scene. Right now, talking low to each other, they were just two ordinary people— although one suspiciously other-gendered—but all it would take was one scream and suddenly those men in top hats and coats who walked past with their noses in the air would know who they were.

And as Winn knew, for George, there was such a thing as bad press.

His hand slackened on her arm. Only slightly, but enough that Winn could wrench it away from him.

And smack said arm directly into the young man who was rushing past them.

"Amomph!" was the muffled, indistinguishable cry from said gentleman, who staggered back some paces.

"Oh my goodness!" was the sharp, anguished cry that came from Winnifred as her folio fell to the paving stones, spilling its contents into disarray. "Oh no!"

"I was thinking the same thing," said the flame-haired gentleman as he squeezed the bridge of his nose in pain.

"Your . . . Your Grace!" stammered George, apparently recognizing the victim of Winnifred's hand as a Duke of some kind. Of course she would accidentally smack a Duke, she thought, flushing red. But could not stop to curtsy. She had to collect her papers before they all flew away! Her articles . . . her letter of introduction!

"I'm so terribly sorry!" George was saying, attempting to bow and neaten the poor man's coat at the same time.

"It's quite all right," His Grace was saying. "I knew I wasn't going to survive the day without being smacked."

"I beg your pardon?" George asked.

"Nothing. And no harm done, I think." He straightened to his full height, then apparently, having noticed Winn's own distress, said, "Do you need any help, miss?"

"I . . ." She stooped to pick up another page, then another. "Oh dear, is that all of them?" She looked around wildly. And her heart stopped when she saw the lone piece of paper, floating in the fountain.

And by the folds in the paper, she knew which one it was.

"My letter!" she cried. She reached out her arm, but it was beyond her grasp. She was about to throw caution to the wind and climb over the edge into the fountain's low pool when a hand on her shoulder stilled her.

"Allow me," the flame-haired Duke said, and reached for the floating paper himself. He had her in height by a foot, but it was nearly out of his reach, as well. At last he managed that final inch and handed the dripping page to Winn.

"Thank you, Your Grace," Winn breathed, but she only had eyes for the paper. *Please don't let it be ruined, please don't let it be ruined . . .*

"No trouble—although now I know the benefit of using a walking cane." He smiled and then gave a short bow. "Miss . . ."

But Winn, her heart in her throat, could not answer. And so, George stumbled into the void.

"Crane, Your . . . Your Grace," he stammered, giving a short bow. "And I am George Bambridge, her cousin. I have often seen you in the Historical Society's rooms, but you always seem so engrossed, I've not wanted to interrupt you to introduce myself."

"Ah. Well, as you seem to be aware, I am Rayne. And Miss, er, Crane." He turned to address her frozen form. "Are you quite well?"

But Winn was not well. Nowhere near it. Because . . .

"It's ruined," she managed in a small voice.

Her letter. Her letter of introduction written to Lord Forrester in her father's own hand was nothing more than a bunch of squiggly, running black lines on wet parchment.

"I'm so sorry," the Duke sympathized. "I take it the page was important."

Important? It was everything. It was what allowed her to be here with legitimacy.

"It's nothing, Your Grace," George toadied, positioning himself by Winn's side. "Just some notes, correct, Winnifred? I apologize, sir, we should be getting back home. My cousin has . . . a dinner to dress for. But, I was wondering, sir, if you would be attending the lecture series this coming week?"

"No," Winn said distractedly.

"No?" the Duke replied when George did not.

"No, I don't have a dinner party to dress for. Nor am I leaving."

"Winnifred . . ." George warned, his voice kept just under angry.

"I have an invitation, George."

"Not anymore, you don't," he replied, flicking his eyes to the wet paper in her hand.

"Actually, George, sadly that piece of paper is still dry."

As a quizzical look crossed her cousin's brow, the Duke's eyebrow went up.

"An invitation?" the Duke said, his interest piqued. And in that moment, Winnifred recognized him. From a decade ago. Jason Cummings, Marquis of . . . something or other. Now the

Duke of Rayne. And George was bending over backward to impress him. Winn almost laughed aloud.

"Yes," she said, her back suddenly straight, her purpose refound. "I have an invitation to call on Lord Forrester at the Society of Historical Art and Architecture of the Known World at my earliest convenience." She narrowed her eyes. "And I find now remarkably convenient."

And with that, she took her folio, her wet page held securely but at arm's length, and neatly sidestepped George and the Duke, moving with all haste to the east entrance of Somerset House.

The two gentlemen fell into step beside her. George to her left, eyeing the damp letter in her hand, trying to make out what the bleeding ink might have been that Winn found so important, while the Duke kept pace to her right. He kept his hands behind his back and his head forward. And, was it possible, the man was whistling?

As their feet struck the stone floor in symphony, she shot a glance at the Duke's profile. A lock of shockingly red hair bounced over his otherwise unexpressive brow—a last mark of boyishness in the fully formed man he now was. The barest of all smiles played over his lips.

"Is this amusing to you, Your Grace?" Winn asked with a scowl.

"Not at all." Then he seemed to reconsider. "Well, somewhat. A little bit."

"I assure you, my meeting with Lord Forrester is not at all amusing to *me*," she replied, her chin going up.

"Oh, I didn't mean to imply that your situation was amusing. I simply find mine so." At her quizzical look, he explained. "This is the closest thing to an adventure I've had in ages."

Winn glanced up at him before smiling a little to herself. "It's the closest I've ever been to an adventure."

"Your Grace, I have to beg you to not encourage her in this," George interjected. "She does not know what she's walking into."

"Obviously, as we just passed the Historical Society's door."

The whole party pulled up short. Winn shot George a dark look as the Duke indicated the door she was meant to enter.

The heavy mahogany weight of the paneled door loomed in front of Winn, its gravity pulling her forward—but her feet wouldn't move. All she could do was stare at that door.

A small collection of gentlemen, moving along the corridor, had gathered at the sight of Winnifred and her two escorts. Small murmuring accompanied their shocked expressions.

"Do you see?" George addressed both Winn and His Grace. "She's already causing a spectacle and she's not even through the door. I told you, Winnifred, no lady has ever entered the Historical Society rooms."

"And I told you there is no rule against it," Winnifred countered, her eyes inexplicably flicking up to the Duke's face.

"That's preposterous," George countered.

"Actually, that's correct," the Duke replied, his eyebrows up, looking impressed.

"How do you know?" Winn asked, astonished.

"I read the charter. Well, I wasn't about to join a club without knowing the rules." The Duke shrugged carelessly. "Call it a quirk. However," he added, quickly redirecting the subject, "Mr. Bambridge is also correct. Some rules are implied."

As George beamed and Winn set her shoulders in determination, the Duke's hand worked over his jaw, considering.

"But, I suppose our lack of specificity is to your advantage, Miss Crane."

George goggled at the man. "You . . . you cannot be taking her side!" And then, remembering, "Sir." He took a deep settling breath. "I know you are a member and I a mere applicant, Your Grace, but you are not an academic, and I am. And academic men like Lord Forrester are very aware of appearance. And they're not going to appreciate my cousin's appearance here. In fact, they . . ." He turned away from the Duke and bent down to Winn.

"Winnifred, this is a mistake."

"Let me make my own mistakes, George."

And with that, Winnifred Crane marched forward and took the door.

Well, what was a man to do but follow?

Jason didn't know why he was shadowing this terribly focused woman and her controlling cousin, or why he felt the need to interfere in their argument. But once enlisted, he couldn't help himself.

Perhaps it was guilt over inadvertently ruining her apparently very important letter. Perhaps it was because she was the first woman in nearly two Seasons who did not look at him with some kind of expectation. Perhaps it was because, when her hand had made contact with his nose, it was as if she'd knocked the weight of the day clean off him—the dreary, boring day that had sat on his shoulders for so long. His dulled mind had sat straight up and said, "Well, this is something interesting, at least."

If she had been one of those bluestockings who banged against male-only institutions simply to make men feel as if they were absolute heels bent on keeping the fairer sex low in esteem, it would have been a different story. But for some reason, he didn't think that was her objective. Such women had a different posture than this tiny female.

And tiny she was—barely brushing Jason's shoulder. She reminded him of nothing so much as a sparrow. And remarkably, all one color. Her tawny light brown hair was capped by a light brown straw hat, which was decorated by light brown ribbon. Her gloves were light brown leather, her spencer a somewhat darker mud. And when she nervously shot a glance in his direction, he was startled to find the lightest of hazel eyes. But everything else—it was as if she had never before sought to stand out.

But as she threw open the doors to the Historical Society's great rooms, stand out she did indeed.

A number of men milled about, standing or sitting in clusters of chairs and sofas, having murmured discussions—whether they discussed the significance of illuminated manuscripts after the invention of the printing press, or a story in today's *Times*, Jason was never to know. Because at the appearance of Miss Winnifred Crane, all conversation abruptly ceased.

He looked down at her—the little sparrow pale and unmoving. Her eyes flicked nervously down to the folio in her hands. But still she remained frozen to her spot.

And suddenly, Jason was taking the reins of the mischief.

He leaned down and whispered in her ear, "Just follow my lead, Miss Crane."

That seemed to shake her out of her reverie. Just in time, too, for the steward of the Historical Society, Edwards—who ran the inner workings of the Society as efficiently as he did quietly—came up to Jason.

"Edwards, my man!" Jason called out jovially, giving the gathering audience a prologue to the play about to be performed. "I think we are in for an interesting afternoon!"

"Your Grace," he greeted with a bow. "Madam," he addressed Miss Crane, "may I be of some assistance?"

Code for "What the hell are you doing here?" Jason thought, squelching the impulse to smile.

To her credit, Miss Crane did not flinch at Edwards's tone. "Yes, I've been invited to converse with Lord Forrester. Could you direct me to him?"

Edwards did not blink before answering. "I'm terribly sorry, but Lord Forrester is not in his offices this afternoon. Would you care to leave a card?"

Maybe it was the look on her face—a fragile breaking, presented with this quandary. Maybe it was the look on George Bambridge's face—relief punctuated by triumph, as if he himself had stopped his cousin's foolishness. But maybe, maybe it was that small part of his brain that still liked to make trouble and hadn't had the opportunity in so damn long.

But whatever the reason, Jason found himself the recipient of every deathly stare in the room when he said, "Really? But it's Thursday. Lord Forrester is always at his offices here on Thursdays. Besides, I just came from a luncheon where his wife and daughter told me he was in residence."

Edwards showed the barest of shocks before flicking his eyes from Miss Crane to Jason to another servant who stood by a door on the far side of the room. Lord Forrester's office door. But that other man's startled countenance offered no assistance. Edwards would simply have to extricate himself from this without his help, Jason surmised, only a little amused by the stoic Edwards being flummoxed.

"If Lord Forrester is not able to receive me today, I can come back," Miss Crane piped up. "Every day. I don't have much to occupy me, so I could simply stand here and wait all day."

As George whimpered in mortification, Jason suppressed a chuckle. And then jumped into her scheme with both feet.

"Indeed?" he said, barely able to keep a straight face. "Would you care for a chair while you wait? Perhaps some tea?"

"Oh no." She smiled at him. "I would not wish to tax the Historical Society's resources. I'll have likely breakfasted before I arrive. But"—she rubbed her chin, pondering—"I do tend to get light-headed and faint in the afternoons without some sustenance."

"That we simply cannot have," Jason replied. "Imagine a lady such as yourself, *fainting* from the length of your wait to attend to your meeting with Lord Forrester. What a terrible story that would be."

"Well then, perhaps it would be best—yes, perhaps it would, if I were to have a chair and table—maybe a small settee, set here for me. Right here, in front of the main doors." She grinned, then turned her suddenly bright eyes to poor Edwards. "A nice blanket over my lap, a tray of tea. I could even bring in my tatting, get that done while I wait."

At the prospect of having a woman faint in their hallway while waiting for an audience—or turn the great rooms of the Historical Society into her sitting room—Edwards conceded a modicum of defeat.

"Perhaps Lord Forrester can be located," Edwards assented in a low voice. "What name shall I give him?"

"Miss Winnifred Crane," she said, her voice clear as a bell. That started a whispering. "Winnifred Crane?" Jason heard from more than one cluster of gentlemen, who had been watching the entertainment with rapt interest.

"Crane?" Edwards's eyebrow shot up.

"I'm the daughter of Alexander Crane," she elaborated. And then she said something so outrageous, so completely undoing, that it stopped the conversation in the room altogether.

"But his lordship may know me better by a different name," she said, her voice suddenly less steady, her face frightened and determined at the same time.

Edwards's face remained impassive. Until she said . . .

"C. W. Marks."

Three

*Wherein our hero cannot
help but become involved.*

C. W. Marks.

It was not a name that held a great deal of interest outside the walls of Somerset House. It wasn't as if she had just
claimed to be the Scarlet Pimpernel or the Blue Raven, for
instance. But inside these walls, inside the realm of learned
societies of Britain and those across Europe, it was a matter of
great speculation, interest, and mystery.

Amazing, Jason thought. Imagine, just a few hours earlier
he had been bored to death at a garden party.

The ripple of Miss Crane's words—*C. W. Marks!*—spread
across the great rooms like wildfire, gaining momentum as Edwards crossed the room to that far door and whispered to the
servant waiting there, who slipped inside. Leaving Edwards to
wait at that door, and leaving Jason to wait with George Bambridge and Miss Crane. Or, it seemed, C. W. Marks.

"Are you really?" he couldn't help but whisper. His eyes
found hers, but before she could answer, George did for her.

"Of course she's not."

Her head whipped around so fast, Jason nearly got smacked

for the second time that day—this time by the brim of a ladies' straw hat.

"How would you know?" she nearly spat.

"I am a professor of the history of art at Oxford, and I am telling you, you are not C. W. Marks."

"You are an associate lecturer and don, not a full professor." She took a deep breath, more confident this time in her declaration, as if repetition strengthened her will. "And I *am* the author of the papers by C. W. Marks."

"Miss Crane." Edwards had rejoined their side, and again Jason had to lean back to avoid being assaulted by woven straw. The steward seemed to hesitate before saying, "This way please."

There seemed no question that Jason was included in that invitation, and he was meant to follow. He had thrown himself in with her lot merely to . . . to what? To see that she got her interview, in spite of her cousin. He shot a look at George, who also felt there was no question of his attending. Her cousin, in the ten minutes he had known the man, did manage to set his back up remarkably well. He seemed the type to dismiss and coddle a woman at the same time.

Obviously the man did not have a sister, Jason thought wryly.

Whatever the reason Jason had taken up Miss Crane's cause, he should have been able to leave her to her own devices once Edwards invited her back to see the president of the Historical Society of Art and Architecture, Lord Forrester. But the prospect that she was C. W. Marks . . . well that changed the game entirely.

Two years ago, just as Jason was presenting his long overdue paper on medieval architecture that would allow for his admittance to this society, C. W. Marks had published three papers.

And set the academic world afire.

The first was a detailed analysis of all pluralistic thought in the court of King Henry VIII, in which intellect seemed to foster brutality. A very well-received work, published in the back half of the Historical Society's quarterly scholastic journal. The second was a piece on the modern glorification of war in battlefield art—the paintings of great ships firing on each other at sea, the epic works of soldiers dying romantically on the battlefield, typified by Benjamin West—and how it refused to reflect the true hardship of war.

This was the paper that had the dusty academics sitting up and taking notice.

It wasn't simply the analysis of the paintings themselves, but how they fit into the broader cultural prism—everything that came before and everything that came after culminating in this one work or movement of art.

And contrary to what conventional wisdom would allow for an academic paper, it was a ripping good read.

This, more than anything, had the name C. W. Marks on everyone's tongue. Academic papers weren't supposed to be interesting! They were by design obscure, so the very educated people who read them could feel superior for having the ability to follow along. But by the time the third treatise came out, this one on Hogarth's *A Rake's Progress*—a collection of paintings often written about, but rarely so amusingly and deeply—everyone within the academic realm was wondering who this C. W. Marks was, and where on earth had he come from?

But that last paper had been over a year ago. While the mystery of the identity of C. W. Marks never died down, the fervor to uncover it did.

Until today, it seemed.

They crossed the great rooms, every single man therein standing at attention and absolutely silent, the only sound the click-clacking of Miss Crane's small boot heels on the polished wooden floorboards. By the time they reached the doors to Lord Forrester's office, Jason thought surely some of their audience's heads would snap off their necks, twisted as they were. Miss Crane, to her utter credit, kept her eyes straight ahead, did not look back nervously as Jason could imagine she wished to. Once they were admitted to the room beyond and the door closed, then and only then did they hear a cacophony of voices from the assembled gentlemen behind them.

But those voices didn't matter anymore. The only voice that did belonged to the man dwarfed by the gargantuan desk before them.

"Miss Winnifred!" Lord Forrester, a man of such girth and general cheerfulness he could pass for Father Christmas if he grew a beard, popped right out of his chair and rushed to greet them.

"You'll have to forgive me the familiarity. Your father wrote to me so often over the course of your life, even though we have never met I feel as though I've watched you grow up in front of me." He took her hand and then, regarding her with as much pride as a favorite uncle might, became a bit wistful. "Your father's passing—left the world without such light. Not only the Historical Society, but Oxford, and of course, he was one of my dearest friends."

Suddenly Jason was hit with a flash of recognition. "Alexander Crane!" he cried, causing the assembled party to look at him queerly. "I completely forgot. Of course, he was one of my professors at Oxford. A damn hard one at that."

"Dean of the History of Art Department, founding member of the Historical Society for Art and Architecture, author of more than a dozen treatises on the British contribution to human culture, of course he was a damn hard professor," Lord Forrester replied jovially. "And he would have been gratified to hear you say so, Your Grace. By the bye, how did you become mixed up in this business?" He wiggled his hand in the air vaguely at "business," as if he himself didn't know what to think of what his servants had relayed to him.

Jason couldn't blame him.

"I suppose I walked right into it, Lord Forrester." Jason smiled. Forrester shrugged, taking that for what it was worth, and turned to the third member of the party.

"And Mr. Bambridge, down from Oxford again, I see."

"I took leave just for the summer courses," George hastened to explain. "My cousin felt a desire to come to London, and I couldn't let her be friendless here."

Jason's glance went straight to Miss Crane's face. She looked murderous but kept her counsel.

"Careful," Lord Forrester chided George. "If you keep taking sabbaticals, your students will forget where your classroom is, and the school will forget why you're the one to teach in it."

While George flushed scarlet, Miss Crane took the opportunity his silence allowed to state her business.

"Lord Forrester, I know you find my appearance here today surprising," she began, her voice stronger than Jason would have expected.

"To say the least," Lord Forrester intoned seriously. "And I'm sorry to say that you will have to leave posthaste. Surely you understand this is a gentleman's learned institution. We chart serious matters of history."

"There's no rule—" she began, but was cut off by Lord Forrester's wave of his hand.

"There are unwritten rules, things that are simply understood," he said. "I do not wish to upset you, but neither do I wish to face a riot from the fellows of the Society."

"Sir," Miss Crane said, her voice stronger still with the conviction of her argument, "I came here today at your expressed invitation." And with that she pulled a piece of paper (not the damp one, thankfully) out of her folio and placed it in front of Lord Forrester.

"This is a letter you wrote to my father, a little over a year ago. It came a month or so before he . . . passed."

Lord Forrester perused the document. He grunted as he read, a small smile coming across his face here and there.

"Well?" George strained, completely overcome with curiosity. "What does it say?"

"It tells him of my family, how they're doing . . . how the

Society is progressing, and of course how greedy the art and antiquaries market has turned in the last year," Lord Forrester drawled. "But I suppose you would like to hear the pertinent bit, Bambridge. Yes, here it is. I wrote: *The Society and I are most impressed by your young protégé C. W. Marks. Please keep sending us his articles; they are most compelling. Better than that, however, bring us Mr. Marks himself, at his earliest convenience. The Society would be overjoyed to receive him, and I would be happy to see my old friend.*"

Lord Forrester put down the letter, a smile on his face even as sadness touched his eyes.

"My father was too ill at the time to travel," Miss Crane said quietly. "But he planned to come when he recovered. Which, unfortunately . . ." She cleared her throat and began again. Reaching into her folio, she produced three thick packets of papers. "Here are my first drafts of my papers written as C. W. Marks. In my handwriting, all my own corrections and cross outs."

"You'll have to forgive me, Miss Winnifred," Lord Forrester said, and he, too, took a moment to clear his throat. "I never thought to wonder why Alexander had not sent me Mr. Marks." He flicked his gaze to George. "Because, you see, I thought he already had."

Winnifred followed his gaze and went pale. George, for his part, looked just as flushed as Miss Crane was white. "I never . . . That is, I never said I was C. W. Marks," George strangled out.

"I asked you once, when you first came to me to apply for membership," Lord Forrester said, "why you were so bold as to published under a pseudonym."

"Yes, and I said I had no idea what you were talking about," George explained, flustered.

"I'm certain you did," Miss Crane replied hotly, "with the barest wink and a nod, and suddenly everyone wants to sponsor your admittance to the Society! I should—I should just . . ." Frustrated, unable to finish that sentence, she took three steps toward George, her free hand a balled-up fist, her intent clear in her eyes.

That, Jason decided, was the signal to intervene.

He quickly stepped forward and steered Miss Crane away from her cousin. Placing a far too familiar and proprietary hand on the back of her neck, he leaned down and whispered in her ear, "You've got him halfway believing you. Don't lose him now."

Her gaze shot to his, that maddening hazel refinding its focus through her anger. She nodded quickly, and Jason removed his hand from her person, once she was steadied.

Unfortunately, the fraction of time it took to calm down Winnifred Crane was just the amount of time George Bambridge needed to tip the scales. The oversized man straightened, cleared his throat, and smiled ingratiatingly at Lord Forrester.

"I never claimed to have been C. W. Marks, my lord," he said smoothly to their genial inquisitor, "because I knew the truth."

"You did?" Forrester asked at the exact same time Miss Crane did.

"Yes. The truth is C. W. Marks is none other than Alexander Crane himself."

A pin could have dropped and been heard across the hall, the room had become so still.

So much for not losing Lord Forrester, Jason thought wryly.

"How da—" Miss Crane began, but her own strangled voice thwarted her efforts.

"I'm afraid my cousin feels the need to make a name for herself now that she is no longer under her father's supervision. I have tried to fill that capacity as best I could—and had I known what she planned today, I would have put a stop to it immediately." His voice was smooth, melodic. Whatever else George Bambridge was, he was a compelling speaker. "But I have long known that my uncle Crane wrote the articles of C. W. Marks."

"But . . . but he didn't," Miss Crane cried. "Lord Forrester, my first drafts . . ."

"Winnifred, isn't it true that in the last years of your father's life, his hands became rather unsteady, due to his illness? And that you became akin to his stenographer, writing his notes on student papers, taking down his thoughts, writing his letters?"

"Yes, but—"

"That's all those first drafts are. You were always a very intrepid assistant to your father in his work, but who can dispute that Alexander Crane possessed the mind necessary for such endeavors as C. W. Marks?"

"And as his daughter, might not I have been granted a similar capacity for deep thought?" Miss Crane countered, sarcasm and impatience seeping into her voice.

"Then why hasn't there been a new article by C. W. Marks since your father's death?" George responded, to Miss Crane's silent outrage.

"You . . . you would have me try to write and publish an article while mourning my father and being removed from the only home I've ever known?" she squeaked, her eyes shooting to Lord Forrester. "Lord Forrester, you must understand . . . with my father's passing, I had no funds to keep renting our house and had to spend the past year not in study but in . . ." But as she explained, she must have seen what Jason saw— that her desperation did more to hinder her argument, and doubt was creeping into the edges of Forrester's expression. A change of tactic was called for.

"And . . . and why would my father publish under a pseudonym?" Miss Crane asked shrewdly, hitting upon a chink in George's argument. "He published widely as Alexander Crane; he wouldn't need—"

"He would if he were to publish articles that ran contrary to several of his other works. Which is half of what C. W. Marks works are."

"My father and I always disagreed about the satirical intent of *A Rake's Progress*." Miss Crane stood up straighter, her spine coming back to her now. "And as for the Tudor era, I am the one who had long arguments with him over dinner about Thomas More's influence on typography. Sir," she said, turning to Lord Forrester, her voice pleading, "if my father wrote to you as I grew up—as you have said he did—then he must have described me as his best pupil."

"He did." Lord Forrester's eyebrow went up. "More than once."

"And I was. I had the benefit of an Oxford education not merely for four years, but for almost thirty. I learned not only at my father's knee but also at the dinner tables of the best and brightest educators in the country. And I promise you, I am the author of the articles by C. W. Marks. I merely wish acknowledgement for it."

"Acknowledgement you cannot have, as you have no proof," George surmised. "And the only person who could provide it has been dead for a year. God rest his soul."

"I have proof!" Miss Crane cried and then, looking at the long neglected wet paper in her had, whispered, "Or I did."

"What is that?" Lord Forrester finally asked. "May I see?"

She laid the page in front of him, its dampness weighing down the edges so it lay flat and lifeless. "It was a letter from my father. He wrote it when he realized he couldn't come to London and introduce me as C. W. Marks himself."

"That's highly convenient," George sneered. A remark that had everyone, even Lord Forrester, looking at him coldly.

"What happened to the letter?" Lord Forrester continued, lifting the edge of the completely illegible paper with the odd end of a quill, and pulling out his spectacles for a closer inspection.

"It blew into the fountain in the plaza outside," Miss Crane barely more than whispered.

"I can corroborate that, at least," Jason piped up. "I fished it out myself."

"And caused it to be knocked in, in the first place," Miss Crane said under her breath.

Jason could not help but be startled. "I beg your pardon, but I'm on your side," he whispered back to her. Miss Crane had the grace to blush and look away.

"I'm sorry, my dear." Lord Forrester sighed, looking up from the page. "But the paper is entirely illegible."

If George Bambridge had not heaved such an audible sigh of relief, Jason was certain he would have been able to hear Miss Winnifred Crane's heart break. She was so utterly stoic, he thought, taking in her countenance. Looking straight ahead at Lord Forrester, her gaze never wavering but her face becoming increasingly pale with every tick of the clock. As if she had suddenly come to understand that her dreams would never be realized.

As if she had just learned she was stuck where she was, and there was no escape. Just the inevitable.

Jason knew that feeling all too well.

They stood there for some moments, the room shattering down about her ears, and yet, still, Miss Crane did not move. Jason began to become concerned—had she fainted . . . standing up?—until he realized she was no longer looking at Lord Forrester. She was looking at the wall behind him.

Like most of the walls in the Historical Society's rooms, the space behind Lord Forrester was crammed with a multitude of paintings, from every conceivable era of history. Jason tried to make out which one she had focused on so intently, but couldn't decipher her gaze. The Poole? The Dürer? The Rembrandt sketches?

"I'm so sorry to have disturbed your afternoon, my lord," George Bambridge said, putting a controlling hand on his cousin's arm. "This is a complicated business. We will endeavor not to disturb you further." He tugged Miss Crane kindly but firmly toward the door, which he opened—and nearly caused the Earl of Salisbury to stumble into the room. To no one's surprise, the audience they had left behind in the great rooms had gathered by Lord Forrester's doors, all hoping to overhear an ounce of the interior conversation.

Say what one will about British stoicism, Jason thought wryly, but he didn't know a single Brit hesitant about eavesdropping. And now that they had a view of the scene, their gazes did not waver.

All the while, Winnifred Crane's eyes remained fixed on the wall behind Lord Forrester's massive desk. Unable to leave well enough alone, George looked to Jason as he tugged. "I know you have some influence over these things, Your Grace, and I do hope this confusion will not affect your decision regarding my application for membership," he said beseechingly.

"Lord Forrester!" Miss Crane spoke up, resisting her cousin's tugging and standing her ground. "I . . . I would make you a proposition."

"Winnifred, please," George whined, "we must be going."

"If I cannot prove to you that I am C. W. Marks," she continued, heedless of George, "can I at least attempt to prove that I have the education, the talent, the creativity . . . the *imagination* necessary to be C. W. Marks? Would you take my suit seriously then?"

Lord Forrester regarded her suspiciously for a moment, his eyes flicking to the black-clad gentlemen crowding the door behind her, looking like a crowd of vultures, waiting to feast upon the remnants of Miss Crane's career.

"I suppose if it was put past doubt, I would have to," he said finally, drawing no amount of angry and scandalized titters from the gathered crowd. "But doubt is a difficult thing to surmount. And I'm not at all certain it can be done away with entirely."

She nodded, swallowing, allowing herself one nervous look down to her hands. But when her eyes came up, they had that sparkle of newfound fire. Of determination.

"That painting behind you"—she pointed—"of Adam and Eve."

"The Dürer?" Lord Forrester replied, following her finger to the appropriate piece. "A particularly splendid representation of the German Renaissance."

"Yes, it is," she agreed. "But what if I told you it was not painted by Albrecht Dürer?"

A jolt of shock rolled through the assembly. Monocles were dropped. Even an utterance of "I say!" drifted over the mutterings and cries.

Meanwhile, Winnifred Crane simply took a deep breath.

"And what if I could prove it?"

Four

Wherein our hero does not appear,
except anecdotally.

"THIS really is the limit, Winnifred, even for you!"

George stomped through Totty's small foyer like a giant fee-fi-fo-fumming his anger out at the world, making small crystal and china knickknacks shake on their various surfaces. Winn followed George through the door quietly, calmly closing it behind her. Now that the interview with Lord Forrester was over—the moment that she had been preparing for, working toward, and building up in her mind for more than a year—Winnifred could feel nothing but a peaceful calm. Let George rant and rave. Let him argue and wheedle—she had done what she set out to do, and now . . .

She was on her way. She had taken the first step down the path to the life she wanted. Now all she had to do was take the others.

"A painting? A bloody painting! That's how you decide to compromise our entire future?" George turned on her, running his hands through his dark hair. "One that *is* a Dürer, no matter how much you pretend otherwise."

She had been caught by that painting, almost from the moment she had entered Lord Forrester's office. She had known that her father had given it to the Society in his will, of course, but the luck of it appearing on Lord Forrester's wall . . .

At first it had amused her. It was as if her father were watching over her even now. But then, as everything began to fall apart around her ears, her hopes of recognition as C. W. Marks fading away, she quickly realized it was the lone, last chance she had to succeed.

"Lord Forrester," she had said, once the murmurs and cries in the Historical Society's rooms subsided at her last announcement, "you must know that my father spent the last few years of his life attempting to compile a comprehensive life history, thesis, and list of works of Albrecht Dürer."

"Of course, he wrote of it often."

"Over many years, he acquired a number of works for Oxford and a few for his personal collection. Including that one." She pointed to the untitled painting, which she had always referred to simply as *the Adam and Eve*. It was a graceful painting, one Winnifred had admired for years. A small canvas, no more than a foot and a half long by two feet wide. Adam to the left, leading the painting, Eve looking youthful and innocent to the right. Fig leaves protected their modesty, and the Tree of Knowledge between them, lit from behind, beckoning like the siren it was. The apple was in Eve's hand, shining and true. But whereas most depictions of this most important moment in human history had the snake hanging from the tree and whispering in Eve's ear, in this version, the snake wound its way around Adam's ankle, securing his fall.

"Yes, and the Society will be eternally grateful that he entrusted us with such an important piece in his will." Lord Forrester replied, his eyebrows rising.

Winnifred smiled kindly, hopefully putting Lord Forrester a bit more at ease—she wasn't planning to take back the painting, and didn't want the head of the Historical Society or any of the other gentlemen listening to think such a thing. The preeminent artisan of the German Renaissance,

Albrecht Dürer was, of course, one of the most popular historical painters right now—one could almost say his renown was reaching a fever pitch—and an original work of his would command a hefty sum. She was already doing enough damage to the Adam and Eve's value simply by questioning its provenance.

"Yes, I'm sure," she demurred. "In assisting my father with his project, I have been corresponding with a number of Dürer enthusiasts throughout Europe." At that, she shot a hard look to George, who could do nothing more than look dumbfounded. Not even he could dispute that she had been working in such a capacity, as her father's aide. "And I have come to believe that this particular painting, while a very fine representation of the German Renaissance, is not a Dürer work."

"This is preposterous!" she heard George swear under his breath. In fact, she was not the only one with keen hearing, because Lord Forrester quelled any further outburst from George's quarter with a spare glance.

"How"—Lord Forrester cleared his throat—"did you come to this conclusion, my dear?"

Well, she had been bold enough to bring it up, no reason to be coy now. Although, with George listening so intently, she did need to be careful.

"There is a gentleman who has been archiving all the Dürer papers he can lay his hands on, and when I mentioned this painting to him, he mentioned a number of letters that he had found associated with it, written by the hand of someone who seemed to be taking credit for the work." She took another deep breath, falling into the flow of the lecture. "And you must admit, there is something marginally . . . different about this painting than other Dürer works. Indeed, even his other depictions of Adam and Eve. The unfinished feeling of the tips of Eve's hands—as if she herself is an unfinished work by God. Dürer was detailed in his oils; the unfinished effect was not of his style. The way Adam turns from the canvas—we see barely a third of his face . . . and here is Dürer, the most influential portraitist of his generation, not showing us a face? And there is the movement depicted in the . . . er . . . foliage."

Winn could not help but blush. One thing about this painting that had always captivated the pubescent Winn, when boys were more a mystery than ever, was how it created the impression that if a breeze blew the wrong way, the painted fig leaves might blow away with it.

Several of the gentlemen present, including Lord Forrester, were peering at the small canvas now, examining it. Wondering.

"To be completely honest, my father debated including this work in his compendium for weeks. Months," Winn added hopefully, and then cursed herself for doing so. Because George took her pause for breath to jump into the fray, arguing.

"Even if your father had questioned the painting's authorship, he obviously came to a conclusion about it, as he never spoke of it to me as anything other than a Dürer."

Winn could only set her mouth in a harsh line, as the men spilling into the room murmured agreements with George. Even one or two giving a "right-o, my good man" and other such inane male encouragements.

Even dead and gone, her father—in the eyes of the Society's members—remained the final word on all things artistically historical. And here she was, admittedly disagreeing with that final word! "All the same," she stated, quelling the ripple of voices, "I hold fast to believing that those letters and documents will prove this work is not a Dürer."

"And may I see these letters?" Lord Forrester frowned, finally tearing his eyes away from the Adam and Eve.

"I . . . I do not have them," Winn had to admit.

"Of course you don't," George replied. "Lord Forrester, you cannot be seriously entertaining this notion that this painting is a fake . . . And that of all the people in all the world, she's the only one to have discovered it!"

"I don't believe it a fake—I believe it mislabeled. And I'm not the only one," Winn countered, glancing to George. "The letters exist. But they are in Basel, Switzerland. Where Dürer was living and studying at the time of this painting." She took another deep breath. "I would have to retrieve them."

That sent a ripple throughout the room and out into the hall. A woman—granted, one well of age—taking on such a task, such a journey, simply to prove a point . . . well, it was ridiculous! Preposterous!

"Your Grace?" Lord Forrester looked to Jason Cummings, lounging against the windowsill. "What are your feelings on the matter?"

Every eye in the room turned to the young Duke. In her desire to put forth her proposal, Winn had somehow forgotten he was there. But now . . . he looked casual, unaffected. But she could tell he had been listening the whole time.

"Well," he drawled, rubbing his chin lazily, "either she is absolutely right, or this is the most complicated lover's quarrel I've ever been witness to."

The room and those beyond sent up a huge guffaw of laughter, and Winn felt her face go up in flames. A lover's quarrel indeed! Over the past year, she had moved about as far away from loving her cousin as a human could manage. But she could not help but sneak a glance at George. His face had reddened as well, but he could not help but show a modicum of relief with it.

"But," the young Duke continued (annoyingly referring to her as if she was not in the room), "she does not ask for the Historical Society to fund her travels or research. Nor does she ask even for admittance to the Society. In fact, the only thing she does ask is for acknowledgement should she succeed. And if she fails . . ." He peered at her then, his dark eyes such a dev-ilish contrast to his bright red hair that in the right light—and of course, if one was not acquainted with him personally—Lord Jason Cummings could be mistaken for Lucifer himself. "If she fails, it's no skin off my nose." He looked to Lord For-rester. "Nor yours. I see no reason *not* to entertain this notion."

And those were the words that had gained Miss Winnifred

Crane her bargain with Lord Forrester. And brought her here, to Totty's home, where George ranted and raved without any hope of denting her joy.

Joy. Excitement. It was bubbling to the surface, threatening to burst forth in a series of adolescent giggles as she worked the knot of her cloak free and handed it to the waiting butler.

"Thank you, Leighton," she murmured, accidentally giving him the most winning smile, such that the unflappable man blinked twice before blushing.

"Winn, darling, you've made Leighton go all red," Arabella Arbuthnot Tottendale, affectionately known as Totty, said as she descended the stairs. "And George. Dare I hope your excursion went well?"

"It did not, Totty," George spoke up as he tried to shrug his oversized shoulders out of his coat. "You will not believe the tangle Winnifred has *willingly*—" But he was interrupted by Totty sweeping past with an upraised hand.

"I can tell already this conversation cannot be had in a foyer—it has an appalling lack of sherry."

Winn caught Leighton deftly rolling his eyes. And the downstairs rumor that Totty had an eye hidden underneath her lace cap must have had some merit, because even though her back was to him, she called out, "Leighton, is there something wrong with your vision?"

Leighton, for his part, had recovered his unflappability and swiftly answered, "No, ma'am."

"Good to hear. I should hate to have to put you in spectacles. Ghastly indulgence for a butler. Oh, and keep Mr. Bambridge's coat handy; he'll have to leave shortly enough if he's to dress and attend the theatre with us this evening."

And with that, Totty crossed into the cozy sitting room, poured herself a liberal glass of sherry, and ensconced herself by the fire. Winnifred and George could do nothing but follow.

"I still don't see why I must bear the expense and put up at a hotel," George grumbled. "There's room enough for me here, and you yourself have told me time and again that your childhood friendship with *both* our mothers extended to her offspring."

Winn caught Totty's eye and shrugged. But the older lady simply winked back at her. Before Totty was a Tottendale, she was just a girl, growing up in a practical and boring village in the south, where luckily, the only thing to defy practicality and boredom could be found just next door: Clara and Margaret. A pair of cousins who were raised practically as sisters. Totty ran wild with them, until their wildness ran out and everyone involved had to become a young lady. A trying loss, but their friendship bore it, and when they were married and had children, gifts and letters were exchanged, visits and holidays spent in each other's company. And when grief came, when Totty lost her son and husband, or Winn her mother Clara, it was shared, and thus eased. And when Winn finally plucked up the courage to leave Oxford and come to London and try her fate, Totty immediately offered to act as chaperone, guide, and friend. And Winn could not be more grateful.

Especially when it came to George.

"Because you have told me time and again that your intentions toward Winn are more than cousinly." She sent a soft look of inquiry to Winn, the same one she offered whenever the subject of her and George's relationship was discussed. Winn dodged it, much as she had all the times before. "And," Totty continued, "while I may not be strictly concerned with appearances in general, both your mothers would rise from the grave and murder me if they thought I had damaged your reputations. So considering I doubt there is sherry in hell, which is, quite frankly, where I know I'm headed, I'll keep myself comfortable here on earth as long as possible. Besides"—she sent George a look of sympathy—"this is a *ladies'* house. You bump your head on the door frames once a day as is."

It was true, even George would have to admit that. The little house on Bloomsbury Street was everything that was comfortable, stylish, and chic. If you were a single gentlewoman.

And Totty had purchased it two years ago for just that reason. She'd told Winn in a letter at the time that it was because while living with Phillippa Worth, she'd discovered "the bigger the house, the fewer options you have in keeping out disagreeable company. At the rate Phillippa involves herself in charitable functions," she wrote, "it is only a matter of time before a sewing circle or some such odious thing takes over a wing and never leaves." So now, Totty had her little house, with its little garden and little stairs, and little door frames that George's gargantuan size simply could not avoid. Now, she could sit by her fire and ignore invitations to charity teas or the theatre if she felt like staying in . . .

"Totty," Winn asked suddenly, "what prompted the desire to go to the theatre this evening? I thought you hated boring lovesick swains pouring their hearts out from the shrubbery."

"Yes, and I have a rather thin tolerance for the plays as well." Totty smiled at her own joke. "But the short answer is you, my dear. I received a note not five minutes before you got home, from Phillippa Worth, saying that we simply had to attend her box this evening—she *had* to be the first person to host *the* Winnifred Crane."

As Winnifred went white and George practically purple, Totty could only purr, "Like I said, dare I assume your excursion went well?"

"It . . . might not have gone exactly as planned," Winn began cautiously.

"You knew about this the whole time, didn't you?" George accused Totty. "You knew she was going to march into the Historical Society and destroy her good name with this joke . . ."

"Now, now, George," Totty soothed, patting his hand in the politest, yet most dismissive manner possible. "I knew only that Winn had an appointment this afternoon, one you were not meant to tag along to—yet somehow you managed to lose me just as we were sitting down to the luncheon Leighton took whole minutes to prepare, and followed her. But I am very curious to find out what did happen."

And so, Winn laid the story out for her. From the authorship of the papers by C. W. Marks to having her father's letter of introduction drown in the fountain, to a Duke, of all people, playing her quiet yet effective champion, to seeing the Adam and Eve on the wall and her utter boldness to offer Lord Forrester a . . . wager of sorts.

"But it really isn't a wager, as he loses nothing if I win and I lose nothing but face if I do not, but it seems I must plan a trip to the Continent posthaste," she concluded. And then, the weight of the story hitting her, "Totty . . . do you think I might have a glass of sherry as well?"

"I'll be damned if you are," George growled like a wounded bear from his corner.

"Now, now," Totty chided. "The girl is thirty years of age. I'm sure she can handle one small glass of sherry," she said, pouring a rather liberally sized *small* glass for Winn.

"Not that!" George barked. "I'll be damned if you think to travel all over the Continent."

"You cannot stop me, George. As Totty said, I'm well past age. I have no need of guardianship."

"I've never met anyone more in need of it!" he cried, practically laughing. "Before last week, you'd never been outside of Oxford—and barely outside of the libraries. It was ridiculously easy to follow you to Somerset House, simply because you had no idea how to get there. You think you can travel on your own to Basel, Switzerland?"

"Maybe, maybe not." She narrowed her eyes. "But I have to try."

"And how do you expect to fund this trip, Winnifred?" George countered. "Totty shouldn't pay for it."

"Can't in any case—I'm a woman on a budget." Totty lifted her glass of sherry to George.

"And you have no funds of your own," he continued, coming to stand over her, looming—and due to his great advantage in height, and Winn's seated position, George was a world-class loomer.

But Winn simply looked up and met his eye in a cold, hard stare. "And whose fault is that?" she accused.

George sucked in his breath and let it out in a great sigh. All the while holding Winn's constant gaze.

"Heavens, if you two are going to talk about money again, I'm going to go scold Leighton for watering down this sherry," Totty supplied, rising and drifting out of the room. Leaving Winn and George to stare daggers at each other.

"The only reason—" Winn began, breaking the silence.

"If your father—"

"The *only* reason I do not have my inheritance in place right now is you," she finished.

"No, it's not. If your father wanted you to have the paintings," George argued, practically by rote, "he would have specified it in his will. He would have sourced the monies used to buy them."

They had had this fight so often by now, Winnifred could almost predict what would be said next. She would argue that her father's private collection of paintings was the result of lifelong dedication and the vast majority of his salary and earned funds. He specified in his will that his estate would go to his daughter—and his estate consisted of those paintings, a few trinkets, and little else. It wasn't an extensive collection—and mostly by minor painters. But there was a Clara Peeters, a Frans Hals, a Jean Fouquet, and several others from the Dutch Golden Age and Northern Renaissance. And worth enough money that, if sold, Winnifred could live off it quite comfortably for the rest of her days . . . but that part she did not mention to George.

George would then argue that her father acquired those paintings under the guise of adding them to the University's impressive collections and thus they belonged to the school.

Winn would counterattack, saying that if that were the case, why had no one kicked up a fuss about the few of his collection that were to willed to entities outside the school (such as the Adam and Eve to the Historical Society)?

George would throw up his hands and say that Winnifred understood nothing of academic politics.

Winnifred would then reply that she understood enough of academic politics to know George was only supporting the school's claims (and indeed, likely instigating them) to further his own ambitions to fill her father's vacant seat and be made a full professor—jumping over several more well-known and well-published dons. His appointment would be secured if he managed to have Alexander Crane's personal collection added to the school's. Leaving Winnifred penniless.

And then George would argue that her father never intended that she not be taken care of.

"Besides, your father knew you would be taken care of," George said, heartfelt.

It seemed they were skipping directly to the end of the argument this time. Intelligent of him, she had to credit. "By me," he continued. "By your husband."

And there it was. The true root of the problem. Oxford professors, aside from the stature of being one, held certain other privileges that dons did not . . . one of them being the option to marry. And so, George needed to become a professor before they could marry, and he could only become a professor if he bargained away Winn's inheritance. It made her feel used. One of the coins on a table in a card game. But more than that—more than the idea of being won or played for—the idea of marrying George . . . hell, the idea of marriage in and of itself . . .

Every time he brought up this topic, all Winn wanted to do was squirm away to a place where she could breathe . . . where she felt free.

"We've been intended for each other since you were fifteen," George said softly.

"Not formally," she whispered, but she doubted George heard it.

"Half your life, you've known we are going to be married. Our mothers planned it. But now that your father . . . quite frankly, no longer needs you to take care of him, you build up these ridiculous notions about running across Europe and being a scholar and you postpone *us*." He came and sat across from her, in the chair Totty had abandoned by the fire. He reached across the gap between them and took Winn's hand, held it, forced her to look at him. "I've loved you my whole life, Winnifred. Please, put this idea of a grand adventure out of your head and come back to Oxford, and we'll get married—we won't worry about your father's paintings anymore, because they'll be right there; you can visit them any time you like. And life will go back to what it should be. It will go back to normal."

Winn looked up into George's face. The same face she had adored as a child, gone angled and scruffy with time, his eagerness pushing itself against her. She should acquiesce. She knew Oxford's ways; she would be a perfect professor's wife. She had been trained to it, some might say. She should give in. Marriage to George was what everyone around her had expected of her. . .

But there was no one around her anymore.

She was the only one left.

"Normal for you," she began quietly, "is to have me correct all your students' essays and to lay out your lesson plans."

"That's not—" He tried to interrupt, but Winnifred would have none of it.

"I have written your lectures, fixed your papers for publication, hell, I've *written* long passages of them . . . Damn it all, no *wonder* Lord Forrester mistook you for C. W. Marks . . ."

"You shouldn't swear, Winnifred," George scolded, but Winn paid him no heed.

"You want me for an assistant, not a wife," she argued.

"That is most certainly not true!" George denied. He would have made a clumsy attempt to kiss her—she could see it in his face—to prove his passion for her had she not immediately stood up and began to pace the length of the carpet.

"And tangentially, how is it that I am intelligent enough

to write your lectures and yet not clever enough to be C. W. Marks? How could you say those things to Lord Forrester? How *could* you?"

"Winnifred, I . . . didn't think you authored . . ."

"Yes you do. Whether or not you think I could have authored those papers, you know I would never try to take credit for my father's work, as you led him to believe. You should be ashamed." She met his gaze and said again for good measure, "You should be ashamed."

And he was. George had the good grace to let his face burn raw, like the young boy she remembered him to be.

"You don't understand . . . How can a man have a wife who is more famous in his field than he is?" George whined weakly. "It's preposterous. You can't be C. W. Marks."

"Now thanks to you I have to go about proving it." She shook her head. "I barely recognize you anymore. This past year . . . I should have been able to rely on you after my father's death, but instead . . . What happened to my cousin? To my friend?"

George's spine stiffened. "Your friend grows tired of waiting for you to grow up. You're not a girl anymore. You can't run after adventures. We have a life waiting for us—it's been planned for ages."

And they came to the same place again. The circuitous argument. One they were too deeply entrenched in to resolve. In the past, she had tried to extricate herself from it. Tried to voice her concerns, but instead of allaying her fears, George had merely dismissed them.

And now, if she said she didn't wish to marry George anymore . . . well, she would never see her father's paintings again, certainly . . . but more than that, she would be saying good-bye to the map that had been laid out before her, by people who wanted only the best. And George . . . He had been her friend once. It was hard to let go of that.

But if she did marry him, that fresh air, where she could breathe . . . the excitement of discovering something new and seeing the world first hand—not just in books . . . it would never be hers.

It was time to bring the argument to an end. Its true end.

"You're right," she said, causing George to look up, startled. "I'm not a girl anymore. I spent my youth in a library. And gained knowledge that I used to make a reckless wager with Lord Forrester this afternoon. So, since I'm in the mood to make reckless wagers, I have one for you."

She took a deep breath, while George waited, perfectly still, for what she had to say.

"Let me go to Europe and try to discover the origin of the Adam and Eve painting. If I manage to prove conclusively that it is not a Dürer work, then you stop backing the university's assertion that the paintings are theirs, thereby letting me have my inheritance." And letting me go, she added silently to herself.

"And if you fail?" George asked, taking two steps forward, closing the gap between them.

"And if I fail . . ." Winn steadied herself. "What do you want?"

"You know what I want, Winnifred."

She swallowed and nodded. "If I fail, I . . . I will come home and marry you immediately."

"No more delays?" His eyebrow went up.

"If that's what you want," Winn declared, her heart racing. "So . . . is it a bargain?"

As the door clicked closed behind George a few minutes later, Winn could not help but let out a huge sigh of relief. More and more the past few months, she had begun to look at George as not her cousin and friend, but as her jailer. As the man trying to keep her in her tidy little box. But now, with this wager in place, at the highest stakes anyone could play, she saw her chance for freedom. She simply had to win it.

"Well, my dear?" Totty said from the staircase. "Did you come to any new conclusions?"

"Some," she replied, then, staring contemplatively at the

door, "I just wish I understood why he's acting this way. Why he feels the need to force my hand in such a manner."

Totty shook her head. "He can feel you slipping away. You have been his future for as long as he's been yours. Some men don't take well to having their plans altered." She came and took Winn by the arm. "Come, we have to dress for the theatre."

"More than that, Totty. I have to plan a trip to the Continent!"

When George stepped out onto Bloomsbury Street, he was whistling. Certain in his heart that Winnifred would fail and he would earn his professorship and, therefore, they would finally marry. Within two to three years, with Winnifred's help, he would be dean of the History of Art Department. He would be admitted to the Historical Society, take his place among men of understanding and learning, and with her as his wife, be able to pontificate on German gilding or Italianate architecture or whatever happened to be modish at the time. Maybe even get appointed to the government for some cushy job as a historical consultant . . . certainly those positions existed. And they would grant him stature, position, and money. And life would go on as he had anticipated.

Now, all he had to do, George thought with a small spike of fear, was make certain that Winnifred failed.

Five

*Wherein our hero makes
a bargain of his own.*

OVER the next few weeks, Jason would have forgotten that afternoon at the Historical Society with Winnifred Crane. He would have gone about his life, his hunt for a bride with the same hope and trepidation that had marked his suit until now. Yes, that afternoon would have faded into a mere anecdote, lost in the back of his brain until some mention of an Adam and Eve painting, or a girl who looked like a sparrow, reminded him.

He would have forgotten. If he had been allowed to.

"I *just* heard!" Jane cried as he walked in the door to Rayne House that evening for supper. Located in Grosvenor, Rayne House was suitably old and suitably large to impress upon their neighbors the magnitude of the Rayne name. It was also suitably cavernous to create an echo effect, so when Jane made her declaration, it was as if thirty women did at the same time.

"Phillippa just left. Apparently she is adamant that she'll be the first to grab Winnifred Crane as an associate. 'I don't care how bluestocking she is,' Phillippa said, 'if she has the gumption to walk into one of those stuffy societies and claim entrance, she'll have the gumption to sit next to me at the theatre.'" Jane beamed. "You were *at* the Historical Society this afternoon, correct? What was it like? What happened?"

"She's not a bluestocking," Jason said absentmindedly. At least, he didn't think she was. Never having really had any contact with bluestocking women, he sort of assumed he'd manage to pick them out by the color of their socks. "She's a . . . direct sort."

Jane's eyes, if possible, went wider. "Did you actually meet her? Winnifred Crane? What was she like? You cannot imagine all the dust this kicks off of every ladies' society and salon in town."

Did he actually meet her? Jason almost laughed aloud. "Yes, I met her. Spoke with her. Sort of . . . maybe blackmailedthestafftoletherinside," he mumbled, surprised to find himself blushing.

Jane's eyes nearly popped out of her head.

"You were *involved*?" she screeched. "Tell me everything. Now! I must have the whole story before Phillippa does . . . er, I mean, before she hears it from someone else . . ."

As Jane pulled him into the sitting room, forced him into a chair, and played the rapt audience, Jason told her how he had spent the afternoon, from getting unceremoniously brained by Miss Crane's errant hand to how she had marched into the Historical Society great rooms, and his small role in the farce of getting her an audience with Lord Forrester.

"Honestly, I thought we were going to have to go across the hall to the Royal—steal some of their medically minded men, because everyone in the room turned a shade of white unseen this side of Queen Elizabeth." Jason sighed, taking the small plate of food handed to him by a very efficient and quiet footman, and shoving the first of many small sandwiches in his mouth. The events of the day had lead to his skipping repast—and he was starving.

"But, Jason, I don't understand," Jane said, shaking her head, taking the baby handed to her by a very efficient and quiet wet nurse. Little Lissa, Jason's newest niece, cooed and gurgled in the pleasant state that followed her feeding—fat, dumb, and happy, Jason had taken to calling it. Watching his sister be a mother was perhaps the greatest argument for marriage. And watching his niece spit up on her was perhaps the best argument against procreation.

"Oh, Lissa," Jane groaned, handing the baby to Jason as she took a rag from a servant and dabbed at the spittle that drenched the shoulder of her deep green gown. "This is a new Madame Le Trois!"

"You're the one who wore it while holding a five-month-old," Jason rationalized.

"So I should give up on looking modish once I've had children?" Jane countered. "No, thank you. And Byrne would agree with me."

"Where is the man responsible for producing this wriggling mass of flesh?" Jason asked, holding up Lissa, who cooed merrily and reached for his nose as he made faces at her.

"Helping his brother with something at the War Department," Jane replied. "And don't try changing the subject. You deeply respect your fellow members of the Historical Society. I don't understand why you decided to give all these old men heart seizures by assisting Miss Crane."

"Why did I do it?" Jason stuttered. "Well . . . I mean, logically . . ."

Why did he do it? A question he'd been asking himself all day. In all honesty, he didn't have a clue. He had been the one assaulted, true. He could have just walked away at that point, accepting her apology. Then, of course, it was only basic manners that had him fishing the wet paper out of the fountain. After that, he could have easily made his escape. But then again, they had been headed to the same place. It would have seemed strange, wouldn't it, if he hadn't escorted her?

But he didn't have to encourage her. He could have agreed with that annoyingly persistent George Bambridge and discouraged Winnifred Crane from her course. But then again . . .

she was correct, the charter did not specifically ban females. And as out of place as a woman was at the Historical Society, Jason had an absurd love of logic, especially the way it turned on autocratic old rules when applied. He could easily rationalize and argue that . . . Oh to hell with it—the truth was . . .

The truth was, he'd done it because it was fun. A small mischief that caused no real harm and caused a great stir.

And it had been so long since he'd had a little mischief.

But as Jason fumbled and flummoxed for an answer to Jane's question, bouncing his niece on his knee, she finished mopping up Lissa's mess and took her back from him.

"Did she make an impression on you?" Jane asked. "Granted, I know little of Miss Crane's people, but if Phillippa has her way she's about to become the most famous debutante this year."

"She's a bit too old to be a debutante," Jason replied. And then, with a pointed look to his sister, "And no—she did not make an impression on me. At least not the kind you imply."

"No, I don't suppose any young lady who lays down a challenge to the head of the Historical Society came to London with marriage on her mind." Jane sighed. "Truthfully, Jason, I don't care why you did it. I'm just pleased you did. Imagine— *you* of all people shaking the dust off the establishment!" She laughed, and Lissa gurgled with her. "At least all those young ladies will have something else to say to you other than to comment on the weather or compliment your eyes. Oh no! Lissa!" Jane cried, her other shoulder now drenched with baby sick. "You couldn't have given that particular gift to your uncle?"

But Jason could only smile mischievously at his niece. Then, not allowing his sister to change the subject . . .

"They compliment my eyes?"

Indeed they did (and his hair, and once, even his teeth, like a prize-winning horse), but over the course of the next few weeks, they also spoke in great detail about the outrageous Miss Winnifred Crane and her challenge. Not only were young ladies and their mothers remarking on her behavior (an unsurprising number of the mothers feared her influence on their daughters), but the fathers, the brothers, the gentlemen of the ton were all discussing it as well, asking Jason who this Miss Winnifred Crane was, and did she really think she could prove that painting wasn't real?

It was about the time that Jason saw the betting book in White's, with Miss Crane's name mentioned on every single line of the front page, and then glanced over at the *London Times*, which, too, bore her name, that Jason realized he was not going to be permitted to forget Miss Crane—as all of England was paying rapt attention.

"You would not believe the people at the theatre," Phillippa had said a few days after his encounter with Miss Crane. They were at a card party, sanctioned by the Worths. And as Jason was chaperoned by Jane, he was fairly safe from the worst of the fawning.

The gossip, of course, was another matter.

"Everyone craning their necks to see this tiniest slip of a woman, and being rebuffed by her gargantuan bodyguard of a cousin. I swear I haven't had so much fun in ages." Phillippa sighed, playing a trump and taking the trick. "*And* she's adorable, and such fun to talk to. She told me that the pattern on the Marchioness of Broughton's gown—you remember Nora, don't you, Jane?—well, the pattern was not French as she supposed, but actually Slavic! Nora was utterly red faced. Well, more so than usual." Phillippa's expression of delight turned into a pretty pout. "If only she would stay in London, I'm certain I could wash the bluestocking right out of her." Then, her turn well played, she took to her old habit of tapping a nail against her teeth, lost in thought. "It's simply too bad she is so intent on her course and going to the Continent. I haven't had a protégée in *years*; there is so much I could do with her . . ."

"Thank God she's set on her course, then," Jane muttered under her breath.

"What's that?" Phillippa replied.

"Nothing. Simply, having *been* a protégée of yours, I can only think Miss Crane is better off on her own."

Phillippa narrowed her eyes. "You were not a protégée, you were a prototype. There are always flaws in the first model."

Sensing the verbal sparring match to come, Jason decided to excuse himself loudly. "Oh look, I'm to sit out this hand." He laid out his cards and scooted his chair back from the table. Jane and Phillippa noticed nothing.

As Jason made his way across the room, he exhaled deeply. It was his third such event in three days, and somehow, Jane and Phillippa managed to start bickering halfway through each time, only to be reconciled ten minutes later, Jane once again focused on keeping him safe in his pursuit of a bride. As thankful as he was for Jane's presence this year, he really despised those ten minutes. He found himself at the refreshment table, pouring himself another cup of too sticky sweet tea, ducking to taste it, then turning and bumping into a soft feminine hand, which had the sad effect of splashing tea on his face and down his front.

"Oh, Your Grace!" Miss Sarah Forrester cried, putting down her own tea. "I'm so sorry—I was reaching for the cream, and I didn't think you were going to turn . . ."

"I have rotten luck with turning, it seems." Jason sighed, taking his now ruined cravat and dabbing at his soaked chin. "One of these days I'll think to go left instead of right."

"It's my fault," Miss Forrester claimed, picking up a napkin from the table and wetting it from a pitcher of water. "I have always favored my left hand, you see, no matter how often I've had it drilled into me to use the right. I have accidentally knocked over more cups of tea than I care to admit." She smiled at him as she dabbed at his neck. A brazen informality that, oddly, Jason found he did not mind. "At least you can take comfort in the fact that this tea is lukewarm at best."

"Yes, the lack of proper refreshments seems to be my saving grace," Jason said as she looked up from her work and met his eyes. And they both smiled.

"Miss Forrester, lovely to see you again," he said, surprised to find he truly meant it. They'd exchanged pleasant hellos only yesterday at a mediocre but proper musicale. He bowed, ridiculous since up until a second ago, she had her hand on his neck, and therefore made her laugh.

"And you, Your Grace," she replied, ducking into a curtsy.

"How are you enjoying the card party?"

"Well," she said, disposing of the wet napkin on the tray of a nearby servant, "I'm losing."

"Oh dear," Jason drawled, watching her face as she sighed and nodded with mock pity. A lovely face, with a smile that could only be answered in kind. "What are the stakes at your table?"

"I had hoped to play for a ha'penny a hand," she explained, "but my mother is my partner and she will not stand for such missish wagers."

Jason's brow furrowed. Was Lady Forrester a closet gambler? Did she play so high that her daughter was to worry for it? And what of Lord Forrester—did he learn his penchant for outlandish wagers from his wife?

"I fear to ask what you've been made to wager." Jason crossed his arms.

"Dances." Miss Forrester cocked a brow.

"Dances?" Jason repeated.

"I've lost three quadrilles, one waltz, and one dance of the gentleman's choosing. And the way I play, I have no hope of winning them back."

"Huh," was all that Jason could think of in reply. "And who did you lose these dances to?"

"Lord Darabont and Mr. Threshing." She pointed discreetly in the direction of her table, where Lady Forrester sat in between Darabont and Threshing—two men whose fortunes and breeding made up for their advanced age and lack of dental hygiene, respectively.

"Oh dear," Jason replied.

"Precisely," Miss Forrester concurred. "The oddest thing is

my mother is normally a magnificent player—routinely winning her table. She must be having an off day," she reflected. "At this rate, I'll not have a free dance to give for a whole week."

Jason's stomach did a little turn. He was not a great dancer; never having had the surety of his steps like his sister, he tended to stick to quadrilles and that was it. But it was on the tip of his tongue to ask Miss Forrester for her next free dance, before she was forced to sell it for a trump card.

"How goes it at your table?" Miss Forrester asked before Jason could give voice to his thought.

"My table?" he squeaked, his eyes falling on the table he had abandoned. "Oh well, it—ah—it goes . . ."

Just then, Jason saw Jane stand up from the table, her voice carrying over the heads of the other players, as if lightly on a breeze, hashing out one of her oldest arguments with Phillippa.

"That midnight tea party was *my* idea, and *you* were the one who was terrified we would get caught by the headmistress, and don't you deny it . . ."

"Miss Forrester," Jason said abruptly, "it has gotten remarkably stuffy in here. Would you care to take a turn out on the terrace?"

Uncertainty crossed her face for the barest of moments. She opened her mouth to reply but was swiftly interrupted by another voice, this one coming from her table.

"Oh la, Lord Darabont!" Lady Forrester's voice reached their ears. "Another waltz? I dare say you will keep my pretty daughter on her toes all evening."

"I would love to," Miss Forrester replied. And taking the arm he offered, out the door they went.

The next evening, Jason managed to run into Miss Forrester at Almack's, in between her dances with Lord Darabont and Mr. Threshing. He also managed a whole five minutes of conversation before Threshing came by to claim his dance partner.

Two days later, he saw her at a lecture and artifact display, her vague interest in the people and culture of India matching Jason's, which came as a surprise and delight.

"My father likes it when I attend lectures like these," she whispered to him as the crowd was gathering and finding their seats. "And my mother detests it. I find that sufficient reason to go—Indian silks and spices aside."

It was at that lecture that he asked her to call him Jason, and she gave him permission to call her Sarah.

Over the next few weeks, Jason ran into Sarah at a number of functions, and at each one she became the highlight of his evening. In fact, if anything or anyone was going to reduce Miss Winnifred Crane and her mission to little more than background chatter in Jason's mind, it was Sarah Forrester.

They talked about the weather, and somehow, it turned into an inane discussion of which person at the assembly looked the wettest, which turned into a fit of giggles at their own ridiculousness.

He told her of the horses he had growing up, and how much he loved riding.

She told him about the cherry tree behind the parsonage near where she grew up, and how many times she had to do penance for stealing the vicar's wife's cherries.

And on those occasions, when her smile was so wide and her eyes were so bright that Jason thought he might just be happy in this moment, she would laugh musically and thus confirm that he was.

He'd hoped to get Jane's opinion of Miss Forrester, but more than once, when he turned to introduce his sister, she was off somewhere arguing with Phillippa. It was only at the Whitford banquet—an evening of such food and wine that it practically wrought its own harvest festival—when Jason left Sarah's side to go fetch his sister and noticed Jane take Phillippa's arm and pinch her, thus beginning another argument, that he became suspicious.

"What are you doing?" he whispered to Jane once he finally got her alone, which happened to be on the carriage ride home that evening.

"Doing?" Jane asked innocently. "Nothing. We're going home. Hopefully the wet nurse got Lissa down in good order, else Byrne will be up half the night with her. He won't let me take her, you know—he always wants to be the one to rock her."

"I don't care about your child-rearing arrangements with your husband. I want to know why is it every time I try to have you speak with Miss Forrester, you are magically in some sort of fight with Phillippa Worth?" he asked, laziness in his voice but directness in his question.

"Oh." Jane blushed. "That."

"Yes, that," Jason replied coldly. "If you have something against Miss Forrester, I warn you, Jane, I'll have none of your snobbishness—"

"Snobbishness?" Jane cried, offended. But then, letting the offense go, raised her hand. "I have nothing against Miss Forrester. Quite to contrary. She seems a lovely young woman."

"But . . ." he supplied for her.

"But, my concern is about you," Jane countered. At Jason's lifted brow, she hemmed a moment before going on. "Byrne told me what he said to you—about having me court the girls for you."

Jason's brow shuttered down. "What he meant was that there would be no chance of getting locked in a cellar again, if you did the courting," he argued.

"Yes, I know," Jane replied drily. "But once I thought about it, I realized that is exactly what would end up happening."

Jason stared at his sister in confusion. "You think I would simply . . . *hand over* the task of choosing a wife to you? Forgive me, Jane, but I doubt we'd have the same taste in wives."

Jane crossed her arms over her chest. "If you were to introduce her to me any time in the past few weeks, I would have invited her to tea, to Mariah's charitable dinner, to just about every event I could think of."

"Which is how I'm told these things go."

"How long before you get bored of attending musicales and afternoon teas and picnics? How long before you start begging them off? You would have considered your duty done, gone off to the Historical Society or maybe one of the estates, and effectively pawned your courting of Miss Forrester off onto me!" Jane cried.

"I would not!"

"For heaven's sake, Jason!" Jane rolled her eyes. "I was told by your valet that before we arrived last month, you left the house intending to attend a play and turned up again only after spending a weekend in Brighton."

"I . . . told my man that I was going."

"You told him, 'This little adventure may take longer than anticipated,'" Jane quoted back to him.

"And it did," Jason countered.

Jane looked at her hands, gathered herself, then replied quietly, "When Father fell ill, I wanted to brain you on a daily basis for behavior like that."

"That's not fair," Jason replied, ashamed enough of how he acted five years ago without being reminded of it. He sighed deeply. "When I went to Brighton, I had just turned over all my account books to my stewards, and I thought I deserved a little fun. I disappointed no one." Jason forced Jane's gaze up with a gentle hand on her chin. He looked her dead in the eye. "I do not . . . abdicate my responsibilities anymore. I hope I've proved that."

"You have. But, you have a tendency—you do, Jase—to delegate. As Duke of Rayne, this is a useful attribute. I cannot think it possible to run half a dozen estates and sit in the House of Lords without delegation to stewards and gamekeepers and secretaries. But while I am more than happy to help keep you safe from the vultures of society while you chose a bride, I will not court her for you. The longer I am more or less un-acquainted with Miss Forrester, the harder you must work to know her and learn if you like her."

Jane sat back in her seat and nonchalantly looked out the window, all the while keeping a suspicious peripheral eye on Jason as he stewed. In many respects, Jane was right—his life required constant delegation, but he hated to think he would delegate *this*.

Then again, how desperate had he been to run away from almost every Jane-sanctioned event before he met Miss Forrester . . . Sarah? He had waited a full year for Jane to be able to come to town and help him choose a bride simply because the entire process made him itching to run. Was his delegation a product of that desperation? Was he less authentic of a man, a Duke, because of it?

Well, no more.

"I suggest you stop fearing my flightlike impulses and start making friends with Sarah," he drawled as Jane's eyebrow went up, matching his own. "I have an audience with Lord Forrester, Sarah's father, tomorrow."

He had the distinct pleasure of watching Jane's eyes nearly pop out of her head. He smiled. "Did you have so little faith in me that you think I would ask permission to marry his daughter via delegation as well?"

Tomorrow came quickly, and before he knew it, Jason found himself sitting in his carriage, rumbling his way up Strand, on his way to the Historical Society.

Truth be told, he had not disclosed everything to Jane in his declaration last evening. Oh, she tried to get him to say more, but eventually gave up—or more to the point, her husband, Byrne, pulled her away from her relentless interrogation.

Sometimes he was awfully glad that Jane had married him. Sometimes.

No, he had not told Jane everything, and one of the most salient points he had not brought up was that Lord Forrester had asked for the audience, not Jason. He had no idea why, but if the man was as savvy as his reputation would lead one to believe, it must have to do with the inordinate amount of time Jason was spending in Sarah's company.

And like any love-struck young swain, Jason was certain he was about to get politely raked over the coals for not having called on Lord Forrester before now. For not having made his intentions clear.

Thus Jason decided that he would not let this opportunity slip by. His intentions would not only be clear, they would also be more than the old man was expecting or indeed, likely could have hoped for. His daughter would marry a Duke! Let Lord Forrester rake him over the coals for that!

It may have been an impulsive decision, borne of his conversation with his sister last evening, but once he'd said the words "permission to marry," it felt . . . right. Or, if not right, then . . . conclusive.

It was what came next.

So as his boot heels clacked down the hallway and he entered the great rooms of the Historical Society, he ignored the stares that followed him as he crossed the room—in fact, he did not see them. He greeted a few gentlemen, unknowingly startling them into returning the greeting and an awkward few moments of small talk as Jason waited for Edwards to inform Lord Forrester of his arrival.

"Erm," said the gentleman to his left, a Sir Gordon, whose most identifiable feature was his oversized mustache. "We have not seen you recently, Your Grace. You missed the lecture on classical reinterpretations of Greek architecture in the Tudor era."

"Yes," agreed the next gentlemen over, who Jason knew sat three rows up and two seats over from him in the House of Lords but whose name eluded him, "would have thought it right up your alley, Your Grace."

"I was sorry to miss it. I was otherwise occupied that evening," Jason replied. And he had been—that had been the evening of a Jane-approved musicale. A routinely painful affair that on any ordinary day he would have avoided and happily attended the lecture, except that . . .

Except that he hadn't really felt comfortable or, dare he say it, welcome at the Historical Society since the afternoon with Miss Crane. And thus hadn't been back since.

"Yes, the last time you were here was rather exciting," Sir Gordon continued. "Perhaps overly so. Perhaps some reflection is required?"

As Sir Gordon and the other gentleman looked at him pointedly, Jason glanced around the room and saw that every other man there was equally curious to hear what he had to say. And that lovely, floating feeling of purpose he had walking into the room smashed flat on the floor and broke into pieces.

It was safe to say he had not thought out the consequences of his actions that fateful day, but really, there was no harm in them. And he certainly hadn't thought he would end up with strange looks and pointed sentences leveled at him. Persona non grata—well, as persona non grata as a wealthy Duke and member could be.

This was why, he thought peevishly, this was why he had avoided coming back to the Society in the past few weeks. Normally, Jason would have felt agitated, confined. Felt like he should run away from the scrutiny of these men for his recklessness in supporting Miss Crane. The establishment never takes well to being rocked. But, running, that was the old Jason.

This Jason was just annoyed.

"I fear reflection would require a mirror, gentlemen. And I'm not surprised this room is without one." He leaned in conspiratorially. Sir Gordon and his companion (and the rest of the room) did the same. "I doubt you'd like what you see."

Sir Gordon sucked in his breath, his face turning redder than the carpeting beneath their feet.

Luckily, before Sir Gordon could become so ruffled as to locate a glove and slap him with it, the butler came over and whispered in Jason's ear.

"Well, gentlemen," Jason said, rising, "I'll leave you to your reflecting."

Jason would have heaved a great sigh of relief upon leaving them. Once away, he would have loosened his cravat, leaned against the door, and sent a thankful word up to the Saint of Sticky Situations.

He would have.

But he could not.

Because he was promptly escorted into Lord Forrester's offices, greeted, and seated across from the father of the young lady he intended to marry.

"Your Grace," Lord Forrester said companionably. "Thank you for coming to see me so quickly."

"My pleasure, sir," Jason replied, equally companionably. Trying to keep himself level. "I am at your service."

"Excellent," Lord Forrester smiled. "Because it is a service I require of you."

Jason's eyebrow went up. Maybe this was not about Sarah after all. "Sir?" he asked, his voice pitched a mite too high for a man of thirty years.

"You have not been to visit us for quite some time," Lord Forrester began, standing and opening the heavy shades on the window. The window faced east, and it was far enough into the day now that no direct sunlight would come streaming in, causing harm to the multitude of paintings situated on the walls.

"I'm afraid I don't understand, Lord Forrester. I have never been to visit you. Although that is a situation I mean to rectify posthaste," Jason rambled. "After all, your daughter and I have been spending a great deal of time in each other's company, it is only right that I call upon . . ."

But at Lord Forrester's look of quizzical amusement, Jason's rambling died.

"Yes, my little Sarah," Lord Forrester said, the smallest of smiles lifting his lips. "Your attention to her has not gone unnoted by her mother, her sisters, or myself. And while I commend your taste, we must save that subject—and your lack in properly calling upon my household—for another time."

Jason's other eyebrow joined his first. At this rate, he was going to go through his entire life looking terribly surprised.

"You meant that I have not been to visit the Society in recent weeks," Jason surmised, and was rewarded with a nod. "I fear that true as well. I confess I did not feel wholly comfortable with my peers after . . . my last visit."

"You mean after you played the logistician and argued on behalf of Miss Crane's suit." Lord Forrester grinned, his oversized belly shaking with mirth at the memory. "My God, that woman walking into this office is the most refreshing bit of air we've had in years. Alexander would be proud. I cannot think of the faces of the fellows without laughing."

"Yes, well, you should see their faces now," Jason muttered, causing Lord Forrester to laugh again. "Is that why you did it?" Jason asked.

Now it was Lord Forrester's turn to look surprised.

"You were under no obligation to accept her bargain. You could have patted her on the head and sent her away without a by-your-leave." Jason regarded the older gentleman. "Did you indulge her to shock the system, and for that look on the old men's faces?"

"Careful, Your Grace, I happen to be a contemporary of most of the 'old' men out there," Lord Forrester cautioned, but kindly. He took a moment, stared out the window at the people milling about the courtyard by the fountains of Somerset House. "Yes, it is interesting just how much attention the Historical Society has garnered in the last few weeks. We've had more than our fair share of press, more people than ever applying for membership, and certainly more than a few museums interested in that." He pointed to the Adam and Eve painting on the wall. So innocent, so innocuous, and yet at the center of the biggest scandal in the Society's existence. "It is amazing how knocking the dust off old men's spectacles makes everything look new. And as president, I have to relish the attention."

He took a deep breath, then turned away from the window and met Jason's gaze.

"You'll forgive me if I speak bluntly, but do you know how many fellows we have that have little or no academic background? Over seventy percent." Lord Forrester sighed. "But they have money, and enjoy stature."

"And I would be included in that seventy percent, I assume," Jason drawled, leaning back in his chair.

"I'm afraid so, yes. You, however, did more than most for your membership. You actually had your paper published," Lord Forrester said, clearly commending him. Jason felt it wise to not mention at this juncture that he had had his paltry ten-page paper published by a press he happened to own. "Like the Royal Society, the Society of Historical Art and Architecture of the Known World was founded with the intention of fostering new ideas and thoughts, of learning about our past with a hope to directing our future. And those gentlemen who were academically minded but underfunded could meet up with better-heeled men who had an interest in this field of study but other obligations that kept them from pursuing it."

"In other words, academics that needed patrons, and patrons who needed a hobby."

"Precisely. And like the Royal, somewhere along the lines we lost sight of that. And so, once more like the Royal, I intend to do what I can to rectify the situation, before our Society becomes little more than a club like White's, simply with better art." Lord Forrester had put his hands behind his back and taken to pacing, as if giving a lecture. Likely one he had been composing for quite some time, Jason thought.

"That is all very admirable," Jason replied, "but I don't understand what that has to do with Miss Crane."

"Because if this is meant to be a learned institution, we cannot reject learning. No matter the package it arrives in." Lord Forrester sighed resignedly, and went back to his chair, adjusting his weight stiffly.

"When the brouhaha began over C. W. Marks's identity," he continued, "Alexander asked me to keep it secret that he had been sending in the articles. And I will admit, I had some suspicion that it might be Alexander himself who was writing them. Marks is his wife's maiden name, you see." Jason nodded, and he carried on. "Perhaps it was a student, perhaps another colleague who wanted to keep his opinions separate from his documented work. But I never thought of his daughter. I should have—he had written quite frequently of her talents. And it disturbs me that I did not. Because those papers . . . !"

"I've read them," Jason supplied knowingly. "They are remarkable works."

"Which is one reason I have chosen you for this task," Lord Forrester concluded.

"And what is this task you speak of?"

"I need an escort."

Jason sat up in his chair. "An escort."

"If the Historical Society has been receiving this much attention, imagine the amount of attention Miss Crane is having to deal with," Lord Forrester replied.

Jason did not have to imagine, he knew. Phillippa Worth had taken Miss Crane under her wing and practically exploded her onto the London scene. According to the papers, she was seen at one party wearing a scarlet dress, and another wearing a blue ensemble. She was asked to come and speak at a number of literary salons. And heaven help any of those more traditionally minded ladies, for if they dared to cut Miss Crane, they cut Phillippa, too. And Phillippa knew how to cut back.

He had actually run into Miss Crane at some affair or another. She was dressed far nicer than she had been when they last met, her all-brown ensemble replaced with a lovely lavender silk-something-or-other that brought out her startling hazel eyes. He was later told that Phillippa—having had two sons—was aching for a girl to play dress-up with, and was directing her attentions and monies toward Miss Crane. And there she was, resplendent, admired, and being hulked over by her formidable cousin at all times.

She looked utterly miserable.

"Yes, she is receiving a great deal of attention. Although I cannot say if she is courting it, or not," Jason replied.

"I don't believe she is courting all of it, for not all of the attention she is receiving is kind," Lord Forrester replied. "There are countless numbers who would like to see her fail. Now, Mr. Bambridge has informed me that he will be going with his cousin on this journey—"

"Then Miss Crane has an escort in place," Jason concluded. "I certainly don't see how I would be of any more use."

Lord Forrester took a quiet moment to regard Jason, rubbing his chin in thought.

"What is your opinion of Mr. Bambridge, Your Grace?"

"I do not know him well—I honestly doubt we exchanged more than five words altogether before that auspicious day when Miss Crane marched in here."

"But a day like that can show a man's character. So, what opinion did you form of him?"

"That he's a politician," Jason said simply.

Lord Forrester threw back his head with laughter.

"An excellent way to put it. I know him to be a man of certain ambitions. And before that auspicious day, I thought he had the talent to back up those ambitions."

"You said you thought that *he* had been C. W. Marks," Jason remarked, pieces of the puzzle falling into place.

"Indeed. Without those C. W. Marks papers to his credit, Mr. Bambridge is sadly under-published for an Oxford don. Looking at him with new eyes, I can see that while he is dedicated to his career, I doubt his dedication to academics. Under the new guidelines for admission to the Historical Society, I wonder if Mr. Bambridge is a good fit at this time."

"Sir." Jason cleared his throat. "While I agree completely with your assessment of Mr. Bambridge"—being a Duke he could recognize sycophants at an easy distance—"I have little idea what it has to do with Miss Crane."

Lord Forrester leaned in conspiratorially. "Out of all those

•

people who would like to see her fail . . . who do you think would top the list?"

George Bambridge. No question about it. He would view Miss Crane's advancement in the field as a hindrance to his own career. However . . .

"While Mr. Bambridge may not wish her to succeed, do you actually see a gentleman of his station doing harm to her?" Jason asked, alarmed.

"Of course not. It would be unconscionable. But Miss Crane is the daughter of one of my oldest friends. And one of the things men do for their friends' daughters is try to keep them as safe as possible. And having a neutral party on the trip is the best protection I can offer."

"Sir," Jason began, his brain finally catching up with the conversation, "I am honored that you would think of me, but I cannot abandon London to journey across the Continent. I have made promises to my family and have obligations here."

"Settle down, young man." Lord Forrester waved Jason's concerns away. "I have a friend ready to meet her once she reaches France. I merely ask that you provide escort to her ship in Dover."

"Dover?" Jason asked. "That's all?"

"I must think also of the Society." The older man sighed. "All the attention this wager is receiving . . . if some misfortune, God forbid, were to befall Miss Crane, the Historical Society would be blamed—our lack of involvement or no. So I have simply arranged for an array of impartial escorts to attend her, on the various stages. And while there is nothing that can be done about her cousin, if you could see her safely deposited on her ship in Dover, I would consider it a great favor."

Dover. That was about a day's journey, through the East Sussex countryside. The Duke of Rayne's ancestral estate, Crow Castle, was in that region, and it had been nearly a year since he had checked in with his steward in the flesh. He could drive down, deposit Miss Crane, and then spend a few days at

Crow Castle, ascertaining that his holdings were in order. This would be little more than a weekend excursion.

He could also, he thought with a wry smile of coincidence, fetch his mother's emerald ring. It would suit Sarah. She'd mentioned something about liking green, hadn't she?

"Is it favor enough to grant me permission to marry your daughter?" Jason asked, surprised at his own boldness, but more so, at his own steadiness.

Lord Forrester regarded him quietly, efficiently. "As I said, my daughter is a topic for another time." That small cherubic smile lifted his lips again. "And that time is after you return from Dover."

Jason swallowed that and rose. Lord Forrester was too intelligent a player to say yes or no outright. But it was good enough for now. He bowed, saying, "I'd best go make arrangements, then."

He headed for the door but was called back by Lord Forrester's voice.

"And when we do have that conversation, Your Grace," he said, "I think you'll like my answer."

Six

Wherein our hero's travels begin.

T HE Great Dover Road, aptly named by some practical and unromantic city planner at some point in last two millennia, was wide, and easily traversed from London. The journey to Dover, with good horses, axles, and changing posts, was a day in length—give or take, depending on the level of leisure one allowed for their travel. The road went from London to Canterbury, and from there to Dover, one of the most active ports in England. It was, on average, a pleasant journey though rolling English fields and small bucolic villages.

But when one is on a mission of protection, charged as such by the father of the woman one intends to marry, the Great Dover Road suddenly seems to carry any number of areas of ambush, sabotage, and treachery.

For about the first hour.

After the first hour, when no perfidy is perpetrated, the journey can become monumentally boring. One grows easily tired of trying to spot highwaymen or suspicious carriages or overly offended men of letters trying to exact revenge upon a petite woman.

One starts to suspect, Jason thought wryly, that Lord Forrester was off his paranoid hat thinking that Miss Winnifred Crane faced a threat from the outside.

But, he had to acknowledge, there was at least the threat to be found inside the carriage. The overgrown cousin whose interest lay in seeing Miss Crane fail, taking up well over half a carriage seat.

The one who sulked and moaned of motion sickness while having his head stuck out a window.

Jason had never felt more superfluous in his life.

Not only because of the occasional retching noises that came from George Bambridge's side of the carriage, but because Winnifred Crane, wrapped in an unseasonably thick, soft brown wool coat, was comfortably ensconced next to Mrs. Tottendale, who had also decided that Miss Crane needed protection from Mr. Bambridge, but for entirely different reasons.

"For heaven's sake, George," Totty said, touching her small flask to her lips. "If you're going to stick your head out the window like a dog, at least stop knocking into your seatmate as you do it. I doubt His Grace appreciates bruises on his shins."

"I'm so sorry, Your Grace," George Bambridge moaned, coming to sit upright while wiping his mouth. "I am perfectly fine sitting on a horse—in fact I'm quite capable. But being inside carriages has never mixed well with my vision."

"Quite understandable, Mr. Bambridge," Jason demurred. After all, as much as he disliked George Bambridge, he was not so uncharitable as to hold something as uncontrollable as a weak stomach on carriage rides against him. Besides, Jason himself preferred riding alongside carriages, rather than in them.

In fact, he would have much preferred to be astride a horse right now. But his driver, Bones, was armed, his outriders trusty, and besides . . . he had thought perhaps Miss Crane might provide interesting conversation. Some juicy tidbit he could take back to Jane and make her jump for. He tried to catch her eye as George held back the curtain and sought air, but she was holding her book suspiciously high, her shoulders shaking mirthfully.

"If you find travel so disagreeable, Mr. Bambridge," Jason continued, taking his cue from those shaking shoulders, "I wonder that you decided to make this journey. If you cannot stand to not be in control of your movements, I doubt crossing the channel via ship and then another carriage ride through the French countryside will be at all easy."

"And over the Alps," came a mirthful voice from behind the book. "Don't forget the Alps."

"It's not usually this bad. Normally, an open window and a fixed point in the distance and I'm fine." George sighed. "But I assure you, I would have preferred it if this journey had never come to pass."

"You didn't have to come," Winn sing-songed, not even looking up from her book.

"Yes I did, and you know it."

"And since he did, I did." Totty yawned. "Promises made to friends past are all well and good, but ridiculously annoying in execution. Who on earth *wants* to go to the Continent?"

"I do," Miss Crane replied immediately, but Totty continued on without hearing.

"Honestly. It's the middle of the Season, and we have to quit London? The best parties, the best food, the best wine . . . do you think that the Alps will have a Burgundy '93?"

"Perhaps we can pick some up on the way. We will be riding through Burgundy. Or thereabouts." Winn tapped her foot, somewhat nervously.

"And how would you expect to purchase a bottle of Burgundy '93?" George grumbled. "Must cost a fortune."

"The same way I purchased passage across the Channel, George." Miss Crane finally looked at him pointedly over the top of her book. That made him turn a rather rashlike shade of red, and he again sought the solace of the breeze from the open window.

Such a look was shared between the two of them, that Jason knew there was more to that comment than was being said. And being brother to a rather notorious gossip, was well honed in his desire to know more.

"Miss Crane, if you are in need of funds for your journey, I would be happy to lend you a few notes," he said, reaching into his breast pocket. He had a small coin purse there. He never carried a fortune on him, but he had enough to see him through a few days in the country, funds he could use to patch tenant roofs or dig a ditch, if required.

"Thank you, sir, but it is unnecessary," Miss Crane replied kindly. "Phillippa—that is, Lady Worth—has insisted on being my sponsor for this trip. She has written ahead and arranged room and board, and carriages for us for every stop we will make. All bills are to be sent to her." She lowered the book then, and directed her hazel gaze at Jason. "I am sorry; I do not mean to speak of something so vulgar as money, but my cousin was unhappy to learn that I had attracted someone—a woman, of all people—willing to sponsor my efforts."

"Not unhappy, Winnifred—but I don't believe we are meant to sit back and enjoy a leisurely trip on her sovereign!" George replied, scandalized. Although Jason had to suspect the man's displeasure stemmed not from the idea of overspending their benefactress's largess, but instead that he had been counting on a lack of funds to be a stumbling block to Miss Crane's ambitions.

"Oh, don't be so missish, George," Totty tried to intervene. "One bottle of burgundy will not bankrupt Lady Worth—as I should know. She wants nothing more than for us to have a marvelous time on this endeavour."

"Now, Totty, this is not a pleasure trip, and you know it. We will not be stopping and taking in the sights," Miss Crane interjected.

"Here, here," George concurred. "You must give Lady Worth no reason to be embarrassed by her generous support of your schemes."

Miss Crane turned her assessing gaze to Mr. Bambridge. "I'm surprised to find you with such morals about spending other people's money. They never stopped you from having supper at my father's table almost nightly on *his* sovereign," she replied calmly.

Jason had to look down at his toes to keep his laugh hidden from the assembled party. But some members of the party had keener eyes than others.

"I'm so sorry, sir," Miss Crane said, her expression aghast. "There is no more unpleasant topic than money."

"Do not apologize, Miss Crane," Jason replied to ease her fears. "On the contrary, I appreciate your candor. I was simply thinking that I have a rather hearty appetite myself."

"You do?" She blinked.

"Yes. I have been known to put quite the dent in a nice rounder of beef." He got lost in thought for a moment, a small gurgle from his stomach giving away the contents of his thoughts. "But I never thought of my oversized appetite in monetary measures before," he finished, snapping back to himself, only to find a small, bemused smile painting Miss Crane's face.

"Men often do not, as they are not the ones to barter with the butcher on Sundays."

"Sad but true." Jason tipped his hat to her. "I must bow to your superior argument."

"Don't bow to her arguments, Your Grace," George mumbled from beyond the window. "At least not yet. Embattled conversation is fun for her. She would debate a pope about the virtues of sin."

"And the devil into a righteous life?" Jason's eyebrow cocked up. "Much like your father, if I recall."

"Yes, in class he adored debating his students. And of course, during the student dinners he held." She smiled at him again. "You could debate well enough yourself then, if I recall. And put away a decent amount of roast at the same time."

Jason could only sit up straighter in delight. "Your father

spoke to you of our shared suppers?" Alexander Crane invited a gathering of students to a meal once monthly, and Jason had been shocked to be invited while he had been Crane's student. He hadn't thought he stood out much, but to have been remembered by Alexander Crane, enough to be mentioned to his daughter, what a delightful and flattering thought.

But a frown simply crossed Miss Crane's brow as she regarded him queerly. "Spoke to me?" she asked, and then shook her head. "Your Grace, you don't remember me at all, do you?"

"Ah . . . erm . . . ," were all the syllables Jason could manage. Miss Crane shook her head again and then returned her eyes to her book, smiling to herself. Whether she was amused at his lack of memory or at his acute embarrassment, he was not to know. Because the subject was rendered forgotten after they hit a bump in the road and George Bambridge, his head still luckily out the window, made a noise unheard of from the human side of the animal kingdom. Apologies were offered, Miss Crane kept her nose in her book, Totty sipped her flask . . . and the whole round started again.

They stopped at a posting inn on the outskirts of Dover for a very late supper and to rest. Morning tide was in a few short hours, but the opportunity to lay down flat in a bed was too tempting to pass up, so they took the rooms Jason had sent a rider ahead to reserve. It had been a beyond exhausting day—George's stomach eventually settling, Totty sipping her flask and dozing at turns, and Winnifred reading, her anxiety over her upcoming trip obvious in the way her foot would wag, the way she occasionally clutched at the small heart-shaped locket around her neck.

As for Jason, he would only be too glad when he had seen Miss Crane safely on her ship, thus fulfilling his duties. And able to go back to London and . . . do what came next.

All members of the party were asleep before their heads hit their pillows.

But, despite Jason's eagerness to deposit his charge and be on his way, when the first few streaks of pale pink light began to lift the sky, it was Miss Winnifred Crane who descended the stairs first.

She was alone in the pub room (which in the mornings was transformed into a breakfast room) when Jason found her. She couldn't have been there for more than a few minutes, as she was mulling over her options at the bar, which was now the freshly stocked breakfast buffet, picking out a scone. She checked over one shoulder, then, seeing no one, knocked the scone on the bar.

"A bit stale, is it?" Jason asked, leaning his arms against the door frame at the base of the stairs.

Miss Crane jumped, only slightly, but enough to make Jason smile. Framed against the morning light streaming in the window, she looked even more like a child caught at mischief. It was hard to imagine that she was a woman, full grown and mature, embarking on a desperate quest.

"A bit. Likely yesterday's scones, but it will do." She put it on her plate and slathered a sufficient amount of jam over it. Jason joined her by the buffet and wrinkled his nose.

"Not hungry?" she asked as he made no move to fill a plate.

"That scone made quite a solid thunk," he said, regarding the oily sausage and eggs speckled with . . . something. Normally, Jason could eat anything, in ridiculous quantities. And frequently did. Once, when he was up at Oxford he had, on a dare, eaten actual boiled shoe leather, paired with a concoction whose full list of ingredients were to this day a mystery to him—though he was certain it had included port, cow's milk, and béarnaise sauce.

However, this particularly unappetizing repast matched with the prospect of another morning ride with George Bambridge's queasy stomach . . . "Maybe it would be better if I waited a few hours to break my fast. After all, we'll be at your ship within an hour or so, and then I'll . . ."

"Be rid of us?" she finished for him, seating herself at a

table. Jason came and sat next to her. The barman appeared, poured him a cup of coffee. At least that, he felt, would be ingestible.

He sipped it.

It was not.

"I don't blame you, you know," she said, taking a bite of a scone and then swallowing, hard. "We are not the most sterling company I could think of."

"No!" Jason cried. "I do not begrudge you the trip. I have business in the area . . . and the conversation in the carriage is wholly agreeable . . . some of the time."

"Of course it is." She laughed. A very pleasant laugh. "As long as I'm not nervously tapping my foot and George isn't retching out the window."

"That's not your fault."

"Actually," she whispered, "it somewhat is."

His eyebrow went up.

"I might have slipped some ipecac into his tea yesterday morning," she confessed.

"Why?" Jason asked. "I don't think your cousin can be dissuaded from accompanying you."

"I had to try," she admitted. "What comes next would be so much easier if I didn't have to worry about George following me."

"What comes next?" he asked.

She flushed, and took another bite of hard scone. "Switzerland, seeking out the letters that prove the painting's authenticity. Or lack thereof."

She became quiet then—either she thought her answer sufficient or she was too occupied chewing. "God, this is awful," she finally said, choking down her bite of scone.

And in that moment, Jason realized, he liked this woman. Not in a romantic sense of course—Winnifred Crane didn't seem to have a romantic bone in her body. But he could respect her desire to seek out her own path in life, as it were. It was an opportunity he had never been granted. And although he could not begrudge the luxuries of a Dukedom, he could appreciate her fervor. It made him . . . think. Of the what-ifs of his own life.

Stop, he told himself. This is nothing but foolish wistfulness. Admire her he did. Still, he would feel better when he no longer had a hand in her affairs.

"Miss Crane," he said, leaning forward, "I truly wish you luck on your journey."

"Thank you," she replied, taken aback.

"And"—he reached into his breast pocket, pulling out a few coins—"if you happen to—"

"Your Grace, please," she said, shaking her head. "It is completely unnecessary, I have enough funds to pay for my trip."

"This isn't for your trip." He took her hand and pressed the coins into her palm. "It's for a bottle of Burgundy '93. If you happen across it." He leaned in ever so slightly closer. "I should hate for your entire trip to be without a little leisure."

They stayed there, frozen for the barest of seconds, their hands connected around a few discs of metal. The smallest zing of electricity passed through their fingers when he met her eyes. Jason's breath caught. And if he wasn't mistaken . . . Miss Crane's did, too.

Curious. The kind of curious that Jason might wonder about, but he would not have the chance.

"Lord love a duck," George said, thundering down the stairs, "I'm starved. Are there any kippers with these eggs?"

"For the love of all that is holy, George," Totty said, following after him, "you spent all yesterday losing your lunch. Do you really think it best to stuff your gullet today?"

And as their hands fell apart, and Miss Crane picked at her scone, the moment passed without comment.

The Port of Dover was a clamor of activity at morning tide. Ships being loaded with passengers and cargo, most heading for Calais, located just across the Channel, but some headed for points further east in Europe, such as Amsterdam or Brussels. Different voices, different languages lapped over each other in a cacophony of noise that tumbled together incomprehensibly. Men supervising pulleys and flats of goods from the Continent made little time or space for novice ship goers, crowding them out of the way.

They had been late setting off from the inn. First Winn wanted to double-check that she had everything, then Totty was certain she was missing one of her trunks.

Jason considered them lucky to have arrived in Dover in the time they did—he must remember to reward Bones's abilities under pressure.

"Stay here," Jason commanded of Bones, who was unable to force their carriage any further into the fray. Jason eyed the teeming masses as he helped Totty and Miss Crane disembark. "This little adventure may take longer than anticipated."

The four of them pushed through the gauntlet of fish sellers, ticket agents, importers inspecting their wares, and sailors still drunk from their shore leave last night. They made a curious line of ants, threading their way along the pier, followed by the porters who carried the travelers' trunks up to the gangplank of the *Phoenix*, the packet that made one round trip daily to Calais, where a ticket agent waited impatiently.

"You all are cutting it rather close. We're off in five minutes," the ticket agent said to the eager Winnifred, the ambivalent Totty, and the begrudged George in turn, issuing them each paper tickets. A quick shrill of his whistle, and the porters jostled past them and were told where to deposit the luggage for loading. It all happened so fast.

Jason hadn't thought that his mission would be executed so cleanly. So quickly. But there they were, standing at the gangplank of her ship, and he was five minutes from being done with Miss Crane and cleared of his obligation to Lord Forrester.

"Oh no, I'll keep this one with me," Miss Crane was saying to a porter as she held fast to her small portmanteau with one hand while worrying at that heart-shaped locket around her neck with the other. She turned to him, saw that he was watching her, and smiled. "It's so crowded here, I simply don't want it to get lost in the shuffle."

"Yes," Jason agreed, "I'm impressed we found the ship in good time."

"I know!" She laughed awkwardly. "It's very confusing. I confess, I thought for a moment we would end up on ship to Denmark or some such thing."

As noisy and crowded as it was on the dock, silence fell between them, as they both searched for something more to say.

"Come along, Winn," Totty called from halfway up the gangplank. "We're about to cast off!"

"Yes, Winnifred," George concurred from in front of her, "and I would like nothing more than to find our accommodations and go back to sleep!"

"Hurry up then, George," Totty grumbled, pushing at the much larger man, urging him up the gangplank.

"Mrs. Tottendale, Mr. Bambridge," Jason called up to them, "best of luck on your journey!"

He didn't know if they heard him, intent as they were on boarding, but Totty turned and waved back, giving a pointed look to Miss Crane as she did so.

"Yes," Miss Crane said, her hand still clasping her locket. "It seems I must go, else miss my own adventure. Thank you for your kindness in escorting me thus far."

Jason gently removed that hand from the piece of gold at her throat, and bowed over it. "Good-bye, Miss Crane. And enjoy your adventure. I'm eager to know how it will turn out."

"You and the rest of the Historical Society, no doubt." She smiled. "I'll do my best to make the story as entertaining as possible."

And with that their hands parted and they parted company. As Miss Winnifred Crane took her first steps up the gangplank of the ship that would convey her to Calais, Jason turned away and wended his way back through the crowds.

It was good, he thought, as he wandered slowly along the pier. His duty was done, and Miss Crane was launched on the world. He was free. And while some small part of him was melancholy at the thought of this unprotected sparrow being thrust out into the world, another small part was jealous of the adventure she would have.

No, that was not fair. He had already had his European tour, he thought as he sidestepped a rather disgusting looking pile of fish guts, which turned his growling and empty stomach over. What came next for him lay in London, in marriage, in the hard work of running a ducal estate.

Well, best of luck to Miss Crane. If he had not *enjoyed* her company, then at least he'd found it surprising, and the comic stock of players and villains she surrounded herself with, amusing. And with that, he banished any further thought of her from his mind.

Partially because he needed to be concerned with his own future. He looked ahead in time and saw himself finding his mother's emerald ring in the family jewel safe. Saw himself slipping it on Sarah Forrester's finger and, soon after, taking an easy, contented stroll down the matrimonial aisle. Saw himself rigorously enjoying what came after a wedding—the time-honored tradition of a wedding night. And the hazy, vision of a calm, quiet life thereafter.

Yes, he allowed himself to forget about Miss Crane, partially for those reasons. But mostly because, as he passed a stall selling hot sticky buns, he realized he was *monumentally* hungry.

He stopped, took in the scent, and nearly ravaged the old lady selling the delightful, sugary treats. He had skipped breakfast, after all. Instead, he contented himself with purchasing half a dozen buns—never having outgrown the propensity to think with his stomach when famished—and the minute he had them in hand, took the first out of the paper wrappings and held it up to his lips.

He didn't bite. Not at first. But there was something so

right about this moment, this one lovely yeasty smell found amid all the horrid dockside odors of fish and foreigners. Representational of him finally finding his path in life? No, he wrinkled his nose. That was far too poetic for so early in the morning. Likely hunger made him wax rhapsodic, and such silliness was easily remedied.

He turned to watch the ships madly loading their cargo and passengers, opened his mouth, and . . .

Something was wrong.

Not with the bun—although he never tasted it. Something must be wrong with his vision, because Jason was certain he was seeing Winnifred Crane, the little sparrow, dart her way up the gangplank of the *wrong* ship.

No, it was hunger that was clouding his vision. It must be. He glanced over to the *Phoenix*, just about to release its moorings. He had deposited Miss Crane there. He was certain of it.

Then why was he equally certain that he saw the petite form of Miss Crane on board this other ship in front of him, clutching her portmanteau and nervously playing with her locket?

The packet of hot, delicious, fragrant, sticky buns was dropped to the ground, and Jason set out at a full run, ducking and weaving his way through the crowds to the ship. He bumped up against a small boy, who gave a quick "Oy!" and then was swatted at by a man whom he presumed was the boy's father. But he had no time to stop or even shout an apology. He ran up this new ship's gangplank, not even stopping when he heard the loud, long whistle of the crew chief fire after him.

Had she gotten lost? Turned around in the shuffle of people, or followed the wrong crewman?

On board the ship, pushing his way through the various sailors and crewmen, most of whom jabbered on in a foreign language Jason hadn't the time to identify, he finally found the small form of the only woman he could see on board.

As he grabbed her by the arm, she turned with a shriek.

Luckily she didn't hit him.

"Oh!" Miss Crane cried, looking up into his face. "Your Grace, it's you. Thank goodness. But, why are you on—"

"On . . . the wrong . . . ship . . ." Jason managed in between heaving gasps, bending at the waist. Crikey, had it really been so long since he had taken exercise that he was this out of breath?

"Beg pardon?" she asked, confused. "I couldn't understand."

"Does this man bothering you, fräulein?" A burly crewman came over, speaking in what Jason recognized as a Prussian accent as thick as the man's biceps.

"No, thank you," she replied. "He's a friend. But I don't know what he's doing here."

"You're on the wrong ship!" Jason repeated, though clearly this time. He stood up straight. "This is not the *Phoenix*."

There was a great deal of commotion around them, men moving to and fro, pulling on this rope and pushing that wheel, but Jason paid no attention. He took Miss Crane by the arm and pulled her through the traffic.

"Totty and Bambridge must be mad looking for you. Come, we can still make it, the *Phoenix* hasn't cast off yet." But the little sparrow resisted with all her strength. The Prussian crewman was in protective pursuit, calling, "*Achtung!* Stop!" to gather the attention of his brethren.

"We have to hurry," Jason cried. "We can still make it, we simply have to move fas—"

But that was all he was destined to hear for a while, because the thick-armed and accented Prussian crewman had caught up to them, making his presence known with a quick blow to the back of Jason's head.

The soft, rocking motions kept Jason's eyes closed far longer than they should have. It was a pleasant, drifting sensation, akin to being in the cradle, and as such, he indulged. Mornings should always be like this. He could sleep in, just a few more minutes . . . the warm sun above, the soft pillow under his head . . . although it didn't feel like his usual feather down pillow. It was soft, yes, but stronger, and radiated its own warmth, like the valley of a lady's lap.

Jason opened one eye, a bare fraction. And realized, when he saw the brown twill fabric on which he rested his head, that it was indeed a lady's lap. The sparrow's.

And just as suddenly, the sounds around him, murmured voices and lapping water, rushed into focus, sharp and painful to his ears.

"He's coming around," she said, leaning into his line of vision. "Oh, Your Grace, I was so worried."

"Why . . . do I keep getting hit around you?" Jason asked blearily.

"I'm so sorry," she replied as another gentleman leaned into vision. The burly Prussian. "Crewman Reinhardt thought you were abducting me."

Jason sat up with a bolt, his head reeling from the action, but having just remembered the circumstances he was in, it was necessary.

"Miss Crane—you're on the wrong ship. This is not the packet to Calais." He spoke in a rush, his gaze darting from Miss Crane to her German protector. "We have to go. Maybe we can still catch the *Phoenix* . . ."

"I'm afraid we cannot," she said calmly. "They have already cast off . . . and so have we."

Jason looked up then. All the commotion, all the movement—the ship had pulled up anchor. That whistle he'd heard, it had not been calling for the watch to stop him from boarding, it had been the signal for the crew to cast off! And suddenly he felt sick, his empty stomach roiling. He stood, bobbled, managed to stumble to the railing, and . . . all he could see was water. And Dover, getting smaller and smaller in the distance.

"Holy hell," Jason breathed. His mind was racing. "Tell them to turn back."

"Nein," said the crewman, "we would lose a day with the tide."

"But you've got passengers on board the wrong ship!"

"It's not the wrong ship," Miss Crane supplied meekly. "At least not for me."

Jason turned his gaze to her then, his muddled mind striking upon the truth, confusion quickly giving way to clarity. "You lost Totty and George in the crowd and then purchased passage on this ship?"

"Yes," she admitted.

"On purpose."

"Yes."

"And, no doubt, given that man's accent, this ship is not headed to Calais, wherein I would be able to return within the space of a day?"

"I don't believe it is, no."

"Miss Crane," he spoke very carefully, all too aware of the docks getting smaller in the distance, "would you please tell me where this ship is going?"

Winnifred turned to the crewman, who stood righteously by. "Herr Reinhardt—where are we headed, sir?"

"Hamburg," he replied.

She turned to him with a trepidatious smile. "Hamburg."

Seven

Wherein our hero loses his temper.

WINN was certain of a few things in her admittedly sheltered life. She was certain that at four o'clock, England stopped for tea. She was certain that Rembrandt had needed better lighting in his house. She was certain that while she was proficient at darning socks, she would never have talent with the needle necessary to embroider so much as a handkerchief.

Yes, these were things she was certain of.

What she was uncertain of, at the moment, was just exactly how angry a human being could become.

Because Jason Cummings, Duke of Rayne, was about to explode like the mountain above Pompeii.

"A week? A whole bloody week to get to Hamburg?" he roared, pacing a small section of the deck, unable to move further as he was surrounded by Winn, the captain of the ship, Reinhardt, and a few gawking crewmen, one of whom was translating Jason's words into German for their entertainment. "You cannot stop at Dunkerque, or even Amsterdam?"

The captain, who luckily spoke very good English, shook his head. "We are due in Hamburg in a week with our shipment or my entire crew will lose half their wages from the company." He shrugged. "And they would not like to lose half their wages, not even to accommodate a Duke."

"The crossing is not a whole week, your grace. Six days, actually," Winn supplied, then when met with the Duke's dark and furious eyes, wisely stepped back.

"I don't want to hear from you. Six bloody days—no it's twice that, because it will take me six days to get back to England. That's a *fortnight* I'll be gone. I cannot be gone for a fortnight. I have . . . responsibilities."

"Then perhaps you should not have stowed away on this ship," Reinhardt grumbled as the captain nodded.

"I didn't stow away! There was no stowing of anyone anywhere! If anything, I was abducted!" He turned to the captain. "Perhaps it should occur to your crewmen that they shouldn't go hitting people about the head without any warning."

"Sir, I apologize, my man was simply acting in protection of one of our passengers," the captain said wearily, for perhaps the sixth time. "One of our *paying* passengers."

Neither Winn nor the Duke missed the implication. "You want me to pay?" His Grace asked, astonished. "For the privilege of being abducted?"

"I am sorry, sir, but the shipping company will keep track of how many passengers disembark. My men's wages are garnished accordingly." The captain shot a glance to the men who surrounded them. Winn looked to her left and right—suddenly the terse yet affable men she had met when she boarded changed into an oversized gang, whose muscles showed the hard work they put in every day . . . and whose expressions showed how much they disliked the idea of having their wages garnished.

His Grace must have noticed, too, because he reached for the coin purse in his coat pocket as he said, "I would take issue with this company you work for. It seems an unkind place to be employed."

"The world is unkind, sir," the captain replied. "But you are more than welcome to ask that your funds be returned from the company's offices. In Hamburg."

His hand emerged from his breast pocket with . . . nothing. He then checked the pockets at his waist, then frantically patted himself down. "Where?" he said to no one in particular. Then announcing to the assembled party, "My coin purse is gone. Someone has stolen it!" He eyed the crowd wildly. "On the docks . . . or when I was unconscious, someone took all my money!"

Before anyone within the crowd could be shocked, appalled, or accused, Winn sighed and stepped forward. "I'll pay for it. I'll pay for his ticket."

She fished in a side pocket of her portmanteau and pulled out the coins he had given her earlier. "Is this sufficient?"

The captain took the money, counted it quickly, and brought his head up with a smile, his entire demeanor changed. "Welcome aboard the *Seestern*. If you have any luggage . . ." His smile faltered somewhat at the mutinous look the Duke gave him. "*Da*, well, please let us know if you require anything. Do the two of you want your berths next to each other?" He waggled his eyebrows and pitched his voice low. But not low enough, because as soon as the translating crewman got through with his work, the men gathered around them sent up a riotous laugh.

"No!" they answered together.

"Good," the captain said, his expression suddenly stern and serious. "My ship is a respectable one. Any instance of bad behavior will be met with an overboard voyage. Fräulein Crane"—he turned his attention to her—"my wife is traveling with me, and since you are alone, she would be pleased to have you as companion for the journey." Then with a few sharp German words barked to his crew, the crowd dispersed, back to their labors and their schedule.

Leaving Winn to face Mount Vesuvius alone.

"Hmm." She giggled nervously. "I didn't know the ship was called the *Seestern*. I know it means starfish, but it sounds like a cis—"

"No," he intoned, the final word on any matter.

She sighed. "I'm terribly sorry that you got muddled up in this. But you shouldn't have chased me!"

"No," he agreed.

"Don't you see I had to do it?" she pleaded. "I had to get rid of George. He would only try to slow me to the point of a crawl, and stop me altogether if he could. Totty knew what I had planned, and while she may not have liked it, she went along with keeping George busy, and this way I can get to those letters and—"

"No!" Jason growled, taking two advancing steps. "Are you out of your idiotic mind? Even if George was trying to stop you, you had an escort waiting for you on the other side of the Channel! You have abandoned your escort, and young ladies cannot gallivant about the Continent alone!"

"I am thirty years old, hardly in need of a chaperone—"

"No!" he said again, this time holding up a hand to silence her. "And what's more, if you were so hard pressed to get to Basel, Switzerland, the fastest way to get there is through France!"

"But I'm not going to Basel," she replied proudly. "I'm going to Nuremberg. Where Dürer lived. I lied when I told Lord Forrester the letters were in Basel, because George was listening and I didn't want—"

"No!" He held up his hand again. "I do not wish to hear any more about your schemes. I will not become involved."

"Your Grace, again I am sorry, I did not intend to involve you—"

This time instead of simply holding up his hand, he used it to cover her mouth. Then he sighed, the sigh of the long suffering.

"I have to confess, from the moment I met you, getting my face smacked by the fountain at Somerset House, I have had an . . . adolescent compulsion to play along. After all, there's no harm in tweaking the nose of the establishment. Just a little fun. And when I was asked to convey you to Dover, it was only a bit of an inconvenience, and I was satisfied that your trip was well laid out, and thanks to Lord Forrester and Totty, you would be well protected. I comforted myself with the thought that your mischief is only academic. Nothing wrong with a little well-planned adventure."

Then, Jason's eyes darkened even further, taking her down into the depths, past their usual warm chocolate and into coal and pitch. "But since I have been abducted, extorted, and *robbed* in the space of the morning, I am now convinced Forrester was right—you do require protection, but from yourself!"

"I beg your pardon, I do *not*—"

But Jason didn't let her get a word in edgewise, replacing the hand that she had wrenched free. "I am no longer in the mood to play along. I refuse to be dragged into your schemes. I am starving, angry, and stuck on this ship, or one much like it, for a fortnight, so for that time, I do not want to hear a single word from you."

And with that, he released her mouth from his soft grip, turned on his heel, and stormed below decks.

Leaving Winn alone.

She rubbed her cheek, still warm from his touch. She shouldn't feel as insulted as she did. After all, Winn was very capable of seeing the situation from his perspective, and he had every right to be angry at his predicament and outraged by her behavior. She *had* run off, leaving her companions to worry. She *had* boarded a ship, a female alone, intent on bearing her to a place she had never been before, where she had no friends to meet her. And he *had* been hit over the head trying to, from his way of seeing things, help her, and forced to journey all the way to Hamburg without so much as a note to his family or servants, displacing him from his life for likely just enough time for said family and servants to go mad with worry.

And since she was magnanimous enough to see the situation from his perspective, perhaps he would, once he calmed down, be gracious enough to try and see it from hers.

All of her actions, every last one, were borne out of necessity.

It had been a year of awakening for Winn, from realizing that the cruelty of time had robbed her of her youth and locked her in a library, to seeing men she had known her entire life turn to bickering and backstabbing, all for want of adding a few paintings to the school's enormous collection. To the utter betrayal of George, who had decided his own interests topped that of his cousin.

Therefore, she had to lie, telling Lord Forrester that the letters were in Switzerland, when really they were in Nuremberg. She'd had to play along when George insisted on accompanying her, even though she secretly tried to dissuade him with expectorants. And she'd had to make a run for it, with Totty's assistance. And to Totty's credit, she had not approved of the plan, but had some experience with mischief of this kind, and had faith in Winn.

That was all Winn wanted from the world. A little faith. That she could have written the papers by C. W. Marks. That she could make this trip on her own, explore the world, and not have to be shut away in some library for her own protection. That, she thought as a gust of wind lifted her hair under her little straw hat and she gripped the railing for support, and the freedom to enjoy it.

The ship listed slightly to port with the wind, and Winn nearly stumbled into a pile of massive rope, being wound by two crewmen around a giant spool. She was not used to the movement of a ship, having never been on one before. She would have to acquire . . . what did Reinhardt call it? Oh, yes, sea legs. She couldn't help but giggle at the thought. Here she was, on a ship! Never having boarded so much as a rowboat before, she was on a ship to Hamburg!

Impulsively, she took the pin from her hat and removed that scratchy covering from her head. And then with an impish smile, and more guts than she knew she had, tossed the hat into the water.

For the first time since her father had passed, Winnifred felt no weight of other people's expectations. Only her own ambitions fueled her. With the wind in her hair she felt free, because she had pulled off her little plan. Thus far, she had succeeded. The only wrench in the works was the surprise appearance of Jason Cummings.

Who would have thought that the gawky, pompous nineteen-year-old Marquis that she remembered from her father's supper parties, whose main focus in life was architecture, whether it be a buttressed cathedral or the impressive cantilevering of a maidservant's breasts, would, a decade later, be the Duke who came to try and play her rescuer? More than once, including his assistance at Somerset House. And still, she couldn't decide if she found his interference bothersome (he did, after all, cost her the price of another ticket—and since Lady Worth's patronage did not fund this hasty secondary plan, money was going to be tight) or kind and useful (would she have made it to Lord Forrester's offices without him?).

However, considering his current sour attitude, Winn doubted that she would have to put up with his interference any longer. Which was exactly how she wanted it. And how it needed to be.

After all, she had come to understand that if she wished to make her way in this world, ultimately, she could rely on no one but herself.

૭ઝ

It was to be a long six days for Jason—a fact he became reconciled to when he discovered his "quarters" were little more than a sleeping berth wedged in between several barrels of salted fish and crates of Shropshire pottery. The other passengers on board had more accommodating accommodations, but, as he was told by the captain when he complained about the salted-fish smell in his space, he *was* the last passenger to purchase a ticket—all the other berths were already assigned.

"But, as a boon to you," the captain said silkily, "I will have the salted fished moved."

And they were. They were replaced by birds. Living, squawking, caged birds.

When he wasn't in his quarters, it wasn't so bad. Aside from the captain and his crew, there were only six other passengers on board, including Miss Crane. They had varying levels of education and English, from a young Hanoverian couple that had visited their aunt in York, to an English pastry chef (a dichotomy in and of itself) who was following his master to Saxe-Coburg for a three-month stay at that duchy. And when Jason tried to make conversation with them, or when they dined, they were all very amiable, sympathized with his situation, and stayed at least six feet away from him at all times.

It was the downside of having only one set of clothes and having to sleep with fish and birds.

But being up on deck was tolerable. Most of the crewmen would look at him, mutter something under their breaths in German, and then laugh and stay out of his way. Having spent a year abroad in his youth, Jason spoke passable German. He had a good handle on the Lower Saxon dialect and could muddle through the Austro-Bavarian, as well as the standard German. As such, he was fairly certain that one comment he overheard from the crew roughly translated to "runaway Duke." They then speculated that he must be a very poor aristocrat, if common little Fräulein Crane had to buy his ticket.

And then he saw her. Fräulein Crane herself. She was leaning on the port-side railing, her face turned to the wind, the sun illuminating her profile and little wisps of hair coming out of her bun and dancing about her ears. He wondered briefly where her little straw hat was, but without it he could see that she was surprisingly lovely in the afternoon light, wearing an expression of utter happiness.

Happiness? Well of course she was happy; she was getting what she wanted. Jason had spent most of his energy the last five days avoiding Winnifred Crane. And she seemed wholly content to let him. There were no hysterics, no "Please forgive me, I've done a terrible thing"; she was simply, silently intent on her course.

It irked him.

Could she be so foolish to think that she could pull this whole gambit off? What he should do is take her aside . . .

No. No, he couldn't let himself get involved. He had done his duty and deposited her in Dover. That was as far as his obligation to Lord Forrester went. When they docked in Hamburg tomorrow, he was quitting himself of her entirely. He had his own life to get back to, of course. And Winnifred . . . she was headstrong, stubborn, and completely mad. She'd have to be to be on this ship, headed for Hamburg, and happy about it!

Perhaps he should speak to the captain's wife. The lady was thoroughly English; perhaps she would understand his concerns. She and Winnifred had been in each other's company the whole journey. Maybe she could find means of procuring Miss Crane some protection on her mad quest.

He could do that. But that would be as far as his involvement would go.

"Probably spends all his money on clothes," one of the crewmen said in German, cutting into his train of thought. The man waggled a brow, eyeing Jason's once-fine driving coat, which now smelled of five days' wear. The men hadn't stopped speculating on his wealth, or lack thereof, it seemed.

"*Nein,*" the other, who happened to be Reinhardt, Miss Crane's erstwhile protector, replied. "He lost it at cards. All English lose their money at cards." He chewed on his cheroot. "Or, he spent all on women, and his fat, ugly wife chased him off the island!"

Oh for God's sake—could no one believe that his coin purse had been lifted? And it was not as if he had been prepared for this particular journey, he thought, narrowing his eyes. As the crewmen were laughing at the image of his fictional rotund wife chasing him onto the ship, Jason sidled up to them. "*Guten tag,*" he said, and continued in his conversational German, "have you another cheroot? May I have it?"

As the unnamed crewman wordlessly fished in his pocket and produced a spare cheroot, Reinhardt had the grace to blush under his glower. "*Tschuss.*" Jason smiled, taking the end of Reinhardt's cheroot to light his. "And for the record, I'm not married." Then for good measure, looked Reinhardt up and down, and winked.

Jason walked quickly away, laughing under his breath, and from the shocked blubberings he heard behind him, felt certain that he had just given the crew of the *Seestern* a hell of a lot more to speculate about than his financial state.

He felt like giggling. What on earth had possessed him to act so ridiculously? Mischief used to be a forte of his. Hell, there was a time when his skills had been surpassed only by those of his sister. That time he and Jane had stolen their neighbor's dinghy and got it on top of the fell . . .

But that was a lifetime ago. Now, he was more or less responsible. Adult.

It must be the five days at sea. It must be the delirium of this maddening situation.

Or maybe it was her.

He made his way over to the port side of the ship, letting the breeze take some of his cares downwind. But as he meandered over, he discovered that while he had been busy disturbing Reinhardt, Miss Crane had moved on from her vantage and disappeared below decks.

Whatever Jason had thought he might say to her was gone. And, he thought as he pulled on his rather tasteless and nasty cheroot, it was better that way.

Because he was *not* entangling himself with Winnifred Crane any further.

❧

The *Seestern* sailed quietly up the Elbe River that night, docking in Hamburg just as dawn broke the sky. And once again, the only person to beat Jason down the stairs (or gangplank, in this instance) was Winnifred Crane. This time, however, they were not met with serenity of an empty breakfast room, but the focused chaos of the Hamburg ports.

It was more like London than Dover, Jason decided. Dover's

seeming sole purpose was shipping, while London (or in this instance, Hamburg) was a thriving metropolis with shipping capabilities. Even though daybreak had barely lit in the sky, the docks teemed with activity, men tying heavy ropes to cleats or posts, calling up to the crewmen on deck, pushing and shoving merchandise onto flats attached to pulleys. It was as it had been six days ago in England, just in reverse, and in German.

Once his feet hit the unmoving surface of the docks, Jason gained his balance and breathed deeply his relief.

And then was pushed by the traffic directly into Miss Crane's small form.

"Ouf!" was the expected, strangled sound from both colliders. Miss Crane turned and looked up at her assailant with murderous eyes. Then seeing it was him, her expression softened into one of awkward bewilderment, as if she did not know how to address the man.

Jason could only imagine his expression was somewhat similar.

"So . . ." he tried, his mind failing to come up with the appropriate thing to say, therefore letting his voice flounder.

"So . . ." she replied, one hand going to the locket at her throat, the other clutching her portmanteau, her eyes focused somewhere around his earlobe.

"You know how to get where you're going from here?" he blurted out.

"Oh!" Her eyes widened in surprise. "Yes. Mrs. Schmidt—that is, the captain's wife—said she'd show me where to catch the public coaches."

"She said she'd show you?" Jason asked, his brow coming down. He had spoken to Mrs. Schmidt. She'd told him she would make certain Miss Crane got to where she needed to go. But did that entail merely putting her on a coach?

No. No, Jason thought. You are not allowed to be concerned. You are not allowed to get involved.

"Yes, I'm sure she'll disembark shortly. She was very concerned about the unloading of her birds. She brought over a menagerie in England, did you know?"

Jason could only nod briefly. Yes, he was all too aware of the menagerie.

"Besides, I studied maps of this city extensively before we came here. The coaches cannot be far," Miss Crane replied. "I would assume most travelers want to get where they are going."

"Yes. And you need to get to—"

"Nuremberg," she supplied. "And you have to go to the shipping company offices. Get your money back for your inconvenience."

"Right," Jason agreed dully. Then, realizing, "Actually, it's your money. You bought my ticket."

"And some day you can buy me a bottle of Burgundy '93 in return." She smiled. "Let's call it even."

Then, a moment held between them. Neither knowing how to end their conversation and start with the farewells. Until . . .

"Ah, Miss Crane!" The trilling voice of the stout English Mrs. Schmidt called, as she regally maneuvered down the gangplank, any number of beleaguered porters behind her, bearing the squawking contents of Jason's ship quarters. "There you are. I thought you had run away from me."

"Understandable," Jason said, his gaze locking with Miss Crane's. She glared at him, but all he could do was shrug his shoulders. *Well*, those shoulders said, *it's true*. And she rolled her eyes, a nonverbal disagreement.

"Well, have no fear, I'm here now," Mrs. Schmidt was saying. "Your Grace, the shipping company offices are that way— take your first three rights and a left. Oh no! Be very careful with that red-breasted woodpecker! Imagine, you'd think they were handling a common sparrow. Now, Miss Crane," she continued without taking a breath, "we need to get you to the south of my adopted country. Never fear, Your Grace, I'll take her where she needs to go."

And with that, their good-byes were said. Mrs. Schmidt

tucked Miss Crane under her arm and conveyed her around the maddening crowds of goods and men, and disappeared.

Three rights and one left later, Jason found himself staring up at the whitewashed doors of the Schmidt und Schmidt Shipping Company, and found himself feeling a little bit the fool. Not simply because it was fast becoming clear that Captain and Mrs. Schmidt were principal shareholders in the company, and therefore *were* the mythical overseers who balanced the books and struck fear into the men by the docking of their pay. But also because, as it was just past dawn, the building was closed. Whatever clerks and secretaries and managers worked there were likely still at their breakfast tables, just starting their days, and would not be at this door for a few hours.

As a peer, Jason should be enraged. He should thunder about and demand his due respect as such. The difficulty was, without a penny on him, no servants, no obvious declaration of his status, no one would believe him. Or if they did, they wouldn't care.

But that did not mean he had to take such disrespect from Captain Schmidt.

What he should do once he got home, he thought as he meandered back toward the docks, was purchase this little outfit and have it stripped into nothingness. But no, that would leave Captain Schmidt far wealthier than he deserved to be. Better still, he should purchase their competitor and grind their business to dust. He was acquainted with a man who made his fortune in shipping, Mr. Holt. He would have his stewards arrange a meeting, ask his opinion . . .

But as it was, he was stuck in Hamburg for at the very least a few hours. His options were limited. However, when he was last here, on his grand tour with Charles and Nevill, the hotel they had stayed at was the only place that traveling aristocracy might stay. If he could find someone he knew there, some Englishman abroad, he would be vouchsafed, surely. He would be able to get back to London . . .

A sensible plan of action. The first bit of sense he'd come across in six days. And so, for the first time in six days, a smile crossed Jason Cummings's face. There might be hope for him yet.

As he turned his last left, he expected to see the Elbe River ablaze with the morning sun and the unceasing activity on the docks. But he must have taken a right somewhere when he should have turned left, because instead of seeing the docks where he would be content to kill some time, he was assaulted by the sight of Miss Winnifred Crane.

Alone.

She had managed to find her way to the coaching yard of a large inn and was speaking very animatedly with a man who was loading luggage onto a public carriage. Other such coaches were being loaded and unloaded, passengers moving to and from the small restaurant attached to the inn. Men yelling, horses being hitched, shoed, fed. And in the middle of it, the little sparrow, waving her arms like a maniac, trying to get her point across, and skittishly jumping every time the horse next to her tried to snuffle her uncovered hair.

Damn it all, she had been out of his sight no more than half an hour, and already she was in some sort of jumble. And where the hell was Mrs. Schmidt?

His mind clicked suddenly on the fact that if he felt Captain Schmidt was less than accommodating, it was probable Mrs. Schmidt followed suit.

Likely what the two saw in each other, he thought grimly.

No, his brain leapt into the fray. Don't do it. Don't get involved in her mad schemes. Just go to the hotel. Continue on your path. You have your plans and she has hers.

Then he saw her shoulders sag and her hand go to that locket around her throat. She seemed to collect herself for a moment and then, with a deep breath, begin trying to communicate to the man again.

And in that instant, he knew that no matter what his mind was trying to tell him, what self-preservation it was trying to enact, he just couldn't do it. He couldn't keep telling himself to not get involved. If he walked away now, his guilt would eat at him, and push him and pull him until his feet brought him right back around to this spot.

He couldn't run.

The idea of finding a friend at the hotel fell from his mind as he took that first step toward the coaching yard. By the time he had crossed it, it was likely common sense had fled him completely. Because when he finally reached Miss Crane's side, and she turned her face up to him in surprise and shock, the only thing he could think to say was—

"So, where are we headed again? Nuremberg, was it?"

Eight

*Wherein our duo contemplates
the economics of travel.*

"YOUR Grace, this is completely unnecessary . . ." she began after a few false starts.

"It likely is, but I'm doing it all the same." Jason looked up at the straight-faced coachman, then let his eyes fall on the sign at the entrance of the coaching yard. It read *Schmidt und Schmidt*. Of course it did. "We are trying to get to Nuremberg, correct?"

"*I* am, Your Grace," she began, but he cut her off.

"Then I have a feeling you are at the wrong coach."

"I am not. I was simply trying to ascertain—"

"Coachman!" he called up to the man and then switched his language to the proper dialect of German. "Does this coach go to Nuremberg?"

"*Da,*" the coachman said.

"You see?" she claimed. "Mrs. Schmidt told me this is the coach I should take, and I was simply trying to find out—"

"How much is the ticket?" Jason asked the coachman in German, who responded with an outrageous sum. "Why so much? We simply wish to go to Nuremberg."

"*Da*, but this coach also goes to Berlin, Leipzig, Dresden, Dusseldorf, Frankfurt . . ."

"I see." Jason's eyebrow went up. "And you go to all these cities before Nuremberg?"

"*Da*," was the only reply. At that point, Jason could no longer ignore the tugging on his sleeve and turned to Miss Crane.

"What on earth did you say to him? And what did he say back? I've spent the last twenty minutes trying to get a straight answer out of him."

"Miss Crane, do you even speak German?" Jason asked, surprised.

"Of course I speak German," she said, affronted.

"Really?" Jason asked coolly. "Which dialect?"

She opened her mouth and closed it, like a fish. "At least, I can read German very well." And then, after a moment, "Renaissance German."

Jason rolled his eyes but withheld from giving in to his great desire to hang his head in his hands.

"In that case," he said, sighing, "did you have any great desire to see all the sights of the Germanic provinces? Because this carriage will have you crisscrossing the land like a row of needlepoint stitches. It's a tourist vehicle."

"But . . . no!" she cried. "I told Mrs. Schmidt specifically I needed to get to Nuremberg as quickly as possible!"

Jason simply pointed to the Schmidt und Schmidt sign above the yard. "And I believe the price of the roundabout ticket was more to Mrs. Schmidt's liking than the more direct path. Whether or not it put you five days behind schedule." He forced her gaze to meet his. "Sometimes people have their own motives for providing assistance, Miss Crane."

She looked up at him sharply then. "If that is the case, Your Grace, what are your motives?"

It was a question he should have expected, but hadn't. And it gave him such pause that in the space before he could answer, she stepped around him. "Thank you so much for your translation services, but I will manage to find the correct coach on my own."

She maneuvered around the people and horses, and had almost made it to the inn's door, where likely she intended to inquire within, when Jason caught up to her.

"For someone so small, you can certainly move fast," he grumbled. "I'm not going to leave, so you can stop running. Do you have friends in Nuremberg, Miss Crane?"

"Do I . . . ?" she replied quizzically. "Of course I do. I have been corresponding with Herr Heider for the last few years—he's a man who has devoted his life to archiving Dürer's works and writings, a true acolyte. And my father corresponded with him for years beforehand."

"A single gentleman?" Jason questioned.

Her eyes narrowed. "No, he has a wife, and he happens to be older than Moses. Tell me, does your mind always tend toward the most prurient evil, or do you simply not trust anyone?"

"I don't trust anyone," he answered bluntly. "The fact of the matter is, to people like the Schmidts and others like them whom you will meet when traveling, you are an easy target. I know, because I've been an easy target in my time." A quick flash of memory of being fleeced by every barmaid, hotelier, and shop purveyor while on his grand tour and unschooled in travel drifted through his mind. "People will try to impose themselves on you."

She threw up her hands. "To be quite frank with you, sir, since I do not know what you want from me, I can only consider *your* continual presence an imposition!"

"The one thing I have *never* done in our short acquaintance is impose myself on you," he countered. "In fact, it's very much the other way around."

"Then why have you pursued me? Are you trying to get me to change my mind and turn around, like George, or are you trying to get me in bed, like all the men you think to protect me from? Honestly, both scenarios give a very different color to your reasons for running after me onto the ship in the first place."

Jason ground his jaw. But he decided to ignore that jab and instead answer her first question. "You asked about my motives. They are simple, Miss Crane. Guilt. I was assigned to help you by Lord Forrester, and until I see you safely deposited in your friend's hands, I will not have acquitted myself of that duty." It was on the tip of his tongue to mention the hopeful familial connection he would have to Lord Forrester, through Miss Sarah. But instead, some impulse kept that information inside. "I have an English upbringing that forbids it," he said instead, "and a sister who would brain me if she ever learned I abandoned *the* Winnifred Crane to the Schmidts of the world."

"Oh," she replied. In fact, that seemed the only reply he was to get, because she had no other.

"So," Jason continued, when she remained silent, "are we done with this venting of frustration? Can we move on now to finding the proper coach? Because as much as I truly wish I could, I cannot abandon you yet."

He made to pull open the door to the inn, but just then, it was thrust outward from the inside, nearly smacking him.

"Watch yourself!" the rotund man said in German as he barreled through the door. Jason harshly yanked on the door, Miss Crane's accusatory words apparently affecting him more than he thought they had.

"You watch yourself!" he yelled back, too irked to bother with anything other than English.

Miss Crane's small hand reached out and held his arm, holding him still.

"Your Grace," she began, "I find myself remarkably cross today. I'm bewildered in an unknown city and annoyed by my inability to make my point. And then you come along gruffly playing savior after pointedly ignoring me for six days on a voyage where I had only Mrs. Schmidt for company, who as it turns out was planning to bilk me for my funds." She gulped as he patiently raised a brow. "Which is a roundabout way of saying I am sorry I snapped at you and questioned your motives. It was unkind of me."

"Oh," he replied, blinking. Amazingly, those simple words managed to bank his anger considerably. "Thank you."

"But please bear in mind I have a . . . a mission. And it has consumed my thoughts for quite some time. I am naturally suspicious." She took a breath, shaking slightly in her thick coat. "And please bear in mind I have to move quickly, that time is a factor for me. And another factor is . . . money."

Jason's other brow lifted in understanding. "I take it Lady Worth was unaware of this rerouting of your trip and did not plan accordingly."

"Indeed, sir."

"Surely she provided you some pin money, for unforeseen expenses."

"She did." Miss Crane nodded. "But George insisted on carrying it, and I couldn't stop him without arousing suspicion. The only money I have on me is my earnings from selling the C. W. Marks articles—fifteen pounds. Less now, since purchasing the ticket on the *Seestern*." She looked up at him then, her eyes a plea. "It should be enough for one person to get to Nuremberg, but not two. Indeed, I think you would be far more comfortable going home."

Jason took her hand and removed it from his sleeve. She wore gloves, and he did not, but even through the kid, he could feel that smallest of zings. The kind he used to get as a child when he would rub his stockinged feet on carpet and then touch a door handle, giddily laughing the whole time.

"Given your language skills," he said letting her hand go, "I think you will find that I will prove expedient for you, not a hindrance. And as for money . . ."

Jason reached into his pockets, felt around for a few moments, and came out with his gold and silver filigreed cardholder (absent, sadly, any calling cards).

"This should fetch us a few bob. This, too," he said, pointing to the stickpin in his wilted and utterly deplorable cravat. His eyes fell on the ducal signet ring on his right hand. "Not this one, unfortunately. I would be disowned by future Dukes of Rayne if I hawked that."

Miss Crane seemed to contemplate for a moment, her expression inscrutable.

"Let me do this," he asked, seriously. Then with a slight smile, "I've come this far accidentally. Might as well complete the task on purpose."

Perhaps the idea of embarking on an adventure alone was a frightening one. Perhaps she had come to the conclusion that his facility with the language would prove useful. But whatever the workings of that convoluted brain, the end result was a simple shrug.

"I suppose"—she sighed resignedly—"I cannot stop you from taking the same carriage to Nuremberg as I am."

"I don't suppose you can," Jason agreed.

"Then perhaps it is best if we . . . find our coach?"

"My dear Miss Crane"—Jason smiled, teasingly—"that sounds suspiciously like permission to come along. How terribly nice to be needed."

Her eyes flew immediately to his face, their hazel hue ablaze with feeling. "I don't need you, Your Grace." She straightened her shoulders. "I don't need anyone."

Jason flinched. Her vehemence was unexpected. She seemed to think so, too, because just as quickly as it had surfaced, it disappeared under a too-bright smile.

"Shall we go . . . and, er, find a pawnbroker?" She glanced at the card case in his hand.

"Yes," he agreed, blinking back any surprise he might still have on his face. Then he took her hand. Impulsive of him, yes. But somehow his skin was curious in a way that his mind had not yet registered. It wondered if that electricity still existed from the merest, slightest touch. He took her hand and pulled her out of the noise and muck of the coaching yard. "And then we find our carriage, and then . . . the proof that you are C. W. Marks."

Needless to say, at this point in the journey, some conversation was required.

The difficulty was, Winn had absolutely no idea what to say.

They had managed to find a merchant willing to trade the Duke's insanely extravagant personal items for a ridiculously low sum. Winn had a feeling that had the cardholder and stickpin been sold for their actual value, they could have financed the entire trip to Nuremberg and perhaps a few weeks in Paris besides. But as it was, they received sufficient funds to purchase tickets on this public coach, which was headed directly to Nuremberg before it continued on to Munich, plus some little left over to cover His Grace's accommodations on the journey—it would be a good two days before they reached their destination. Their coach was only half full, the only other occupant being the rotund German man who had nearly overset Jason earlier. Luckily, he seemed content to slumber through the journey.

Unluckily, he snored with a fierceness that rivaled any orchestra.

Winn snuck a peek at the small watch pinned to the breast of her brown woolen coat. Two days. Two days of a snoring German. Two days with Lord Jason Cummings, Duke of Rayne, staring back at her from the facing seat.

Winn did not know what to make of the man. She found herself believing his motive. After all, he had no personal care for her or her cause, he had no stake in seeing her succeed or fail. Unless, of course, he'd laid some wager on her in one of those gentlemen's clubs, but somehow she could not think that he had. Not that he seemed a man above such gentlemanly pursuits as wagering on every little thing, but more . . . that he did not seem to care if she succeeded over much. So long as he did.

He had spent six days on a ship, ignoring her mightily, after all. His company now was insisted upon, duty bound.

Was she meant to say thank you to someone who was so dutiful? Was she meant to say thank you to someone whose presence was superfluous? Or, due to such superfluousness, was she meant to ignore him?

Even if his presence, dutiful and superfluous, was a curious comfort?

After all, no matter what he believed, she did not need him.

True, her German was less than fluent, but she would have managed. Her funds were low, but her ingenuity never would be. She did not need him, and better still, for the first blissful time in her life, no one needed her.

But it was so ridiculously awkward! Up until now, they had either been in the company of Totty and George or he had been ignoring her on board the ship. This felt like the first time they were truly . . . together. Thus, Winn was completely at a loss to find some subject to talk about. Which was a shame, because . . . she thought, selfishly . . . she was on the adventure of her life. She wanted to enjoy it!

She snuck another peek at her watch. Only thirty seconds had passed. This was to be a long two days. Two days with Jason Cummings, Duke of Rayne, staring back at her from the facing seat. And two days of that smell.

Winn was not one of those delicate flowers who carried around a scented pouch to hold to her nose when she met people whose personal hygiene did not match her own. But for this one moment, God how she wished she was!

As she tried to breathe through her mouth, tried to position herself a mite closer to the window, tried to slide the curtain open just a hair more.

"You can say it you know," the Duke drawled. "You're not sneaky enough to be polite in this instance."

"Your Grace, you smell something terrible," she said in a great rush.

He laughed at that, throwing his head back and giving a bark of full-throated amusement. "God, I know. I'm beginning to repulse myself." He rubbed a hand across his beard, which over the course of six days had come in thick, stubbly, and bright red. Another week and it would rival the most venerated of philosopher's beards. Strangely, it defined his jaw in a surprisingly pleasing way. He could even be described as somewhat rakish . . . if he didn't smell so bad, that is.

"I confess I could smell something in the coaching yard, but I could not account for it being you until . . ."

"You were forced into a confined space with me?"

"Exactly. It . . . it smells like fish, and . . . and something else I can't quite—"

"That something else is bird." Off her expression, he continued. "I was housed with Mrs. Schmidt's menagerie."

"I imagine the birds were quite taken with you, Your Grace, considering your fishlike scent."

"You imagine correctly." He shook his head. Then, eyeing the gentleman who snored indelicately next to him, he leaned forward and beckoned her to meet him. She did—holding her breath. "I think it best, if, considering our reduced circumstances, if you not address me as 'Your Grace.' "

"Why?"

He hedged a moment, then said, "Because people—innkeepers, coachmen—tend to expect to put forth the best to the aristocracy, and hike up the rates accordingly. Something I learned when I took my grand tour."

She considered him, pulling on her locket as she did so. Something she did when she was thinking over a problem, and a habit that had forced her to replace the chain twice in just the past year. "I thought that aristocrats never paid their bills."

"We do eventually. And if we are on top of our business, we actually *read* our bills. Call it a quirk." He waved his hand, dismissing the line of inquiry. "But I doubt anywhere we stop is going to be willing to delay payment . . . Suffice to say I would rather avoid the trouble altogether."

She regarded him, tilting her head to one side. "Then how should I address you?"

He shrugged noncommittally. "Sir? Jason? 'Hey, you?' "

"How about Mr. Cummings?" she ventured. The idea of calling him Jason (whether or not it was how she thought of him) was at once too interesting and too overwhelming to consider. "I don't think you'd answer to 'Hey, you,' " she offered with a wry smile.

"Mr. Cummings," he tried the words on his tongue. "Sounds . . ."

"Common?"

"Clunky," he countered. "But it is the best option, I suppose."

They fell silent again, the carriage rumbling along. They were well out of the city now, and the window (which Winn had opened fully as soon as His Grace—no, Mr. Cummings—had given her the freedom to acknowledge the stench) offered a view of pastoral countryside. Rolling green hills, small villages in the distance. Cows. Many, many cows.

Discreetly, Winn checked her watch again. Oh heavens, this was going to take forever.

"It's only been sixty seconds since you last checked the time."

She looked up and found his eyes on her. She must not have been as discreet as she thought. Then she saw that his eyes were more on the watch at her breast than on her, and she felt herself blushing . . . for a few reasons.

"It's tin. The watch," she clarified. "If I thought it was worth anything, I would have sold it—not just this morning, but weeks ago, as I was planning the trip." She saw his eyebrow go up. "Truly. I sold anything I could of value to supplement my C. W. Marks money . . . I had to spend some of it getting to London in the first place and making myself presentable. And the only thing I kept of any worth was this locket, and it was my mother's—it's really the only thing I have of hers—so I wasn't about to give it up . . ." she rambled to a stop only when she noticed the set of his jaw and the direct gaze of his dark eye.

"Miss Crane, did I say anything about your watch or its value?"

"No, but I could tell you were looking, and—"

"I was looking because I was curious if we were close to luncheon and wondering if we were going to stop for it."

"Oh," was all she could muster. She looked sheepishly at her little tin watch for a moment, then could think of nothing else to do but look out the window again.

"I'm curious," Jason drawled, breaking through the snores

of their companion. "You mentioned you received your current funds for publishing the C. W. Marks articles. You could have offered up that money as proof of authorship."

"Ah, I did consider that. Unfortunately, the bank notes were sent care of my father, and he cashed them without signing them over to me, instead giving me coin. No bank in the world can trace a coin's lineage, unlike bank notes."

"Very true," Jason conceded. "But the fact that you have the money itself must have *some* weight."

She just laughed at that. "According to George, I could have just as easily gotten the money from selling my hair."

Jason peered at the mass she had loosely pinned at the back of her neck. "Strange. I do not see that you cut your hair."

"I haven't." Her hand went unconsciously to a fallen tendril. "But logic was never George's strongest suit."

As she smoothed that tendril back into place, she looked away briefly, lost in a memory. "I almost did though. To supplement my funds for this journey. However, I may not have a claim to any just vanity, but I do like my hair."

She blushed herself mute when she realized what she had said. It was one thing to fill a silence with inane chatter, but another to reveal yourself as vain in the process!

"But it does bring to mind a question," he supplied, bringing a quick end to the silence, which had been magnifying her mortification. "If your funds are so very tight, why risk the trip in the first place?"

She blinked twice, astonished at his bluntness. "Because I am very good at what I do and would like the credit for it," she stated matter-of-factly.

"No. That is one reason, but it is not *the* reason." He leaned forward again. "Why the . . . desperation?"

She met his eye then. "Because I want my freedom."

As his eyebrow went up, she knew he was asking for the whole story. And while some part of her acknowledged that telling him this information was an act of intimacy far more personal than calling someone by his Christian name, another part of her could only think it somehow inevitable that she let him in. After all, he had taken her to Dover, jumped on the wrong ship after her, and now was rolling down to the southern provinces with her. For better or for worse, he was on this journey, too, and he might as well know why.

"It's a bit of a long story," she began, glancing over at the German, reassured in the consistency of his snores. "Were you aware that my father collected paintings?"

And so she told him. Haltingly at first, but the whole story rumbled out eventually. About the school tying up her inheritance with its claim, and George's support of it. Of George's machinations to move into the vacant professorship at the school. Then she told him of her bargain with George, and the stakes involved.

"Wait a moment," Jason interrupted. "You've been engaged to George Bambridge since you were fifteen?"

"Not engaged." She sighed. "Intended, perhaps. And I don't intend to be any longer."

"For God's sake"—a look of disbelief crossed his face—"what were you doing in the intervening years?"

"Helping my father," she replied. "He had a long decline, and without my mother, someone had to look after him. Besides, he loved nothing more than to teach, and I proved to be his best student. He needed an assistant for his work, I was there for him. He needed someone to keep his house, I was there for him. And as his illness progressed . . ." She broke off, unwilling or unable to complete that sentence. "He needed me," she finished simply. "For a very long time, he needed me."

"And that was burdensome to you."

She blinked, taken aback. "No . . . no. I love my father. It was my duty to care for him."

"But it was still a burden." He shook his head. "Be as polite as you please, but my sister and I went through the same thing with our own father. There is a weight to that need. And it can crush you if you let it."

She found herself nodding, awed by his honesty and the

truth of his assessment. "Yes, all right. Perhaps that weight was a bit heavy. Perhaps that's why I invented C. W. Marks—to give voice to all this education I had . . . and to find an outlet, so I would not be crushed under the weight of my father's needs." Her eyes narrowed, and she filled her voice with conviction. "And while I miss him, now that the weight is gone, I refuse to be tied back down again, to the same place."

He nodded at that. Seemed to digest, to understand. And a curious sensation spread through her body. What a strange thing, to find someone who would understand.

"I understand, you know," he said, somehow snatching the thought out of her brain. "The need to prove yourself."

She could not help it, she had to laugh. "Please, Your Gr—*Mr.* Cummings. When have you ever had to prove yourself?"

He seemed stumped by that, his mouth gaping but no sound coming out. Until . . .

"Your father's class," he declared. "I never worked harder in my life."

"I remember how he spoke about you," she replied with a smile. "He said it was a pity that you were a Duke—or I suppose a Marquis at the time. 'A waste of a good mind,' he would say."

"You seem to remember me rather well from Oxford," he drawled. "Did I cut such a dashing figure?"

She could barely keep from snorting in derision. The boy she remembered could hardly cut a dash through anything. Gawky, self-important, maudlin, and dressed in the most ridiculous fashions of the time. And puffed up enough to believe he was the next Brummell in a puce-colored coat.

"I remember you because I attended those dinners my father held for his favorite students."

"You did?" He blinked back his surprise.

"Yes, and you mistook me for the cook's eleven-year-old daughter." Her lips twisted wryly. "Twice. A product of my height I'm used to living with."

As he began to gape, she took pity on him and continued. "I think my father decided when I was about eighteen that he should introduce me to some gentlemen my own age. Hence, the dinners."

His eyebrow quirked at that. "What about poor Bambridge? Or didn't your father know of his . . . intentions?"

"He did," she replied, but then swallowed the rest of the explanation. After all, she couldn't claim to know her father's mind, his best student or no. Instead, she avoided the Duke's eyes by folding her hands in her lap. "But it was proved time and again that the vast majority of young men at school were interested in their books and their barmaids, but not respectable professors' daughters." She shrugged. "In any case, I stopped going after a few years—I was constantly getting older and all the students remained annoyingly young. But the years I attended overlapped with yours. Hence, I remember you."

"And what do you remember?" Jason asked with a grin. "My fierce intellect? My witty repartee?"

"I remember you ate so much you practically devoured whole platters of food." She smiled. "I also remember you were so thin, I speculated to my father that you must be wearing a corset."

The grin vanished almost immediately. His expression became so contemplative, so serious, that Winn began to panic. Oh dear, had she overstepped some bounds?

"But you're not now!" she blurted. "Wearing a corset, I mean. Obviously." If possible, she turned even redder. "Not that you need one! You have become very . . . even. Balanced."

"Miss Crane, would you care to change the subject?" Jason asked.

"Yes, please," she replied immediately.

But the trouble was, what topic of conversation could they move on to? Despite their few moments of shared history (which he did not remember, she thought wryly), common subjects were eluding her. And awkwardness descended again.

It really was going to be a very long trip, she thought, her gaze finding the window yet again.

Apparently, Winn was not the only one to note the uncomfortable silence (well, as silent as it could be with the crocodilian snores beside them), because Jason was the first to venture into the void.

"Is it all you hoped it would be?" he asked.

"Hmm?" was her quizzical reply.

"The Continent." He blushed, pointing to the pastoral vista that surrounded them. "You mentioned you had not travelled much—"

"Never out of the country, and rarely out of Oxford," she supplied helpfully.

"Right. And I . . . wonder if the German countryside is living up to your expectations."

"Oh! Yes," she said immediately, but then a frown creased her brow as she looked out over the rolling hills of pasture, the sheep and cows that dotted the landscape. They were too far from the Alps to see mountains in the distance, and as such . . . "Actually, it reminds me rather closely of England. I thought it would be different."

He smiled at that, possibly suppressing a chuckle. "Yes, sadly. Sheep and cows on a hill look like sheep and cows on a hill no matter what country you happen to be in. But the mountains to the west and south change the landscape." Then his face turned introspective, his hand went to his new beard, stroking his chin. "Italy looks different. So does France—well, the countryside doesn't so much look different as *feel* different. Some sort of intoxication in the air. The southern parts of Spain . . . once you reach the Mediterranean, the world is a blue that you have never seen before and will never find thereafter, no matter how hard you search."

She could picture it in her mind's eye—the breeze on the wide-leafed trees that dotted the white sand shores of a sea so blue . . . She'd seen it before, but only in paintings. Only in the library.

"You've been? To the Mediterranean, and all these places?"

He nodded. "The way the sun hits the water . . . Trust me, watercolors cannot do it true justice."

"And yet you choose to stay in England?" she inquired. And watched as he found something of remarkable interest on the toes of his shoe—so much so, his eyes would not stray from it.

"It's my home. Everyone needs a home. Besides, I am the head of one of the largest ducal estates in the country. Living in England isn't so much a choice as it is—"

"A duty?" she guessed with a smile. "You do seem rather caught up in doing your duty."

Either he decided to ignore that sideways comment or he tacitly acknowledged it—in any case, something dark flashed through his eyes, before they changed to an expression of wistful remembrance. "But I am glad I got to see it. The sea. I don't think I would be content with my life without having seen that color blue."

"Then that's the first place I'm going to go, once I complete this journey." She smiled.

"You should make a list." Jason smiled back at her.

"Oh, I already have one."

"Can I see it?" He sat up in his seat, his interest peaked.

"It's not written down," she countered. "But it exists. A list of places I've yet to go and things I've yet to try or see."

An eyebrow went up. "List of things you've yet to try? Give me an example."

She thought for a minute. "Ice cream. I'd never had opportunity to try it until a party two weeks ago that Phillippa— Lady Worth—made me attend. Marvelous stuff." Then, she qualified, "The ice cream, not the party."

He laughed, just a little, just enough to make Winn's brow furrow. "Now, why is that funny?"

"Because I imagine if this list starts with ice cream, then it is as long as the road to Damascus. And I hope that toward the end of this list you have some . . . more interesting items in mind."

"Ice cream is awfully interesting to someone who has never had it," she countered. "What items did you think I had on my list?"

And for some reason that made him laugh harder.

And then . . . like sunlight coming through the curtains, she understood. "Oh . . . a list of things I've yet to try. And more interesting than ice cream. Very good, Mr. Cummings, you managed to blanket the entire conversation with innuendo. At least in your mind."

"I'm sorry, I couldn't help it." He laughed, unable to help it. "My sister Jane always hated it when I pulled her pigtails— metaphorically—but I couldn't help it then, either. I don't think you've ever been teased in your entire life."

"Not often." She couldn't help smiling at his juvenile laughter. "And yet somehow you managed. Aren't you proud of yourself?"

"Terribly so."

And then, she had to laugh, too. And it was as simple as that. The tension, the awkwardness, dispelled with talk of travel and innuendo. She could be easy in his presence, the forced intimacy of their proximity giving way to the beginnings of mutual friendship.

Of course, it could not last.

"Since you have so many items to check off this list of yours, let us hope that good George Bambridge does not catch up to us anytime soon," Jason commented as he stretched his legs out, settled into a more comfortable position for sleep, and closed his eyes.

George. Heavens, for perhaps two whole minutes, she had managed to not think about George.

"Do you really think he'll try to follow after us?" she asked, alarmed.

He opened one eye. "After that wager you told me about? Of course he will. Besides, do you honestly think we are going to be that difficult to track? You're a distinctive-looking English female. Luckily, he doesn't know I'm on this journey, so he still might think you're traveling alone, but . . ." But then he shrugged. "But, you know the man better than I do. The real question is, do *you* think he'll follow after you, Miss Crane?"

She grew silent for some minutes as she pondered his question. Yes, Winn had to acknowledge. Yes, George would. Moreover, he would be able to. He had more funds at his disposal, he spoke the language better than she, and his tendency to eschew book study for taking a weekend hunting trip was about to come in handy.

She had been so stupid! What on earth had made her think she could give him the slip in Dover and that would be the end of it? Her lack of caution was deplorable. Well, no more.

Her eyes fell on the still and trying-to-sleep form of Jason Cummings. Winn, however limited her worldly experience, was not unfamiliar with subterfuge or military tactics. She had read whole books on the subject. And one of the first rules was to use whatever cover was available to you.

"In that case, Mr. Cummings"—she cleared her throat—"I think it perhaps best if you call me by another name. My cousin will be looking for a Winnifred Crane, and as such I should probably no longer use that one."

He opened his eyes again. "Sounds reasonable." He shrugged. "What would you prefer? I suppose C. W. Marks is unusable as well. Perhaps a different bird name? Lark? Sparrow?"

"I was thinking"—she bit her lip as she tugged on the locket at her neck—"what about Mrs. Cummings?"

Nine

Wherein our hero declares himself wed.

"THIS is ridiculous," Jason claimed under his breath. They waited in the busy, shuffling coaching yard of the Stellzburg Inn. Their coach had stopped for the evening in a small town called, unsurprisingly, Stellzburg, whose sole purpose it seemed was to be a stopping point in between larger cities, and whose size was little more than the coaching yard they stood in. As their driver spoke with the head stableman, greeting him as a friend, and helped him unhitch the horses, he waved his passengers toward the inn's door, where the innkeeper, a stern-faced and practical-looking man, awaited his newest customers.

"We would do better to say we are brother and sister," Jason argued in a whisper.

"Maybe if I was six inches taller and had red hair," Winnifred countered. "Married, we have the benefit of cheaper accommodations, one room instead of two. And George is less likely to question a false married couple than a false brother and sister."

"Yes, and if anyone ever hears of it, your reputation will

be shredded, and mine won't fare much better." Jason shook his head.

Winn held her breath as they neared the innkeeper. As Jason was the one who spoke the language fluently, he was the one who ultimately would approach the man. Would he go along with her plan? She could pull him aside and roll her eyes at him, give him what she knew to be sound arguments. That first of all, being as they were so far removed from London, no one would find out. Second, as a woman of thirty, she felt vaguely insulted at the idea that her reputation required protection. She had, after all, been in charge of her own reputation so far, and had done very well with it. And third, his reputation wouldn't even come up in the conversation.

But, while she had sound logic on her side, Winn knew Jason had the theoretical right of it on several points . . . and some that were not mentioned. That she hadn't the practice or the nature to pretend to be married. That she was too uneasy to call him by his Christian name. That she wasn't entirely certain he knew *her* Christian name.

But, as they found themselves in front of their somber innkeeper and soporific fellow traveler, Winnifred smiled and did her best to seem a pleasant, unnoticeable traveler. And she sought, found, and squeezed Jason's hand.

It was terribly odd, the feeling that she could and should take this man's hand—a veritable stranger. But up until now, he'd had no qualms about touching her, his hand taking hers in the coach yard in Hamburg, his fingers grazing hers when he gave her money for a bottle of Burgundy—and each time, she was highly aware of the sensation. Maybe he was raised in a more affectionate environment, she thought briefly. Winn had been adored as a child, but her father was not one to express his love for her physically. Hugs and touches, little kisses on the cheek died away when her mother passed. She was not used to being touched.

And yet, she took his hand. And when he looked down at her, she knew he was as surprised as she was.

"And how can I help you?" the stern innkeeper asked in English, no trace of a smile to his face.

While on the one hand, Winn was beyond relieved that he spoke English, she really had to wonder . . . what happened to a little geniality?

"Ah! Good, English!" Jason cried, snapping Winn back to more pertinent things. "We desire accommodations for the night. I am Mr. Cummings." Then with a glance to Winn, he took a deep breath. "And this is my wife, Mrs. Cummings."

As he declared them man and wife, Jason removed his hand from Winn's and placed it on the back of her neck. That small stretch of skin that lay exposed between the nape of her hair and the collar of her dress. Winn couldn't help it; she jumped.

Just the barest, most fractional jump. But it caught in her blood, making her blush. And making the innkeeper turn suddenly hawkeyed.

"And how long have you been married?" the innkeeper asked, unable to keep the suspicion from his voice (or perhaps, it was merely the German accent that lent suspicion to every syllable).

"Not long," Jason supplied, his hand pressing ever so gently on her neck, willing her not to jump again, his thumb stroking a stray wisp of hair . . . and making her blush all the deeper.

"Four days," Winn piped up.

"And still getting used to her new name, you see," Jason finished, looking down into her face. His smile was for the innkeeper's benefit, but his eyes bore into hers, begging for . . . something. Her silence? Asking her to relax? Before she was to figure it out, Jason turned his smile back to the innkeeper, and Winn pasted her own smile on and followed suit.

"Mein Herr!" The innkeeper greeted the other occupant of their carriage, the sleeping, snoring German, who was for the first time since they had become his traveling companions, awake and alert. He embraced the innkeeper like a long lost friend. Their conversation continued at such a rapid pace, and in German, that Winn could not possibly follow it.

"He's asking how the ride was," Jason leaned down and whispered in her ear. "Apparently our fellow passenger has to travel these roads several times a year. Now, the innkeeper is asking . . . oh hell."

There was a pause. Winn watched in frightened anticipation as the rotund snorer they had shared their carriage with eyed them—first Winn and then, speculatively, Jason. Then, turning to the innkeeper, he said a flurry of words that had the innkeeper smiling.

"Welcome, Mr. and Mrs. Cummings," the innkeeper said, turning to them. "Follow me and I'll show you to a very nice room."

"What just happened?" Winn asked in a hurried whisper as she trotted to keep up with Jason's long strides. He saw that she was falling behind and immediately slowed his pace.

"The innkeeper asked if we were truly married."

Her eyes went wide. "And what did the other man—the snorer—say?"

Jason smirked then. "He said, of course we were married. We bickered the entire ride down, he could barely sleep."

She smiled then, relief flooding through her body. Jason took her hand again. "Come on. I don't know about you, but I am dying for a meal and a bath."

As they hurried after the innkeeper, Winn turned her head and found the eyes of the Snorer (as she had taken to calling him in her head) following them from his seat in the taproom, a large plate of food in front of him and a large pint to match. As she found his gaze, she nodded.

Winn couldn't be sure. The inn was terribly busy and jostling, people crossing through her vision constantly. But later on, when she remembered this moment long enough to put it to paper, she could swear that the Snorer, over his spaetzle and beer, across a crowded room, had winked at her.

❦

The Stellzburg Inn, for all its accommodation, was found to be one of those roadside stops that charged for every little service. There were no bathtubs to be had—at least not that they could afford. But there was a cool, clean stream fifty yards away, in the woods behind the inn, where Jason promptly submerged himself. A pitcher of hot water was purchased and brought up to the room for Winn, and that was enough for her to wipe away a week's worth of travel.

It was decided that it was prudent—nay, necessary—to spend the coin to have Jason's clothes washed and pressed, removing any trace of fish or bird smell. He was lent (for a small fee) some of the innkeeper's clothes to wear in the meantime.

Jason reported to Winn that he had seen a maid smacking his shirt on a rock while he was swimming. "The finest linen in the world!" he bemoaned, only to be greeted by an eye roll from Winn.

It was decided unnecessary to have a blade and soap brought up so Jason could shave. One bed, two pillows, one blanket . . . all added up to more coin in small increments, but given that these were the only rooms to be had for many miles, there was very little to be done about it.

They went down to the taproom that evening, and engaged in the debate of splitting a plate of sausage and spaetzle.

"There is no possible way that I am going to be satisfied on half a plate of food, Mrs. Cummings," Jason said pointedly as Winn crossed her arms.

"And there is no way I can possibly finish an entire plate of food, Mr. Cummings," Winn countered, waving a hand over herself to indicate her smaller stature. "I've never eaten very much, and right now it would simply be wasteful."

"Of course you would eat like a sparrow, too," Jason grumbled under his breath.

"What was that?" Winn asked, unable to hear properly in the overloud environs of the taproom.

"Nothing." Then, as a tray of heavenly smelling sausages

was brought out for a nearby table, "I cannot believe that one extra plate of food would bankrupt us," he whined.

"Spoken like someone who has never worried about money."

Jason threw up his hands. Well, at the very least, they were making a convincing show of being a couple.

"Let me see what I can convince the cook to give us," Jason said, patting her shoulder and stepping up from the table. She thought she could hear him grumble as he left, "Now I know how George Bambridge feels."

When he was gone, she could still feel the impression of his hand on her shoulder. The resonant heat that had passed from his hand through her serviceable twill dress to the skin underneath. She had left her coat in the room—for once the atmosphere was warm enough that she felt easy without it. But the shiver down her spine would have to be owed to something else. It seemed so easy for him to casually throw out little touches like that. So easy for him to unnerve her.

Well, she simply wouldn't allow it, she thought as a barmaid brought over their drinks—a half glass of beer for her, a full pint for Jason. Not being terribly familiar with beer, she slowly took a sip of the stuff. The weight of it made her grimace, and the foam that touched her nose made her laugh. Automatically she looked up. No one noticed her unexpected giggling.

Left by herself in the taproom, Winn took the opportunity to look around her. It was the first time in many weeks that she had been alone, even for the barest moments. No George hovering, no people in London fawning over the newest, latest discovery of Phillippa Worth. Oh, Jason had left her alone on board the *Seestern*, but in truth she had been as hovered and watched over by the Schmidts as she had been by others back in London.

Alone was Winn's natural state. As she had acted as her father's faithful assistant and caretaker, the deans of the colleges, with a wink and a nod, and letting her gender slip their minds, had allowed her access to the Bodleian Library, Christ

Church, and other collections. And perhaps, when she'd found what her father was looking for, she would look for her own pleasure . . . Thus she'd had hours upon hours left to her own devices, all by herself in a library, losing herself in books. She was a natural observer.

But the library never let her observe anything like this.

The taproom of the Stellzburg Inn was full of *life*. Life that had eluded Winn up until this time. The energy and excitement that she sought. Travelers, mostly men, and mostly strangers to one another, were drinking, laughing. The innkeeper, his wife, and their servers threaded themselves through the crowd, delivering drinks and food with smiles, and sometimes a wry comment that made the customers laugh.

But it was all perfectly aboveboard. Respectable even.

Somewhat disappointing, that.

"For a minute there you looked blissfully happy, so how is it I rejoin you and you're wearing a frown?" Jason asked as he returned to the table. "Er . . . you have foam on your nose."

"Oh!" Winn said as she turned bright red. Jason reached in his pocket but came up empty.

"Damn," he said, handing her a cloth napkin from their table. "I keep forgetting these are not my own clothes and my handkerchiefs are not where I expect them to be. No, you missed." He indicated her face. She wiped again but must have missed the offending foam again, because Jason took the napkin from her hand and, cupping her chin, wiped the end of her nose gently. "There, you're perfect. Now, why were you scowling before?"

"I was?" she asked, her face remarkably hot. Must be the beer, she decided. "Oh, I was reflecting."

"Reflecting?" he asked, bemused. "On what, pray tell?"

"That reality rarely lives up to expectations." At his quizzical expression, she continued. "I thought the taproom of an inn would be . . . bawdier. More like a public house."

Jason turned completely still. "You've been to a public house?"

"No, but I've seen illustrations," she argued. "Someone playing a fast fiddle in the corner, barmaids with their breasts spilling out. Also, I would like to have some illusions preserved. But here we are in the German countryside, and I have not even seen one pair of lederhosen," she finished mournfully.

Jason threw back his head in laughter, his deep-throated guffaws drawing the attention that Winn's hesitant giggle had not.

"Expectations are a heavy lot. Perhaps we can find you some lederhosen in Nuremberg. But for now, just be happy that we are amongst actual Germans."

"Why?" she asked, her eyebrow going up.

"Because they are logical enough to bring us—and charge us for—only one and a half plates of food." He smiled.

"Thank you," she replied with a nod of acknowledgement. And it was not some few minutes later that the innkeeper himself brought over their food—smelling so good and buttery that Winn for a few seconds considered that maybe she could have made use of a full plate.

"Danke," she said to the innkeeper in anticipation of being served her eagerly awaited meal. Jason casually put his arm around her back, some proprietary instinct letting the innkeeper know they were indeed coupled.

"Bitte." The innkeeper smiled back at them. Strange, for the first time since they had met, the innkeeper's stern countenance had fled, lending him a sort of elfin charm. "I hope you are enjoying yourselves, yes?" he continued in English, still holding the food on his tray.

"Yes," "Very much," she and Jason replied in turn.

"Four days married." The innkeeper shook his head with a smile.

"Five tomorrow," Jason said. "That tray looks terribly heavy," he continued, practically salivating—for which Winn could not blame him. "You should set it down . . ."

But the innkeeper was lost in his own line of thought to even consider placing the tray of food in front of two famished customers. "I remember when I was four days married! My wife—she was so young and lovely we did not emerge from our rooms for the whole week!"

"Er, right," Winn piped up. "But we were a bit hungry, you see . . . from all the . . . staying in. So if you could—"

Then the innkeeper turned and addressed the whole room in his booming voice in German. The room gave a solid cheer and then began clapping in time, chanting the same word. The last one the innkeeper had said to them: *"Kuss."*

"What on earth?" Winn asked, utterly confused.

"He told the room we are newlyweds," Jason whispered to her and then hesitated. "And then he said that . . . oh, just follow my lead."

And he leaned down and kissed her.

It wasn't romantic. It wasn't even kind. It was his mouth pressed up against hers for a hale and hearty smack. But it was enough to have the room erupting in cheers. And it was enough to knock the wind right out of her.

Jason released her mouth and greeted the room with a cheer of his own and a raised glass, which he promptly downed. Winn, more than a little confused, turned her eyes to the innkeeper and saw in them the shrewd glint of the skeptic. It had been a test. He'd had the room egg them into kissing to test the boundaries of their comfort—the Snorer's testimony had not wholly convinced him. But the kiss apparently had, because the innkeeper put down the tray of food and said with a smile, *"Tschuss.* Enjoy your meal. You will be hungrier at breakfast, I know."

And as the innkeeper left them alone, to the toasting and cheers of the entire room, the buzzing in Winn's ears died, and she dully realized she had another new experience to tick off her list of new things to try: being kissed in public.

She was certain she had jumped over several things meant to lead up to it.

"That was close," Jason whispered, his eyes on his plate. Then they flicked over to hers. "Can I entice you to take my carrots? I've never been able to stand the things. In the spirit of making use of every penny, of course."

"Ah . . . certainly," she replied, her mind catching up to the present. "And what is your stance on turnips?"

"Decidedly pro."

"Excellent, then please make use of mine." She breathed easier. Much simpler of course to talk of things of benign interest—turnips and carrots—than to give in to this impulse to lose all composure. To smile or giggle—or panic. Because of course, Jason did not seem prone to smiling, giggling, or panicking. On the contrary, he seemed relaxed, jovial even, as he exchanged his carrots for her turnips.

Then again, Jason had the distinct advantage over her. Not because he might be better versed at kissing someone in public taprooms than she. No, his single-minded focus was expected of his gender. From the lowliest cretin to the most educated, erudite genius, man becomes utterly transfixed when hungry and confronted with food.

But as Jason dug into his meal, and Winn stared bewilderedly at hers, a single thought crossed her mind.

Maybe faking a marriage had been a risky proposition after all.

Ten

*Wherein our duo negotiates
the politics of bedclothes.*

THEY retired shortly after emptying their plates, to the cheers and good wishes of the room. Winn was a shade of red previously unknown to the human eye as she walked quickly out of the room with her head down, while Jason waved to the crowd, even shaking hands with a few of the more intoxicated gentlemen.

When they reached their little room, Winn relished the silence, for as long as it lasted.

Which, with Jason there, wasn't very long.

"I thought the innkeeper had us for a second." Jason smiled as he sat on the edge of the bed and removed his boots. "You know what I think almost gave us away?" One boot hit the ground, followed by the other in loud thuds. "When I went and asked to have a small plate fixed for you. I may have insinuated that I was unfamiliar with your eating habits. And the innkeeper's wife said that any man four days married knows exactly how much his wife eats. Although, the innkeeper's wife is a bit stout, I think she might have aimed that comment at her husband and not me, but it certainly made his ears perk up."

He removed his jacket next and placed it to the side. "You did very well playing the blushing bride, by the by."

"Thank you," she said quietly. "But I don't think you needed to play the bridegroom so . . . jovially."

His head came up. "I was simply playing along. With a ruse of *your* chosing."

Her hands came up. "True."

"It's not as if I intended to kiss you. The innkeeper practically demanded it. And if other men want to shake my hand in congratulations, I couldn't stop them, now could I?"

"I said you're right," she countered, coming off the door.

"Oh," he stuttered. "I am?"

She kept silent, simply quirked an eyebrow at him, and went to the chair, where her portmanteau sat. Opening it, she searched for the flannel nightdress amidst her few necessary belongings, pulling out objects in her way. She could feel his eyes on her back the whole time.

"I'm sorry, it's just so very rare I hear those words coming from a female mouth, could you perhaps say them again?" he said, a grin in his voice. Then, the grin fled. "Winnifred, what is that?"

She turned to him, the object of his attention in her hands. "That is the Adam and Eve painting."

He leapt off the bed, took the one and a half steps across the room to her, and grabbed the frameless canvas out of her hands. "Did you . . . did you *steal* this? How? Good God, does Forrester know?"

"I didn't steal it—it's a reproduction. For reference. And of course Lord Forrester knows; he's the one who had it made for me." She shot a wry look at him. "And if you had been paying attention, you would have noticed that it's three-quarters the size of the original. Full sized, small though it is, would not fit in my suitcase."

As he handled the painting, she went back to her portmanteau and pulled out her flannel nightdress. As she maneuvered herself behind the small, sturdy screen in the corner, she called out.

"And please, don't call me Winnifred. I prefer Winn."

"You do?" his disembodied voice replied. "But I heard Bambridge—"

"I know," she countered from behind the screen. "He's the only one who refuses to call me Winn. I think he dislikes the idea of a name and verb being one and the same. Especially for a female."

"True, you should limit yourselves to adjectives—or nouns, perhaps." He replied, a smile in his voice. "Prudence."

"Violet."

"Sunny."

She emerged from behind the screen nervously. Although nervousness was ridiculous. She was covered neck to toe, and for good measure, had kept her chemise on under the night-dress, as well as her stockings. And as it turned out, nervousness was unnecessary as well—Jason did not look up from the painting in his hands.

"I simply do not see it, Winn," he said at last. "It looks like a Dürer to me."

"But there are some tells that point to a different artist."

"Like what?" Jason asked, holding out the portrait for her. "Show me."

"Well, first of all, it's unsigned. And Dürer had a very distinctive monogram." A capital "D" swallowed by a large, flat "A." It was a mathematical, symbolic signature—and wholly recognizable.

"That means very little," he countered. "Dürer did not sign all his works. Some of the triptychs and his earlier portraiture."

She shook her head. "Usually the signature can be found if one looks closely enough—and those that bear no signature are generally found to be unfinished works. But, all right," she conceded. Then, standing closely next to him, her cheek almost touching his arm, she allowed her finger to trace the lines of Eve's form. "Look at the fluidity of form, the movement. Dürer suggests movement but not action. Here, you can practically feel Eve pulling on the apple from the tree."

She pointed to the figure, trying to show him what she meant, but when she looked up, Jason's eyes were not studying the painting. Instead, they rested on her. But he quickly darted his gaze back to the painting in his hands. "Ah . . . but Dürer has movement in his works. Look at his *Martyrdom of the Ten Thousand* or any of his Italian watercolors. You cannot say that Dürer was not a painter of magnificent breath, a portrait artist whose rendition of hair alone marks him as . . . why are you looking at me like that?"

She couldn't help it, she was smiling at him. "You actually have studied, haven't you?"

An eyebrow went up, even as he blushed at the compliment. "More like your father's lectures left a deep impression."

They held for a moment. Nothing more than the barest tick of a clock, but one where his eyes met hers and they were unable to do anything other than stay as they were. But then, the earth spun on its axis, and movement became necessary.

They each took a step back. Winn took the picture from his hands and turned away, stuffing it back into her bag.

"In any case, I'm not disputing the genius of Dürer. Only that this painting *is* a Dürer. And I understand why it's been mistaken for one." She latched the bag and placed it on the floor before turning back around. "What on earth do you think you're doing?"

Jason lay down on the bed, his long body stretching as far as it could go, like a cat settling down before it slept.

"What do you think I'm doing?" he asked. "I'm going to sleep."

"Not there!" she replied, appalled.

His head came up. "If not here, then where?"

"The chair?" she suggested, waving to the stuffed chair she had just cleared free for him.

He simply chuckled. "Not on your life, wifey dear."

"But . . . But . . ." she sputtered.

"Oh for God's sake," he groaned. "I have not slept in an actual bed, or even something resembling a *pallet*, in over a week. Now this bed may be lumpy and uneven, but it's the best damn thing I've laid eyes on since England. I have absolutely no intention of ravishing you—I am too exhausted to even contemplate it. In fact, I have no intention of getting further undressed than this. But I also have no intention of sleeping in that chair. If you would feel more proper doing so, by all means indulge, and enjoy the cramped back you'll have in the morning."

Winn eyed the chair, then the bed, then Jason, murderously. He sighed.

"If it will make you feel any better, I'll stay above the covers, and you can sleep below."

Her murderous look turned merely dubious. But with a last glance back to the chair (which Winn had to admit, did look remarkably uncomfortable), she stiffened her spine and glided regally over to what was now her side of the bed. He grinned at her as she lay down, then pulled the covers up to practically her nose. And then promptly laughed at herself and pulled the covers back to midchest, and blew out the candle.

And they simply laid there.

Winn closed her eyes, but as tired as she was, every inch of her body was very still aware of the fact that she was sleeping a foot away from another person. Another person of the male persuasion. And even if her mind could accept that he had no intentions toward her, and they were separated by the barrier of clothes and bedclothes alike, her nerves still found it exceedingly awkward.

And he was right. The bed was lumpy. And uneven.

She burrowed deeper into the covers, trying to get warm. Then, she opened one eye and spared a look at Jason. His eyes were closed, the rise and fall of his chest even and deep. He was the picture of comfort and ease, unruffled by his current situation—and Winn had never been more envious in her life.

But before she could fantasize about whacking the somniferous Duke with a pillow, or perhaps engage in any of those childish antics that she'd never had the opportunity to engage in, such as putting his hand in a bowl of water, Jason proved that looks can be deceiving, and spoke.

"For God's sake, woman, I can feel you thinking."

What was she to say? That she was thinking about his nearness, his chest, rising and falling . . . the way his red beard defined his jaw?

"I think we chose the wrong name," she blurted out.

"Cummings?" Jason replied, still not opening his eyes. "Whatever is wrong with it? It's my name after all."

"Precisely. If George manages to follow us this far, he might grow suspicious of a young English couple with, coincidentally, your surname. Lack of title or no."

Jason just stretched again, opened one eye, and placed his hands behind his head in the most annoyingly unconcerned manner. "You chose it—and we cannot change it now in any case." He reached down and patted her on the head patronizingly. "Don't worry—we'll be in Nuremberg soon enough, and you can give my name back to me when I deposit you with your friends."

She swatted his hand away, saying, "Thank you ever so."

He grinned at that and, closing his eyes, settled back down to sleep.

Winn tried to do the same.

Until, of course, Jason spoke again.

"You know," he drawled, "there is one thing I don't understand." He turned his head and met her gaze. "If you've been corresponding with this man in Nuremberg, why not simply take up a pen and paper for your cause? You do seem, mostly, an intelligent, sensible woman. Get your proof from your desk in your library and then your money from Bambridge, and *then* embark on your adventures. Why the need for this mad journey?"

Whether he knew it or not, Jason was asking her the most fundamental question about Winn Crane. So it was only natural that she would take a moment to answer.

"Because if I didn't go now, I would never leave." She sighed. "I would have stayed in my library."

"Yes, but . . . it'd be a hell of a lot more comfortable for both of us, if you stayed in your library," Jason replied, closing his eyes again and adjusting himself on the mattress.

Winn's brow furrowed as she brought herself up on her elbows.

"So you would have me be retiring, quiet in my country life?" she countered. "All for want of an even mattress?"

His eyes flew open. "Honestly? Maybe."

Her eyes narrowed. "You are the one who insisted on accompanying me. You are free to leave at any time."

"Am I?" he countered. "You are far too dewy-eyed and naïve. What have you learned today? That people want to bilk you, they will steer you wrong if it's a benefit to them. A woman traveling alone might as well save time and purchase a ticket for the Turkish harem she'll end up in."

"First of all, we are not traveling anywhere near Turkey," she replied hotly. "And second . . . excuse me, but you can't have it both ways. Either I am a young naïve girl, foolishly headstrong, careening into adventure, or a spinster who should not bore the world with her presence but who should instead retire to her library, ever to remain in the background."

She took a deep breath, wanting her argument to be reasoned and not angry—an emotion she was closely venturing into. Odd . . . she so very rarely became angry. Likely a product of exhaustion, she told herself.

"Think of it this way," she continued calmly. "You're thirty, correct? My age. And yet you are just now considering marriage. Considering retirement to a quiet country life." She laughed a little. "It's strange, but of the two of us, you are the one who thinks to retire and I am the one who seeks out the world."

Jason turned on his side, facing her. "That's not really a fair assessment. You have a list of things to do and see and try . . . and so do I. But my list is full of responsibilities. Besides," he continued, "I don't consider marriage an ending, in and of itself."

"Neither do I," she was quick to agree. "But the world has different expectations for us. And I'm well aware of how the world sees me. A spinster, whose life is in a library, who missed my window for happiness by caring more for old men than young ones. My life is over.

"But you, the world sees as young and virile—your life laid out before you. You can do anything you wish. Even if you contemplate marriage, you are just beginning."

"Winn"—Jason sighed wearily—"what are you trying to say?" The desire for sleep seemed to be winning out over the desire for answers. For her, too.

So, as she settled deeper beneath the covers, she made her conclusion softly, simply.

"Why, if we are the same age, am I considered done and you just getting started?"

Two Days Later

The docks at Hamburg were as uninteresting to George Bambridge as the docks of London or Dover. Seamen and fishmongers with their cries and rhythms did not delight him the way they did his cousin, and add in the foreign tongue, and George found all the noise just an annoying buzz in his ear. But he had made it: he had tracked her thus far.

The packet from Dover to Calais had been at sea about twenty minutes before George realized Winnifred was missing. Always crowded, the packet seemed that day to be more so, with young men heading out for adventure, their grand tours. Since these were young men of good family, George found it prudent to stop and chat with them—it was only solicitous, after all. George was not one to waste any opportunity to ingratiate himself. He was soon to be a professor at the most prestigious institution in the country. One never knew. One of these young men could be or have been a student. One who could happen to have a parent who was influential with the deans.

They talked for some minutes—and all of the young gentlemen, having recently spent some weeks in London, knew of Miss Winnifred Crane. They mentioned that her expedition's beginning had made that day's *Times*. George's chest puffed with pride when he explained that he was traveling with her. Maybe this little adventure wasn't so bad an idea after all. Of course, its outcome would be terribly anticlimactic for his cousin and all the people following it in the papers, but if it afforded him the chance to see his name in the *Times*, perhaps described as an impassioned art historian, and also perhaps, downplaying Winnifred's role in the whole thing . . .

But then the young gentlemen asked if they could meet Miss Crane. George's eyes narrowed at that, his chest giving way to that sinking impression that always accompanied anyone's curiosity in his betrothed. But he smiled and told them she went below decks with her companion, and obliged the young men by moving to fetch her.

However, she wasn't there to be fetched.

"Winn? She was up on deck with you." Totty waved at him. "Can you fetch me my bag from up there?" She pointed to where her valise rested on a high shelf. "All these people bumping into me, I could use a drink."

"Totty, Winnifred is not up on deck," George said, his expression darkening.

Totty's eyebrow went up. "Oh dear. In that case, I really could use a drink."

By the time the entire ship was searched top to bottom, they were too far out to sea to do anything other than complete the journey. Once they landed in Calais, they jumped on the first ship headed back to Dover. After all, once George had discovered she had never boarded the ship, other conclusions fell into place like pieces to a puzzle. She had been lying to him, to everyone the entire time. She was not going to Basel, Switzerland—else misdirection was unnecessary, he would have simply caught up to her there. So the question was, where was she headed?

At times like these, George wished he'd studied his field more. If he knew more about Dürer, he might have some idea about where Winnifred would likely go to track down his papers.

"Well, didn't he paint some in Italy?" Totty offered in an effort to be helpful. "Perhaps she caught a ship to Italy. Which would be wonderful!" She pulled him along the Dover docks to the few Italian ships. "An Italian holiday, warm weather, good wine . . ."

"I don't think so," George replied. "Most ships to Italy leave from the west of the country—Plymouth and the like. We should start with the German ships. After all, Dürer was German, wasn't he?"

Thereafter, it wasn't difficult to find the Dover offices of Schmidt und Schmidt Shipping, nor was the copy of the *Seestern*'s passenger manifest with a Miss Crane listed as having purchased a ticket before setting sail at yesterday's tide. And George spared no time or expense booking his own ticket to Hamburg.

Much to his chagrin, neither did Totty.

"For heaven's sake, of course I'm coming," Totty argued when she saw the somewhat disturbed expression on George's face. "What if she's been kidnapped? I'm not about to sit at home and wait for news."

"She hasn't been kidnapped," George replied crossly. "She's gone off on her own, and when I get my hands on her—"

"Which is the other reason I'm coming along," Totty interjected. "As rash as her actions may seem, there is no way I am going to allow you to meet her alone."

"Dammit, Totty," he yelled, "you'll slow me down!"

Totty flinched at his words, and George immediately regretted his show of temper. It was not seemly, not the cultivated, educated gentleman's way, to yell at elderly matrons.

But he had been thwarted for so long, and here was the latest example of it.

"I have no intention of slowing you down, George," she said slowly, deliberately. "But I am coming."

And there it was. He was backed into a corner. And when backed into a corner, George was a surly beast. But instead of taking his frustrations out on Totty (or Winnifred, as he truly wished to do), he simply took them out on the ship's railing later in the evening, as they set out to sea.

And now, they were in Hamburg. And finding Winnifred, and where she went, would be as simple as finding the Schmidt und Schmidt offices here. After all, he knew his cousin. When freed of fear, she spoke and acted without caution. She had to have talked to someone. Told them her plans, where she was headed.

Totty might try to talk him into waiting a day, getting some rest at a hotel. But he would not oblige.

He couldn't be more than two days behind her, maybe three.

Eleven

*Wherein our hero takes up
fishing as an occupation.*

"WINN. Winn, wake up." Jason nudged the sleeping form off his shoulder. She didn't stir immediately; instead, she nestled herself deeper.

Jason didn't blame her. The last two days of carriage travel had been wearying. His suit of clothes, cleaned and pressed just the night before last, was as wrinkled as an old man's face; they had been cooped up and cramped in this carriage for so long.

Needless to say, this was not the manner to which Jason was accustomed to traveling. Normally, if he were to go abroad, letters would be sent out ahead of time to secure passage and the best rooms at the best posting inns available. Those letters would have been affixed with the seal of the Duke of Rayne, and when he arrived, it would have been with servants in his livery, telling the innkeepers and ostlers exactly who he was without him having to say a word.

But now—he has no men in livery attending him. No letters had been sent out in advance on fine paper and paid for at a penny a page. No one assuring the posting houses that the bills would be settled to their satisfaction. He had little more than an old ring on his finger, which to a provincial innkeeper in rural Germany meant much less than the fact that he had very little money.

It was strangely freeing. Simple.

Although what was not simple was pretending to be a married commoner with a new bride on his arm.

Sometime yesterday they crossed into Hesse from Lower Saxony. They had made another stop last evening, at another roadside inn, and repeated the same performance they had in Stellzburg. Although this time they must have been well practiced enough to successfully sell themselves as a married couple, because no one questioned it, no one drew attention to them . . . no one slapped him on the back as they made their way upstairs, which he knew made Winn happy. And once up in the room, there was no negotiating for bed space, no thoughtful conversation. They were too tired for it.

It was in the morning, when he was well rested and clear-eyed, that he came to realize just how disturbing the situation had become.

Yesterday morning, Winn, for all her exhaustion, had again been up before him and banging about the room, trying her best, albeit unsuccessfully, to be quiet. But it wasn't the noise that had alerted him to the day—he had slept too blissfully for that. It was the dent in the mattress. It was Winn-sized and circular, as if she had been curled up in a ball—and it was situated alarmingly close to his own body.

But he did not allow himself to speculate on the positioning of the mattress dent relative to his sleep space, or the fact that he was awoken by her getting up and thus its discovery. But the next morning—that morning—he was confronted with it head on.

Something, some small noise outside woke him briefly before dawn, and Jason discovered something truly shocking: Despite the bedclothes that separated them, somehow his arm had found its way under her head, cradling her in its crook.

And she, curled up in a ball at his side, her knees prodding his hip, seeking his heat.

He had been awake from the moment on.

Today they crossed into Bavaria, the principality that housed Nuremberg. They had picked up a few more travelers at this second inn—a mother and her young son. There was very little conversation, as their rotund German Snorer was . . . snoring, and the mother was preoccupied with keeping her son from getting anything sticky on his fingers, and therefore, the whole of the interior of the carriage. Jason had moved next to Winn to protect her (oh, all right, and himself) from said stickiness.

It did not allow for relaxation.

It was odd, but being this close to Winn, her slight frame against his side—as aware and awake as it made him—it was becoming natural for him. When she didn't occupy that space, he was far too aware of the cool air that rushed in and filled it. When they had begun this together, when he had touched her hand in the breakfast room before they reached Dover, the electricity that passed between them was pleasantly shocking. Intriguing, too. After taking her hand in the coaching yard, he had consciously decided to try and touch her again, on the hand, on the back of the neck, wiping beer from the end of her nose, to see if that curious shock that spread through his nerves would still be there.

But now, mere days later, those little jolts, those little touches, they were like a drug to him. Something he needed to have in his system, daily. Something that kept his side warm, and the cool air from invading the space.

He just couldn't stop doing it.

Apparently, even in his sleep.

"Winn," he said a little more sternly, even as his thumb caressed her shoulder. "Winnifred, we're here."

"I told you not to call me that," she mumbled, her eyes blinking open.

"Desperate times call for desperate measures," he answered wryly. "Besides, I thought you would have been sitting up with your head out the window like a puppy. We've reached Nuremberg."

That brought her head off his shoulder, just as the carriage rumbled to a halt in the coaching yard. The other passengers were eager to disembark, but Winnifred beat them to the door, leaping out with so much passion that she nearly knocked over the young servant who was just setting down blocks for them.

And that cool air rushed in, occupying the space she had just fled.

By the time he reached her side again, she had made it halfway to the coaching yard gate, her feet hitting the cobblestones of Nuremberg's streets with vigor and intensity.

"Forget something?" he drawled, coming to walk beside her.

"Oh, I knew you'd catch up eventually," she said, waving her hand absently as her eyes searched the streets, looking for signs and postings most likely. Trying to find her way.

"I meant this," Jason replied, holding up her portmanteau, the sight of which brought her to an immediate stop.

"Oh my goodness!" she cried, reaching to take the bag from his hands. "I'm such a goose today."

"Why?" he asked, smiling, not releasing the bag to her. Instead it allowed his fingers to knock up against hers, and he wasn't about to let go just yet.

"Forgetting my bag, of course, and . . . falling asleep on you." She blushed, talking faster to cover her embarrassment. "It must be the excitement of the day. You see, I'm finally here! In Nuremberg, and we just have to get to Herr Heider and I can get the letters, and—"

"Yes, most people fall dead asleep when excited," Jason replied, sarcasm dripping, but with a smile. "And let go, woman. I can carry your bag. This way if you drift off in the middle of the street from excitement, you won't drop it and leave it behind."

She raised a skeptical brow at that but let go of the bag, allowing Jason to take control of it.

"Excellent," he said, his eyes darting up to the sides of the buildings that surrounded them. Small placards gave the names of the streets on the corners. "Now, where to?"

"Now we go find Herr Heider," she replied, beginning to walk east.

He fell into step beside her. "And where does Herr Heider live?"

She looked at him askance. "At the Dürer House, of course."

Nuremberg (or Nürnberg, to the locals) was a medieval town, with a formal medieval town wall, castle, and all the trappings. It was built along the Pegnitz River, a city made of brown brick and stone. But it was small enough that it could be walked easily, and if one were a particularly good walker, entirely. And Winn's country life and Jason's health made them both quite adept.

They crossed over walking bridges that not only spanned the river but also carried the weight of buildings. It was a clear, blue-sky day. The flowers and trees in full bloom, the towns-people out and conducting business, their voices raised in a cacophony of commerce and life. As they fell into step, Winn and Jason passed a park where ladies of good family strolled under parasols; it was, Winn thought, much like Hyde Park in London, though the strollers' fashions and voices were un-quantifiably different than those seen and heard in England. They crossed through the Hauptmarkt at the beautiful cathe-dral of the Church of Our Lady, the market row after row of stalls of fresh produce, meats from local farmers, and fish from the rivers. And the toys! Winn stopped in her tracks when she saw the clever wooden dolls with mechanical parts that made them clap or walk a few steps when wound.

And Winn's stopping in her tracks had the unfortunate ef-fect of making Jason bump directly into the back of her.

"Oof!" one or both of them cried. Jason caught Winn's arm to keep her steady, then straightened.

Jason recovered himself first. "You know, we can stop and look at the market if you like."

Winn, whose eyes had been trying to take in everything—the movement of the market, the medieval architecture of the buildings—suddenly cast her eyes to the ground.

"No," she replied, "we should be going. There is much to do, I cannot dawdle." Her eyes fell on one of the clockwork toys again. "But it's all so interesting, and . . . different."

"This really is the first foreign city you're experiencing," Jason realized. "We were in Hamburg for barely a few hours, and Stellzburg and the other roadside stops don't even count. Of course you would wish to linger."

"Yes, but I should not," she replied, pulling away, her hand going to the locket at her throat. "I want to see everything, but I can do so later. After . . ."

After she located the necessary letters, of course. After she made her stake in the world. Then she could wander the marketplaces of Nuremberg, Rome, and Timbuktu if she so desired. But . . .

"Come on . . ." His voice a temptation. "Take off your coat. Stay for a bit." And then he smiled at her, that lopsided charm that had eluded him in his youth (or at the very least, been utterly ineffective on Winn) brought forth into full bloom—and damn effective, whether he knew it or not.

"Oh!" she stuttered. "I, ah . . . I wear the coat because I get cold easily—even though it is June, I simply find it more practical to—"

"Yes, having managed to feel your ice blocks of feet through layers of socks and bedclothes for the past two nights, I am aware of your . . . temperature," Jason drawled. "However, I meant 'take off your coat' as a metaphor, for 'stop a moment and enjoy yourself.'"

"Oh." Winn's brows came down. "I knew that."

"Uh-huh. In any case, seems a shame you should have

to ignore the beauty of the city the first time around," Jason argued agreeably. "So, how about a compromise? We won't stop, but why don't we walk a little slower?" He offered her his arm, and with a tentative smile, she took it.

"But we are still determined on our course," Winn qualified after a few steps.

"Mrs. Cummings, it couldn't be any other way."

They managed to find their way to the Dürer House in the Zisselgasse, but only after taking the not so direct path up toward Nuremberg Castle, which still had its castle walls intact and served as an active market and tourist destination. They might have also stopped for a pastry and cream . . . but only because they were both so famished from the trip. (And perhaps Jason managed to shove three such pastries in his mouth, but that is neither here nor there.) It had only really been a few minutes of a detour, but as they strolled arm and arm up to the Dürer House, a five-story timber-framed structure standing proud on the corner of its street, Jason almost immediately regretted it.

Because standing at the entrance to the house was a group of several young gentlemen looking on as a native-speaking man exchanged harsh and angry words through a half door with an older woman, whose steely-eyed glare belied her fluttery hands and blousy manner. The man continued his vehement speech as he tried to pull the bottom half of the door open, while the woman on the inside constantly swatted at his hands.

Winn's fingers gripped Jason's arm, pulling him to a halt.

"What's going on?" she asked.

"I don't know . . ." Jason mused. "Excuse me," he called out to the nearest of the young gentlemen, who Jason realized could not have been more than twenty, and self-important enough to make him cringe.

"Ah, thank Christ, someone who speaks English!" the young man cried, drawing the attention of some of his friends.

Jason watched wryly as the young man pocketed a small flask. "Do you speak German?" At Jason's nod, he continued. "Can you tell us what on earth our guide is saying?" He waved his hand toward the two arguing Germans. "We paid him to show us the sights, and Henry over there—we're all studying at Cambridge, but he's the only one who really studies—insisted we see this stupid house. And now it seems that this . . . house-keeper won't let us in."

Jason quirked a brow at him. "Well, I . . ."

The young man eyed Jason's wrinkled and Winn's serviceable clothes, and obviously made some sort of decision. "We're taking our grand tour. Do you know what that is?"

"I think so," Jason replied, trying to keep the sarcasm out of his voice. "Darling, you know what he means, correct?"

"I believe so," Winn answered, playing along naturally. "Young men travel the Continent and see the world's wonders."

"Yes, well, I'd much rather we see the wonders inside a pub right now," the young man replied. "But Henry won't leave, and we don't understand a word that's being said."

"Should have paid better attention in your language classes," Jason admonished kindly, but was met with a cold glare by the young man.

"Yes, well, I find that being a member of the aristocracy is time-consuming enough. I am Frederick Sutton, son of Baron Sutton?" His supercilious raised brow said that it was a name Jason should recognize. Sadly, he couldn't. "And you, sir? May I ask your . . . profession?"

"A bank clerk," Jason answered, just as Winn said, "Fishmonger."

"I'm a bank clerk who used to work for her father . . . as a fishmonger," Jason quickly amended.

"Fishmonger to bank clerk. That's terribly ambitious of you," Frederick Sutton replied. Then he fished in his pocket and held out a few coins. "Since you are so ambitious a person, perhaps you would be so kind as to translate for us?"

Jason looked at the shillings, then to Winn, who was admirably holding back a smile as she just shrugged. She reached forward, took the coins, and shoved them into the top of her dress. Then, with an alarmingly broad accent, said, "Oh, thank ye, sir. Yer grand. Me pap will never believe we met with a real live baron. Darling, go listen to the Germans and tell us what they say?"

She nudged Jason toward the arguing men, who had kept up a steady stream of undifferentiating conversation this whole time.

"Your guide is saying he'll give the lady a higher cut of the money," Jason drawled. "And the lady, the . . . she says she's the owner of the house . . . is saying there is no way, she will not allow any more guests . . . the last group the guide brought in destroyed . . ." His gaze immediately went to Winn. "They destroyed some papers."

He watched as Winn went desperately pale. Then she straightened her spine and steeled her jaw. Jason almost smiled at her, oddly touched by her resolve. But before he could turn back and follow more of the conversation, it abruptly ended with a *"Nein!"*, a slammed top portion of a door, and the finality of hearing locks turn.

"That seems to be your answer," Jason supplied for young Frederick Sutton.

Frederick gave a sigh of relief. "Finally. Well, lads!" he called to the group. "I think we've had enough education for today."

"But Freddy," replied the one who must be the studious Henry, "we haven't seen anything yet, not the castle, not St. Lorenz Church . . ."

"Education tends a different way, Henry," Frederick answered. "Time to learn about the local varieties of that delicacy known as beer!"

Most of the young men cheered, while Henry moped, "But it's not even ten thirty! Oh all right—but only if it's in a pub with some historical influence . . ." And so, Henry was appeased, and the motley group of young gentlemen went on their way without a glance back at the fishmonger-turned-bank clerk and his wife.

"So what's it like?" Winn asked after the group turned the corner out of sight.

"What's what like?"

"Meeting your younger self."

Jason scoffed for a moment. "I wasn't . . . that is, I was never that bad when I was twenty." Then he hedged, uncertain. "You think I was?"

Winn simply shrugged and smiled sympathetically.

"Well, that's highly disconcerting," Jason answered glumly. But Winn had already moved forward and knocked on the door to the Dürer House.

No one came to the door, so she knocked again. And again.

"Herr Heider!" she finally yelled. "Herr Heider, I know you are in there!"

The locks finally rumbled and the half door was cracked open.

"English, yes?" The lady who had been guarding the door from the assault of young marauding English university students only minutes before peeked out through the small opening.

"Yes, I'm here to see—" Winn began with relief but was abruptly cut off by the half door being thrown wide open.

"No more English! No more tourists! This house is closed to the public! Go . . . make migration elsewhere!" The woman's eyes flashed steel again, and she made to slam the top portion of the door shut again, but this time, it was stopped.

By Jason's hand. And rather painfully, too.

"Madam," Jason ground out through his teeth. "Before, you said you own this house. Are you, perhaps, Frau Heider?" he asked with a pointed look to Winn.

"*Da*," Frau Heider replied, alleviating the pressure on Jason's hand. "*Ich bin Frau Heider.*"

"Frau Heider, I'm here to see your husband," Winn cried, not wasting any more time. "It's Winnifred Crane . . . Alexander Crane's daughter!"

❧

As they were admitted into the house where Albrecht Dürer
had lived and painted, Jason expected to be awed. To feel
the hallowed light of residual genius. Instead, he was fairly
certain he entered a regular, albeit messy and disorganized,
Nuremberg town house under basic construction.

And under a shroud.

Black drapes covered wall hangings, mirrors, clocks . . .
black tablecloths fell in folds over surfaces. Even the relative
clutter of stalled construction work could not mask the grief
this house existed in.

"I apologize for the mess, Miss Crane, but ever since my
husband purchased the house we have been invaded by students and artists from every single country!" Frau Heider explained in her strong English, stopping to rest at one of the
two massive pillars that marked the entrance to the home. She
dabbed at her brow with the edge of her serviceable apron,
weary from a trying morning.

"Herr Heider was originally from Berlin, but is a Dürer
enthusiast," Winn explained to Jason. "So much so that when
he made a pilgrimage to Nuremberg a year or two ago and saw
this house, he purchased it."

"*Da*, my Wilhelm had to save it, he told me. He sold my
father's business that *I* inherited in Berlin, our house there . . ."
Frau Heider paused for a moment, her gray eyes lost in
thought. Then, she fluttered her hands, smoothed her apron.
"But he did do a great deal. You should have seen this place
before—falling down around its elbows. It cost so much and
took so long to simply get it habitable!"

"The tour money must have helped financed the repairs,"
Jason surmised, and watched Frau Heider's face blush.

"Wilhelm, he wanted all the travelers—migrators . . . ?"
she said, asking tacitly if she had the correct word.

Jason smiled kindly and supplied, "I think you mean 'pilgrims,' ma'am."

"*Da*—pilgrims. Students, lovers of Master Dürer, they come, and my husband cannot in good faith turn them away. People of study are good, nice . . . but school boys drunk add more to the repairs," Frau Heider replied. "We had been asking the city of Nuremberg to purchase the house, as a historical place, but the city, it has no money. So instead we try make repairs, and make lives here, and move my husband's Dürer collection in, *da*?"

"Yes, Frau Heider, the correspondence is why I came to see your husband," Winn began, but the woman was not listening.

"And then, last month, while unloading trunks of letters from Berlin . . . he collapsed . . . and left me." Frau Heider's fluttery hand came up to her eyes, covering them. Jason glanced at Winn. Winn's sympathetic heart—and perhaps her own affections for the man—wore plain on her face.

"Oh, Frau Heider, I am so sorry—if only we had known."

"Left me to deal with that scrounging, not good"—then Frau Heider said a word in German that Jason decided he would not translate for Winn, no matter how much she gave him that inquiring look—"tour guide and his drunken charges!"

"I do hope you don't include us in that group," Jason asked with a smile.

Frau Heider blinked a moment, and her shoulders relaxed. "Of course, good sir, of course. I am sorry, I have been the neglectful host. Please, follow me." She ushered them to a set of chairs by a small fireplace in an adjoining room. "How did you know my husband?" she asked Jason.

Jason managed a, "Well, I . . ." before Winn jumped in.

"You see, Frau Heider, I am the daughter of Alexander Crane, and have been writing your husband for several years now."

Frau Heider's eyebrow went up. "You. Have been writing my husband?"

"Yes," Winn said in a rush. "We have been corresponding on the works of Dürer for some time, especially since my father is a scholar—"

"I am sorry, but are you telling me that my husband has been writing with young ladies, for how long?"

"Oh, many years. And, I don't think he wrote other young ladies, just me. I am astonished to hear of his death. He always seemed so vigorous in his correspondence."

"Vigorous?"

"Lively. Impassioned."

"Passioned?" Frau Heider's voice came out as the barest strangle.

"Yes!" Winn cried, oblivious. "Why, I remember one time he wrote to me of a particular nude sketch that he had discovered—"

As Jason saw the farce playing out before him, two things became abundantly clear: First, Herr Heider had kept his correspondence to himself, and second, to keep the already emotional Frau Heider from breaking, he was apparently to lend Winn his name a few days longer.

"Darling!" Jason interrupted, smiling tightly at the look of palest, abject horror on Frau Heider's face. "Perhaps it would be a good time to mention to Frau Heider that we are currently on our wedding trip. And the purpose of it."

Winn looked up at him curiously, her face awash in confusion. He leaned down and kissed her cheek, at the same time whispering in her ear, "After all, you won't get what you want if the lady thinks you've cuckolded her."

"Oh?" Winn asked. Then for the first time, seeing the look of complete horror and confusion on Frau Heider's face, understood. "Oh!" she cried again, this time with understanding. "I assure you, Frau Heider, my correspondence with your husband was purely academic. After all, I've only ever had eyes for . . . my darling Jason, here." She latched her hand onto his and squeezed. The act of which crushed his fingers even as it relieved the pressure on Frau Heider's face, and she relaxed.

"Of course," Frau Heider said, sighing. "How silly of me. My Wilhelm only ever had eyes for Master Dürer and, if I could get his attention, for me."

"In fact," Winn said kindly, "we do not wish to impose, but we are on something of a mission."

"A mission?" Frau Heider's eyes lit up. "A mission involving my husband?"

"Precisely."

"A mystery!" Frau Heider cried joyfully. "I love nothing more than a good mystery. Tell me, my dear, how can I help?"

"Your husband told me about some letters," she said, taking her portmanteau from Jason's hands and fishing out the Adam and Eve copy. "Ones he found, written to Master Dürer, about this Adam and Eve painting."

Frau Heider took the painting from Winn's hands and peered at it with those keen gray eyes. "I do not recognize it, but I did not involve myself in my husband's work," Frau Heider said.

"Well, you see, the letters he found say . . ."

As Winn laid out the purpose of her visit—leaving out the less than pertinent information regarding George and various wagers—Frau Heider followed the conversation carefully, only occasionally stopping her, asking her to speak slower or for Jason to provide a translation.

"Frau Heider, please, tell me you still have those letters. I would be eternally grateful," Winn concluded.

Frau Heider slid her eyes between Jason and Winn once more, and Jason held his breath. "Yes, my dear, I do. At least, I hope so."

At that pronouncement, she rose and beckoned for Winn and Jason to follow her. And they did, up the stairs to the third floor, where the repairs had not gotten as far as they had on the rooms downstairs, but which at least seemed sturdy and clean. Except for one space.

They stopped at one door, at the very end of the hall. Frau Heider took a large ring of keys out of her apron pocket and, finding the appropriate one, fitted it into the new brass lock on the door.

"I had to put new locks on this door," Frau Heider explained.

She opened the door and let them into utter chaos.

Papers stacked in boxes everywhere, paintings and etchings in half-open crates, everything piled floor to ceiling.

"My husband's life's work," Frau Heider said grimly.

"Did drunken school boys do all this?" Jason asked, following Winn as she delicately moved into the space.

"Only partly. I fear my Wilhelm did not get very far in his reorganization this time."

"This time?" Jason asked.

"He reorganized everything once a year. The move from Berlin made it especially . . . mixed up? Yes, mixed up."

Jason looked to Winn, who had gone still, her fingers gingerly picking up a piece of aged vellum, its ink almost indecipherable. It was likely a few centuries old—if it came from Durer's time.

"Winn?" Jason ventured gently. "Are you all right?"

Her head came up, and he saw the resolve in her eyes. "I'm fine," she stated clearly. "Let's get to work."

Twelve

*Wherein letters are found, hope is lost,
and unexpected visitors arrive.*

Two days. That's how long it took for Winn to find what she was looking for. Two days that she spent encased in the small room on the third floor, fully immersed in her quest. Two days that Jason spent below stairs with Frau Heider, wondering what on earth was going on in that tiny, cramped space.

Of course, he had been in there. He had tried to assist Winn as best he could, but four hours of deciphering tight German handwriting in fading ink on aged, browning paper was his limit before he needed some air. Of course, Winn would not let the windows be open in the room, nor would she allow anyone to touch the papers without soft cotton gloves on. Frau Heider, with absolutely no enthusiasm for Dürer and having similar limits to Jason's, removed herself as well and got out of Miss Crane's way.

"You think it the best thing?" Jason asked, no longer trying to mask the concern in his voice. "That she is working herself so hard?" They were in the kitchen rooms, cutting up the bread, cheese, and vegetables that Frau Heider had just fetched from the market, leaving Jason to fend off yet another

group of eager students (French ones, this time) and their enthusiastic guide. It was decided that a young stern man would
be far more adept at dissuading visitors than an older matron.
They were correct in this assumption.

"She's not even sleeping," he added, removing the hot iron
pot from the woodstove and pouring its piping contents into a
teapot to steep.

Frau Heider, once assured of their marital status and the
work cut out for Winn, had decreed that they would stay in
her guest bedroom, which luckily had a bed. Old and not often
used, and therefore lumpy and uneven, but a bed nonetheless.
Winn and Jason had simply shrugged at each other—strangely,
they were becoming accustomed to their imposed sleeping arrangements. Or at least, Jason thought, he was.

That first night, when Frau Heider had gone up to bed,
he sat downstairs for some minutes, trying to decide if he
should go to bed or go to Winn—but he had already spent
several hours with her that day, his eyes straining to decipher
unintelligible handwriting, his lids drooping in exhaustion.
As such, he decided on sleep, thinking that Winn would join
him shortly. After all, after dinner she had said she was only
going to spend an hour or so in the little room at the end of
the hall.

It was just before dawn when he awoke and saw she wasn't
there, no circular, Winn-sized dent in the mattress beside him.
If he had known she wouldn't be there, he thought peevishly,
he would have allowed himself to sleep beneath the sheets.

The next night was similar, Winn going up to the small
room after dinner, leaving Jason with Frau Heider. It wasn't as
if he could stop her—the exhaustion sinking into her eyes or
no. Winn's entire body was a tensed wire, her entire focus on
pawing through the contents of Herr Heider's collection. So
he went to bed alone again . . . but he didn't stay there. After
midnight, when the house was still, he went to the small room
at the end of the hall and knocked gently.

There was no answer. He tipped his head in and found

Winn with her head down on the desk, her candle burning precariously low. He went and rocked her shoulder.

She didn't move.

"Winn," he whispered.

Still no movement.

"Winnifred," he tried, louder.

"Stop calling me that," she complained weakly, keeping her eyes tightly shut.

"Come along, you need to sleep," he argued, but she pushed his hands away.

"I'm just resting my eyes."

"And Napoleon just had a mild interest in foreign policy. Come on." And, brooking no opposition, he took her up into his arms and carried her—she couldn't weigh more than a bird's wing—down to their shared bedchamber. She was dead asleep before her head hit the pillow, curling into the Winn-sized ball that he knew well now.

And again, when he woke up before dawn, it was because there was no Winn in the bed, just, this time, her impression.

"This is her passion." Frau Heider shrugged kindly. "And passionate people, they are blind to everything else. Like my Wilhelm. He would sometimes go days, weeks without emerging from his study. I brought him food, I made him sleep . . . I was the only person who could connect him to the world." She smiled the sad, wistful smile that painted her face whenever she spoke of her Wilhelm, which was a dominant topic of conversation the past few days.

"I cannot lie—in some ways, she is the answer to my prayers. A talented person, taking care of that mess of paintings and papers and sketches that I cannot," she mused.

"I know she's talented, of course. I've read her papers, I just didn't—"

"Didn't think of the work that went into them?" Frau Heider chuckled. "Trust me, Mr. Cummings," she said, placing a small plate of stewed turnips on the tray. "My Wilhelm, he would be in his books for days, ruining his eyes on old words. And while he was here, I had use . . ." She paused for a moment, sadly looked at her hands. As if her fingers missed the purpose she sued to put them to.

"People like Wilhelm, and your Winnifred," she continued after a moment, "they can have all the talent in the world, but they need someone like us to care for them. As you will discover."

"Winn keeps saying she doesn't need anyone." Jason shook his head.

"And you believe her? You do not know your wife very much." Frau Heider chuckled.

"I know her well enough to know that she doesn't like turnips," he replied, and removed the small plate of turnips from the tray, replaced it with the teapot, and hefting it, headed for the stairs.

Two days, Jason thought as he climbed the steps to the third floor, the plate of food in his hands. Two days, and he didn't even know if Winn had slept four hours total during them. Frau Heider was right; as much as he enjoyed dabbling in the Historical Society's interests and taking in a lecture here and there, he really had no notion of the work that went into the process of discovery. He could only marvel, and try to help, and make trays of food.

How well did he really know this woman he was escorting all over the Continent? They had met, barely, a decade ago, but unfortunately not to his recollection. And it had been, what, a month ago? that he ran into her outstretched hand in the courtyard of Somerset House. But still, she kept earning his surprise.

He knew she was a fighter, determined and focused to an almost frightening degree of intensity. Demanding her independence and holding fast to that freedom on the basis of her ability to argue. And he knew she was oddly sheltered, her curiosity the reason he saw her as a sparrow, darting about from here to there, her attention fixed on the next, the new, the unknown. Absorbing the world with childlike wonder.

The wonder she still had in the world. He liked that best.

Jason knocked on the door at the end of the hall and quietly let himself into the small room.

Two days, and to Jason's eye, it looked like she had barely made a dent.

Papers were in new piles, spread out around the room in neat lines, some form of chronological charting going on. The crated paintings had been moved into an adjoining room (Jason had been the one to do the moving, of course), allowing Winn to concentrate solely on the papers. The small desk had been moved in yesterday with a chair, and there, like yesterday, in between two piles of old work orders and supply lists written in Renaissance-era German, lay the head of Winnifred Crane, sound asleep.

She looked so tiny asleep. She was small in any case, but asleep, the bravado that filled her frame was in hiding, and she was as soft and fragile as a doll. Jason put the plate down by her head and gently placed his hand on the back of her neck, that small stretch of exposed skin that he had subconsciously claimed as his own. She didn't jump, didn't stir. He leaned down closer, a small part of him wanting to make sure that she was still breathing.

One other thing Jason knew about Winn—the woman could sleep like the dead.

"Winn!" He shook her shoulder gently and then when that did nothing, harder. "Winn, the letters are on fire!"

That brought her head up. Quickly, forcefully. So quickly and so forcefully that her head connected with his nose, and he stumbled back, his eyes watering like mad.

"Ow!" he cried, the sound muffled by the fact that he was holding his nose.

"Ow, yourself!" she replied, holding the back of her head. "You have the pointiest nose in Christendom!" Before he could vehemently protest, Winn whipped her head around the room. "The papers . . . Fire?"

"No . . . no fire," Jason answered, adjusting his nose. Finding it without breakage and thankfully not bleeding, he felt well enough to release his hand. "We have to stop meeting like this."

"Oh, thank goodness." Winnifred sighed, her gloved hand coming to gently rest on one of the piles of paper on the desk. Then, with a sidelong glance to Jason, she asked, "Are you crying?"

"What? No," Jason said quickly, blinking up any stray moisture from his eyes. "I . . . we thought you should eat." He waved his hand to the plate on the desk, next to her elbow. As she inspected the food, he looked around the room. "You should really open up a window, let some air in here. No wonder you fell asleep. Again."

If she remembered being carried to bed the previous night, her face gave no hint of it. "We cannot open the windows. Do you understand how delicate these papers are? The wrong breeze hits them and tears them . . ." She gave a small shudder.

As she delicately stripped off one of her cotton gloves and picked up a piece of bread and cheese, he peered over the papers on the floor. "Have you found what you're looking for?" he asked.

"Sadly no." Winn sighed, frustrated. "But I have managed to sort out which letters are in Master Dürer's hand and which are not. That pile there"—she indicated where he stood—"are notes and notations on mathematics. Those"—she pointed to another pile—"are markings on human proportion. Nothing conclusive, certainly not drafts of anything that made it into Dürer's *Four Books*, but these are the types of things that most people would normally think worthless and have burned. And Herr Heider found them in a trunk, in an antiques shop. Amazing, don't you think?"

"Yes," Jason agreed, bending to look at the papers. "But where are your letters? The ones about the Adam and Eve painting?"

"That's another problem," Winn replied, taking another bite of bread and cheese, closing her eyes and making a small noise of sheer pleasure in sating her hunger. It took Jason a moment to notice she was still talking. "Albrecht Dürer depicted Adam and Eve several times. Including a painting, done in 1507, and an engraving, done in 1504, both undeniably his. So any letters he received mentioning an Adam and Eve could be about them."

"But you thought our Adam and Eve was done in the 1490s, correct? Can't we simply go by the dates of the correspondence?" Jason asked as he lifted letter after letter, careful to be delicate.

"We could," Winn said, smiling, "if only our forefathers had been so kind as to date every letter they sent. Besides, who's to say Dürer received the letters around the time of the painting? Things aren't always done in good time. I've written theory and criticism on thousand-year-old works." Then she looked down at the piece of bread in her hand. "Add in that the pages are nearly illegible, and that my Renaissance German skills are not as strong as I'd thought," she admitted ruefully, "I'm near to going cross-eyed on these."

"You lasted about thirty hours longer than anyone else—or, at least, I—would," Jason admitted. "But . . . you have always said that these letters exist, yes?"

"Of course they exist!" Winn cried, frustrated. "I am not going to fail now!"

"No, you misunderstand!" Jason replied quickly. "I meant to point out that you said 'letters.' Plural."

"Yes," Winn replied, realization dawning. "Herr Heider told me of letters, a correspondence. So there would be more than one letter in the same hand."

"You need to categorize these differently. You need to find the letters in the same handwriting, not the same subject matter."

Winn dropped her sandwich, her eyes glued to Jason's face, her expression complete astonishment. "Oh, Jason, that's brilliant. Utterly and completely brilliant." And before he knew it—likely even before she knew it—she had leapt from her chair and taken the two short steps across the room and kissed him.

It was like being hit by a wave. When he had kissed her in the taproom of the Stellzburg Inn, his mind had been tuned to the idea of survival. And her reaction had been one of surprise, and from what he could recall, little else. But this . . . this was pure emotion. Gratitude, joy, desperation . . . all coming from this trim body against his, those arms that wound around his neck, those sweet lips pressed up to his own.

She broke away mere seconds later, her eyes searching out his, confused and more than a little embarrassed. Somehow, his arms had come around her back and he was actively holding her to him. Keeping her there, keeping the cold air from filling that space. Then, he let her go.

She backed herself all the way to the other side of the room. Unfortunately, Jason thought, the room was too small to put any worthwhile distance between them. All he could do was stare at her, and all she could do was look at the space of floor between them.

It must be the air, Jason thought. The heavy air that in the last few seconds had burned up like fire.

"I, ah . . . I need some air," Jason said finally, filling the void that had been previously occupied by only the sounds of their breathing. "So I'm going to . . . go take a walk."

He didn't check to see her reaction. He didn't even spare her a glance as he wrenched open the door and passed through to the other side. And as he stepped downstairs and out onto the street, his mind kept going over and over the last few minutes on a never-ending loop. And one coherent thought managed to make it through his wreckage of a brain:

What the hell had just happened?

She could have kissed Jason. Again. If he'd been in the room.

It was barely an hour later that Winn located the letters she was looking for. There they were, having been moved into different piles because one spoke mainly about Dürer's engraving education in Basel, Switzerland, and the other has the barest mention of an Adam and Eve painting. Her eyes were burning, and her mind beyond tasked, but it was there. She knew it.

Since Jason was not in attendance, instead she contented herself with running downstairs, the two letters in hand, and accosting Frau Heider with her delightful find.

"Frau Heider!" she called out, finding her in the kitchen, taking a trowel and plaster to a crumbling corner of the room. "I found them! I found them!" she cried, entering the room.

"Ah, wunderbar," Frau Heider replied. "May I see?" She held out a hand, covered in plaster, and Winn's eyes went wide with horror. "Ah, no—you are right. Best not touch."

"Where is Jason?" Winn asked, her heart beating in her throat. "I must show him!"

"He went out, child," Frau Heider replied, waving her trowel in the direction of the door. "Said he needed air."

Winn blushed and then ran for the door, the letter, her precious careful letters, still in her hands.

"He went in the direction of the Hauptmarkt, my dear!" Frau Heider called out and then, as the girl burst through the door, could only chuckle to herself. Discovery, whether a letter or a feeling, was ever an inspiration.

❧

Winn had never had much luck at finding people in crowds. Being on the shorter side of the human spectrum, she could only hop on her toes and pray for a glimpse of red hair and beard. It was just past noon, and the market was bustling with women purchasing meat for that night's supper, men bartering and trading for feed and seed for the farms just outside the city walls. Others strolled the craft stalls, small dolls and clockwork toys, carved wooden buttons and small treasure chests that had no purpose other than to look pretty and remind people that they had once been to the market on a warm summer day.

And in the middle of it all was Jason.

She found him after some minutes, exiting a small shop on the northeast side of the square. He had a package wrapped in paper in his hand, that Winn could only assume was a sandwich of some kind. She ran up to him, into him, with such force that it set Jason back on his heels.

"Oof!" The air came rushing out of his chest as he backed away from the door frame that had caught his weight. "For such a small person you really pack an enormous wallop," Jason grumbled as he discreetly hid the package behind his back. "Is it in your plans to cause me as much bodily injury as possible?"

"I'm sorry!" Winn cried, giggling. "Well, not really. I found them!"

"You found them," Jason repeated dumbly. Then, understanding, "You found them? The letters?"

She nodded, and produced the letters from her skirt pocket. "It's very small, the section that I need, but it's right here." She indicated the lines she sought on the page, her hands still gloved in plain white cotton. Jason came to stand behind her and peered over her shoulder.

"It's nearly illegible," he said finally, his breath in her ear. "Can you make it out at all?" At her nod, he responded, "Read the passage to me."

And as she met his eye, his face alarmingly close to hers, Winn forgot for a moment that they were in the crowded Hauptmarkt. "I think . . . at least, I am sure I am right, but I think it says this." She cleared her throat and read. *"I wish to honor the master and my friend for his sympathies. Once you said you admired my work, so I send to you my last work, a First of Man and Woman. My mother, who is my superior in all things, has proclaimed pride my sin, and that I must rid myself of the paints, that I honor myself more than God. When we met in Basel, you suggested I study—"* Winn paused here and squinted. "I think this next word means 'horticulture,' but I honestly have no idea." Then she cleared her throat and continued. *"And my practicing I hope has met with your agreement."*

Winn looked up then, carefully refolding and pocketing the letter as she did so. "And then they discuss Lutheranism in veiled terms for a while, and that's it."

"That's it?" Jason asked, a little too skeptical for Winn's liking. "There are no other letters in this handwriting?"

"Yes, there is one," she replied, carefully fishing it out of her pocket, "but it mainly discussed etching techniques Dürer studied in Switzerland and some other commonplace things. Not the Adam and Eve painting."

"That's not enough," Jason replied, taking her hand. "Come on. Let's go back to the house, see if there are any other letters in any of Frau Heider's other trunks."

"What do you mean, that's not enough?" she asked as he pulled her through the crowds of the Hauptmarkt.

"That's not enough to prove that your Adam and Eve painting is the one being discussed."

"Of course it is!" she countered. "It is exactly what Herr Heider described to me. It says that they met in Basel, that this painter sent an Adam and Eve—a First of Man and Woman—to Dürer."

"It's exactly what Herr Heider described? Are you telling me you crossed the Continent on a whim and the belief that that much was proof of a painting's . . . authorship?" Jason asked, his face complete astonishment. "Are there any dates on that letter? Any discussion of form and technique beyond studying horticulture? Any proof of receipt of the painting? Is the author of the letters recognized as an artist otherwise?"

"I don't think so," Winn replied. "But then again, there are not a lot of female painters recognized from this era, period."

That brought Jason up short, stopping in the dead center of one of Nuremberg's famous stone bridges. "The painter is a woman?"

Winn nodded. "They are signed by a Maria F. I can't make out the last name beyond the first letter."

Jason threw back his head and laughed. "Oh for God's sake! That's even worse!"

"How is that worse?" Winn asked, her brown brows coming down.

"Because the Historical Society is going to write those letters off as coming from a young girl overly impressed by a master artist, one who sent him a sketch she did in her adoration. Not this painting, not a serious work, nor someone to be taken seriously."

As Winn felt her blood rise, she wrenched her hand free of Jason's. "It will be enough to cast doubt."

"No it won't," Jason intoned seriously. "So you had better hope there is more conversation between Dürer and this Maria F., and that it is a detailed account of Maria's talents as an artist and their relationship, because otherwise . . ."

Winn could only narrow her eyes and harrumphed. And then, of course, turned and walked briskly in the direction of the Dürer House, Jason close at her heels.

They rounded the corner, coming onto the view of the Dürer House just as they had a few short days ago, when they had met with the crowd of students paying homage. Only this time there were no students.

There was instead an instructor.

George. Next to him stood Totty, looking, if possible, both concerned *and* bored. They had been met at the half door by Frau Heider, her banked caution apparent to Winn and Jason, if no one else.

Winn froze solid upon seeing George, unable to move forward or backward. Luckily, Jason had the sense to pull her back beside the next building—hidden from view in the alley but within earshot.

"My affianced bride, you see, is terribly admiring of Master Dürer," George was saying with a smile, his practiced charm diffusing any fear Frau Heider might have from his size. "But she is somewhat scatterbrained. We became separated recently, and I wondered if perhaps she had come here."

He placed a concerned hand over the older woman's, eliciting a blush.

"Scatterbrained?" Winn whispered indignantly, forcing Jason to shush her.

"What is it with you English and your fascination with Dürer?" Frau Heider was saying kindly, her stern visage warming to George's affecting countenance. "But I am sorry, there has been no single ladies here."

"Are you certain?" George replied earnestly. "She's small in stature, brown haired, somewhat plain?"

"Somewhat plain?" Winn couldn't help but repeat, incredulous. At this point, Jason rolled his eyes and gave up on shushing her, and instead simply placed a hand over her mouth.

"Small in stature?" Frau Heider replied, the wheels visibly turning in her brain.

"Yes!" George cried. "Her name is Winnifred Crane. I'm sorry, I never introduced myself. I am George Bambridge, professor at Oxford. Winnifred's father was my mentor . . ."

As George explained, the understanding on Frau Heider's face turned to surprised understanding, then anger. Jason and Winn watched as the older woman sputtered indignantly, then opened the door fully, admitting George and Totty.

"We have to go. Now," Winn said quietly after removing Jason's warm hand from her mouth.

"Right. We'll come back after they leave," Jason agreed.

"No, you don't understand, we have to leave Nuremberg," Winn replied, hedging out into the street. Then seeing that there was no one spying on them from the Dürer House windows, shot out at a breakneck pace, running as fast as her feet could carry her.

"Winn, where are you going?" Jason cried, trying to catch up. "Winn!"

Arabella Arbuthnot Tottendale, affectionately known as Totty, was not a woman to be unseated, literally (she sat remarkably well upon a horse, and always had, despite her lack of practice in recent years) or metaphorically.

She had been utterly and completely shocked by Winn's plans to travel to the Continent alone, but not unseated by them. She had followed along and helped as best she could. Besides, Totty surmised, she had always been horrid at stopping mischief, so why not facilitate it instead, and make certain it was the least outrageous version possible?

Of course, somehow, her darling friend Winn had managed to find the most outrageous form of trouble possible by teaming up with an unmarried Duke on her cross-continent adventures, but then again, that child had always exceeded expectations. Still, said actions were not capable of unseating Totty. What left her dumbfounded, bewildered, and yes, unseated, was George Bambridge's reaction to them.

They had made the annoyingly tedious journey from Dover to Hamburg, following Winn's footsteps without so much of a trace of the flash of temper George had showed ever so briefly before they left. A flash that Totty had never been privy to before . . . but she feared Winn knew of it, more than she spoke.

Which was why Totty insisted on coming along. She would do her best to slow George down (counter to her promise to him), but she feared they would catch up with Winn all too easily, and there was no way she was going to let Winn face George alone.

Perhaps Winn had the same notion, and that was why she had the Duke of Rayne following after her like a lover on a lead.

At least, they assumed it was the Duke of Rayne. When they got to the Schmidt und Schmidt offices in Hamburg, they had met with a stereotypically efficient German—yet surprisingly English by birth—woman, Mrs. Schmidt.

"Yes, I directed the girl to a coaching yard," Mrs. Schmidt had told them after being assured not only of their interests in Winn but in their financial solvency. She pocketed the coin George had tossed her. "She was desperate to get to Nuremberg. Although what awaited her there, I do not know. She was always jabbering about old paintings and bothering the crew about mundane things, like what the rigging did or how they navigated by the stars. Oddly naïve, that one."

George nodded sympathetically and agreed. "And do you happen to know where in Nuremberg she intended to go?"

"No," Mrs. Schmidt replied, "but that Duke fellow might know."

Both George and Totty froze at her words.

"What Duke fellow?" George asked finally. And at Mrs. Schmidt's shrug, put another coin in front of her.

"At least, I think he was a Duke. That's what he said he was, but he presented no card to me, or any such thing. Ran right on board the ship after Miss Crane, just as we were about to cast off."

"Did he happen to have red hair? A good height?" George continued. "Not as good as me, of course," he said with an offhand grin that Totty knew was intended to set people at ease.

"Yes," Mrs. Schmidt agreed. "Hair as red as the blazing sun. Miss Crane and the gentleman rarely spoke on board the ship, mind, but rumors were rampant that they were—"

Totty finally found her voice. "Yes, we have some idea as to the rumors, thank you."

"Don't know if you do, as one of the crewmen said the gentleman winked at *him*, but that's neither here nor there," Mrs. Schmidt continued pertly, unhappy to have been interrupted in telling her juicy story. "I wish my husband were here, but he had to set out on another voyage. He could tell you more about the chap, but I really had very little to do with him."

After they left the offices of Schmidt und Schmidt Shipping, and rid themselves of their money-grubbing company, George grew alarmingly silent as they stalked in the direction of the coaching yard Mrs. Schmidt said she had directed Winn toward.

He remained alarmingly silent while they were told by the stable lad at the coaching yard that a woman matching Winn's description had purchased tickets to Nuremberg with a man with red hair.

And silence reigned now, as Frau Heider sat across her kitchen table from them and told them that Winn had introduced herself as Mrs. Cummings, and the red-haired gentleman as her husband.

It was the silence that worried Totty more than anything. Mr. Tottendale, God rest his soul, was a genial sort who had an occasional hot head . . . one that Totty herself seemed to set off more than any other person. He would stomp around the house in a fit of pique but then be back to himself.

George was not stomping around the house, burning off his justified frustration. And from that flash of unreasonable anger that she had seen earlier, she knew he was capable of such stomping. No, instead he was keeping it bottled up. And playing Frau Heider like a fiddle.

"I cannot believe Mrs. Cummings would be so heartless as to jilt her fiancé and marry another man," Frau Heider said after George had laid out a particularly glassy-eyed version of his romance with Winn to his captive audience. Totty couldn't help but be impressed by George's eloquence in German. The things that boy could have done if he'd actually cared to apply himself.

"It is not heartlessness on her part. I am afraid it is my fault. We quarreled about these letters, and she took off. I did not support her as I should. And she has been so sheltered and naïve . . . I fear this man with the red hair, Mr. Cummings, is taking great advantage of her. Tell me," George said, his voice warm and controlled, "did Miss Crane . . . er, Mrs. Cummings, did she, perhaps, find these letters?"

Frau Heider hesitated a moment. A moment long enough for George to make his voice crack with emotion. "I'm so sorry, I just . . . finding those letters was her father's dying wish . . . He put all of these notions into her head, and all I want is my darling Winnifred back, and if she found those letters perhaps . . . perhaps there is no marriage. Perhaps she will return home."

Frau Heider looked to Totty for confirmation of George's story. And what was she to do? He was not lying to the woman, merely playing it out from a different side. "He's very upset," Totty said dryly, in her schoolgirl German. "And was wondering if Winn had found the letters she sought."

Frau Heider clucked at George's almost teary eyes and stood up to fetch the teapot. As she poured hot water into the pot and left it to steep, she placed a tray of bread and cheese in front of George with a sympathetic smile.

"Yes," she told Totty and George, "Miss . . . Mrs. . . . Winn left here not a half hour ago, saying she found the letters and she had to go tell her husband. He had walked to the market."

George wasted no time standing and oversetting the chair on his bid to get out the door.

"They should be back soon!" Frau Heider cried to his retreating form. "At least I hope so. Oh dear, oh dear." The delicate-looking woman worried her hands in a decidedly un-German fashion. "Did that young woman truly get married? Or didn't she? I should like to get this whole thing sorted out."

"As would I, Frau Heider," Totty agreed from her chair. She would have gotten up to follow George, chase right after him and make certain he did not find Winn immediately . . . if she hadn't already seen, out of the corner of her eye, Winn and—lo and behold—the Duke of Rayne, when they were still outside.

"Don't worry, he won't find her," she said, only to receive a quizzical look from Frau Heider. "You don't happen to have anything stronger than tea, do you?"

Thirteen

Wherein our hero's attempt
at subterfuge goes awry.

"Winn, stop!" Jason hissed, finally catching up to her halfway across town, near the entrance to the coaching yard where they had first come into town two days ago. His legs might be longer, he thought grimly, but that did absolutely no good when she was not only able to duck and weave through the flow of traffic with impunity, but also desperate enough to do so.

"Winn!" He managed to grab her arm, pulling her to a stop. Then, bending over, gasping for breath, "Hold on . . . one . . . moment . . ."

She was breathing as heavily as he, her skin flushed aglow from her exertions. But whereas Jason needed a minute to recover from his running after her—and possibly from her appearance—Winn apparently did not.

"We haven't got a moment, Jason. We have to get out of here now!" Winn replied in a rush, her eyes shining with fear and excitement.

And before Jason could ask why or how or where they

were going, Winn pulled her arm free and set off into the madness of the coaching yard.

Almost a week in Germany, and two days of doing nothing but reading cramped Renaissance German handwriting must have elevated Winn's skills with the language considerably, because she read down the chalkboard list of coaches and their destinations, chose one, and headed for it decisively.

That or she was quickly choosing at random.

But whatever the explanation, Winn had chosen the one carriage that was rigged to depart. It would be leaving in very few minutes.

"Why that one?" he whispered in her ear.

"It's going to Vienna," she whispered back. "And it's the only one going today."

"Vienna?!" he exclaimed, causing no small number of heads to turn their way. "Why on earth are we going to Vienna?"

"I'll explain on the way, but it's about to leave . . . Come on!" she cried, taking his hand and pulling him toward the carriage door.

"Wait." He pulled her up short. "You don't have your bag."

"A sacrifice we'll have to live without," she replied.

"All of the money is in your bag," he hissed in her ear. "We can't purchase tickets."

As he watched her turn pale, then tug at the heart-shaped locket around her neck, Jason groaned. "All right," he said with resolve. "Just follow my lead."

He took a few seconds to eye the situation. There was no driver on the carriage yet, but all the luggage was loaded on the back. The last of the porters turned away and started to load packages onto a different carriage. The only one watching the Vienna carriage was a young boy, holding the leads of the horses while taking the fares handed him by passengers who then loaded themselves on.

Jason straightened, and turned to the young boy who was

holding the horses. "Excuse me!" he called out jovially in German. The young boy looked up, and the horses danced and shuffled. Jason realized his luck when he saw just how young the boy was and how unused he was to controlling horses. Perhaps he was new enough to his position that he could be intimidated.

"Where is the driver? I absolutely must speak with him about these appalling accommodations!"

The young boy looked left and right, blanching. He stuttered a moment before saying, "He's gone inside . . . to get his kit for the voyage."

More likely to finish off his pint, but Jason declined to dwell on that.

"Well, I'll talk to you, then. What kind of slipshod business is it when I am expected to *share* carriage space with others? I am the son of a baron. Surely you have something better for the likes of us?" Jason continued in what he hoped was a dead-on impression of Frederick Sutton, son of Baron Sutton, turning the young boy away from facing the carriage door.

"It's . . . it's a public carriage," the boy answered, uncertain of himself.

"It's a disgrace is what it is. All I want to do is go see the opera dancers in Vienna, but do I have to put up with this madness to do it? Crammed next to any old fishmonger or bank clerk?" As he gave this speech, Jason fleetingly locked eyes with Winn and urged her into the carriage.

"The upholstery isn't even velvet!" Jason decried with a sigh.

The young boy could only shrug and say, "I'm sorry, sir."

Jason sighed the sigh of the righteously put-upon. "I'll be the laughingstock of all my friends. You're lucky I don't make a mockery of this whole operation and *walk* to Vienna."

"No sir! Please don't do that!" the young boy cried, terrified. "I just got this job, and I'll lose it for certain if a passenger decides to walk."

Jason eyed the young boy circumspectly. "Well, just this

once, I suppose I can be accommodating. I won't mention it to your driver if you don't."

The boy nodded vigorously, and Jason turned on his heel and stepped up into the carriage.

Inside he was met by indifference from the few other travelers, and the decidedly interested gaze of Winnifred Crane. He held up a hand as she opened her mouth to ask one of probably four thousand questions, cutting her off into silence. The seconds ticked by, falling into a few minutes, before the sound of shuffling feet outside the carriage met his straining ears.

"Hans," a deep German voice called out, followed by a belch. "Are we ready? Everyone loaded?"

"Yes, sir," the young boy replied.

Then there was the sound and motion of a significant amount of weight climbing up to the driver's seat.

"Good!" the driver replied. "Any problems?"

There was the slightest of pauses, wherein Jason could feel the tiny bead of sweat form at the back of his neck. But before it could break, the tiny voice of Hans the stable lad answered directly. "No, sir. No problems," the boy said from beside the driver.

The driver snapped the reins, and they were off, Jason and Winn comfortably aboard.

Of course, it was not two hours later that they were uncomfortably kicked off board.

It couldn't have lasted, in any case. They would have never made it all the way to Vienna. There would be stops to change horses, feed the passengers . . . and an overnight stop wherein they would be discovered as not paying and not able to afford the rooms they were made to take. But still, Jason had hoped to make it farther than they did.

It did not assist that he still had no idea why they were going to Vienna. Winn was unable to give her explanation in the carriage, as two of the other passengers, ladies, began a conversation that did not stop, except for every time Jason or Winn tried to open their mouths to say something. Then it got so quiet Jason could swear that he could hear the ladies listening.

So Winn and Jason had to ignore each other, until finally the ladies settled down into snoozing. Which turned out to be Winn and Jason's undoing.

Really, they would have been better off just keeping quiet the entire time.

"Now, do you mind telling me why we had to escape Nuremberg so quickly that we had to leave all our money behind?"

And that was it. That was the one sentence that had to be said that shouldn't have been said. Because, as Jason should have learned by now, snoozing, carriage-bound Germans have the suspicious ability to hear (and understand) English extremely well.

"Driver!" one of the ladies cried, sitting bolt upright and banging on the roof of the carriage. The carriage lurched to an immediate stop, and the driver climbed down, followed by the light footsteps of Hans, the boy Jason had to bamboozle.

While the boisterous and, now that Jason thought about it, ugly and warted woman divulged—in rapid German, of course—through the window of the carriage everything she had just heard Jason say, he watched as the young boy's eyes grew wide, and then as his face paled when the driver turned to him, his hand raised in a fist.

"No!" Jason bellowed as he leapt from the carriage, ran around to the other side, and came in between the driver and the boy. "He did nothing to earn a beating," Jason growled, catching the driver's arm.

"He cost me money!" the driver sneered. "He needs to learn a lesson. Or do you want to learn it for him?"

Jason breathed in the fumes of the beer on the driver's breath and eminently regretted his decision to put his nose in the man's face.

Now, Jason had only ever been in a single fight in his life, and it had been decidedly one-sided. And that side was his, facedown in the mud outside of a pub called the Oddsfellow Arms near his sister's home. But he liked to think he could hold his own in one-on-one combat.

He was wrong.

Even a lifetime of beer drinking could not allay the sheer strength the driver had earned from controlling a team of horses all day, every day. Even as Jason managed to land a combination of blows to the man's impressive gut, the driver's fist came down onto Jason's face and ribs in quick succession, felling him to his knees. Followed by a swift kick to the body, and Jason was sprawled on the side of the dusty road, reeling in pain.

Out of the corner of his red, addled vision, Jason could see the driver raise his fist again to little Hans. He moved to come between them, tried to sit up in time, but he had been incapacitated too neatly. He could not save Hans from his beating.

But Winn could.

She leapt out of the carriage and wedged the whole of her petite frame in between the large driver and his frightened charge.

"Don't you dare!" Winn ground out, her eyes boring into the driver's face. "Shame on you." Jason struggled to his feet and watched as the sparrow confronted the elephant. "Shame on you!" she yelled, loud enough that it echoed through the rolling hills of the empty countryside.

Even though the driver may not have understood Winn's English words, he understood the look in her eyes and lowered his arm, hesitating. He turned his head when he heard shuffling from the carriage.

"I knew they were trouble when they first boarded, didn't I tell you, Uta?" the more rotund of the two ladies was saying in German as she maneuvered her weight to better see the dramatics unfold outside.

"Oh, leave them, driver!" the other lady, Uta, said. "We must be on our way." She held up a pocket watch and shook it at him, as if to remind him of the time.

"Not worth it in any case," the driver grumbled. He shot one last disparaging look at Jason, who had struggled to his feet and come to stand next to Winn, between the driver and the boy, his breaths coming in sharp, painful bursts. Whatever his condition, the driver dismissed it, and them, by climbing up to his seat on the carriage, flicking the reins, and pulling away with all possible haste, disappearing down the road.

Leaving Jason, Winn, and the young Hans on the dusty side of the long road, Nuremberg behind them, Vienna in front of them, and nothing but rolling hills dotted with farm animals in between.

Now, Jason liked to think of himself as a fairly reasonable man. He had only truly lost his temper once, and to be fair, alcohol had been involved, and the result had been, as it was so mentioned, to find himself facedown in the mud. But having, in just the past few hours, been forced into becoming a fugitive, his nerves a fraying wire, and then subsequently beaten by an oversized Bavarian, he was holding on to his good sense with both hands.

But there was Winn to think about—and the small, soft fingers prodding at him.

"Gah!" he cried when said fingers not so gently came across a sore spot on his ribs.

"Oh! I'm sorry," Winn cried, immediately poking him again in the same spot. "Does it hurt there?"

"Yes, that's what 'gah!' means!" Jason growled, enough of a warning so that Winn backed away. Instead, she turned to the boy, Hans, who was standing silent, shaking.

"Oh, Hans!" she said in English, so whether or not the boy understood her was suspect, but he looked up into her face with his big innocent eyes. "Are you quite well? No bumps and bruises? You should be thanking Jase—er, Mr. Cummings for his help. He took a beating for you."

Hans nodded solemnly and, escorted by Winn, took tentative steps toward Jason . . . and promptly kicked him in the shin.

"You cost me my job!" the child cried, and then, turning on his heel, began running in the other direction, back toward Nuremberg.

"Wait!" Winn cried after him. "Where are you going?"

"Home!" the boy shouted behind him, and continued down the path, faster than either Jason or Winn would be able to catch up with him.

"What do we do?" Winn asked, the worry creeping into her voice. "Should we go after him?"

And it was the worry that did it. That small change in her pitch, the concern, the fear. It broke his anger free like no punch or blow ever could.

He began to laugh. But not his normal, amused laugh. This laugh sounded as though it were coming from another body, one that was quickly losing any sense of self-control.

"What the—?" Winn asked. "Did you get hit in the head? Have you gone addled?"

"Have I gone addled?" Jason repeated with disbelief. "Probably. But it's nothing compared to you."

"What—"

But she didn't get very far into whatever question she was going to ask, because Jason's laughter abruptly stopped.

"You! You are finally, *finally*, worried about something, and it's *him*?"

"He's a child."

"He's a native speaker who actually has some idea what he's doing and where he's going! And yet you worry about him." Jason began to advance on Winn in small, methodical steps. Even in the middle of the road, with every direction to run, she couldn't escape him. It had taken two weeks of travel, but he was finally, legitimately angry, and this conversation was long overdue.

"Now, I've seen you pull at your locket in a worrying way

as you try to figure out your next move, I've seen you process through a thousand emotions, but I have never heard anything close to concern in your voice.

"No, you are too focused on your mission to think to worry—not only about me, and I have sacrificed a ridiculous amount to be here, but for yourself. But you *would* worry about this small boy! The only one of us who has a destination and knows how to get there. The boy will be fine!"

Winn stiffened her spine, her eyes flaring wide in indignation. "As I have told you before, you don't need to be here—I do not need you to escort me across the Continent!"

"Oh yes, you bloody do!" Jason crowed. "And that's the most frightening part of this whole thing. I know for a fact I am not the world's best protector, but if I weren't here, I cannot imagine what you would do or where you would be right now—you don't speak the language, you don't know when someone is bilking you . . . you never *think*, Winn. Oh, you think about your paintings and your letters and the history you learned from books, but you are never . . . practical!"

"You think to lecture me on practicality?" Winn scoffed. "You, who ran willy-nilly onto a ship that was setting sail for ports unknown?"

"Yes, because you are the one who ran willy-nilly onto a carriage heading for Vienna of all places! Would you care to finally tell me why you did that?"

"Happily," she spat back, her hand gingerly digging into her pocket and pulling out the letters she had showed him so proudly just that morning. "Because *you* said I needed more definitive proof—you said I had better pray that there were more letters about the painting. And since George invaded the Dürer House, we couldn't go back there . . . so, it occurred to me that there would be other letters—in Vienna."

Jason quirked an eyebrow, a cynical invitation for her to explain further.

"These letters"—she gently waved them in his direction—"when they start talking about Lutheranism, there is a mention of attending services at Stephansdom—St. Stephen's Cathedral, in Vienna. That's where the artist who painted the Adam and Eve lived. That's where we would find the other half of this correspondence—letters written in Dürer's own hand."

"Wonderful," Jason drawled, clapping his hands slowly. "No, no, don't look so peevish, I actually commend your reasoning. It's wholly sound. Except for a few things."

"Such as?" Winn's brow went up.

"Such as, *if* these letters from Dürer exist in the first place, there is no guarantee that the family of Maria F., whomever she is, has kept them for the last *three hundred years*. And if they did—don't you think letters written by Master Dürer would have come to light sooner?"

"Possibly not—after all, the Adam and Eve painting was not discovered until fifty years ago, and then ascribed to Dürer mistakenly . . ." Winn argued, her confidence beginning to waver.

"But your reasoning," Jason continued, heedless of her argument, "does not explain why the hell we had to run from Nuremberg immediately! Leaving behind your bag, which had your clothes, your copy of the painting, and *all* our money!"

"Because!" Winn shot back. "George was there! He managed to find us already—we had to move!"

"But George would not always be there," Jason yelled. "He would have left eventually. Nuremberg is a big town; we could have found a place to hide for the afternoon and come back in the night and gotten our things before haring out of town as if being chased by the Four Horsemen of the Apocalypse!"

"He would have found us." Winn shook her head. "And if he didn't, he would have managed to get Frau Heider eating out of the palm of his hand—the minute we turned up there, she would have notified him. You don't know him at all."

"You're right, I don't know him—but I know enough to feel sorry for him," Jason retaliated. He knew, when he saw the shock of pain in her eyes, that *this*—not maligning her

common sense or her plans to find the accompanying letters—
was the bridge too far, but he couldn't stop himself. It just
felt too good, too right to vent his spleen in this manner, that
he plowed through any objection the small voice of his good
sense might have had.

"That's right, George Bambridge, I feel sorry for him.
Because of you. You: tiny, little, five-foot-nothing Winnifred
Crane, have been playing him for a fool. Of *course* he followed you here—if he knows you at all, the way I am getting
to know you, he probably lost his mind with worry thinking of
you traveling across the Continent alone. But the blasted thing
is, if you'd had, at any point in the last *fifteen years*, the guts
to mention to George that you no longer wished to marry him,
you could have avoided this mess altogether!"

And that was the point at which Winn slapped him.

Over the course of their acquaintance, Jason had been hit
accidentally by her hand, and hit purposefully multiple times
by many other people. But he'd never felt the sting quite so
harshly as when Winnifred Crane put the full weight of her
five-foot-nothing fury behind her intentions.

It wasn't the hand that hurt, nor the reddening impression
that it left on the side of his unshaven face. It was the tears
welling in her eyes, threatening to fall down her cheeks.

Jason could only stare, could only rein in the emotions that
had been running out of control for the last few minutes. The
last few weeks. His breath came in jerky gulps as his hand
went to his burning cheek. Her breathing was the opposite—
not erratic, but deep, furious, and controlled.

"You think I do not know I am in a mess of my own making?" she said quietly. "I'm well aware. But I am happy to
report, it is a mess that no longer concerns you."

And with that, she straightened her spine, in that Winn-
some manner, and began to march down the road, in the direction their abandoning carriage had rumbled not ten minutes
earlier.

"Winn . . . Winn, wait . . . Where do you think you're going?" Jason called after her.

"Vienna!" she retorted.

She didn't turn around as she spoke. So she didn't see Jason rub his cheek gently, and with a resolved sigh to the heavens, begin to take stiff, painful steps after her.

Fourteen

Wherein our duo contemplates misperception.

THE sun was setting in the west, casting Winn's shadow long before her as she set out on her path toward Vienna. She could hear the shuffling footsteps of Jason behind her. He kept a safe distance, about twenty paces—close enough that he could keep an easy eye on her, but far enough that if she happened to decide to strike him again, he would have time to set up defenses.

Not that she cared that he was following behind her. As she intended to keep her distance, he would, she concluded, eventually grow tired of seeing her backside, and when they reached some sort of civilization, he would see the futility of following her further. She was setting out on the rest of this journey alone, and intended to complete it that way. Alone.

Nor did she care that she had, for the first time in her life, willingly struck someone. He had deserved it, utterly and completely. How could someone—how could *Jason*—who had practically begged to accompany her on her adventure, decide now to call her gutless and of all things, impractical?

Gutless. It had been the scariest act of her life to set out on this journey. To leave the comfort of the known in Oxford and the friendship of Totty, and march resolutely toward her own independence. And to rest that independence on something as frighteningly flimsy as a wager . . .

A niggling voice, tiny and persistent, in the back of her mind reminded her that Jason's gutless comment was in reference to her treatment of George. And the little voice transformed itself into a pebble of guilt, annoyingly stuck in some crevice and impossible to rid herself of. But she would not allow herself to think of that now. She had to hold on to what righteous anger she had. It was what was forcing one foot to fall in front of the other.

The truth was, while "gutless" made her seethe, "impractical" at least had the ability to make her snort with laughter. Impractical. Out of the two of them, which one had some idea of the value of a shilling? Which one got his pocket picked on the docks of Dover, making Winn take on the burden of his expenses (no matter what little money his hawked items contributed)? Which one had at least planned on this adventure and secretly undertook weeks of research on how best to accomplish it, while the other decided to come along as little more than an afterthought, as if he simply decided that this week, instead of running his estates or sitting in the House of Lords, he'd rather frolic across Bavaria?

True, she had been impractical enough to leave her bag at the Dürer House with Frau Heider, but at least she was lucky enough to have the necessary letters in her pocket. And at least, she thought with a small shiver as the sun dipped below the horizon, her dress was warm, and her boots sturdy and durable. And since she had her anger to warm her blood, she didn't even miss her thick wool coat—also left back at the Dürer House, in the care of Frau Heider. She almost snuck a peak behind her, to see if Jason was shivering in his now well-worn, summer-weight coat.

Almost.

She kept walking. Two more hours, maybe three, before

she was tired enough to think of stopping for the evening. They had passed very little in the way of shelter in the intervening hours, and been passed by very few in the way of carriages.

The one time she managed to get a vehicle to stop for her—a horse and cart loaded with summer wheat to use as feed for farm animals—she was mollified into admitting that she had nothing in the way of funds. When the driver of the cart (a much kinder, more sober-looking man than the previous) had glanced down at her gold locket, she blanched and clasped it, her hesitation just enough for the driver to shake his head and snick his horses back into a trot. All the while Jason had been looking on, having shortened the gap between them to about ten paces.

She stepped more briskly after that, determined to restore their original distance.

But now, as the chill of night settled over the land and Winn struggled to keep her feet moving and her eyes open, she had determined she must stop. But where? They seemed to be fairly far from a town or a village or even the farmhouse of whomever owned the endless fields they were walking past. She was so far from everything . . . and so very, very tired. Her anger had been burnt hollow about an hour ago, leaving her emotionally and physically spent. All she had to do was rest somewhere. And, as her eyes drifted off the road, over the field dotted with piles of yet-to-be-baled hay, this was as good a place as any.

Resolutely, she stepped off the road, into the field beyond. She heard Jason's footsteps—they did not hesitate to follow her, no startled shuffling questioning her motives. If one could read expressions in footsteps, Winn could almost swear that his gave echoes of relief. But as she approached a particular pile of hay, she turned and glared at him, the first time she had looked at him since her slap vibrated across the German countryside. It was a warning, and one Jason was smart enough to heed. He removed himself to the closest hay bale to hers and promptly set about pulling down an amount of straw, making himself a bed of the stuff. Winn, watching out of the corner of her eye, followed suit.

When she laid her head down, Winn looked up at the thankfully cloudless sky, lit with stars as bright as diamonds. The moon was barely half; it would develop into its full self in little more than a week. And when it did, it would blanket the sky with its stark light, overpowering the stars, making them less impressive, less vast.

But now, with the Milky Way above her, billions upon billions of points of light swirling in their own cosmos, Winn could only feel small, and alone.

This was the first time in her life she was sleeping outside. She should have relished the experience, viewed it with a sense of adventure. Sleeping in hay under the stars! How marvelous! Something new to be checked off her list! But the truth was, it was the first time that things had been dire enough to warrant it. She shivered slightly, as it was less comfortable than she had imagined. Her mistakes had led them to this place. What other mistakes was she making, or going to make?

This was the first moment in her whole journey that Winn did not know what came next. Where a hint of doubt made its way through her confidence. What if there were no letters to be found in Vienna? What if they could not even discover the identity of Maria F.?

No, not *they*, she admonished herself. *I.* She was continuing this journey alone. After all, she had intended to do the whole of it alone, and she had started out that way.

But that wasn't true, she thought. She had spent approximately three minutes of this trip without Jason Cummings, Duke of Rayne, involved in some respect. Hell, it was the first time in a week she was even sleeping alone.

A pit of ice dropped in her stomach, making her shiver harder against the chill of the night. It was curious. As an only child, she had never had to share her bed with anyone. She was used to sleeping alone, but to feel so keenly the void that separated her from Jason after only . . . five days? Was it really only five days?

It felt like he had been there forever, his presence infiltrating every aspect of her life. Sleeping in his clothes on top of the covers while she slept beneath. His hand falling gently on the back of her neck. She had never sought his touches, but now that she was without them, she felt as if the tide of her body had ebbed out to sea, and could only pray for the return to shore. At some point, without knowing how she arrived there, Winn had become addicted to Jason's touch.

Disconcerting, to say the least.

But it was no matter—not anymore. As she told herself again and again, as she shivered against the night and burrowed into her pile of hay, she was by herself from here on. After all, even once this mission was complete, she intended to follow her own path. One that did not include a Duke, a peer of the realm. She was fighting for her independence tooth and nail, and she would not allow anything, not even the curious effect Jason Cummings's touch had on her, to get in her way.

All she had to do, right now, was get through this night. All she had to do was fall asleep and when she woke up, start walking again. She would worry about hunger when she felt its pangs. She would worry about money when it became necessary. Right now, all she had to do was sleep.

If only it hadn't become so cold!

Where was her coat? Oh, maybe she should have risked George and gone back to the house—if only for the warmth of that thick coat. She shivered and burrowed, shivered and burrowed. Just sleep, Winn told herself. When you are asleep, you won't feel the cold as much. And the sun will be up and shining soon enough . . . Just sleep . . .

Suddenly, softly, she felt warmth against the line of her back, wrapping itself around her. Or rather, wrapping himself around her.

"What are you doing?" Winn whispered through chattering teeth. "Get off me. Go away."

"Your anger isn't keeping you warm enough," Jason replied in her ear, his own teeth clacking ever so slightly. "And I'm not going to let you freeze to death to spite me. You can still despise me in the morning."

Winn thought over her options for a moment. She could kick him away, get up, move to the next hay bale, or start walking down the road again, guided by the paltry half moon.

But he was so warm.

"I'm still going to Vienna alone," Winn finally said, her head coming to rest in the cradle his arm provided.

"Duly noted," Jason replied, his beard scratching against the top of her head.

And as Winn stopped shivering and relaxed into his warmth, she felt her despair fall away, and she fell to sleep like a stone.

෨

The next morning, with dawn breaking over the sky and warming their skin, they began their silent journey. But this time, Jason was in step beside Winn.

However, the silence that governed their mouths did not apply to their stomachs. About an hour into their walking, the morning air was rent by the most horrible gurgle coming from the vague area of Jason's midsection.

Winnifred sent him a silent glare.

"Apologies," Jason grumbled. "Haven't eaten since breakfast yesterday."

"I thought you had a sandwich," Winn accused, forgetfully breaking her self-imposed moratorium on speech. When Jason only looked at her strangely, she rolled her eyes and explained, "Yesterday, when I found you in the square? You were coming out of a shop with a package, which I thought to be some sort of food, since you seem to require feeding every hour on the hour. Don't tell me you ate it already." She sighed with disappointment.

"Oh," Jason replied, realizing. "That wasn't food."

"You spent our money on something other than food?" Winn's eyes went wide, her head falling into her hands. "Jason, and you called *me* impractical."

"It wasn't our money. It was the few coins Frederick Sutton threw at me," Jason replied peevishly, rummaging in his coat pocket and coming out with the small package wrapped in brown paper. "And it may be impractical, but it was for you," he mumbled, and held out the package to her.

Winn's head came up. "For me?" She delicately took the package, which she could see now was far too small and oblong to be a sandwich. One touch and Winn could tell it was fragile.

As she unwrapped it gently, Jason watched her face carefully. "I figured everyone needs a souvenir to remind them of their first trip abroad."

It was a doll. One of the small wooden dolls that stood upright and had clockwork parts that allowed it to move its head side to side, its arms up and down. It had been one of the dolls she had admired, however briefly, when they took their initial stroll through Nuremberg to find the Dürer House, however many short days ago.

And the doll was, laudably, painted as though it were dressed in lederhosen.

A small, stunned smile painted Winn's face in wonder. She wound the small key on its back, watched as the toy jerkily moved its arms and head, an oddly stationary dance meant to delight children. And apparently Winn herself, because she could not help but feel something inside of her click into place, her own inner clockwork kicking to life, and all she could feel was warmth bubbling up inside her. And it was due to this little doll. How it had survived the events of yesterday and last evening, she had no idea, but she could not help but be overjoyed that it had.

"Thank you," she managed to say shyly, her eyes flicking up to Jason's face—who was trying awfully hard to not look overly invested in her reaction.

"Well," he replied gruffly, "like I said, it wasn't expensive. Nor was it my money, technically."

"Then, thank you, Frederick Sutton," she replied.

Unable to say anything else on the subject, and unsure of any other course of action, they began walking again. They fell back into their silence, and Winn could not help but be acutely aware of it. The day was crisp and clear, undeniable in its beauty, but every breeze was punctuated by the sound of Jason's feet falling on dirt next to hers, his pace kept even with her obviously shorter one. She couldn't help but also be entirely too concerned with where his hand fell at his side, swinging lightly . . . if he swung it a hair wider, his knuckles would graze hers . . .

Not that she wanted him to, of course. She crossed her arms over herself, putting her hand out of harm's way. She was still chewing over his accusations from the day before, and her reaction to them. If it had been anyone other than Jason . . . if, for example, Totty had expressed concerns over her actions, would she have reacted the way she did? Would she have become as deeply incensed as she did?

"And that's another thing," Jason's voice broke through the silent walk and Winn's own thoughts. Upon seeing her raised brows, he continued haltingly. "Speaking of Frederick Sutton, that is. When we met him, you said I had been exactly like him."

"I . . . I didn't mean to offend—" she began, but he held up a hand.

"I know you didn't, and it didn't. Mostly because it was untrue. When I was Frederick Sutton's age, I wasn't like him. I was like his friend Henry."

"Henry . . ." Winn's brain relived the encounter. "The one who actually *wanted* to see the Dürer House?"

"But was easily dissuaded and then persuaded into mischief," Jason concluded. "In some ways, I think I would have rather been Frederick. At least he didn't make a pretense of his intentions."

Winn came to a stop, turning to face Jason. "But I said that days ago. You can't have been thinking of it all this time."

Jason shrugged. "It has been bothering me. I wanted to clear it up."

"Oh," Winn replied. And then, as they resumed their walking, "As long as we are clearing up misconceptions, there is something that has been bothering me."

Jason then quirked his brow and nodded for her to continue.

"I'm not five-foot nothing," she declared. Then, with a concessionary grumble, "I'm five-foot-one."

"Oh," Jason replied in kind. And then, he couldn't help it. He began laughing. A small chuckle that was all Winn needed in way of an apology. And perhaps, when she joined in laughing, too, he would know she apologized as well.

They resumed walking, continued chuckling, right up until Jason's stomach growled again, adding a third voice to their wordless conversation.

"We need to get you fed," Winn surmised, putting her hands on her hips.

"You as well, little sparrow," Jason replied.

Winn paused as she gave Jason a curious look. "Sparrow?"

But Jason ducked his head, blushing under his beard, unwilling to answer Winn's question.

"Come on," he said gruffly. "We have to come to a village or town eventually."

And this time, when Winn put her hand to her side, his hand fell right beside hers, and when their knuckles grazed like she thought they might, his hand grabbed on to hers under the pretense of pulling her along quicker to their unknown destination.

And as she fell into a trot beside him, Winn could not say that she minded in the least.

Fifteen

*Wherein our duo makes
a spectacle of themselves.*

THE little village of Lupburg was as unpretentious and, at the same time, as staunchly Bavarian as they come. Built into a small hillside in the rolling farmland that dominated the eastern parts of Bavaria (as opposed to the Alp-ridden southwest), it was dominated by a medieval, now crenellated keep on top of the hill. Just below the keep was the town church, and just below that, the winding main street, marked on one end by the bakery, and on the other by the butcher's shop. The village square was anchored on one corner by a shrine to the Virgin Mary, and on the other by a posting board for local news. Under the blazing blue summer sky, the town was a ribbon of neatly whitewashed buildings, and a beacon of hope to two weary travelers who veered off the main road when they saw it.

Or rather, heard it.

As Jason and Winn had been walking along the road, every footfall accompanied by either a stomach rumble or an annoying hunger pang, their discussion had waxed and waned as they each thought of misconceptions they wanted corrected.

"I think that you think that I don't know the value of a shilling," Jason said, his brain making sense of that convoluted sentence, and hoping Winn's did the same.

"So you *do* know the value of a shilling?" Winn asked Jason, who nodded vigorously.

"Absolutely. It's the value of a dozen pounds, if I win at cards that day."

"That's horrible." Winn laughed, shaking her head. She looked at him out of the corner of her eye. "I think that you think that I have absolutely no concept of time."

"Only when you're in a library," Jason replied. His hand was still wound around hers, and he gave her a small squeeze. "Or searching through three-hundred-year-old letters. Or perhaps, when I'm trying to sleep in the morning and you're banging around like a giant in the forest. Other times you are as precise as clockwork." Searching for other topics, his free hand came to his chin, rubbing the now almost two weeks' worth of growth there.

"I think that you think that I need a shave," he said finally.

Winn paused, considering his face. Jason felt himself blush underneath his beard and her scrutiny. "Never mind," he mumbled before she could answer. "That one happens to be true."

Winn smiled at him, that odd, considering smile that lit up her eyes like amber jewels. "Oh, I don't know . . ." she whispered, then let the thought drift off. Her eyes played over his face, his jaw . . . Then, after thinking for a brief moment, she hesitated before venturing into the gulf. "I think that you think that I haven't been kissed before."

Jason's vision turned dark, his body stuttered. What was she up to?

"Not true," he countered, deciding to play along.

"You don't?"

"I know you've been kissed," Jason smiled lazily. "By me. Twice. Although once was sort of you kissing me, so I don't know if that counts . . . hey!"

His teasing line of thought was cut off by her playful punch to his arm, but then, self-consciously, she pulled back. Perhaps remembering the last time she hit him, and its less than friendly intent. Jason did the only thing he could do, which was give her hand another kind squeeze.

"You may have been kissed before, but I know you are new to being teased," Jason replied softly.

It was one of those moments that had been happening all too frequently in Nuremberg, and perhaps, before, where they had both stopped talking, both stopped searching, and simply stayed in each other's gaze. Jason wanted to take that half step closer to her, pull her to his side, and fill the gap of cool air that separated them with her warmth. And if he didn't misread the light in her eyes, she wanted something similar.

But before he could move, before he could take that half step, Winn's head cocked to one side, like the sparrow he knew her to be, as she listened to the wind.

"Do you hear that?" she asked, looking past him, her body taking shuffling steps around him, away from him, that dratted cool space growing wider between them. "It sounds like . . . horns."

Jason concentrated, putting his ear to the breeze. "And . . . cheering?" he asked, surprised.

"It's coming from this way," Winn said after a few more minutes of listening. She pointed through a thicket of woods, separating the road from what lay beyond. She began to move toward the woods, but Jason, his hand still wrapped around hers, pulled her to a stop.

"Hold a moment. You want to cross through a darkly shrouded wood in rural Bavaria?" Jason asked, his entire body wired with skepticism.

"Yes," Winn answered slowly. "Why shouldn't I?"

"Tell me," Jason replied, "in all your time in the library, did you ever come across any folktales? They tend to heavily feature Bavarian forests. And the things you find in them."

Winn smiled at him again, this time in a quizzical, disbelieving fashion that, if possible, lit her face further. "You know what I think about you right now?" she asked, closing the gap between them, her sudden nearness momentarily fluttering Jason's thoughts.

"I think you're a little too old to believe in folktales." And with that, she pulled him into the forest.

As it turned out, in this particular patch of trees, there was very little in the way of ogres, monsters, talking wolves, fairies, or anything else one might think to find in a Bavarian forest. Which Jason found slightly disappointing. As much as Winn had spent their walk through Nuremberg craning her neck for the sight of lederhosen, Jason would have loved to take back to England a story about his trek through a Bavarian forest, and the ogre he met there. Not that he believed in ogres. But still, some childhood glee at scary thoughts never really goes away.

No, they simply followed the sounds of trumpets and cheers, which got louder as they wound their way through the woods, and came out on the other side, finding a similar road to the one they had just left, but instead of leading toward unending farmland, this road led directly to a small hillside dotted with that ribbon of whitewashed houses that bespoke of a village. The sound of trumpets and cheering were now accompanied by the sight of people and flags moving slowly up what Jason guessed was the village's main road.

"It's some kind of parade."

Just then, Jason's stomach grumbled, louder than previously. Hell, likely louder than it ever had.

"My goodness," Winn said, her eyes wide with astonishment. "It's as if your stomach knows that food is within a mile perimeter."

"Ha-ha," Jason replied, unable to quiet his internal growling.

"You see?" Winn grinned up at him. "I may be new to it, but I think I'm getting the concept of this teasing thing you value so highly."

"I will have you know," Jason said, following after Winn

as she took to the road that led to the village in the distance, "that there is a decided echo in this forest."

Jason's guess of a parade turned out to be correct, but only partially. When he and Winn entered the village of Lupburg, they found themselves entering a full-blown village festival. Ribbons strung between roofs hung over the main street, the entire town turned out on the sidelines to see their chosen sons march up and down the parade path that lead from the main street up to the church, blowing horns and making merry. There was even a giant paper and leather cow, operated by four men, one for each of the cow's legs, mooing and careening down the street, a girl upon its back tossing sweets to the children in the audience.

And everyone was eating and drinking.

Jason nearly doubled over in bliss at the smell of the fatted chicken legs held in the greasy hands of some of the laughing townsfolk nearby. The loud guffaws were silenced only when the people took a swig of beer from the tankards they held in the other hand.

"Oh my God, this is torture," Jason moaned. He turned to Winn, surprised to see her attention entirely caught and held by what looked like a marzipan turtle being stuffed into the greedy mouth of a young child. Jason held back a grin, and he yanked her back to face him.

"Hmm . . . What did you say?" she asked finally, her attention now removed from the sweets.

"You looked like you were seriously contemplating *literally* taking candy from a baby," he said sardonically. Then, "Come on, let's find the source."

They wound their way through the crowd, and Jason pigeonholed a local and asked him where the food came from. He was pointed in the direction of the food stalls on the other side of the parade route, near a pub and inn that was packed to the gills with people enjoying the festivities, the view, and most of all, the beer.

"How can everyone be intoxicated already?" Winn asked

with one eyebrow up in the air. "It cannot be later than ten o'clock in the morning."

"It's also a festival of . . . something," Jason replied. "Revelry starts early when there's a party to be had." When she looked up at him quizzically, Jason had to sigh. "Don't tell me you've never been to a festival. Oxford had them all the time! I know, I attended them!"

"They tended to be for the students, not the professors' daughters," Winn replied.

"Well then, another thing to cross off your list—'attend a village festival.' "

"If only I knew what it was for," Winn grumbled, and then *her* stomach joined in the complaining.

"Aha!" Jason crowed. "You do get hungry! For a while there I thought you were one of those inhuman, abstaining types who can go a month on a crust of bread."

"Just because I don't have to eat an entire *cow* for every meal . . ."

But their burgeoning bickering would have to wait, because just then Jason spied the latest tray of chicken legs being delivered by a stout woman to a beefy, happy man, who was quickly attacked by the joyful crowd, throwing coins at him in exchange for his delicious goods.

"That stall, right there," Jason leaned down and whispered in her ear, directing her attention to the spectacle before them. "If you can distract them, I can nab a piece or five, and then we hare out of here."

"How would you have me distract them?" Winn asked, the worry pricking through her voice.

"I don't know. Scream? Faint? Do something womanly?" her replied, and was met by the hard stare of the unamused Winn. "You know what I mean. Do you think you can do it?"

Winn nodded, her hand going to the locket at her neck, giving it a slight tug.

"What is it?" Jason asked, his face suddenly concerned.

"You only pull at your locket when you are contemplating something."

"It's just . . . why do we have to steal the food?" she asked quietly.

"Because we have no money?" Jason replied, his eyebrow up. He was a little surprised at having to explain the obvious to her, especially considering how tightly she had tracked her funds the whole journey.

"I know that, but hear me out." She pulled him to one side, so they were not in the midst of the jostling crowd angling to get nearer the parade route for better access to the goodies that were being tossed out. "If we steal this food and are spotted, we are going to have to run—and we have nowhere to run to, especially with the entire town chasing after us. But if we instead attempt to *earn* some money, then we will be able to purchase not only the food but maybe a coach ticket as well—maybe not all the way to Vienna, but at least we won't have to walk the whole distance."

Jason was only able to blink at her as he chewed over her argument. Meanwhile, Winn shifted her weight on her feet, apparently uncomfortable under his gaze. "I know you think I never think things through, but perhaps this time—"

"No," Jason interrupted. "No, it's a good plan. I'm just trying to think of what we could possibly do to earn money."

Earning money itself being a foreign concept to a Duke, Jason thought with a grimace, or else he'd like to think he would have come up with this plan himself. But, if he had, he would not have gotten to see the relieved smile on Winn's face, creasing so wide as to cause a dimple in her left cheek—a sight he hadn't seen before. A worthy sight, indeed.

"Ah . . . I don't know," Winn replied. "What can you do?"

"Head one of the largest estates in England and vote in the House of Lords," Jason replied. "And brush down a horse. What can you do?"

"Write a paper on the difference between Brunelleschi's

and Ghiberti's bronze work," Winn quipped and then, after a thought, "and argue with the butcher."

"Well . . . we are two utterly useless people," Jason surmised. "Except for the butcher."

"And the horses."

Just then, both Jason's and Winn's stomach grumbled in harmony.

"We had better find something we can do fairly quickly," Jason said in answer to his hunger's loudly asked question. "Else thievery may be our only option."

❧

They asked at the inn on the main street, crowded with townsfolk drinking merrily, if they needed any additional servers. They were told no. They asked if the vendors at the various stalls needed someone to watch their wares while they took a break. They were thoroughly rebuffed. They even asked the village priest if he needed any assistance cleaning up the rectory—they were told a kind negative and to go with God.

"So much for Christian charity," Jason grumbled.

"It's not that they are mean people," Winn replied, biting down on a hard candy. They had luckily managed to scrounge enough of the sweets being tossed by the parade participants into the crowd to quell the worst of Winn's hunger, but the little treats had only served to whet Jason's appetite. He was, if possible, hungrier than before. "It's that they don't know us. We are outsiders on their day of celebration."

"Are you telling me that the juggler that was in the parade and the man walking on stilts are from this town?"

"No, but they were hired. We are asking for work. There's a difference."

Jason couldn't argue. They stood out like sore thumbs in this little place. Winn's constant English and Jason's well-made (if completely ruined and soiled) clothes made them objects of curiosity. More than a few of the celebrating villagers (and what they were celebrating was still undetermined) had shot them looks of suspicion. After all, a festival brought out not only the hardworking members of the community but the less desirable ones as well—pickpockets and petty thieves were a well-known danger.

"Perhaps we should give up and find a different town," Winn whispered, defeated.

Jason sent her a look of utter horror. "Winn, I am not venturing any closer to Vienna until we get either some money or food or both. Now come along. We tried all the businesses on the parade route—maybe we should try some place off the beaten path."

And so they did, turning up a side street, and being met quite quickly by an innkeeper so enthusiastic for their presence that Jason was physically set back on his heels.

"Mein Herr! Fräulein!" the man cried. He continued in his native tongue, so excited and rushed that Jason had a hard time keeping up. "Are you hungry? Tired? Come, come rest your boots, come and sit and eat and watch the parade . . . through that tiny alley there."

They were ushered in through the main inn yard, past the stables, and to an outdoor table that overlooked a small alley that allowed a slight view of the parade passing by.

"We have the best cuts of meat and the best spaetzle in all Lupburg. My beloved Heidi, she had the largest cow slaughtered just for the occasion." The eager gentleman, who seemed to have no hair upon his head at all, save that which came out of his ears, virtually forced them into their seats, and with a single clap of his hands, had two steaming, overstuffed plates of the most delicious food Jason had ever seen placed in front of them.

"Would you like ale? Of course you would! Best ale in all Bavaria! Aged in barrels in my own cellar!" they were told, and with another clap of his hands, two foamy delicious tankards of ale were placed in front of them.

And well . . . Jason couldn't help it. He was too hungry to *not* dig into the pile of food placed before him. It was beyond temptation, beyond delight, beyond satisfaction, to have the weight of meat and potatoes slide across his tongue, down his throat, and into his stomach. He was three bites in before he heard the startled, strangled sound from across the table and looked up, meeting Winn's pointed look.

"Wunderbar!" the hairless innkeeper cried, upon seeing Jason's appetite. "You are going to want seconds." He turned over his shoulder and called to the kitchens, "Heidi, my love, more food!"

"No!" Jason said immediately, his mouth so full of food, he had to chew and swallow before he could continue. But one last longing look at the food still on his plate earned him a kick in the shins from Winn, and reluctantly he continued. "I'm sorry, sir," he said in the innkeeper's dialect, "but I should not have eaten this food. We cannot pay for it."

They watched as the hairless innkeeper's face went from gleeful hope to inconsolable depression in a mere fraction of a second. Then, the man's entire posture collapsed into despair as he flopped down on the bench next to Winn.

"Of course you can't pay!" he said to Jason. "The first customers we've had all day, and they are beggars!"

He threw his face into his hands and began a terrifically undignified bawl. From the kitchens beyond, they heard a cabinet slam. His beloved Heidi, Jason thought ruefully, obviously a compassionate individual.

Winn's eyes sought his and from her look he knew she wanted desperately to know what was going on, but Jason could only shrug.

"Uh, I'd be more than happy to work for the food . . ." Jason ventured in German to the innkeeper. "Herr . . ."

"Wurtzer," the innkeeper answered. "And I'm sorry, but I have no work to give you. Every year, the festival of *Sonnenwende* is the biggest event for my pub and inn. People come from three villages over to try my beloved Heidi's spaetzle."

"Sonnenwende?" Winn asked, managing to catch one word out of the thicket of Herr Wurtzer's speech. "Of course!—

Jason, how could we be so stupid. It's the twenty-second of June, the solstice. It's the midsummer festival!"

"Excellent," he responded, only a touch sarcastically. "Now that that mystery is solved, perhaps we can return to the problem at hand." He nodded toward the weeping Wurtzer, now snorting in great hunks of air in between his sobs.

"Every year, we have hundreds and hundreds of people! But this year? This year, the village decides to change the parade route! Now it goes past Brauer's pub . . . whose son just married the daughter of the town mayor, so I have *no idea* how that decision was made . . . after all, Brauer's is not on the main route of town—here is where there are the largest tables, the best rooms, here are the changing horses for the post!" Wurtzer went from mournful to seething in the flash of an instant. "Brauer. His ale is practically water, but since people can see the parade from there, they all flock to him. Even my own servants! They abandon me—with no one here to serve, they go down to watch the parade and buy Brauer's watered ale and stale meats! And why? Because Brauer has the parade route—and he hired the magicians and the jugglers to make sure the crowd stayed there, even after the parade is over."

Winn's eyes told Jason she needed a translation, and so he provided her a more succinct version than Wurtzer had given. And almost immediately, Winn's hand went to her locket, tugging. There was, after all, a problem to be solved.

"It sounds like Herr Wurtzer needs something to attract people to his establishment once the parade ends," Winn said. "Something even more outrageous than jugglers and magicians."

"I suppose," Jason replied, "but neither your list of accomplishments nor mine includes things more outrageous than jugglers or magicians."

"No," Winn answered slowly, "but you did mention your facility with horses."

A nod of her head indicated that he should look over his shoulder. Doing so, he spied the small stables. Twelve stalls, neatly in a row, lining the main yard of the inn, the horses in them either nickering or slowly chewing the oats and hay in their buckets, as bored of the view as any potential customer might have been.

"So?" Jason asked. "Having me work with the horses is not much of sight, I assure you."

"Not you, no," Winn countered. "But having the Duke of Rayne working in the stables is something of a spectacle." Off his shocked look, Winn continued. "You know sometimes I think you forget you have that title."

"I know very well I have that title," Jason drawled. "But I thought we long ago agreed it would be better if I didn't use it. Anonymity and all that."

"Desperate times call for desperate measures?" She shrugged. "Besides, that was when we did not want to draw attention to ourselves. Herr Wurtzer *needs* attention—attention you can provide."

"How? By forking straw bedding?" he argued.

"By . . . performing," Winn rationalized.

Jason took a deep breath, pinching the bridge of his nose between his fingers. And as he did so, he saw the plate of food in front of him, its smell still an intoxication. But he also saw, edging out from beneath the table, Winn's shoes. Scuffed raw. If he did this, maybe he could save her feet—and his—from a more arduous journey than necessary. However, there was one more piece of argument to be made.

"What about George?" he asked, and watched as her eyes flew to his face.

Winn's shoulders collapsed. "George managed to track us to Nuremberg without us using your title. I think we need to give up the ghost of the idea that we have any talent for subterfuge."

He had to smile at the truth of that, exhale a breath of laughter.

"If we're lucky," Jason mulled, "George thinks you've headed back for England, proof in hand."

"And if we are not, our best hope now is to outrun him."

She bit her lip, watching his face for his reaction. "And we'll move faster with money."

He chewed this over. "What do you propose?"

Winn sat up straight, ready to engage in negotiations. "Herr Wurtzer," she began, and after a pointed look to Jason, he translated. "You may not be aware, but you are in the presence of one of the most famous aristocrats in Britain. This man is the Duke of Rayne, known far and wide as the bender of wills and breaker of hearts."

"Now hold on," Jason interrupted, but the sharp toe of her scuffed boot told him to simply continue translating.

"Unfortunate circumstances have lead him to your door," Winn continued. "But despite his noble upbringing, he is a man of morality and willing to work for what he owes . . . and then some."

Wurtzer looked utterly dubious as he eyed Jason. Took in his bearded visage, his rumpled, dirty clothes. As the innkeeper perused Jason's unimpressive form, Winn cleared her throat and conspicuously nodded to the gold ducal signet ring, the only thing of any worth Jason had left on him, on his right hand.

While Wurtzer's eyebrow went up, he still held the posture of a man unconvinced. "You could have stolen that," he said, pursing his lips in disapproval.

When Jason translated that little bit of (to be truthful, angering) information, Winn squared her shoulders and looked him dead in the eye.

"Jason," she whispered. "You have to prove you're a Duke."

"And how do I do that?" he argued.

"I don't know—act like a Duke!"

"I *am* a Duke, I don't have to act like one."

"Then put your nose in the air and act like Frederick Sutton. Oh, give him a court bow!" she exclaimed.

Jason glared at her, but he stood abruptly, his nose in the air as directed, and gave his best flourishing court bow, as if Herr Wurtzer was King George IV himself. And just for good measure, Jason then twisted the ring on his finger, showing the skeptical innkeeper the line where tan skin met pale—this ring had been on his hand for years.

Luckily, whether it was the bow or the show of skin, Herr Wurtzer seemed impressed enough to believe them, his ear hair twitching in thoughtful anticipation.

"Imagine it," Winn was saying, "the entire village drawn away from Brauer's watered-down beverages and second-rate meat pies, all to see an English Duke, tacking horses in your stables."

"Tacking horses?" Jason said.

"Isn't that the term?" Winn asked, wide-eyed.

"No—tack is the equipment you use to . . . never mind, I'll explain later." Jason sighed, and continued translating for Herr Wurtzer, but conspicuously changing Winn's more uninformed phrasing.

"Of course, once they are here, the customers will realize the superiority of your fare." Winn smiled at the mulling Wurtzer, his ears twitching with every mental cog falling into place. "And they'll stay."

"How much?" Wurtzer asked, his eyes narrowed shrewdly, calculating.

"Ah—this is the best part!" Winn cried. "No up-front fee."

"No up-front fee!" Jason's voice nearly cracked—something that had not happened in over a decade, such was his surprise.

"No up-front fee beyond the food in front of us," Winn clarified. "But, we get fifteen percent of your profits at the end of the day."

As Herr Wurtzer scoffed, Winn jumped quickly into the fray. "If this experiment doesn't work, there's no harm to you. You end up with clean stables and well-tended horses—all for the price of two plates of food.

"But, if it does work," she continued, her voice taking on this strangely seductive, persuasive quality that set Jason's nerves to tingling, "and you steal all of Brauer's customers . . . isn't that worth fifteen percent of your day's business?"

"Fifteen percent?" Wurtzer replied. "*Nein*. But ten percent . . ."

"Twelve," Winn negotiated, adding, "and a room for the night."

"Twelve," Wurtzer agreed, "and you can bunk in the stables. There's a space in the loft for the stable hands. Which is what the Duke is today."

Winn listened as Jason finished translating. He held his breath as he watched her face, alight with the excitement of the barter, the art of the deal . . . He couldn't help but imagine how glorious she would be in the markets of Budapest, Morocco, or Egypt.

When she said, "Deal," and stuck out her hand for the sealing handshake, rather than be delighted by her broad, transformative smile, or the idea that he got to finish his plate of food, he was instead struck by a lowering, (almost) appetite-killing thought.

That when the time came, he would not see her bargain in the markets of Egypt.

Because he wouldn't be there.

Sixteen

*Wherein our duo eats, drinks,
and makes ... merry.*

THAT evening, after a long day of stable work, Jason decided that his and Winn's comfortable spots near the warmth of the bonfire in the town square were well earned. As were the tankards of beer that Herr Wurtzer had winkingly given them, along with the promise of continual refills. All part of their payment, Wurtzer said. They sat on bales of hay, mixed in with other couples and townsfolk, watching as the dancers performed the last of the unstructured *Sonnenwende* rituals, hopping and moving in happy circles around the fire that rose so high it obscured the stars. Musicians, all local men and women, none professional, played their instruments with joy and vigor, if not skill.

And Winnifred Crane sat opposite him, a hay bale serving as their makeshift table, the light of the fire reflecting the utter peace on her face.

So this was Winn content, he thought, a small smile peeking out through his beard. Normally he could see the thoughts whizzing past, going faster than a gallop ... even in her sleep. Although after the events of the day, there was little reason for such contented bliss on her features, but there it was.

"How can you know they won't trample me?" Winn had shrieked in the stables as one of the horses showed a decided interest in chewing on her hair.

Jason had just laughed heartily, as did the massive gathering of townsfolk watching and eating and laughing nearby.

Winn's plan had worked marvelously, although not necessarily as she had intended. After they had downed their meals, Jason took to the stables immediately, wanting to see what he was working with. What he found was a fairly well-maintained set of boarding stables and a dozen bored, unattended carriage horses. Unattended, he assumed, because without any of the festival's delights coming this way, the stable lads had abandoned their posts to chase said delights.

While Jason had located the feedbags, the oats and hay mixture that made up the feed, the brushes, and the brooms, Wurtzer had commandeered his beloved Heidi to start spreading the word of their newest hire. A younger woman than Jason had expected, she immediately went down to the bakery and told the extraordinary story of the starving young man and his diminutive companion, who in true folk-story fashion, had turned out to be a man of nobility from distant shores. Beloved Heidi, being a native to the village of Lupburg and therefore well ingratiated with the other women therein, knew well enough that her visit to the baker's wife, and shortly thereafter, the butcher's wife, and then a sprinkled word here and there throughout the crowd would be more than enough to start a wildfire of gossip and piqued curiosity.

After all, there is not a Bavarian in the world who can resist a good story.

But when the crowd began to gather and saw a well-dressed if unkempt man of strong disposition forking away old straw and strewing new onto the stall floors, they were bemused but not delighted. Oh, at the whispered words of Wurtzer, they strained for a view of the gold ducal ring on his hand (he had been told to leave off the thick leather gloves he had found, a circumstance his palms would pay for later) and took casual sips of the ale they purchased, but there was very little in the way of a show.

That is, until Winn entered the stables, bringing Jason his own tankard of ale.

The small English woman seemed deeply ill at ease in the presence of horses, but the horses were the exact opposite. Every single one, given the opportunity, nudged her, nickered as she passed their stalls, and when they were out of the stalls (so Jason could thoroughly clean them) danced right up to her, delighted by her presence.

And *her* antics—her screeching, her skittishness, her running away from what had to be the gentlest animals in all of Bavaria—not the Duke's brushing down work and carriage horses, became the entertainment that kept the masses engaged, and kept them purchasing food and drink. So much so that when she had made a move to escape the barn, Jason had to stop her.

"They are not going to trample you, Winn. They like you too much."

"No, they like how I taste. Just let me leave . . ." she moaned, biting her lip as one horse—an older lady with a lovely gray mane named Blume, which meant "flower"— nudged at Winn's hand to see if she had any treats.

"You're right." Jason sighed as he shoveled another forking of old hay into a pile to be removed later. "I'm certain Wurtzer has earned enough by now for our twelve percent to get us to Vienna . . ."

Winn's eyes went directly to the crowd, who it seemed she had just noticed, and saw they were not watching Jason but her, and every strange little thing she did, every little squeak she made . . . their eyes following with laughing engrossment.

She had become the show—not him.

Sighing, her shoulders raised tensely, she turned back to Blume and hesitantly reached out her hand.

And drew it back immediately when Blume tried to nip at her, sending up a roar of laughter from the growing observers.

"You'd think they had never seen someone who was afraid of horses before," she mumbled.

"They probably haven't. Horses are a way of life in the country—you can't be afraid of them when you have to work with them every day," Jason responded, wiping his brow with his sleeve. "Which begs the question—you grew up in the country. How is that you are so unacquainted with horses?"

"I am not unacquainted. I have ridden in carriages, they have horses," Winn answered petulantly, taking hedging steps back from Blume . . . which had the effect of putting her within hair-chewing reach of the horse in the next stall, who was named Wolfgang (and couldn't have been less of a wolf, given that he practically bent in half in his plea to get Winn to pet him).

"I think you're not answering the question," Jason countered with a smile.

"I think you're being purposefully annoying!" Winn cried—but when Jason turned to look at her, he could see that that particular comment had been directed at poor Wolfgang. "And I didn't grow up in the country," Winn argued—this time to Jason. "I grew up in Oxford. Practically on the university. And as you know, since you went there, Oxford is very much not the country. I never had to go very far for what I needed, and when I did, I walked."

"Yes, but what about visiting people?" Jason countered. "Surely you went to seek a change of scene and society once or twice."

But Winn simply shook her head, which attracted far too much of Wolfgang's attention. "Oxford has a new group of people invade every year—I never had to seek a change of scenery. The scenery in Oxford changed on its own."

Jason stopped working for a moment and could only contemplate what she had told him. He knew that she had not been to London prior to her trip to the Historical Society, and she had said that she had not travelled before, but he didn't think that it had meant *ever* or *anywhere*. But before he could comment, Winn started squeaking again, as Wolfgang had managed what none of his stable mates had managed, and pulled Winn's hair out of its haphazard, half-fallen bun and commenced chewing.

"No! Stop it! Bad horse! Bad horse!" she wailed, pulling her hair free but unfortunately coming within Blume's reach in the process.

"Take two steps this way." Jason sighed, pulling her toward him. "Stay directly in front of them. Their field of vision is weakest there."

"This begs the question," she repeated dubiously, "how is it that you are so good with horses? Don't you have fifty stable hands to do this kind of work for you?"

Jason just laughed out loud. "Not fifty." Then his brow furrowed. "At least not fifty all at one residence. It's quite possible I have fifty stable hands in total."

"Jason . . ." Winn said warningly.

"I am good at this." Jason smiled as he finished up one newly clean stall and began on another, "because my father made certain I knew how to do various jobs all over the estate. He thought it terribly important that I know how to do things."

"Really?" Winn asked.

"When I was growing up. As you can see, only one of those things truly stuck with me." Jason could remember his father . . . his father from before the man's health had begun to decline, this large, imposing, gregarious figure whose sternness was matched only by his indulgence. When Jason had been ten or so, in between fencing masters and Latin lessons, his father would send him out with the groundsmen, so the boy would learn how to mend a fence. Then he turned Jason over to the gardeners, so he would learn how to plant a hedge or a tree. Then he was turned over to the falconer, then the gamekeeper, and then the head butler, to learn how to . . . polish silver, apparently.

And he had been bored to death by all of it. Almost as bored as he had been by fencing masters and Latin lessons.

But the one person he had not been bored by was the stable master. A thin wire of a man, the stable master had awed Jason with his ability to calm and control any horse, no matter how unruly and wild. And when Jason had insisted, as a nose-in-the-air ten-year-old lord and master was want to do, that he be taught how to mesmerize an animal like that, the stable master had said he would, just as soon as Jason could prove his worth in the stables.

So Jason had learned. He had learned to brush down a horse and clean its stall. He had learned how to pick out rocks in its shoes. He had learned how to take a horse through its paces in a training pen. Hell, he could even act as farrier in a pinch. And in the end, he'd found himself addicted to horses, to riding, to life in the stables.

"You know, I even find it somewhat soothing," he said as he finished telling Winn about the wiry stable master and his demanding training. "Cleaning out stalls and such. It clears the head."

"Clears the head?" Winn repeated, taking a step backward to allow Jason—and his dirtied pitchfork—to pass with ease. "How can it possibly, with the stench?"

Jason forked another pile of soiled straw. "You get used to it." He looked pensively for a moment, his mind going back in time. "It reminds me of my home."

"Well, I can promise you, I will never get used to it." She crossed her arms over her chest and shook her head.

Which she should have learned by then, was a mistake.

Having stepped backward to allow Jason to pass, and having shook her head to make her point, Winn was now within reach and within sight. So much so, that both Blume and Wolfgang reached out and found a chunk of her hair to chew on lazily.

"Think of it this way," Jason said cheerfully. "You said once that you liked your hair. Well, the horses simply concur."

As Winn moaned in agony again, the crowd laughed and cheered, and one or two gentlemen called out advice.

"What did they say?" she asked Jason, her voice slowly pitching up to panic.

"They said Blume and Wolfgang won't leave you alone because your hair is the color of summer hay."

"No, it's not." She frowned. "My hair is brown. Plain brown."

But it wasn't. At least it wasn't anymore. At some point in their travels—and possibly because he hadn't seen her in a bonnet since they were on board the *Seestern*, her hair, which had indeed been a plain pale brown when they had first met, had taken on lighter strands, honeyed, sun-kissed tendrils drifting down and framing her face.

She had changed.

Even now, as he looked at her in the reflected light of the bonfire, across their makeshift hay bale table, he could see the change in her. Her hair was no longer plain brown. Her face was no longer small and lost under a hat, but instead open and bright. Those eyes—those startling light brown eyes, had grown to sparkle like amber in the sun, darkening to burgundy in the evening, and shifting to nearly black when she read intensely by candlelight.

But one mustn't suppose his observations about her changes were reserved for above the neck.

At some point, Winnifred Crane had grown breasts.

Not that she hadn't had them before, because obviously a woman of thirty didn't grow breasts overnight. But that is to say, Jason hadn't taken particular notice of them before. At least, not when she was this little bird of a woman in the courtyard of Somerset House—nor when she was traveling with Bambridge and Totty to Dover, exasperated but accepting of her companions. No, it must have happened sometime between their arrival at the Stellzburg Inn, where their marriage ruse began, and their departure from Nuremberg. He remembered very clearly her breasts heaving with her labored breath as she ran up to him in the marketplace, the discovery of her letters filling her body with energy and light. And of course, he remembered them with perfect clarity moving up and down in cool, systematic anger after she had slapped him some hours later.

But the reality of them, of her easy curves on her small body, came into his mind when he had held her last night, kept her from shivering to death. It awoke something in him— something that his sleeping self had been well aware of, and now his mind had to acknowledge.

Never before had she looked like she did in the light of the bonfire. Her body being completely at ease, watching the dancers, did something to Winn—something Jason was not poetic enough to describe nor artistic enough to put to paint. But it was glorious, glowing. And her breasts . . .

Her dress—the one she had worn for the last two weeks— mimicked a man's shirt on top, with a row of buttons up the middle to a starched collar. Normally, she wore it buttoned all the way to the collar, practically to her chin, with her coat over it. (And her nightdress, in the few glimpses Jason had allowed himself before she dove under the covers every night, boasted a similar restraining neckline.) But her coat was long gone, and today, after a morning of walking and an afternoon of being mooned over by a stable full of horses, after an evening of joyfully imbibing a full pint of Wurtzer's excellent beer, she had opened the first few buttons of her dress's collar, allowing a tantalizing glimpse of elegant neck. The light from the bonfire played off the hollow at its base, where her mother's locket rested, the point on the end of its heart shape directing where Jason's gaze should continue . . . down into a valley, disappearing beneath unfortunately still-closed buttons . . .

His fingers twitched, just looking at those buttons. They were nothing special, just small, round, and white. But, oh, what lay beneath them! His hands became tight as every nerve ending became enraptured with the idea of touching those buttons . . . working them free . . . the soft skin to be found beneath . . .

"Did I spill some?" Winn asked, breaking through Jason's hazy thoughts.

"I'm sorry?" he stuttered, his eyes flying to her face.

"Did I spill some ale?" she clarified, straightening and looking down at her shirt, where his gaze had been but a moment ago.

"I, uh . . . I don't . . ." Jason mumbled, taking a swig of his own beer. Where the hell had his brain been? It was the ale, he decided. Strong Bavarian beer, the undoing of better men than he, had clouded his brain and had him thinking things he shouldn't. That, combined with the hard labor he had performed for hours that afternoon, had weakened his resolve. After all, it was very hard to think of Winn as a little sparrow who he could tuck under his arm and who needed his help and protection (whether she admitted it or not) when taking far too much notice of her breasts.

And a little bird she would have to remain, he thought as his eyes flicked downward once again. It would be . . . healthier for all involved.

"No matter." Winn shrugged, the inspection of her shirt-front coming up with little to spare him the embarrassment of having been caught staring. "I'm sure I'll manage to before the night is over," she said with a laughing smile, before taking another swig of her beer.

Jason cocked his head to one side. "I think you're a little drunk."

"I think you're right," she replied easily, then her brow came down in concentration. "But only a little." She cocked a brow at him. "I think you think I've never been drunk before."

"I . . . I wouldn't presume to know—"

"I think you'd be right, again," Winn interrupted before he could continue. "What a terribly boring life I've led, don't you think?"

She smiled at him, that grin practically taking his breath away. (It must be the beer. It had to be.) And he found himself smiling lazily back. "Well, it's another thing you can check off your list," he drawled.

"Hmm?" she asked, her eyes flying to his face. Strange,

but they had seemed to be fixated in the general vicinity of his mouth, and when he had smiled at her, she'd . . .

That same strange darkening took over the edges of his vision, directing all light to fall on Winn. It was the same focused sensation that had occurred when she had unexpectedly kissed him in the Dürer House and when she had asked him if he thought she'd ever been kissed before, just that morning on the road. That unsettling . . .

Jason immediately set his face in a stern expression. Oh, this wasn't good. This wasn't good at all. It was fine if he reacted to her in certain ways, he was certain he could control it. But if she began reacting back . . .

"Is there any water here?" Jason asked, clearing his throat conspicuously. "This beer is a little, heavy."

"I think there is some wine, over in those jugs." Winn gestured to the far side of the bonfire, where other revelers made merry watching the dancers, occasionally joining in themselves.

Wine was not a viable replacement, so Jason simply shrugged again and took another swig of his beer. It may be the cause of his current mindset, but drinking it kept his hands and mouth otherwise engaged; therefore, it was the lesser of the evils presented.

"You think the beer too heavy?" Her eyebrow went up as she questioned him.

"It is," he hedged, and, not about to tell her the true reasons behind his gulping, continued. "I doubt even a giant like George Bambridge could down it like a local. But it's better than nothing."

Her face went still, contemplative. She looked down at her beer, her fingers tapping lightly against the tankard in a slightly nervous rhythm.

"What is it?" he asked.

"Something you said yesterday." She took a deep breath. "I think you think I have been cruel to George Bambridge." She bit her lip. "That I've been playing games with his affections."

Jason blinked twice, gaping. "Winn, I never meant to infer—"

"It's all right," she said in a rush, waving away anything he might say. "I know what it seems like—that I've strung him along . . . that I would position myself so that if I don't succeed in this mad scheme, that I would at least land comfortably, into a marriage with a man who I may not love, but at least know." She exhaled a great rush of air. "Women throughout time have done much worse for their own comfort. Why would you think any different of me?"

Jason opened his mouth to speak, to protest—but then he thought better of it. There was an explanation coming, and he was eager to hear it. But she stalled, her mouth opening, her lips moving, but her voice getting stuck in her throat.

And so Jason reached his hand across the hay bale table and sought hers. Taking it into his, he began to rub his thumb gently across the back of her hand, trying to soothe her fears. Never mind that his own nerve endings sighed in relief from the contact. Never mind that having her watch his thumb's movements was almost as entrancing as the act itself.

"Winn, you have no obligation to tell me anything. I am not owed an explanation."

"But I want to tell you!" she cried, looking up from their joined hands. "I want you to understand . . . but to understand, I'd have to take you back to the beginning."

"The beginning?" he asked, teasing. "Are you going to regale me with a lecture on the origins of man? Adam and Eve from the painting?"

"No." She smiled, which had been his intention. "I'm afraid you'll have to settle for the origins of Winn Crane." Her face grew serious then. "I was a very headstrong girl, and sometimes very lonely because if it. And there was a time when George Bambridge was the only friend I had.

"I don't claim to have many now, or to have thrown him over for better society—nothing like that. But when you're fifteen, every feeling feels ridiculously important. A thousand young men around me and none of them taking notice—it left the rather indelible impression that something was lacking in me. Height, beauty, a winning personality, breasts . . ." (Jason could not deny that his eyes flicked down to those entrancing buttons at that point—but he just as quickly brought them up again.) "Whatever it was, I did not have it."

"So eventually," Winn continued, "when a man takes notice—even if your mothers are cousins and he is therefore forced to acknowledge your presence—it means something."

"When you're fifteen," Jason surmised.

"When you're fifteen," Winn agreed. "Although I grew out of this particularly depressing mindset within a few years, just in case you were frightened for me."

"Frightened for you?" Jason replied. "Never. Frightened *of* you, maybe. . . . Ow!" he cried with a laugh, Winn taking his teasing back with a bit of bite, and pinching the thumb that had been lazily stroking over her hand. "All right . . . all right, you win, Winn." He shook out his hand. "You are getting alarmingly better at being teased."

She giggled—Winn Crane giggled! Like the coquettish child she hadn't known how to be, and for the briefest of moments, Jason was completely certain his heart had stopped beating. Just a second, frozen still, the world around them lost, and the only thing that occupied it was Winn's happy, girlish laugh.

So. This is trouble, he thought, his body slowly catching up to the rest of life. Slowly drifting down into someone's laugh, until you realize you're stuck.

But just as soon as the giggle had occurred, it was over, and the serious, slightly vulnerable expression took over her features once again.

"George could never tease me like that, you know. He would think it unseemly."

After all, she still had a story to tell.

"I could not say if he proposed out of true, deep feeling for me, or if it was because it was expected of him, but I had only enough stars in my eyes to hope it was the former and suspect it was the latter. And my father suspected the same." She looked down at their joined hands and sighed. "My father did many marvelous things for me—made me his prize pupil, didn't send me to live with a relative when my mother died— but the best thing he ever did was insist that the betrothal not be made public—that is, that there would be no formal engagement until I was older. And then he didn't specify when older would be.

"Shockingly, George didn't mind. Once he had secured my hand, he put me aside. After all, he had what he wanted. And while one year turned into three or four, my father started having those dinner parties for his students, partially because he wanted me to realize there were other people in the world."

"But you didn't enjoy those," Jason recalled.

"No, it all seemed embarrassingly obvious to me. But then again, I barely thought about George then, either. I was too busy studying. Too busy dreaming of old paintings and what life was like outside of Oxford, outside of England. George may have put pressure on my father, but it was pressure I was shielded from. And then another decade passed . . . and when my father died, I then came to understand that George had certain expectations about how we would live. And suffice to say, they did not involve me pursuing my own studies, or even the outside world. The best I could hope for with him is writing papers under someone else's name, while correcting my husband's work."

She took a deep breath, the air coming out from her lungs on a laugh. "It's harder than you think to let go of the life that was planned ahead of time. It may have taken far too long to come to this conclusion, but come to it I have."

She looked down at her hands again, her voice soft but resolved. "I am not doing this out of a desire to teach him a lesson, or anything so characteristically female. I just know I want something different from my life . . . something grander, and more frightening."

"But why didn't you walk away the moment you discovered this about yourself?" Jason asked. "Why did you give him the hope of you losing this wager and coming back to him?"

She laughed, a little sadly. "At some point—whether it be in the last year or the last decade—George stopped listening when I spoke. He . . . can be very dictatorial. And so, when I would broach the subject, he simply patted me head and said, 'It's the grief, Winnifred. Don't worry, I shall take care of you.'"

"Well, that settles it," Jason said with mock severity. "Such condescension tells me what I had long suspected."

"Which is . . ."

"That George Bambridge was not raised with the benefit of a sister."

She laughed at that, a happy sound, coming in the midst of this bleak story. Her laughter died quickly though, and she grew serious again.

"But the next thing I knew," she said, sighing, "George had exercised his influence over my inheritance. And I cannot be who I wish to be without it. To walk into the world with nothing: no money, position, or friends . . ." She bit her lip. "A man could do it, but not a woman. I will earn the other two through hard work, but I need to start with one. And without the hope of winning me back, he would never have made the wager in the first place."

"I take your point," Jason said after a moment, with an easy shrug.

"You do?" She looked up, bewildered.

"Yes," he replied, somewhat bemused by her shock. "One of the reasons I have been at your heels this entire journey is because I know that the world is so much harder on the fairer sex. Whether or not you require a man's protection, people are far more willing to give you the benefit of the doubt when you have it. You're right—a woman needs one or other of money, position, and friends to make her way on her own. And if you've had to resort to some muddleheaded things to get what you need out of life . . . well, we shall simply have to make sure that you succeed in winning your wager. Simple as that."

"Simple as that," she repeated dully. Then suddenly, her eyes welled with emotion. "Thank you."

"You're welcome," Jason said warily, not being at ease with the threat of female emotions. "Er . . . what for?"

"For understanding," she replied, sniffing away any sign of tears. "I would have judged myself far more harshly."

He leaned across the table, beckoning her closer, as if to tell a secret. She leaned in.

"That's what friends are for, Winn."

Her gaze, already moist, threatened to become water again. A circumstance Jason would avoid heartily if he could. And so he leaned back and turned his eyes to the fire.

A silence fell between them, and Jason struggled with what he wanted to ask next. Why he wanted to ask it, but as soon as the idea popped into his head, it would not do him the courtesy of popping back out.

"Er," he said, then coughed, and started again. "So, you never loved him?"

"Loved who?" Winn asked dazedly. "George?" she asked as her eyes grew wide. "No. Of course not. At least not in that respect."

"In what respect?" Jason asked, suspicious. "Because I warn you, running across a continent after you is the act of a man in love."

"Or the act of a man corralling what he thinks of as his belongings," she replied tartly. Then, she grew pensive. "I never loved him romantically. In fact, I don't think I know what love is. I know the love a parent gives a child, and vice versa, and the love of friendship, and, growing up in a place with a high volume of young men, I am familiar with physical lust . . ."

Jason nearly choked on his beer, almost unmanned then and there at the thought.

". . . But to be *in* love?" she continued. "Romantic love?" Winn shrugged, a quiet little movement that bespoke of both innocence and sadness. "I've studied hundreds of paintings that supposedly depict the moment of love, and still its understanding eludes me. I have no idea what it's like to fall openly to someone like that."

The corner of Jason's mouth went up, his mind fuzzing over in memory. "It is surprisingly easy," he said. "You simply sort of, leap. Open yourself up to the other person. Start telling them things about yourself you didn't even know, and yet they still accept you, and vice versa. It's heady and quiet and a secret you want to shout to the world."

Winn met his eyes then, and again, as it had all evening, his breath caught.

"So, you've been in love? Er . . . are in love?"

Jason's mind flashed briefly to Sarah Forrester—her cool, quiet loveliness and her happy wit. The person he was supposed to be falling madly for. And yet . . . she was so far away. Not just the miles that spanned continents, but she had been a distant thought in his mind for weeks now. And meanwhile, at the forefront of his thoughts, consuming his every waking beat of his pulse, had been this strange woman in front of him, keeping him constantly on his toes and making him laugh at the most curious moments. The one whose hand for the past two weeks he had not been able to let go of.

Too many thoughts, running too deep, he admonished himself. Instead, looking into Winn's eyes, Jason took his first step out on the tightrope and answered honestly.

"No, I'm not in love. But I have been. As in love as a boy of nineteen can be, I expect." He blushed a little at the rose-tinted memories. "Penelope Wilton. I wrote some particularly bad poetry and saccharine letters. A summer romance—at the end of which I went back to school, and later she married a nice barrister in Manchester. I loved her before I knew what it was to be in love with someone."

Winn's gaze did not falter from his, as she asked him, in her most academic, dry tone, "And now?"

Jason had to pause and think for a moment. "I've seen my

friends paired off into marriages, some turning out very happily, others turning into little more than a steady dinner companion, others barely speaking to each other, living separate lives. And I've seen my sister's marriage, to a man of lower status, one who shouldn't have even contemplated a Duke's daughter for a mate—and yet, they fought for what they have. And I shall not lie—initially, I was one of the more obstinate obstacles they had to combat. But with each other in their back pockets, the fight . . . well, it looked easy. Looking at her, I think I know better what romantic love is."

Again, in that clinical, academic tone, as if she were studying him like she would a painting, examining for unseen secrets, she asked, "And what is it?"

"It is parental love," he answered thoughtfully. "Wanting to protect and keep the other person safe. As well as the love of friendship—esteeming the other person, even desiring each other's company beyond all others. And it is lust," he said, meeting her eyes, and was rewarded by seeing them darken, her breath becoming slightly unsteady, one little word jerking her out of her clinical assessment. He smiled, a predatory, seductive grin. "The physical needing of the other person, the quickened pulse, the sweaty heat." His hand, which still rested on hers, began slowly moving, his fingers dancing over her skin. "Combining them makes the result greater than its individual parts. Because it produces something else. It creates . . . a steadiness. A strength. I can't explain it well—being only an outside observer—but I only know that out of all my friends' relationships, my sister's marriage is the epitome of grace."

He held her gaze as she studied him, her analytical sense locking something into place. What, he did not know, but she smiled at him then—that knowing half smile, that turn of her lips that made her seem the possessor of all knowledge. She leaned forward, willing him to do the same.

"It sounds marvelous," she said, her voice pitched low for the telling of secrets, and seductive in a way that she likely didn't even realize. "But I don't know if I could do it."

"Do it?" he asked.

"Fight for the whole. I can manage the parts—parental love, friendship. I can manage lust."

She looked him dead in the eye when intoning that last word, making Jason think that Winn Crane—bookish, scholarly Winn Crane—knew *exactly* what she was doing to him. "But I don't know if I am destined to find them all together. Make myself responsible for someone else's happiness. I don't think I'm built for it."

Built for it. Jason wanted to counter, to disagree. To assure her that anyone who cared as diligently for her father and as passionately about her work as she did, indeed had the capacity for love. And the will to fight for it.

But when he opened his mouth for such a speech, he found his throat dry and his courage fleeting. Because one thought flew to the front of his mind. One niggling little thought that displace all others:

While he was certain Winn had the strength to fight for what she loved, he didn't know if he did. And he doubted it.

Better to joke. Better to stay on an even keel. Than admit to fears out loud.

"I don't think I could, either," Jason agreed, with a smile. "Try and make one other person happy? Might as well tell me to read all my estates' account books cover to cover. I'm far too lazy and irresponsible an individual," he replied, silently exhaling a sigh of relief. Whether it be the air or the ale, the conversation had become far too close to meaningful, and he was glad for the chance to be a bit jovial. But Winn did not laugh at that bit of sarcasm, as expected. Instead, she looked at him queerly.

"Are you?" she asked.

"Am I what? Lazy? Irresponsible?"

"As . . . self-deprecating as that statement was meant to be, I think you think you *are* irresponsible and lazy."

Jason didn't quite know how to respond to that, so he bought time with a slow drag on his ale.

"And what do you think?" he asked slowly, unable to meet her eyes.

"I'm not entirely sure. You claim to not know how many stable hands are in your employ, yet you cleaned and maintained those horse stalls today with pride and accuracy. You pretend to have no head for details, but quirk or no, you keep track of your bills. Hell, you read the Historical Society's charter before you joined; I doubt there is one man in a hundred who can say the same.

"You pay lip service to duty," she continued shrewdly, "and don't seem to have any pressing obligations in life beyond your own pleasure, and yet you abandoned those pleasures and comforts to go out of your way to help me. Say what you will, but those are not the acts of the lazy."

Jason was caught for a moment. In her hazel eyes, firelight dancing in their depths, and in the accuracy of her assessment.

"Why did you do it?" she asked. "Why have you been helping me? And don't say it's because Lord Forrester asked you to. I think we both know you have gone above and beyond that particular call of duty."

He could play it off. Shrug casually, make another sad attempt at a joke. But they had breached new ground with their honesty tonight, and Jason . . .

He didn't want it to end.

"Many reasons," he said on a laugh, which did nothing to hide his vulnerability. "I felt a bit guilty. It was my fault your father's letter of introduction got knocked into the fountain."

"No, we lay the blame for that at George's door," she argued, a twinkle coming into her eye.

"And if I hadn't egged you on once you got into the Historical Society's doors, you wouldn't have managed to see Forrester and challenge him into this crazed journey."

"First you blame yourself for hindering me and then for *helping* me? For giving me something I wanted?" Winn mused. "The workings of the male mind are twisted indeed."

Jason's gaze flicked down to the buttons of her shirt again as he replied, "You have no idea. But . . ."

"But . . . ?"

"I became involved," he explained. "With you. And your scheme, at a very early stage. And I think . . . for once I wanted to be the person to finish something. My sister—she made a comment I don't think she realized would stick with me the way it did."

At her unblinking and rapt gaze, he continued awkwardly. "When I was younger, and my father was falling into ill heath, I wasn't like you. I didn't care for him or help run the estates in his stead. I avoided responsibility altogether."

"But . . . surely you don't avoid it anymore."

"No, I don't, but that was a hard lesson learned. Yet according to my sister, while I no longer abdicate responsibility, I do . . . delegate it. I don't have to pay particularly close attention to my life—I have stewards and secretaries and butlers and gardeners that run the machine. And I could have easily done that with you. I could have left you in Dover and driven away, handing you off to the next person. But, I think some part of me looked for you on the docks, and spotted you on the wrong ship, stayed with you in Hamburg, then Nuremberg, because . . . I didn't want to delegate this. I want to see this through."

He held his breath while she watched him. The fire cast the shadows of those dancing around it, flickering light across her face—giving her expressions that might not be there. One moment she looked pensive, another lost, another powerful—all without changing the set of her mouth, the slight rise of the corner of her brow, the tiny, wicked purse to her mouth.

It was only a moment, bare seconds passing. But later, in the cold air of winter, when Lupburg and *Sonnenwende* were just a distant memory, Jason would come to recall this moment—the firelight and shadow playing across her features as the moment that he knew.

But it passed, as moments tend to do. This one pleasantly, as Winn's sly smile came back to her face.

"So," she drawled. "I suppose that's one thing we can cross off your list of new things to try."

"What?" he asked, his eyebrow going up, matching her smile.

"Seeing something through."

"But I'm not finished yet," he countered.

"And I'm not finished getting drunk," she said, raising her glass of ale, "yet you've already crossed that one off mine."

"Yes, well"—he laughed, gently pulling her stein back down to their hay table—"feeling the effects of alcohol is something better judged from outside."

"As is nobility," she replied, far more sober than Jason feared he was.

He held her gaze again as the musicians started up a new tune, fast and lively. Her eyes flicked over to the sound, where the drum and violin players were being met by cheers and, of course, more dancing.

"There is something else I would like to cross off my list," Winn said confidingly.

Jason's other eyebrow joined his first, his mind going places they should not, but would not alter from.

"Dancing around a bonfire at a *Sonnenwende* festival," she breathed.

Jason immediately leaned back, recoiled at the idea, even as she stood and tugged on his hand, trying to pull him out of his seat.

"No, no, no, no," he protested.

"Please?" she begged. "It will be fun."

"I . . . I don't dance, Winn."

"Neither do I. Let's do it."

"Winn—"

"This is not a ballroom. No one is going to force you to remember the steps of the waltz. Which is something I cannot do either, by the way."

Jason threw a glance to the dancers behind her. True, any formality to the dancing had dissolved as the evening had worn on and the thick German beer had flowed with impunity. Now, it was simply an expression of happiness, of tradition, and the summer night.

But still, Jason was not confident that he could manage even that.

Winn must have recognized his hesitance, because she smiled at him, that half smile that held all the world's knowledge, and then leaned down the short distance between his sitting height and her standing. Her face close, so close to his, she whispered in his ear.

"Come now, Your Grace. Do not delegate *this* responsibility. Just . . . follow my lead."

He felt the warm, soft pressure of her lips against his cheek. Just a peck, a kindness. But it was enough to get his blood moving and his legs propelling him out of his seat.

She winked at him, and whether the alcohol or the night or the length of the day was responsible for his bewitchment, for the transformation of Winn Crane, scholar, into Winn Crane, temptation, he did not care. Because he was happy enough in that moment to trust her, his heart pounding in time to the music, and pulled along by their joined hands . . . and begin to dance.

Seventeen

Wherein decisions made
are acted upon, and fortunes change.

THEY stumbled into the loft of Wurtzer's barn, groping for purchase even as they clung desperately to each other. Lips found lips, hands found hands, and bodies pressed against each other with intention. In the swirling haze of feeling that seemed to blind Winn to everything—including the slumbering horses—everything but Jason, she rejoiced in how she had actually managed to get here, and the bravery it took to do it.

Although the actual, physical act of getting here, to the loft of the barn, was slightly unclear. But then again, her focus had been elsewhere.

They had been dancing. Terribly. The confidence the ale gave her was undermined by her own lack of skill, but then again, it was matched by Jason's, which somehow made everything fun and funny and all right. Other couples danced around them, their steps sure and known, and so, for a minute or so Jason and Winn tried to mimic them. But after bumping into their third couple, they caught each other's eyes and started laughing.

"I told you, I can not dance!" Jason shouted over the music, the fire, the voices.

"I told you, I do not care!" Winn replied. And then, something—be it the ale or the atmosphere, the stars overhead or the company beside her—made Winn feel . . . free. Free to move however her body dictated, to the rhythms of a song played on a horn or a fiddle.

And so she did.

She stepped without knowing where she would step next. Moved without a prescribed idea of what followed after. She twirled, stepped, leaped with more grace than she ever had before. Later, much later, reflection would ascribe her oddly superb balance and lack of fear of falling to the alcohol, but in that moment it felt glorious. She took the ties and pins out of her hair, letting it fall freely, messily down over her shoulders. Her poor, chewed upon hair, she thought—its loose tendrils a desperate temptation to poor Wolfgang the horse, and now . . .

She turned and saw the expression on Jason's face. The way his eyes were following her movements, her hands, her hair . . . now she was a temptation to him.

How strange, how utterly strange to see want in his eyes. A want that she had never seen directed at her, but as basic and recognizable as a smile or a frown or a grimace. Want. Desire.

And he desired *her.* It made her feel tingly all over. Little pinpricks of fire flushing across her skin, as her body woke up to the idea of being desired. Of being beautiful.

How strange . . . and how powerful.

He followed after her, her jumping steps, her out-of-style but in-time movements, holding to the beat set by fingers plucking strings. They were free of the expectations of society's judgment, free of their own concerns, and for the brief, glorious moments the music afforded, they simply danced.

Soon enough, they were not the only ones who had given up the steps in favor of easy, joyful dancing by the light of the bonfire. Other couples, fueled by happiness and alcohol, mimicked their unknown steps, and the tune played became livelier and the crowd's jubilation matched.

Jason came round, caught her by the waist, causing her to squeak with surprise and delight. Then he took her hands and spun her around, like children did to make themselves dizzy. And dizzy she was indeed—the blinding swirl of feeling mixed with the alcohol to turn the stars into white streaks of paint on a dark canvas, and she had to stop, to steady herself, to catch her breath. And to smile. Tremendously. Deliriously.

She caught Jason looking at her. He was always looking at her.

"What is it?" he asked, concerned, over the music and laughter.

"Nothing like that!" She giggled at the worry in his voice. "I just think we've all suddenly become pagans!"

She indicated the crowd, the hopping, happy dancing, the bonfire that would burn well into the night. But when she turned back, she saw that Jason's gaze had never left her face. It was dark and intense and burning into her skin.

"You know," he said, closing the half-step gulf of space between them, his voice pitched low and honeyed, "I think you're right. I think we are all pagans."

She looked up at him, curiously. Her eyes finding his intent . . . and then with a quick glance down at his lips, allowing it.

He didn't need to be told twice.

This kiss . . . it wasn't the quick press of flesh that had appeased a crowd in Stellzburg. Nor was it the impulsive display of gratitude she had unsettled him with at the Dürer House. This kiss . . .

So, this was passion. This was want acted upon, need and hope churned up, groped for, held fast to. His lips pressed into hers with no kindness. And when she finally began to press back, it was with no ease. It was new and exploding in her body and brain, like the time an anonymous Oxford student had let fireworks fly over the Radcliffe Camera: completely unexpected, completely spectacular.

Something you can cross off your list—the thought popped

into her brain, causing her to smile sheepishly against his mouth, his beard scratching against her cheek.

It was the smile that did it. When she opened her lips just that bare amount, he wasted no time in swooping in, invading her with his tongue. And suddenly, as she let her tongue dance in unknown steps with his, all of those sensations—those fireworks spectaculars that had taken over her body—felt dim in comparison.

Yes, it was something that she could check off her list. If only she didn't want more.

At that thought, her body went still, shock coursing through her system. Jason felt it, because he pulled back, met her gaze. And held.

And suddenly, Winn knew exactly what it was she wanted to do.

And she decided to do it.

"Come with me," she said, her voice soft and thick. Taking his hand she pulled him away from the bonfire.

"Winn—wait, where are we going?" Jason said, tripping after her, the smile in his voice masked by confusion.

They came to the corner of the village square—away from the voices, the movement, the fire. The cool air coming to touch her reddened cheeks, her skin.

"Winn, I'm sorry, I didn't mean to frighten—"

She came up short, forcing Jason to an abrupt stop. Then, with all the bravery the journey, the night, and the ale had unleashed from her soul, she brought his head down to hers and kissed him.

Slowly, deeply. Her hand snaking up around his neck and pressing herself into his body—that body that she had spent night after night sleeping next to but not feeling, until last night, when he held her close, kept her from shivering to death. The body that she had spent hours today watching as he lifted forks of straw, shook out blankets . . . by rolling up his sleeves and unknowingly exposing his strong, capable arms. By lifting and sweating, making his shirt stick to the planes and muscles of his back in the most curiously satisfying way.

As she clung to that back, she lifted her face away from his, to find and hold his gaze.

"Follow me," she breathed, her voice thready and low.

His eyes, dark already in the banked firelight, became charcoal as they changed from astonished to understanding in the barest fraction of a second. He nodded mutely, his face completely stone . . . except for the tiniest smile, awed and knowing, peaking through his beard.

They were a clamor of hands and soft laughter all the way back to the barn. A tumble of rushed footholds and kisses as they made their way up the ladder to the loft. And now . . . now they were a rush of fingers pulling at ties and buttons—those enticing buttons.

Those *entrapping* buttons, Jason thought as he marveled at their engineering, all the while cursing their existence. He had managed to get one free of its mooring, but that only made him want to get them all free, and damned if his fingers weren't too big and clumsy for their delicacy.

"Stupid . . . buttons," he breathed, while Winn rained soft kisses down on his temple.

"Problems?" She smiled against his skin, her hands slipping under his coat at the shoulders and ruthlessly shoving it to the ground, leaving him in his shirt . . . leaving him to wrestle with those damn buttons.

"No—I . . . I just want to feel all of you."

The next few buttons miraculously came free, enough for him to slip his hand beneath the surface of twill and find skin made of silk. His finger pads and palms, roughened by two weeks of travel and that day's worth of hard labor, brushed against the skin of her breast, making her gasp at the sensation.

That little noise filled his blood with fire, rushing directly to his groin, making him harder than stone. His body wanted more little noises, more little gasps, more soft, silky skin. He dipped his head to her neck, settling into that sweet crook,

while his fingers explored the valley of her breasts, their surprising fullness (really, where had this little slip of a woman
been keeping *these*?), finding his way over to her nipple.

That elicited such a gasp, Jason could not help but chuckle
against her neck.

"You like that?" he asked huskily, using his other hand to
free another button, and yet another.

She nodded sheepishly, her chest still unbearably exposed
to him.

"Good," he said, doing it again, "I want to find out everything you like."

"Everything?" she asked, her voice barely a squeak.

"Everything," he said again. "For instance . . ." He put his
hand at the back of her neck, the delicate jointure that he had
long ago claimed as his own, and began to nibble on her ear,
as his thumb stroked lazily against the fine tendons along her
neck. "Do you like that?"

He was rewarded by a small hum of agreement and her
wrapping her arms around his neck, pulling her to him.

"How about this?" he whispered in her ear, and then pulled
at the small ties that held her now-exposed chemise together,
exposing her breasts to the cool air. He ducked his head and
blew gently on their tips.

"Ha-ah, that feels a little funny." She giggled but still caressed his shoulders, ran her fingers through his hair.

"What about . . . this?" He ran his hand down her spine,
finding her pert bottom and pressing her against his hard
length.

"Stop!" she cried, her eyes flying open, suddenly going
completely still, completely tense.

"What? Ah . . . yes . . ." Jason sighed, his blood thrum-
ming in protest against every word. But words that had to be
said. "Yes, you're right. Too far . . . We should stop . . . This is
likely a bad idea . . . You've had too much to drink and I . . ."

But even as his body cried out in agonized disagreement,
his mind rationalized his actions. Although they had only had

a few beers each, her relative size and inexperience with alcohol made her far more easily influenced than he. This might feel good now—really, incredibly, undeniably better than anything he'd ever felt before in his entire life good—but regrets would come in the morning. He would simply have to stop running his hand up and down the line of her back . . . finding her firm bottom and pressing her to him . . . stop searching out her lips with his . . .

"I didn't mean stop entirely," she corrected, her eyes going wide at the mistaken impression. Then, following the line of his hand down to her hip, she veered off course and reached into her pocket, drawing out her precious packet of letters that had been stored there.

"These need a better place, somewhere where they won't get crushed," she explained. Then, bending down, allowing a truly mind-bendingly wicked image to pop into Jason's mind, she took his coat that she had only moments before shoved ruthlessly to the ground. She stood and shook it out, and placed the packet of letters neatly in his breast pocket, next to the toy doll that lived there.

"Considering I had my coin purse lifted from there, I cannot claim that my coat pocket is the safest place."

"Who is going to lift your coin purse here? Wolfgang?" She smiled and then, stepping away from him—just a few fatal steps but enough to have him regretting the distance—hung his coat from a nail on the wall, generally reserved for pieces of tack.

Then she came back to him, closed the distance between them, and put herself right back in his arms.

"Now then," she said, her voice, usually so dry and academic, taking on the sweet alto of seduction, "where were we?"

Where had they been indeed? Let's see . . . his one hand was here . . . and his other hand was there . . . and his mind had been thinking that this was perhaps not the best idea . . .

Damn it.

Doubt. Just a drop of it, just a grain, but some little ethical part of his brain was still awake and functioning.

"Winn," he said, cursing every syllable that fell from his tongue. "Maybe we shouldn't do this."

"Why not?" she asked, her lips finding the way to his ear, mimicking his earlier seduction of her. Damn effectively.

"Ah . . . because . . ." His hazy brain tried to focus. "Because . . . we've been drinking . . . and we still have a ways to go before we get to Vienna, so this—"

"You're not frightened, are you?" she replied, her lips moving from his ear to his neck.

"No." He shook his head, his entire body laughing at the notion. Yet, his brain still froze with hesitation. "But . . . you are not—that is . . . this is new, and . . ."

But his body overruled and effectively shut down his brain when she dipped her fingers beneath the waistband of his trousers, grabbed his ass, and pulled him to her.

"How do I convince you I want this?" she asked, moving her body against his length, seeking warmth . . . seeking pressure . . . "And that I want it with you?"

It was the look in her eyes that did it. Slightly predatory, wholly confident . . . except for the smallest speck of vulnerability, just behind their hazel depths. Well hidden, to be sure. Winn was always careful to hide well what she truly felt, but somehow, Jason always managed to find it.

Vulnerable. Unsure. But wanting. As eager as she was, there was still some part of her that had to be coaxed out of hiding.

"Do you think you can?" He smiled at her with lopsided charm. "Convince me?"

It was his smile that did it. That teasing, playing smile that made everything a game, made it fun. Winn's pounding heart was full of fear—fear of what they would do, fear that they would stop—but when he teased her, everything felt easy. It felt free.

"Hmm"—she smiled up at him—"let's see if I can find

something convincing . . . how about this?" She pulled at the buttons on his linen shirt, her fingers working far more nimbly than his had managed with hers. The buttons now free their moorings, she slipped her hand beneath his shirt, over the rough hairs on his chest, the hard planes of his muscles.

"That's . . . nice . . ." he breathed, smiling down at her, the hitch in his voice making her giggle.

"What about . . . this?" she whispered, lowering her head to kiss a line down his chest, playfully mimicking him again, but with her own twist—letting her teeth graze against the sensitive tip of his nipple.

He grabbed her as he felt his knees buckle, and brought her to the ground, to the pile of blankets that Wurtzer had thrown up to the loft for their comfort. He landed on top of her, careful not to crush her with his weight, and looked down into her eyes.

"That's not fair—I wanted to do that to you first," he groaned, and then lowered his head to her breast.

She giggled, delirious with her power. Everything except the man on top of her, cradling her head in his arm, had taken on sort of a bleary, hazy tone. Jason was in sharp focus, his red hair in the small fraction of half moonlight that came through the slats of the barn; his nose, which up this close, had the oddest smattering of freckles, the last vestige of his youth to be found on his person. It was as if her eyes had discovered that nothing else in the world mattered beyond him. And in this moment, nothing did.

He sought her mouth then, and took what she had to give. This . . . this was exactly what she had felt when spinning and dancing next to the bonfire. Why did people drink if they had kissing available to them? But then again, not everyone kissed like Jason Cummings.

More buttons came free, a frantic rush of need, of wanting to feel skin against skin. Jason came up on his elbows, to free himself of his shirt, tossing it recklessly aside. He found her eyes again and held for a moment, hesitating.

"This is a bad idea," Jason warned.

"On the contrary." Winn leaned up and kissed him with all the passion she had at her disposal. "I think it the best idea I've had in a while."

Oh, fuck it, Jason thought. Let regret come. After all, what is life without a few regrets? Let him have this one moment. This one delirious, swirling moment, lost to ale and to *her*. To Winn. The crazed bluestockingish woman who had infected his blood with her smile and her schemes. And as he dove for her . . . since there was no longer anything to stop them, stop they did not.

Clothes were determined to be wholly unnecessary. Winn, for all her proclivity to cold, was likely to set the dry tinder of Wurtzer's stables on fire, her skin was all slick heat. Therefore, it was decided her dress simply had to go. His shoes and her stockings, his trousers and her petticoat, all gathered into hapless mixed up piles across the floor of the loft. Each article of clothing shed another inhibition, another fear, and suddenly, there they were, wholly exposed to each other.

"You look like a statue," she said, awed, with only the barest hint of tipsy laughter.

"A statue?" he asked. Well, he was certainly as stiff as one, that was for damn sure.

"All those Greek and Roman statues in the British Museum collections at Montague House . . . Totty lives remarkably near, I made sure to visit in London when I was there, and you are—mmm . . ."

He kissed her—partially because he wanted to, partially because he didn't want her rambling herself into awkwardness. But he had to take this slow, he realized, as slow as he could manage.

"And you are so beautiful," Jason rasped, his gaze raking across every curve, every swell.

She blushed, biting her lip. "I'm too . . . little to be beautiful."

How odd, how astonishing to find this pinpoint of insecurity in the brash Miss Winnifred Crane, who marched into the Historical Society and demanded an audience. He grinned at her. "Maybe when you were younger," he countered, kissing her neck, letting his roughened hand dance its way down her body. "But not now! Obviously. You have become very . . . even. Balanced."

She stared up at him, bemusement on her features. "I said that to you ages ago. You can't have been thinking of it."

He shrugged. "It's been bothering me."

He expected a smart, cynical response, but just then, his hand slid its way down over her belly, into that sweet valley, and found its goal. Winn sucked in her breath and was lost to speech.

From there on, there were no more teasing words. They let their hands and bodies do what their quips and conversation had been playing at for so long. Touching, pressing, grappling for what would get them closer to what they both wanted. He nudged her legs further open with his knee—and as long as he kept touching her *there*, she would do anything that he directed.

Jason knew, he knew he was being greedy, but he was straining against the effort of holding back and simply taking her, that tight little body that had been sleeping next to him and yet out of his reach for the past week. He let his body tease her, let his hard shaft nudge its way in between her legs, let his hand coax her open, all the while raining kisses down her eyes, her neck, her breasts.

As for Winn, there was something profound, she could sense it, some great discovery, coming just over the rise, just out of her grasp . . .

She clung to him and before she knew it, was urging his hardness into her softness, climbing for what she wanted. And Jason . . . he didn't have the strength to fight her.

He entered her swiftly—his body winning the war with his mind and unable any longer to move slowly or with any grace.

Of course, that was when it all went to hell.

She stiffened, her entire body reacting to the invasion. To the pain.

"Um," she squeaked, her body refusing to relax, refusing to unfreeze.

Jason lowered his head to her shoulder, trying like hell to hold still. But she was so *tight*. It took all of his effort to say through gritted teeth, "I'm sorry. I'm so sorry. It's just this once, though."

She closed her eyes, let herself adjust to this new fullness. All the while Jason fought every fiber of his being that was telling him to move, as he held murderously still.

"Can we . . . hold still, for just another moment?" she asked meekly, a blush spreading up her face unlike anything Jason had ever seen before.

Jason kissed her forehead gently. He would do it. He would fight this bloody war against his body and win. He would gain control over it, and he would stay as still as the statue she thought he was until . . .

Until she moved beneath him.

It was the smallest shift, something that would have gone unnoticed if he hadn't been fortunate to have such an excellent vantage point, but shift she did. Then, trying again, moved with a little more confidence. A slight arch of the back, a raise of her hips . . . motions that every woman knows instinctively, that have bewitched man for millennia. He began moving in time with her . . . these steps, they both knew.

And as they dance higher, both lost to touch and sensation, the most curious thing happened. At least, Winn thought it was curious. That feeling of fullness yet straining, that profound discovery that she reached for, searched for . . . it found her.

It found her pulse, her heartbeats, and pushed them to their absolute limit. It found her core and grew there, the epicenter of waves of pleasure, pulsating out, spreading through her body, through the loft, through the tiny town that danced around a bonfire. And as she touched down with light steps, the newness of her body coming to her in full, Winn held tight to Jason.

He marveled at her, at her utter abandon. His body wanted to take her passion as the invitation it was—to bury himself deep and stay there, spill himself entirely into her tight, welcoming body. But in the war between his body and his mind, his mind had the last shred of strength, and knew he couldn't. At the crucial moment, he withdrew and spilled himself on the straw beside them.

His heart began to slow down, as his body was consumed in numb, sated pleasure. It was a few moments before he could turn and seek her eyes, but when he did, his heart stopped completely.

She looked at him, confusion filling her features, but completely mute.

I'm a complete heel, Jason thought. Then reaching down to their feet, where one of the unused blankets rested, he pulled it up over her.

"You must be freezing," he whispered, tucking in the edge of the blanket around them, letting his body warm her side. But still she said nothing.

"Winn . . . you're scaring me a bit. I don't think you've ever been silent this long before," Jason said with a small laugh, trying to inject some levity to the moment. But he could not keep the concern out of his voice. "Are you all right?"

"Yes," she finally replied with a small nod. "I'm fine. A little tired, I think."

Jason had to believe her. After all, what choice was there? So, regardless of his true feelings, and letting his body once again take the reigns over his mind, he wrapped his arms around her and submitted to his dizzying desire to rest.

Winn was tired. But more than that, she was stunned. Stunned by her body's reaction to him, stunned by how much she liked having his arms around her. Normally she would pounce on this new information, process it into what she knew before, but this . . . this was too big, and her mind was too mixed. Instead, she told herself she would sleep. She had to.

But even as she let herself drift off, the world spinning before her eyes as much from the drink as it was from her bold actions, she settled on one thing with absolute certainty:

She felt too much.

Too much of the cool air on her glistening, hot skin. Too much of his weight on her, too much of his heart beating in time with hers. But it went deeper than the body. It was as if, by invading her person, he had managed to take up residence in some part of her that she had always held close, held safe.

It was her heart.

And that . . . that was not allowed to happen.

That frightened her more than anything.

Eighteen

*Wherein our duo's proclivity
to run comes greatly in handy.*

JASON came to with his wits wholly intact. There was no bleary minute or two of closed-eye bliss, thinking he was in a bed, in his home, his cheek resting against the top of the head of a beautiful woman. Only that last part was true.

No, Jason knew exactly where he was, whom he was with, how he got there, and what they had been doing a mere few hours previous. And he knew it had only been a few hours, as the sky was only just lightening to gray, the sun still not yet out of its own bed.

But someone else was, and was rapping furiously on the trap door to the loft.

"Herr Duke!" Wurtzer's desperate whisper came through the floorboards. "Herr Duke, you must go! Now!"

Jason's brow furrowed. Go? But it wasn't even dawn. But Wurtzer's knocking did not cease, forcing Jason to quickly but gently unwrap himself from around Winn, who was being blearily roused by the noise now, too. Jason found his trousers, hopped into them.

"What's . . . ?" Winn asked, her voice barely a rasp.

"I don't know." Jason shook his head. "Just stay there. I'll find out."

He fastened his trousers as he moved briskly barefoot across the splintery, strawed floorboards of the loft. He wrenched open the door, revealing a very worried-looking Wurtzer at the top of the ladder.

"Oh, Herr Duke," Wurtzer said in German, relief apparent in his voice, but not staying long. "I just came back from the bonfire—or its ashes, as it died out. But Brauer was still there and very drunk, and he says he's going to come after the Englishman who stole his business."

Jason's mind, alert though it was, had to focus back to find Brauer in his memory (as his mind, during the bonfire, had been predictably elsewhere). A younger man, true, but a shorter one, too. Hell, Winn could likely best him in a fair fight. "I wouldn't worry too much about Brauer," Jason drawled in the man's language. "Drunken boasting has felled more than one man."

"It's not Brauer I worry about—he has brothers. Seven of them. And all are very protective of their 'little' brother—and their family's income, which is from the pub . . ."

Right then, Jason heard a noise. Some revelry, out in the distance, beyond the loft, beyond the street Wurtzer's establishment sat on. He rose and peered out the window. There in the distance, he could see the last embers of the bonfire in the town square, and a contingent of what had to be the burliest, drunkest men in the town. Awake, and walking directly toward them.

"Right . . ." Jason drawled, coming back down on his haunches to face Wurtzer, "we should probably go."

"I'll have my beloved Heidi try and distract them in the main court. You can take the back way out of the barn, and through the alley to the street below, yes?"

"Yes, but"—Jason narrowed his eyes and reached out, catching Wurtzer's arm, preventing him from leaving in all haste, as the older man obviously wished to do—"we haven't been paid yet for our services yesterday."

Wurtzer nervously patted his pockets, coming up with a small pouch, jingling with coins. "Here—this is all I have on me. The rest is in the safe, and I don't think there is time to get it."

Jason weighed the pouch in his hand. "This isn't nearly enough. We agreed upon—"

"I know, I'm sorry!" Wurtzer cried. "But please, you have to go—I told them you left last evening, but if they find you here, they will tear apart my barn, wreck my taproom . . . and Brauer's son is married to the mayor's daughter, I would not be able to . . ."

Jason rolled his eyes. Not only was he losing the argument, they were losing time.

"All right then, what about some horses?" he asked. "Just to borrow. I'll make sure they get back to you."

Wurtzer seemed to mull this for far too long a time, considering how much closer the angry voices of the brothers Brauer got with every tick of the clock. "Which direction do you go?" Wurtzer asked finally.

"Southeast."

"Take two horses. Head toward Regensburg. Leave them at the posting house on Hohenfelser Strasse. A man named Hecht runs the place, he'll make sure they get back to me."

That was fair, Jason decided, and considering the speed with which the drunken march approached them, it was a deal worth taking. He shook Wurtzer's hand.

"Remember—side door to barn, through the alley. Hurry!" And with that Wurtzer was gone.

Jason turned back, finding Winn already lacing up her boots.

"We have to go?" she asked, seemingly already knowing the answer.

"Yes," Jason said, locating his own shoes and socks. "He paid us what he could and has given us leave to borrow some horses, but yes, we need to go and go now."

"You mean horse, singular," she amended, grabbing Jason's coat off its makeshift hook and locating the packet of letters in the breast pocket. She gently transferred them to her dress pocket before tossing him his jacket.

"Winn, we don't have time to argue about your silly fear of horses—"

"You're right, we don't," she countered. "But believe me when I tell you that I have never sat successfully on a horse by myself, and if I have to ride one, I will fall off and break my neck. And while that would annoy, it would also slow us down considerably."

"So will riding two to a horse!" Jason replied in a rushed whisper.

"Then I will walk beside you," she countered. And brooking no further opposition, she marched to the loft door, wrenched it open, and proceeded down the ladder.

Jason's brow came down. The last thing he wanted to do was argue with her right now. In fact, this is not what he had in mind for the morning after—he would have much rather have awoken with the sun, and awoken her with . . . other activities. But instead, a mad dash out the door was required, and therefore any other activities, as well as any arguing, would have to wait its turn.

"Fine," Jason grumbled (to himself it seemed, as Winn was already down the ladder) as he followed after her, "but the first thing I'm doing when we get back to England is teaching you to ride."

❧

"Truly, Winn—riding is not that difficult. I'll have you seated on your own and at a gallop in a fortnight, three weeks at the most," Jason said nonchalantly, shading his eyes from the midmorning sun as he settled in more comfortably to his spot against the fir tree he had commandeered for a nap.

"We should not dawdle here," Winn said as she tugged at

her locket, pacing back and forth in front of Jason. "We have to keep moving, get to Regensburg, then—"

"Then Vienna, I know." Jason sighed.

"Then why have we even stopped? We should be on the road!"

"And we will be—as soon as Wolfgang has had a bit of a rest. He's not a machine, you realize."

Wolfgang, munching on the bit of grass within his reach, tethered to the tree as he was, looked up in what Jason liked to think was agreement. Then of course, went back to his munching ways.

"You simply *had* to choose the one horse in the stables that wants to eat me," Winnifred grumbled.

"No, I simply had to choose the one horse in the stables that was of a size to carry both of us," Jason retorted. "And as he is carrying both of us, Wolfgang gets tired more easily and has to rest a bit, and we move slower than you'd like to Regensburg." He opened one eye and regarded Winn carefully. Her tense shoulders, her labored, sharp pacing—something was decidedly off about her today.

"What's wrong?" he asked softly, making her stumble ever so briefly on her well-worn path.

"Nothing," she replied. "Just eager to be on the road."

But it wasn't nothing. Something odd had overtaken her almost since the moment they woke up. Ever since they managed to saddle and sneak Wolfgang out of Wurtzer's stables and through the alley, down the quiet streets of Lupburg and into the new day. Winn had said little to Jason once they were on the road, and he had more than once envied the position she had, sitting across his lap, thinking that she would use the time to sleep a few more hours. But instead, she was wide awake and unbearably stiff in her seat, as if she were trying to maintain some distance and decorum between the two of them. And as such, she wasn't really moving with them, she was moving against them. Every time they hit a bump in the road or he wanted to urge Wolfgang from a trot into a gallop, her stiff form would bang against him, knocking his chin into the back of her head or her temple against his nose.

It was trying, to say the least.

And how different from how she had been the night before!

Jason was not one to feel the after effects of only a few beers, and as such, he remembered the night before with amazing clarity. Every gasp, every moan, every inch of her body exposed to the moonlight was seared on his brain like a cattle brand. Every moment, every smooth, eager movement of said moonlit body belonged to him, and would forever. She had been so free the night before, giving herself to him, and he took it, every single inch that he could . . .

"Oh God, I'm an idiot," Jason scolded himself, scooting upright against the tree.

"Why?" Winn asked, not stalling in her pacing.

"Come, sit down," he said coaxingly, but only earning a cocked eyebrow from Winn.

"Again, why? I'll be sitting enough once we're back on that bloody horse," she retorted, earning her a hurt look from Wolfgang, whose admiration of Winn was dwindling by the minute.

"I am an absolute brute and a moron. Winn"—he looked at her imploringly—"you must be sore. After . . . last night. Riding a horse all morning must have been the last thing you wished to do."

But Winn only looked at him strangely, the continued pacing. "Don't be ridiculous, I'm fine."

"You are?" he replied skeptically. "I know it . . . I know *I* caused you some pain last night."

"Did you?"

"Yes, and by the stiffness of your pacing I'd say you can feel the effects of it."

She shook her head. "I've simply been sitting on a horse too long. Again, I'm fine."

Then a thought dawned on him. He might have a perfectly clear recollection of the previous evening, but she had drunk a great deal more, was a good deal smaller, and was less used to it than he. "Winn—last night, what we did . . . you remember what we did, don't you?"

"Of course I remember," she said immediately, her face going up in flames. "But I don't know why you persist in talking about it."

"Fine," Jason replied, holding up his hands. "We do not have to talk about it." And then, while his male brain took a huge sigh of relief in that he did not have to chitchat about the meanings behind last evening's activities, his conscience, his damn moral soul, knew that he could not run from this conversation . . . and neither could she.

"At some point, however," he drawled, stalling Winn yet again in her stiff pacing. "It is a subject we should likely broach."

"I do not see why," Winn replied on a sigh.

"Because it changes things between us. That's why," Jason replied, sitting up. Then, with a smile, "Really, for someone so intelligent, you can be terrifically dense at times."

That did it. A light bit of teasing earned him her full attention. She stopped pacing then and regarded him through narrowed eyes. Then, deciding between delaying the inevitable and giving in to it, and obviously choosing the latter, asked, "How does it change anything?"

How does it change anything? Jason stared at her, nonplussed. It changed everything. And for some unknown reason, an act that should have brought them closer together only managed to have the skittish sparrow pulling away from him. It made it so he felt that he couldn't touch her—even though he had laid claim to taking her hand or letting his fingers fall on that spot at the back of her neck for weeks now.

"It changes things because it makes us . . . involved."

"And how were we not involved with each other before? You and I have been joined at the hip ever since leaving Dover. I'd say we are fairly involved."

"Oh for God's sake." Jason rolled his eyes, knowing full

well that his explanations were inept at best. "Why the hell is it that women talk about their feelings all the time, and I get the one woman in the world who would rather do anything but?" He stood, brushing off his pants and came to stand in front of her. And then, testing her limits, reached out and took her by the shoulders. She did flinch, ever so slightly, causing Jason's nerves to prick up, but she did not pull away.

"I meant that . . . our feelings are involved. Something happened between us. Something basic and primal and—"

"And drunken," Winn concluded. She looked him dead in the eyes. "And it happened. And that's all there is to it."

"No, that is not," Jason countered, his voice taking on an edge of annoyance. "But in some respects, you are correct. It *did* happen. And we *were* drinking, and as such it shouldn't have, but it cannot be denied, so—"

"Wait." Winn held up a hand, stopping his speech. "Why shouldn't it have?"

"Because . . . you were . . . untouched, as it were." Goddamn but finding tentative words for this conversation was difficult, and as such, Jason decided to give up on it. "Oh, to hell with it. You were a virgin, Winn. You didn't know what you were doing. And I took advantage of that, and you."

Winn, still holding his eyes, her hand still up in the air, froze. Then, a giggle. Then another one. Then complete, doubled-over laughing.

"Not the reaction I was expecting," Jason replied, taking his hands off Winn's shoulders and crossing them over his chest.

"Oh, Jason. Did you honestly think that I didn't know what I was doing? Taking you by the hand and leading you back to the loft?"

"Well . . . sort of," he replied, his brow coming down. He remembered her glassy-eyed approach last night, her siren dancing, newfound and graceful all at once. It was the movements of someone stepping into a brave new world.

"Sadly, you have confused innocence with ignorance.

Jason," she said, looking up at him, "I have read every book to be found in the Bodleian Library. I've read all the poetry and studied all the paintings. I knew exactly what I was doing." Then she looked down and gathered her courage before meeting his eyes again. "And there were no feelings . . . no emotions involved whatsoever."

She held his gaze as Jason felt something shift beneath his feet, and he fought to keep steady. "That cannot be true," he rasped finally, his voice coming back to him.

"Oh, I like you!" she cried, taking a step forward, but Jason, not wanting to be comforted at the moment, took a step back. "Of course I like you. I don't think I could do what we did with someone I disliked, surely."

"Surely not," Jason replied snidely.

"And of course, I liked it," she continued in a bid to soothe his wounded pride, and yet somehow every word she said just plunged the knife deeper. "At least, I found the entire evening very . . . interesting. And, and nice. But it was just an experience." She looked up at him sadly, trying to find his eyes, but he gave her no quarter. "I just wanted to know what it was like. But I still want the independent life I'm fighting for. One night doesn't change that."

Jason looked over at her then, let his gaze rake coolly, dispassionately over her body. "You'll have to forgive me, Winnifred, but I don't take very well to being used."

Winn flinched backward, as if struck. "I wasn't . . . that is, it wasn't my intention—"

"Oh really?" he replied coldly, imbuing his voice with all the authority a dukedom gives it. "Are you saying you did not take my hand and pull me to the loft in an attempt to check me off your imaginary list?"

She blinked, unable to deny it, her inability to hold his gaze serving instead as an admission.

"You did," he intoned, understanding finally, finally breaching his thick skull. "Oh holy hell, you did. You thought,

'Here's something new I haven't yet accomplished, I'll do it and cross it off my list and be done with it.' "

"That's not fair—" Winn began, but Jason, for all his cold demeanor, was becoming remarkably hot underneath his collar.

"*Goddammit*, Winn!" he yelled, startling Wolfgang from his munching and Winn from her reasonableness. "Are you really this selfish? This unfeeling?"

"I told you last night, I don't think I have what it takes to love someone, so why are you—"

"Because, I, unlike you, have feelings." His anger was unparalleled, but it was more than that. It was pain, a slicing through his skin and deep into his chest, making his blood run thick and hot. He breathed deep, trying to keep his anger and his pain under control. "I knew, I *knew* last night, that I would regret my actions come morning, but I certainly didn't think it would be in quite this manner."

"I'm sorry," she said meekly, eliciting scornful laughter from Jason.

"And that's the true irony of it all!" Jason crowed. "I'm the one that's supposed to be begging forgiveness from *you*. If you were any other woman in the world, and if you were at all *sane*, you would be railing against me for my brutish, drunken actions!"

"For heaven's sake, are you mad at me now? For *not* being angry with you?" Then Winn threw up her hands. "Fine. Perfect. I'll just wait over here with Wolfgang until it's over, if you don't mind."

"And what is that supposed to mean?" Jason spat out as Winn tentatively crossed to the besotted horse, who was more than happy to have his beloved closer and therefore under his protection.

Winn regarded him with an unnerving sense of calm. "It means . . . when is it my turn to be mad at you?" She sighed tiredly. "You yell at me on the deck of the *Seestern*, chide me at every opportunity, and nearly take my head off once we were outside of Nuremberg. And even though you've managed to make my journey a *hell* of a lot more complicated, I like to think I've kept my temper very even." Jason wanted to point out that she was glossing over the slap that echoed across lower Bavaria just two days prior, but held his tongue. "So since you have the protocol of argument down, do let me know when it is my turn to be mad at you," she concluded with a shrug, crossing her arms over her chest.

It was as if the world had turned upside down on him, Jason thought as he rubbed his eyes, which had suddenly grown oversensitive to the light, a sure sign of an impending headache. "Winn, you *should* be mad at me! I took your virginity last night."

"I offered it, fairly thoroughly."

"And I should have been gentleman enough to refuse what you offered! Because actions . . . especially actions like these, have consequences."

"If you mean a child," Winn countered, "I was aware enough to realize you spilled yourself on the straw. Therefore, I am not particularly worried about the consequences."

"For God's sake! Your relatives should be calling me out right now—they should be forcing us to the altar!"

"But my father is not here to do such a thing. And I refuse to be forced anywhere or into anything." She looked up at him, standing close to him—close enough to touch, but she did not reach out. "I wanted to find out what they write poems about—what inspired the masters to take up their brushes. And so I did. And now, we move on."

"We move on," he repeated dully. "Winn, you think of yourself as free from society, living just below its notice, but you are not. You and I should be mar—"

"Don't you dare say it," she said, putting a hand over his mouth. "I would never do that to you. I would never . . . *trap* you in that way." Her eyes became suspiciously bright. "So don't you dare do that to me."

"Winn, I—"

"No. Don't you see? I took the opportunity that was before me simply *because* I don't have to worry about being in your life. After this is over, you are not going to take me back to England and teach me to ride a horse . . . That's just folly. You are going to go back to your dukedom and a lovely, appropriate young lady who will agree to marry you. You, *Your Grace*, are going to go back to your life . . . and I intend to start mine."

He was unable to tear his gaze away from her earnest hazel eyes, and as such, she was the one to falter first and lower her gaze. "Oh, we might run into each other at a Historical Society function . . . assuming I can gain admittance after all this madness"—she laughed a little at that—"but our paths veer away from each other."

And at that moment, Jason felt something inside him sink, forcing his knees to buckle. Sink past the soles of his feet and into the dark German earth, put to rest there. Because she was right. This was an interlude for him. A holiday—albeit a mad one—away from the pressures of choosing a bride and living his life at home. He had done what he had promised Jane he would not do—he had run. And as soon as it was over, he was going to have to return home.

But the idea that she had effectively *used* him in the process of elemental discovery . . . that rang as false to him. No, hang it. That was complete and utter bullshit.

However, he didn't say anything more to her, or she to him, while he paced in the dirt, and she, exhausted, took a seat next to the tree he had abandoned. Nor did they say anything to each other, when, some minutes later, Jason abruptly stopped pacing and untethered Wolfgang from the tree. He didn't say a single word to her until she was situated on his lap, his arm wrapped securely around her waist. Then, ignoring her stiffness, her desperate desire to maintain some distance between them, he pulled her close to his body, his mouth fractions of an inch away from her ear.

"I don't give a damn what you say," he whispered, causing

her to take in a sharp breath. "We were both there last night, Winn. And we both know it was more than 'interesting,' more than 'nice.' And more than just an experiment."

Before she could reply, before she could even breathe, Jason urged Wolfgang into a trot. After all, the interlude had ended.

They had a journey to continue.

Nineteen

Wherein...

THEY arrived in Regensburg before nightfall and found the inn on Hohenfelser Strasse fairly easily, only stopping once for directions. Regensburg was a city growing in wealth and population, still rebuilding from the Battle of Ratisbon in 1809, where famously Napoleon himself was wounded by a bullet to the ankle. Regensburg didn't have the bustle of Nuremberg, but it was certainly not allowing itself to be stuck in the past. Older, Tudor-esque structures were giving way to Georgian columned buildings with alarming speed, painted in pastels that sat brightly against the dull landscape. The streets were becoming cobbled by stone, and Hohenfelser Strasse was located right off one of the main paths.

Winn wanted to ask what the city had looked like the last time Jason was here, if he had come through here, six years ago when he took his grand tour of Europe. She wanted to ask but didn't. Even that light bit of banal conversation was too heavy a weight to carry right now.

Once in the yard of the inn, they disembarked from Wolfgang, Winn admittedly more at ease with the animal after spending the better part of the entire day on his back. He hadn't tried to eat her hair once during their periodic stops to let Wolfgang lap some water from a nearby stream. Now, as then, Jason dismounted first and then took Winn by the waist and lifted her down. Then, as now, he didn't say a word to her, just turned away, this time stalking toward the door to the inn.

And without the distraction of conversation, all Winn had were those last words that he had whispered to her, echoing through her brain. *More than nice . . . More than interesting . . . More than an experiment.* Hours of silence, hours of road in front of them, and she could not concentrate on Dürer, or who Maria F. was, or where she might find her letters, if they still existed. No, the only thing running through her brain was Jason's words.

She left a mournful Wolfgang in the hands of a young stable hand and crossed the yard (slowly—because no matter what she had told Jason earlier, she was a tad sore from the previous evening, and a tad more sore from sitting on a horse all day), following Jason inside. She found him bent over in conversation, his head dipped to meet the one belonging to the proprietor, Hecht.

The setting sun filtered through the window and hit his red hair, making it seem a flame. His long, lean frame, stretching under the worn and dirty linen shirt, the muscles hidden there more known to Winn than she cared to admit at the moment, but still her eyes could not look away. Jason talked with his hands, his most charming smile occasionally breaking through as, Winn assumed, he explained how they had come into possession of Wolfgang, and his instructions for leaving him here. Hecht responded back with laughter, and suddenly both men were chuckling at fate or folly or some such male thing.

And some part of Winn yearned, traitorously, to go and be near him. To wind her arm around his, to listen patiently to the conversation he was having and ask for translation. To feel his hand fall casually on the back of her neck, and for everything to be *normal* again.

But she couldn't. She knew she couldn't. Because those long hours of uncomfortable contemplation had taught her one fundamental thing: that even if the night before had been an experiment, she was wholly unprepared for the results.

She had felt too much. Why had no one ever written poetry about the overwhelming draw on her soul that resulted from lovemaking? Or, rather, perhaps they had, and she simply hadn't paid attention, considering that part of it ridiculous. She, and no one else, governed her soul, after all. And she was determined to do so now, shaking off any sentimental notions about Jason's form in the setting sunlight.

But the want she had! The basest physical desires were overrun by the deep-seated feeling that she could fall so easily into his arms and tell herself that it was where she was meant to be—and she was *not* meant for it, or for him. Therefore, that could not and would not happen. And so, she kept herself silent all trip. She kept herself protected.

Which was why she had been so utterly cruel to him, she knew in retrospect. Whatever impression he had of her now, she deserved. Not for wanting her independence, not even for taking the opportunity of last night to its inevitable conclusion—but perhaps, for the smallest lie, of telling him that her feelings were not involved in the process.

However, the walls must be maintained, and held.

But she couldn't keep herself from the want.

"Good news," Jason said, breaking into her thoughts, and breaking the silence that had existed between them since he had whispered those words in her ear. Goodness, her brain was so addled, she hadn't even seen him cross to her. "There is a public coach leaving for Linz, Austria, in an hour. The tickets are a little out of our price range, but Hecht has offered us a deal."

"What kind of deal?" she asked, surprised at her own lack of voice.

Jason grimaced. "It will take most if not all of our remaining funds. Unfortunately, Herr Wurtzer didn't give me nearly what he had promised us, even with the borrowing of Wolfgang—but nothing to be done about it now."

Winn nodded dully, processing the information.

"Good," Jason replied. "I'll just go . . . and purchase our fares . . . Here," he said, reaching into his pocket and pulling out a spare coin. "Go get some food. You haven't eaten all day."

Neither have you, she wanted to say, but instead, as she turned, she impulsively reached out and caught his arm. "Jason, wait."

He turned to her, one eyebrow raised expectantly.

"What if—what if I continued on alone," she blurted out, her eyes never going any higher than his waist. "You . . . you've done so much for me already. You could take half the money and stay here in Regensburg for a bit of time— write your stewards to send you funds to get you home . . . I wouldn't blame you, you know. Especially . . . especially after last night, and what I said earlier. You deserve to . . . Well, you deserve to. That's all."

Jason stared down at her for a hard second, then took her gently but firmly by the arm and pulled her out of the way of the comings and goings of the busy inn's front rooms, into a small alcove two steps away. There, expression set along hard lines, he bent his head and kissed her.

It was a brutish, forceful kiss. Something claiming, branding her with his mouth. But just as soon as Winn had wrapped her mind around its occurrence, it was over.

She met his gaze, flushed hot, bewildered. His breathing had become harder, but his expression had not changed.

"I told you," he said softly, yet iron laced his voice, "I intend to finish this."

Then without another word, he left her in the alcove to seek out Hecht and buy their tickets to Austria. Left her with a coin in her hand, and a hunger that did not originate from her stomach.

Left her breathless.

Winn decided it best that conversation be relegated to the weather. Luckily, it began to rain.

It started just outside of Linz. Previous to that, conversation was stilted at best; jammed into a hot carriage with several other passengers, Winn tried to maintain as much physical distance as possible—she did not allow herself to lean into him or slack against his strong side.

The carriage they took made many regular stops in small towns, and the axles were somewhat delicate, slowing its travels—to the point that a trip that should have taken a day and a half took over two. Winn felt herself growing antsy at their pace . . . but found she could not speak of it to Jason, could not even seek the calming comfort of his hand over hers.

That kiss in the alcove was the last time he had touched her.

She could feel Jason's eyes conspicuously not on her, holding himself away. Because it was what she had wanted. What she had dictated. They spoke only of what was necessary. What was polite. And the ache she felt, as if she had plunged a knife in his side and ended up nicking herself. Guilt and resolution, all in one.

But then, a heavy summer storm started, with thick droplets coming down in violent fury, thunder and lightning shaking and blazing the sky at turns. Having been in a carriage for two days straight, the cut to the thick air was a welcome relief . . . for the first twenty minutes. After that, the rain became soaking, even within the confines of the carriage. Everyone in the public coach—a varied assortment of travelers that rotated and altered when various stops were made—were terribly happy to decamp to the coaching inn that served as their destination in Linz.

"I'm practically drowning!" Winn cried in the hubbub of the inn's entryway. Their carriage was not the only one to seek refuge from the storm. The taproom and stairs were crowded with equally saturated guests, packed in humidity and misery.

"There's no way we can sleep in the hall tonight," Jason grumbled, running a hand through his hair, shaking off the wet. The previous two nights, when the carriage stopped for the evening and everyone put up for the night, Jason and Winn were entirely without funds for a room. The last coin they had was the one that Winn used to purchase a loaf of bread . . . which lasted them up until yesterday. At the first inn, they were permitted to sleep in the taproom—but had to wait until it cleared out, well after midnight. At the second inn, they were allowed two somewhat comfortable chairs in the main entranceway on which to sleep.

Winn woke up every time the door opened. Which was regularly.

Lord, but did she need a good night's sleep.

"You seem to be correct . . ." Winn said, her eyes taking in the crowded space. The door whipped open with every new entrance, letting in a burst of wind and rain that soaked the floor six feet into the room. And sometimes, the wind opened the door of its own volition.

"I'll go and ask about the stables," Jason said, bumping into her as he himself was bumped by another traveler, eager to make his way to the innkeeper at the front desk. He pulled back immediately—the past two days of distance forced on him by Winn having had its desired effect. He no longer sought to touch her. "See if I cannot trade work for a place to sleep."

She nodded. "And I shall ask the same about the kitchens."

Jason turned and ducked back out into the weather.

Winn felt the tide of guilt crash against her once he was out of sight. As strained as she had been toward him, he was still doing everything in his power to protect her, to provide for her. Even now, having arrived in Linz, when they had no more money and no easy way of earning any (true to form, they had not come across any small towns in need of a Duke to clean their stables, or even a regular Englishman; nor did they require the butcher batering or kitchen cleaning Winn could provide), he was trying. For her. Doing what he needed to do.

Ever since they crossed the border into Austria, Winn had felt that she was so close to her goal. So desperately close. All she had to do was get to Vienna. And they would, she thought, her hand going to her locket, pulling at it in her worrisome way. Once they had a good night's sleep, they would be on their way.

She eyed the innkeeper, swamped with travelers applying for rooms.

Squaring her shoulders, she approached him.

Now, it was time for her to do what *she* needed to do.

"I do not understand," Jason said as Winn lead him into the small room she had procured from the innkeeper. The smallest room they had, and boasting a window so thin it would not serve as an archer's post on an old castle. But it did not leak, and was above the kitchens, therefore benefitting from the warmth of the stove fires below. Add to that the clean linens and—she sat gingerly on the bed—not too uncomfortable straw ticking, and it was the most beautiful place she'd seen in days.

"What did the innkeeper say?" Jason asked, confused skepticism on his features.

"He said this room was barely used in any case, and that if we promise to help clean up the gardens in the morning— they'll be fairly ruined in the downpour—there will be breakfast in it for us, as well as supper tonight."

"That's awfully kind," Jason replied, standing still in the doorway. There was nowhere but the bed to sit and he was still dripping. "But considering the number of people downstairs, a bit *too* kind."

"I . . . I don't think so," Winn said, unable to meet his discerning eye. "Sometimes people are kind without cause. Think of Frau Heider or Herr Wurtzer. Both of them kinder than they needed to be. Perhaps the innkeeper is just the same."

He advanced on her. Not in a predatory way, just slow, considering steps that made Winn want to squirm in her seat.

Standing directly in front of her, he tilted his head to one side, regarding. Studying. Then finally he asked, "Winnifred, where is your locket?"

She jarred at the sound of her full name on his lips, even as her hand went automatically to that space at the base of her throat, knowing she would find it empty. She sighed, letting her shoulders sag. "Perhaps the innkeeper does not deal strictly in kindness, but nor is he unfair. We get this room and supper for the evening. And, again, if we help with the gardens, breakfast in the morning. Indeed, I doubt a pawnbroker would have given us the equivalent."

When he didn't say anything, his mouth set in that hard, considering line, she felt the impulsive need to fill the oppressive space.

"And consider the clamor downstairs! Neither of us would have been able to sleep, and given the last few nights, sleep is of the utmost importance. I know . . . Jason I *know* we could get to Vienna if we just had a decent night's sleep and a meal. So I traded my mother's locket. It's worth it. Heavens, we can *walk* to Vienna—the Danube connects the two cities. All we have to do is follow the river east for a few days." She looked up at him, saw his gaze falling dispassionately down on her as she rambled.

"Stop looking at me like that," she ordered. "I did what was necessary. That is all. I thought you'd be pleased. To be dry and safe for a night." She threw her hands in the air. "Well, say something!"

He nodded, his mouth still pressed into that line, his jaw clenching beneath his beard.

"Wait here," he finally said. And with that, stalked out the door, closing it behind him.

Leaving Winn alone in the small room, seated on the bed, unmoving. Certain of only one thing: Even with all her study, the male of the species was still a complete mystery.

Twenty

Wherein our travelers get a good night's sleep.

IT was two hours later before Jason made his way back to the coaching inn. The rain still came down in sheets; he was soaked to the skin. He looked at no one, not the innkeeper that Winn thought "fair-minded," not the other patrons in the taproom, as he plodded up the stairs to the small room Winn had traded her one heirloom for.

Her necklace. Jason didn't know what enraged him so much when he saw that it was gone . . . just that she did not look herself without it. She had nothing to hold on to when she was thinking, nothing else in her wardrobe that was remotely feminine—even her dress was shaped after a man's shirt—but, still the idea of her slim neck without its shine disturbed him in a way he did not like.

And so he did something stupid.

He opened the door of the tiny room to find Winn sitting on the bed in the same position as when he'd left her. The only sign of movement was the tray of half-eaten stew and potatoes that sat beside her.

"Where did you go?" she asked.

In response, he dropped her locket on the tray next to her. She tried to seem unaffected as she touched it reverently, picked it up, and held its weight in her hand. She tried, but to his trained eye, she failed.

"But I only gave it to the innkeeper . . ." she started, her voice impossibly thick.

"And he had already given it to a lad to hock. I had to track him down and then the shop he sold it to," Jason replied gruffly.

"But we have no money, how did you . . ." And then her eyes shifted from the locket to him. He could feel her gaze rake down his body and land on his hand.

His naked hand.

She stood up abruptly, rattling the tray of food. "You should not have done that!" she scolded, her face flying to his face.

"Probably," he agreed spitefully, and then turned to the door.

"Jason, you should not have done that—that is your ducal signet ring!" She followed after him. "That's worth a hundred times my necklace!"

"Then it's too bad the lad sold it to a swindler," Jason replied, anger lacing his tone. "I couldn't get more than your necklace for it."

"Why?" she cried, throwing up her hands. "Jason, why couldn't you have just let me do this . . . so we could get a good night's sleep and go on in the morning?"

"I. Don't. Know," Jason replied, throwing open the door and stomping down the first few steps, knowing full well Winn was on his heels. "Maybe it's because I have a hundred thousand reminders of my title at home, where as you only have that stupid necklace to remember your mother by. Maybe it's because you don't seem to have any other heart than that one, and so I thought it best you keep it. Maybe it's because I'll be *damned* if I'm going to let you sacrifice anything more to get to Vienna, because while I go back to my stately houses and silk cravats and all the other ridiculous things that I own once this is over, you have really little more than that locket and your own will to guide you through the rest of life. So I did it, and I'm not about to tell you which shop has my ring, so you'd best get used to it."

She pulled back as if struck, blinking at the fury of his speech. Of his feeling. Jason, too, was surprised by the strength of his argument. They stared into each other, on the cramped staircase leading down to the noisy kitchens, his breath coming hard and hers coming not at all. Finally, he turned and continued stomping his wet boots down the stairs.

"Wait . . . where are you going?" Winn cried, skipping after him.

"You said we were allotted supper—I'm going to the taproom to drink it."

"Wait . . . Jason, would you stand still a moment?" She caught up to him, caught his arm. He turned. Still on the stairs, she was one or two above him and therefore at a height with him. And therefore, did not have to stand on tiptoe to kiss him.

Gently, kindly, her lips pressed to his.

"Thank you," she said, into his shocked gaze.

It was the space of a breath, the length of a decision. And then, Jason knew . . . he could hold back politely no longer.

He tore at her mouth, whether she wanted it or not. And from the way she wound her arm around his neck, he knew that she was as desperate as he. He took the steps, taking her with him, backing her against the staircase wall, his strength holding her small weight up to his height. He cared nothing for the clamor of the kitchens, the voices in foreign tongues, growing less foreign by the day, calling out orders for roast and chicken, or the threat that the owners of those voices could step around the corner and they would be seen. He cared only that after two days of hell, sitting next to her in the carriage, he was finally able to touch her—truly touch her in ways that were more than polite, or necessary.

But then again, this . . . *this* was necessary. He moved from her lips to her neck, taking in her scent and pulse. She gasped for air, then plunged her hands beneath his wet coat, grasping to get closer to skin.

"Tell me you want me," he growled into her ear.

She nodded desperately.

"Say it."

"I . . . I want you," she breathed.

It was like fire in his blood. He lifted her in the air—God, how was it that someone who weighed so little could have such a force on his life? With her legs over one arm and her body cradled in the other, he carried her up the steps, all the while never stopping kissing her, she never stopping running her hands through his hair.

Never stopping when he kicked the door to their room open.

Never stopping when he dropped her on the mattress, placing the tray of half-eaten food on the floor.

Never stopping as boots came off, wet shirts, a dress, trousers.

Never stopping . . . until he had her gloriously naked, and all to himself.

The candle was still lit, flickering its light against her gorgeous skin.

The rain beat down, the only sound made other than their breathing.

He lay his own naked body next to her, and suddenly . . . the rush was gone from him.

Oh, the need was there. The need was ever present and at attention. But, it was as if he had been holding his breath and then allowed himself a great gulp of air, and now . . . now he needed to breath steadily again. Slowly.

"What is it?" she asked nervously, making to cross her arms over her chest.

"No, don't." He stopped her hand. "I want to look."

Her eyes darted back and forth, confused, frightened. He kissed her eyelids closed, smoothed her nerves. "Keep your eyes closed," he commanded.

She lay still, wearing only candlelight, her eyelids opening briefly and then fluttering trustingly shut. Achingly gentle, he let his fingers drift over that skin, barely skimming its surface. He started at her waist, narrow and soft. She jumped at his touch, startled by it, but eased herself back down, accepting his hand smoothing over her flesh.

His fingers danced their way up, over her ribs, up to the soft mounds of flesh shaped like raindrops, that responded to his touch as he responded to her.

"These are perfect, you know," he breathed, his thumb playing with one's peak.

She lifted her eyebrow skeptically at that, kept her eyes closed. He grinned madly.

"I've dreamt of having you like this. Riding Wolfgang with you pressed against me, my arm around you just . . . about . . . here. But you, keeping yourself rigid. Forever out of reach."

She opened her eyes then, met his.

"I won't spend the next few days at arm's length, Winn," he admonished softly. "I can't do it anymore. I haven't the discipline."

"I don't want you to," she whispered.

He leaned down and kissed her then, reverently, but heat building inside of him. His hand moved up her body, over her shoulder, dancing lightly against her neck . . .

"Wait." He pulled away and began looking feverishly around them on the bed.

"What's wrong?" she asked worriedly, trying to come up to sit, but being kissed back down onto the bed.

"You're missing something."

And then he found it. In the pile of her clothes on the floor, he plucked out the shine of gold on a chain. He resumed his leisurely position beside her, resting his hand on his head as he dangled the necklace above her, letting it come to rest in that notch at the base of her throat, its cool weight making her suck in her breath sharply. He let the chain fall against her skin and then, with more dexterity than he knew he had, reached around her neck and clasped it.

And she was perfect.

After that, nothing came between them. He became bold, letting his hands roam over her body, dipping down below her waist, grazing her navel, her soft patch of light brown fur that marked her womanhood.

She became ever bolder, let her hands mark his body, perverse in their strength. How could she have held herself back from him for so long? Two days of stiff posture, of jumping at every accidental brush . . . when all she'd wanted was *this*. This glorious touch.

Emboldened by need, she let her hands fall down his body, down to that hard shaft that had made her feel full and frantic all at once. He made a strangling sound when she stroked him, hesitantly, tentatively. She giggled softly.

Whether it was the courageousness of her touch or the gentleness of her laugh, something drove him mad enough to grab her hand by the wrist and place her arm over her head as he pushed her into the cushions. The thrill of it sent a spike though her body, and she smiled dazedly in her shock.

"What has you smiling?" he asked.

"I didn't know"—she grinned at him—"how much power there was in a touch. In the tips of my fingers."

His face broke into that devilish, charming grin as he took his free hand and dipped it between her legs, reveling in her sharp gasp of pleasure.

"Or mine," he countered, skillfully working his fingers there, in ways she could not see and did not comprehend, only that she wanted more of it, more of his touch, more of him.

And then, just when she thought she could not live without that "more" any longer, he gave it to her.

There was no pain this time, no ache or tear, just the overwhelming feeling that she was exactly where she wanted and needed to be. She lifted her legs around his strong thighs, his slim hips, pulling him tighter to her, trying to get closer, as he moved with old rhythms, touched her here, pushed and pulled there, driving her closer to an edge that seemed impossible to climb.

Jason, for his part, considered it his very good luck that he had lowered his head to kiss her at that moment, effectively taking her cries into himself when she finally allowed herself to break free. Her warmth, her aching tightness pulsated around him, and he allowed himself a few glorious moments of reveling in her joyous abandon before removing himself from her sweet, tight body, and spilling himself away, joining in the abandon himself.

In the moments after, as he wrapped his body around hers and their senses and wits returned to them, they realized that it was still raining outside. Realized also that they had been in such a frantic state that they had not even availed themselves of the covers—and yet a singular, albeit separate thought occurred to each of them individually.

For Winn, it was that she could feel Jason's heart beating through his chest, in time with hers.

For Jason, it was that for someone who had lived his life carelessly, leisurely, somehow he had still managed to find his way into this moment, and know it was exactly where it was he was supposed to be.

And it didn't frighten him at all.

Winn awoke just before dawn, her body entwined with Jason's. It was no longer raining; instead, she could feel a cool cut of sweet air coming from the tiny window and assaulting her uncovered backside. As she rose to adjust the covers, Jason moaned in protest and pulled her back into his arms.

"Stay here," he commanded, not even opening his eyes.

It was all she wanted to do. To stay in their little room, in their little world. But . . .

"You know we cannot stay here forever," she intoned, her words weighted.

Her meaning sad but clear.

They could not stay. Their paths would veer.

"I know," Jason said, sad as well, but accepting. "But stay for now."

"For now," she agreed.

Twenty-one

Wherein we meet new players,
interesting in their familiarity.

THIS, the last leg of the journey, would perhaps prove the most difficult.

They set off on foot the next morning, after their chores were completed and the innkeeper kept to his bargain and gave them a decent breakfast. The innkeeper's wife slipped them hot rolls from the oven, which they accepted gratefully, and managed to save until that evening, when they ate under a tree on the banks of the Danube, miles away from any town or village.

"We shouldn't have stopped," Winn said as she bit into her roll. "I could easily walk another two hours tonight."

"We've walked for the last twelve. Give your feet a rest," Jason replied, kissing the top of her head.

It was as if a détente had been issued. As if they had both silently discussed and agreed that as long as they were still on their journey, they had no idea when the journey would end. And if they had no idea when it would end, there was no reason to act as if they were mere acquaintances stuck together. So Jason felt free to kiss the top of Winn's head, and Winn felt free to press herself against his side, taking up the empty space under his wing that was made to fit her shape, and only hers.

There was no holding themselves apart, no awkwardness or pretense. But they both knew the time was coming when they would have to give up their comfort with each other. And Jason had a feeling that time would come when they reached Vienna.

If only Winn wasn't in such a hurry to get there!

It was over a hundred miles down the Danube from Linz to Vienna, and Winn seemed to think they could conquer it in a day and a half. The next morning when they woke up, Winn as per usual before him, she was fifty yards down the road before he caught up to her, eager as she was to start the day.

The next morning she was a hundred yards in front of him.

These days were heady, sun filled. And Jason knew that despite their hardship they were magic. They talked. About books read, races attended. About home. Opening up parts of their lives they wanted known to the other.

They occasionally managed a ride. A journeyman or farmer with a bit of kindness in his soul would allow them to ride as far as the next town in the back of his ox cart, allowing them a little relief. But most of the time was spent on foot, his hand holding hers, or his arm around her shoulder or him caressing that small spot at the back of her neck.

But the magic lasted only as long as they had the strength and temper for it, and the road sapped them both quickly.

The difficulty was not the road they travelled on—indeed, following the river made it so the road did not traverse any steep hills or unexpected detours—rather, it was that as the days went on, they were increasingly hungry and therefore slower in their movements. And thirsty. Terribly, gut-wrenchingly thirsty.

"We have a river," Jason argued.

"We need a well," Winn countered.

"The last town we found a well in was Melk, and it was

yesterday," Jason reasoned. "The river is here, it's fine. The fish drink it. Have a sip."

Jason decided it was thirst that drove him to this decision, one he knew was risky, and likely foolish. Therefore, thirst was to blame for the pain that occurred thereafter.

Both he and Winn were struck at the same time, the meager contents of their stomach revolting and demanding exit from their bodies, through whatever egress was closest.

"Oh God," Jason moaned, for perhaps the fortieth time that hour.

"I told you . . ." Winn admonished, before practically crawling behind a tree and a horrible retching sound told Jason of her state.

"Then you should not have listened to me," Jason replied, agonized.

But tortured as they were, they could not stay by the river that was the cause of their distress.

"We have to go inland," Jason said, his face sweating from the strain of standing. "The road veered away from the river. We have to find it."

"Why?" Winn asked. "Why can't we just die here?"

"Because if we don't get help, death is a distinct possibility," Jason replied.

She looked up at him, pale under the sheen of perspiration. "You're being serious."

"I am." They hadn't had food or (good) water in long enough time that if they didn't get help, they would be dehydrated to the point of immobility. They had to find the road. They had to hope for help.

"All right," Winn said with as much strength as she could muster. "Let's go."

They moved. One step in front of the other, due north. Cutting across pastureland. Hoping that the road was not too far from the river . . . hoping that it was only just over that rise.

An hour passed, they had gone maybe a mile.

Another hour passed, they had travelled nearly two.

Winn leaned on Jason, on his arm, using strength he didn't know he had left. But she never stopped. Never gave in to the exhaustion.

Until the road was in view.

"Oh, thank God," she whispered, and fell against him.

"It's all right." Jason sighed. "We made it."

He picked her up and carried her the last few yards, and then set her down next to a fallen log by the road.

"Thank you," she murmured, falling deeply asleep.

Making sure she was comfortable—or at least, her head was not resting on any rocks—he sat on the log and took up a position of watch.

"Don't worry, Winn," he said, his body heavy from his own weakened state. "Any minute now, a carriage is going to come down this road, and I'll jump up and flag it down. You rest. I'll be here. I'll be right here."

∂⌀

"What on earth is that?" he heard the girl's voice cry.

He had heard the carriage rumble to a stop some seconds prior, heard the shuffling and moving of disembarkment, but Jason really couldn't say he cared to move himself. Or that he could, if he tried. So instead, he stayed where he was, laying next to the log about ten yards off the side of the road, his arm wrapped around Winn's equally exhausted and sleeping form.

"It's just a pile of dirt," he heard another young female voice say. "I told you we shouldn't have stopped. Father *is* expecting us to be in the city before nightfall."

"I'll tell him I wanted to wait for the right light to paint the mountains," the other girl replied vaguely. "And it is not a pile of dirt . . . it's moving."

It took a moment for Jason's brain to register that the girls were talking about himself and Winn. It would make sense after all—after three days walking, and another three before that without being able to take a proper bath or even so much as shake out their clothes, Jason and Winn had taken on the burnished hue of their environment. The other thing that took a few moments to soak into his head was that these two girls were speaking English.

"Moving!" the one a further distance away exclaimed. "Evie, come back here! Don't go near it!"

"It's not an it, it's a he," the one named Evie replied. "And a she, apparently."

"I'm afraid I must insist," came the voice of a man, and a shuffling that told Jason he was the coachman, lifting himself to the ground from the driver's perch, "that you go no closer, Miss Alton. Your father would not be pleased to find you assaulted by a vagrant."

Jason decided at that point, it was time to speak.

"I'm afraid I am in no position to assault anyone," he drawled weakly, his mouth dry. He opened his eyes and was met by the blue, wide-eyed stare of a young lady of some means, judging by her wardrobe—and of some sympathy, judging by her proximity to him.

"Heavens, he's British!" Evie Alton exclaimed, turning back to the other, darker-haired girl, who had climbed out of the carriage but stood tentatively a few steps behind. "Gail, they're British!"

"And judging by his accent, a gentleman," Gail surmised, cocking her head to one side.

"Sir, are you and your companion all right? Whatever are you doing on the side of the road?" Evie asked, perhaps a bit too loudly.

"For heaven's sake, Evie, you don't have to yell." Gail smiled, shaking her head.

"Oh!" she exclaimed. "Forgive me, it's my first time attempting a rescue," Evie said to Jason, blushing.

Jason actually managed a smile. "It's quite all right," he said, nodding. God, but his throat was dry. Then, he looked to Winn, curled up in his arms, seeking his warmth, even in her deep, hungry, exhausted sleep. But she wasn't stirred by the commotion. A result that was far more worrisome than any hunger or parchedness of his own. "I beg your pardon, but we could use some water . . . ?" he asked Evie.

Evie looked toward Gail and then turned back to him, her face breaking into a mischievous smile.

"Water we do indeed have. But I think we can do you one better."

Twenty-two

Wherein identifying articles are argued.

Winn woke up in a room fit for a queen. Or at least one of her ladies-in-waiting. Still, it was grander than any room she had ever occupied previously, and therefore this was obviously heaven and she was dead. Strange, she thought dully. She had no expectations whatsoever of going to heaven.

And, curiouser still, heaven was . . . yellow. The famous Austrian shade of yellow, found on buildings from Salzburg to Innsbruck to Graz. And chintz draperies. Heaven seemed such an odd place for chintz.

"Oh good, miss, you're awake!" a cheerful voice, spoken with the clipped tones from northern England, called out from the door. "We thought you were going to sleep all through the day."

Winn turned her head to see a young maid enter, bearing towels and linens.

"Where am I?" Winn asked, her wits restored to the point where she could recognize that heaven would likely be an egalitarian place, and therefore maids would be obsolete.

"You don't remember a thing do you? I don't blame you,"

the young maid chattered as she placed the linens in various drawers, then went to the wardrobe and pulled out a set of clothes. "You were completely passed out, exhausted, or so said His Grace, from walking all day and night with no food. When the young misses found you, you didn't move a muscle."

"Found me?" Winn replied.

"Hmm. On the side of the road, with His Grace. The misses—Miss Evangeline and Miss Gail Alton, that is, found you, discovered you were English, and decided that since their father is a diplomatic envoy, that it was their Christian duty to attend to you."

"Diplomatic envoy?" Winn shook off the fuzziness in her brain.

"Aye—Sir Geoffrey. This is his house." The young maid chuckled.

"Oh, but I can't stay here!" Winn cried, coming off the bed and then immediately regretting it. Dizzy and weak, she sat herself back down on the soft feather palate.

"Sit back, miss—here, drink this." The maid handed her a cup of lukewarm weak tea, which from the moment it touched Winn's lips, she downed in huge greedy gulps.

"His Grace said you did the exact same thing, in your sleep, when they gave you water by the road." The maid chuckled.

"Where is His Grace?" Winn asked, holding her empty cup out for more tea. "Thank you for your hospitality, but we truly cannot stay here—we must get to Vienna."

"His Grace said you'd say that, too," the maid replied. "As luck would have it—you are in Vienna."

"I am?" Winn cried, excited. "We are?"

"Yes." The maid nodded, Winn's enthusiasm proving infectious. "Let's get you cleaned up—and some new clothes, as the ones you had on were so dirty they have been burned—"

"Burned?" Winn cried. For the first time she looked down at herself. Sure enough, she was wearing an unfamiliar nightdress, surprisingly well sized to her small form. Even though

she knew they were not there, she still patted frantically at her sides, where her pockets should be.

"Do not worry!" the maid replied. "His Grace made sure to remove the letters from your pocket before we took your clothes. I have to say, His Grace was terribly considerate of you, my lady, took care of dressing and undressing you himself, as gently as if you were a babe."

Winn's eyebrow went up as she turned a burning shade of red. "Er, I am not 'my lady.' I am simply a 'miss.' Miss Crane, as a matter of fact."

The maid's eyes went wide—wider than could really be healthy, Winn thought.

"Oh . . . this is more interesting than the time my sister went out one night with her beau and came back with her petticoat on backward," the maid said, a grin breaking out over her face. "I'm sorry, I forgot. I'm Olive."

Er . . . Hello, Olive, I'm Winn Crane."

"Well, now that we are properly introduced, I'm going to draw you a bath, and you are going to tell me everything!"

Winn emerged from the yellow bedroom an hour later, having been fed, at intervals, tea and the story of how she got to where she was. Olive's enthusiasm for gossip translated into her giving a dramatic retelling of Winn and Jason's relative states of collapse and the heroism of her two young mistresses, as Winn bathed. Considering she admittedly was not present at the event, she managed a particularly colorful recounting. Then of course, Olive's enthusiasm for gossip turned to intrigue . . . specifically Winn's.

Winn did her best to avoid the more probing questions, but the luxury of hot water and rose-scented soap relaxed not only her shoulders but also her tongue. Luckily, the restorative powers of tea enabled Winn to keep her wits about her and the more, er, pertinent details to herself.

But Olive was not to be deterred, and so by the time Winn

had dressed in the clean under things and lavender dress that had been laid out for her (Gail, the younger sister, was also the taller, and it seemed that a tall eleven-year-old was approximately the same size as a short thirty-year-old), she was more than willing to face the world, if not precisely ready for it.

Nor was she precisely ready for the sight that greeted her when she stepped into the hall.

Jason.

He was heading down the hall toward her, presumably from the chamber he had been assigned. He had been given the same grace of a bath and clean, serviceable clothes, but he had also been given . . .

"Oh my God!" Winn cried, immediately covering her mouth with her hands but unable to tear her hand away.

Jason's hand went immediately, and self-consciously, to his clean-shaven jaw.

"I know. And I so wanted to keep it, to torment Jane."

"I hardly recognized you," Winn said, awed. Indeed, the Jason she had come to know was scruffy, rakish, with a dirty shirt missing the first few buttons, and his red beard, white teeth peeping through in a charmed smile. But this Jason—this Jason in his clean clothes and clean-scraped jaw, his posture straight—this was the Jason from London.

This Jason was a Duke.

And right now, the Duke was looking her over, a small smile playing over his lips.

"I hardly recognized you, either," he drawled. "Why on earth are you dressed like a child?"

"What do you mean?" she asked, fingering her skirt. "The gown goes to the floor, as is proper."

"But it's so . . . cheerful. And there are ruffles. You just look so young." Jason looked her up and down once again. "Makes me feel like a lecherous old man, knowing what hides underneath."

Winn blushed wildly, barely managing a glance up at Jason. His teasing would not have managed to elicit such a reaction if she hadn't spent the last hour so assiduously avoiding the topic, and therefore thinking of nothing else.

"Yes. Ah, well . . . I don't think beggars can be choosers in this situation," she mumbled. And then, adding, "Your Grace."

Jason just smiled at her, and came and took her arm.

"Olive—that is, my chambermaid," Winn began, "kept calling you 'Your Grace.' I'm ashamed to admit it took me a moment to discern she was speaking about you."

"Yes, well, the most shocking thing happened," Jason said conversationally as he escorted her down the stairs. "Even under all the dirt and grime, someone actually recognized me as a Duke."

❧

"Of course I recognized him!" Gruff, gregarious Sir Geoffrey Alton said as he forked another serving of roast onto his plate. "We met once three years ago over a card game at White's. And because of my work, I know better than to forget a face. Especially one to whom I lost twenty quid."

Sir Geoffrey Alton, diplomatic envoy of Britain to Austria, chuckled at his own joke. To either side of him, his daughters— the young girls who had played their saviors—either laughed along, or took pity on him and did so.

Sir Geoffrey and his daughters were a happily situated family. Apparently his wife had died some years prior, and unwilling to leave his girls in the upbringing of a relative, instead brought them, and the appropriate number of household servants, with him wherever his services were required. And the girls seemed to benefit from it—they were both able to hold easy polite conversation, on a range of topics. Evangeline— called Evie by her sister—was thirteen, and in the midst of growing into a true English beauty, fair of hair and face and temperament. Her younger and yet taller sister Gail was a curious mix of intelligence, silliness, and vulnerability. If Jason wasn't mistaken, Sir Geoffrey was going to have his hands full with both of them once they came of age.

But he didn't really think terribly long on the marriage prospects of the Alton daughters as his attention had naturally and rightly fallen to the food in front of him. Supper was a hearty and yet sumptuous affair. Jason was in his own personal brand of heaven. There was roast, duck, lamb. There were breads, potatoes, vegetables, wine. *English* custard. Say what one will about the lack of culinary graces in English cuisine, but there was no better sight than a pudding when one had been without its gelatinous wobbling for weeks on end.

He had three helpings.

"I couldn't live without English fare, myself," Sir Geoffrey declared, patting his own stuffed belly. "I make sure to bring along my own cook when I am assigned to different posts."

"It's true," Evangeline Alton interjected shyly. "We were living in Paris, surrounded by the best chefs in the world, and my father is livid that there are no peas in his stew."

"Good Lord, Geoffrey, I knew you were a philistine, but I didn't know how far it extended." The drawling voice from the other end of the table called out, eliciting giggles from his dinner companion, the younger, taller Gail Alton. "Please tell me that you have not taught your daughters to consider nothing more horrible than a pealess stew," Mr. Henry Ellis said with a grin.

While Jason had been surprised to be recognized by Sir Geoffrey Alton, the more significant surprise was that Sir Geoffrey's visiting friend, Mr. Henry Ellis, recognized Winn.

"Of course I recognize you," he had said when they first met as dinner was being served. "In fact, Lord Forrester asked me to act as escort on your journey once you reached Calais." A twinkle appeared in the older gentleman's eye. "But you never made it to Calais, did you?"

"Henry is much in your line, Miss Crane," Sir Geoffrey supplied. "He is a fellow of the London Society of Antiquaries— your rival learned society, I believe, Your Grace—and is newly named as the curator of the British Museum. I'm surprised your paths have not crossed yet."

"I'm sure they would have had I been in London during the weeks Miss Crane made such an impression on the Historical Society," Mr. Ellis replied. "But I was in France. But once I received Lord Forrester's letter and managed to get my hands on a few English newspapers, I was quite eager to meet you. You cannot imagine my devastation when you were not on your ship! I was told by some excessively large gentleman that you had chosen to take another vessel to a different destination."

"Ah, yes," Winn hedged. "It seemed my path veered in a different direction, with different companions."

Unbeknownst to Winn, that tidbit of information was already known to their host. Earlier in the evening, while Winn was still dressing, Sir Geoffrey had called Jason into his library. Jason had never felt more like a guilty schoolboy in his life.

"I understand from my maids and daughters that you have kept the young lady close in your company . . . Perhaps too close?" Sir Geoffrey had questioned.

What was Jason to have said? Was he to tell Sir Geoffrey that while they had been in each other's company the whole trip, nothing untoward had happened? It had. Or was he to tell him that Miss Crane was an independently minded female, and watch the man sneer in well-bred criticism?

Apparently, however, Jason's silence on the subject was the best answer he could have given, as Sir Geoffrey had merely looked at him and said, "It is impossible to know what occurred on the road to here, so I will not question you. London may care, but we are well removed from London, and therefore I have decided to keep my council on the subject. But, while in this house . . ."

He hadn't needed to finish the sentence. Jason had nodded, relieved that he was no longer a schoolboy in trouble.

"Well, since I intended to drop you in Switzerland on my way to Vienna," Mr. Ellis was saying, "I decided to simply travel straight here instead. And of all the luck, you end up in my friend's care, and I get to meet you after all!"

Winn smiled then, as Mr. Ellis's obvious good humor put everyone at ease.

"Now then, I have read only a little about your journey and its cause, so tell me everything I missed," Mr. Ellis said.

And Winn obliged. Over supper, she held the entire table rapt in her retelling of her trials in getting to London, her first meeting with Lord Forrester (and incidentally, Jason) that had set the academic world alight, including the small lie she told about the location of the letters. The two girls gasped at that.

"Oh, how exciting!" Gail said. "The start to an adventure."

"You mean how frightening," Evangeline countered. "Having to hide your destination as you set off into the world alone?"

"Well, as luck would have it, I was not alone." Winn shot Jason a look from under her lashes. But before that look could be remarked upon by the audience, she continued with their dramatic trip to Hamburg, then Nuremberg—and what they found there.

This caught Mr. Ellis's attention.

"May I see these letters?" he asked, and Winn produced them.

"They've been in your pocket? For the whole journey?" he asked, aghast.

"I know, I'm horrified," Winn replied. "I would have killed for some kidskin or vellum to protect them with. But I had no choice—my cousin had caught up to us in Nuremberg, and we had to run. I've been extremely careful with them . . . even when we had to sleep on the side of the road or work as stable hands for a meal."

"As I recall," Jason had to interject, "I did most of that stable-hand work."

He could tell that Winn was about to counter teasingly, but the girls spoke before she could.

"This is better than any of Mrs. Rothschild's books," Gail squealed to Evangeline's eager nodding.

"She could take a page from you, Miss Crane. And to think, the whole thing over a painting!"

Sir Geoffrey chuckled heartily at that. "My Evie is mad about her paintings . . . and my Gail about her history. I think you've hit upon the one story they both would sit still for."

And then, the story concluded with their rescue, already well known to all in attendance, attention turned to the neglected food in front of them, and conversation began to be colored by comments on card games at White's, English pudding, and peas in stew.

But it was after most of the plates had been cleared that attention again returned to Winn's story of their adventures, and Mr. Ellis—free from the possibility of a splattered pudding—produced the letters from the safety of drawer he had placed them in and began to inspect them.

"They have held up remarkably well, given their age," Winn commented.

"True . . ." Mr. Ellis commented, his eyes never leaving the page. "But you are right to seek a secondary evidence. These provide doubt but not proof of your painting's authorship." Then he looked up and addressed another member of the party. "Gail, would you come and look at this? My German is atrocious."

"If you need a translation, I think I've managed the whole," Winn said, but a chuckle from Sir Geoffrey deterred her.

"Don't worry about the letters, Miss Crane," he said. "My Gaily girl knows how to handle herself with such important things, don't you?"

"Yes, Papa," the girl replied, her jaw setting as she became quite serious, stilling her normal, eleven-year-old bounciness.

"Besides, Gail has a bit of a knack for languages. We've been here only two months and I'd swear up and down she was a native Austrian if I hadn't seen her every day of my life."

Gail sat down next to Mr. Ellis and began to peruse.

"There is no last name to her signature—where do you intend to start looking?"

"I have to surmise that this woman met Master Dürer first and perhaps only in Basel, when he was apprenticing, but they

kept up a correspondence, even though these were the only
two letters found. The simple fact that it is a literate woman in
the year 1500 points to her being well-off. Add to it that she
is obviously trained in art, and since they met in Basel, at one
time had means to travel, she must have been very wealthy
indeed," Winn explained. "The only location mentioned is St.
Stephen's Cathedral, so perhaps there is a slim chance they
still have some records of who the wealthy or aristocratic fam-
ilies were who worshipped there."

"You won't find her family at St. Stephen's," Gail piped up
from her position bent over Mr. Ellis's shoulder. "At least not
her biological one."

"What do you mean? She mentions her mother in one letter, doesn't she?" Jason asked, trying to remember the exact
phrasing from Winn's excited retelling in Nuremberg.

"*My mother who is my superior in all things*—when she
has been scolded for having too much pride in her work,"
Winn added, apparently reading Jason's thoughts . . . but then,
a funny look crossed her face and her hand went to her locket.
"Unless . . ."

"Exactly." Gail smiled at Winn. "You misidentified the article. Understandable, since it's a bit smudged, but . . . there
it is."

Mr. Ellis beamed at Winn the way an instructor looked on
his favorite pupil, and Winn was shaking her head, practically
laughing at her own foolishness, but the rest of the table was
on the edge of their seats, eager to be clued in.

Unsurprisingly, Jason was the one who couldn't hold his
tongue any longer. "Well then, what does it really say?" he
cried impatiently.

"It says *my Mother Superior*," Winn answered, smiling.
"The author of this letter is a nun."

"Which makes sense," Mr. Ellis supplied for the edification
of all. "In that era, a woman of talent would have had more of
a chance in a nunnery to foster it than in a marriage."

"Excellent," Jason said. "But is there an abbey associated with St. Stephen's?" he asked the table.

"Er . . . well, there are dozens of nunneries in Vienna who worship at St. Stephen's at major ecclesiastical holidays," Sir Geoffrey supplied. "Let me reach out to some people, see if I cannot get the parish priest to provide you with a list."

"So, to paraphrase Shakespeare, we shall get ourselves to a nunnery." Winn smiled.

"Nunneries, it sounds like," Jason grumbled. But the rest of the table was far too taken with excitement to note his skepticism.

"Oh, Jason, this is wonderful. This might actually work!" Winn cried excitedly. Jason let her voice saying his name, which she had refrained from using over dinner, wash over him, settling into that place in his spine that relaxed at the sound.

"How so?" he asked. "I'm sorry to play devil's advocate, but we still have to locate half of a three-hundred-year-old correspondence that it is very unlikely to have been kept as important, if at all."

"True," Winn agreed, "but when have you ever known a church to throw anything away?"

"I'll toast to that!" Sir Geoffrey called out. "Richards"—he addressed a servant who had blended effortlessly into a wall—"bring out the Burgundy. A '93, I should think!"

Jason's gaze shot to Winn's. And together, the both of them burst into starry-eyed laughter, leaving the rest of the room out on the joke.

And if they had been alone, he would have taken her into his arms then and held her there. For as long as he could.

Because as they toasted with the long-ago promised Burgundy '93, Jason could not help thinking with a touch of melancholy that tomorrow . . . tomorrow was the beginning of the end of the adventure.

Twenty-three

Wherein we catch up with other travelers.

TOTTY was fairly certain that George's head was shortly going to explode. Which would be a tragedy, as it would be impossible to get blood and brain matter out of her travel gown, and she only had three with her.

Of course, Frau Heider could lend her one, and the two of them were of a size. But really, she would prefer it if George's brain stayed in his head altogether.

Yes, Frau Heider had taken up a place as a co-traveler on this journey. Well, it had been so long since Totty had had a friend her own age to chat with, and George was not the best of company on this journey, as he was becoming progressively more surly and erratic as every day ticked on.

The search for Winn had not gone well in Nuremberg. George was unable to locate any trace of her for almost two days—and indeed, had almost assumed they'd headed for England, letters in hand—when his inquiries at the stable yard bore fruit. They had yielded a young boy who had been duped by a woman and her flame-haired companion, and the child was scathingly eager to tell them where they went—or rather, where the coachman had left them on the side of the road.

"And we are off!" Frau Heider had cried. "Oh, how exciting!"

This elicited strange looks from both Totty and George.

"Well," Frau Heider reasoned, "I am owed a holiday. Besides, I am keenly interested to learn if the young lady really was married to the nice young gentlemen she travelled with."

When she said that, Totty could hear George's teeth grinding.

And so, against George's increased objections, the Dürer House was closed, shutters put up on the windows (this took an extra half day, as George told them more than once), and all the poor drunken students for the next several days would simply have to be disappointed.

The spot where the lad said Winn and the Duke had been dropped revealed little information, but at least it put them in the same direction as the objects of their pursuit. They travelled down the roads, toward Munich, and had stopped for the evening in a little village near the Austrian border before they discovered they had to turn around.

It was Frau Heider's happiness to be among people that lead them in the right direction. While George was always eager to be conversational with men he felt the need to impress, he was not one to bother speaking to those he felt could not be of use, and so took a private dining room, where the rabble would not annoy him.

Totty, likewise, was one for the avoidance of rabble, and finding it best to keep an eye on George at this juncture, who was becoming increasingly on edge, ate with him.

She had just been sipping on the heaviest beer she'd sampled this side of Ireland when Frau Heider came through the dining room door with two pleasant looking, if working-class, men in her wake.

"Tell her what you just told me," Frau Heider said, in her native tongue.

"We were at our sister's, in the village of Lupburg, for the

Sonnenwende festival," the more egregiously smiling of the two gentlemen said, "and you'll never guess what we saw."

"No they never will, so I'll tell you," Frau Heider interjected. "They saw an English Duke cleaning out stables, and his companion lady being chased by the horses."

Suddenly Totty's beer tasted very sour indeed.

But Frau Heider was so pleased with herself and so happy to have been of use on the journey, that Totty had to wait until George, who popped out of his chair immediately at the news, was readying the horses to dampen her enthusiasm.

"My dear—the next time you discover something like this," she said in a whisper, "come to me first, and me only."

"But why?" Frau Heider asked wide-eyed.

"Because I feel it might be necessary to buy Winn and her friend some time to find what she's looking for," Totty reasoned, shooting a pointed look in George's direction, who yelled in his agitated German at the slow pace of his loading of the trunks.

She turned back toward her new friend and found her nodding solemnly, looking somewhat fearful and heartbroken—so much so that Totty, in a manner quite unlike herself, felt the need to pacify her. "Never fear, you did no wrong. We will find them . . . but why such a rush? No reason we can't be a bit leisurely about the matter, is there?"

But leisurely was not George's state of mind. One would have thought that since Frau Heider was instrumental in discovering the direction of Winn and the Duke, George would have been more tolerant of her presence.

One would be wrong.

"Why do I feel certain this will be another waste of time," George grumbled. "Coming back the way we came to follow a rumor?"

"It's better than anything else we have, George," Totty said pointedly. "Besides, the following of a rumor is simply another name for research . . . a skill your profession prizes, does it not?"

George settled against the cushions of the carriage and grumbled. But at least it stopped his glaring at Frau Heider.

The rumor of Lupburg boasted the true article, as everyone in town pointed them quickly in the direction of an inn owned by a man named Wurtzer.

And Wurtzer pointed them in the direction of Regensburg. Even gave them the name of the stable yard where they'd stopped next. Although, he felt he would not be able to tell them precisely where to find it and so decided it best that he himself accompany them in the carriage, to point out the exact turns to take to find Hohenfelser Strasse.

"After all," the kind innkeeper reasoned, "I did not pay them the amount I owed them, and I would like to settle accounts. My beloved Heidi would not hear of me shortchanging the young lovers."

While George's expression darkened, Frau Heider's expression—with whom Herr Wurtzer had been having the most enjoyable conversation—took on a more quizzical vulnerability. "Oh? You have a beloved Heidi?"

"*Da.* My daughter. My wife passed some years ago, I'm afraid."

After that, a great deal of conversation was had between Frau Heider and Herr Wurtzer, in German rapid enough to be completely unfollowable by even the most fluent of the nonnative members of the quickly crowding carriage.

Regensburg pointed them to Linz, Austria. Totty did her best, with some assistance from Frau Heider (although truth be told, that lady was now very much engaged with Wurtzer), to require George to stop the carriage perhaps an hour earlier than he might normally, or that they make certain to have the horses' shoes checked and then double-checked when hiring them. But they travelled on at a pace that made it seem as if they were bearing down upon Winn's heels.

That is, of course, until they got to Linz. In Linz they had to look for clues. And it was in Linz that Totty found one.

And it was in Linz that everything changed.

They had been there for two days, unable to find any trace of Winn and her fictitious husband. They apparently had left the posting inn and disappeared into thin air. All inquiries at local inns and hotels yielded nothing, although that was considered a long shot to begin with, as Wurtzer had provided them with particulars of their financial state, or lack thereof.

"I cannot bear to think of the poor girl, sleeping out in the cold night!" Frau Heider cried, clutching Wurtzer's arm tighter.

"She deserves it," George growled, "for disobeying me."

"What was that?" Totty replied, turning her quizzical gaze on George. And for once George did not turn away in chagrin. Instead, he met her gaze dead on, as if daring her to question him.

It was at a small pawnshop, on a row of shops and restaurants in the shadow of the Pöstlingberg Church's double spires, that it happened. George had gone up the street, inquiring at a small dining room if they had seen a petite woman with a red-haired companion. Herr Wurtzer and Frau Heider had decided to wander up to Pöstlingberg Church, to see if Winn and the Duke had sought sanctuary there. And Totty had decided to do a little shopping.

Besides, what was a holiday across the Continent without collecting a few trinkets?

She was browsing the selection of trinkets, brass lockets, earrings, and the like, when she saw a beautiful gold ring. With a decidedly familiar insignia on it.

Now, Totty was not always the most observant creature. Her butler Leighton had more than once decried his mistress's senses when she poured whiskey into a brandy snifter. But she had taken note of that ring, had in fact focused on it, as they drove from London to Dover, distracting herself from having to listen to George's retching out the window.

"Where did you get this?" she asked the rotund proprietor behind the counter, in his own dialect.

The proprietor, smelling a customer, smiled ingratiatingly. "That belonged to an Austrian count in the Holy Roman Empire. It has been in my family for centuries. A truly priceless artifact."

"Don't be an idiot," Totty rebuffed him. "I know it's English, and I know you purchased it within the past fortnight. But I don't care. I will pay your advertised price if you tell me what you know about the man who sold it to you, and then forget you ever saw it, or him."

The proprietor grinned lasciviously. After all, a desperate customer was far preferable to a stupid one.

"Oh, I do not know if I could part with it . . ."

Just then, on the fringes of her vision, she could see George's hulking form through the window, stalking up the street toward the shop.

"Twice your price." She turned to the proprietor, speaking in a hushed whisper as George threw open the door of the shop. "Just hide the ring, now!"

"Well, that was a waste of time," George sneered, his face fixed in its perpetual scowl. "Find any trinkets for yourself? Or did you perhaps do something useful instead?"

"No, I don't think I did. Nothing but junk in here. Shall we be off?" Totty said perhaps too brightly.

"Wait . . . what is that?" George said, his shrewd vision catching the proprietor shuffling the tray of trinkets from the display to a shelf below.

"Nothing, George," Totty tried again, but he would not be deterred.

"Bring it out," he told the proprietor. "Bring. It. Out," he growled, and the smaller man did so.

Just then, as George was sifting through the items, Herr Wurtzer and Frau Heider came through the shop door, setting its bell jangling.

"There was nothing at the church," Frau Heider cried, "but there was a lovely cart selling meat pies on our way out, and—"

"What is this?" George interrupted, the ring in his hand. "This is Rayne's ring! How could you miss it?"

"I, ah—" Totty tried, but it was of no use.

"There is no possible way you would have missed it. You meant to hide it from me," George surmised. He held it up to her face, his fingers shaking with the pressure of restraint.

"Now, Herr Bambridge," Frau Heider jumped into the silence. "She wouldn't have hidden it from you. Not forever."

"Not forever?" George asked, now actively stalking forward, forcing Totty to take steps backward. "Not forever. Which means you would have for a time. Maybe once Winn had found that proof that she's looking all over the Continent for, you would have revealed it? Maybe once we were back in England and I am in *disgrace*?"

"Now, George, stop it!" Totty said forcefully. But this time . . . no, this time George was not going to be shamed into propriety.

"I will not stop it! You have been holding me back with your *coddling* this entire journey! *You* have been trying to stop me from finding Winnifred, and *you* have involved these hangers-on"—he threw his arm out at their friends, knocking over a vase in his anger but not caring—"in your schemes! And therefore you are to blame for what happens to her now."

"George don't be ridiculous—" Totty tried, ignoring the belly-deep fear that George—who she had seen grow from a boy into the angry oversized man before her—was igniting inside of her. But she shouldn't have ignored it, because George was past reasoning. With one swipe of his great paw, he struck Totty across the face, throwing her into a glass lamp and crashing her to the ground.

The horrified cries of the gathered party echoed in Totty's ears as the light faded in and out in front of her eyes, colors stirring with dark.

"Oh shut up, all of you!" George yelled, a stuttering panic in his voice. Then Totty could hear a shuffling as he leaned over the counter, and a thunk and cry as he pulled the proprietor to him by the collar. "Now, you will tell me *exactly* what you know about this ring." And then the light faded away entirely.

৵

Totty came to with a splitting headache, and Frau Heider bending over her.

"Oh, she's awake! Günter, she's awake!" Frau Heider cried, bringing Herr Wurtzer to her side.

"Where is he?" she asked, trying to sit up and finding it impossible, as the whole world spun. "Oh—this is the worst hangover I've ever had."

"Don't try to move," Frau Heider said. "You have a cut under your hair from the glass, and a large bump. There was even blood—we were so frightened for you. Herr Bambridge is gone. Günter tried to restrain him but—" She shrugged, which was all the explanation for why a sixty-year-old man was not able to stop one half his age who happened to have the size and strength of a gorilla.

"You couldn't have hidden that ring any quicker?" she said to the proprietor, who was anxiously wringing his hands. Totty couldn't blame him. Having an Englishwoman die in your shop is not good for business.

"I'm sorry, I didn't realize. I . . . He made me tell him what I knew. That the man asked for an amount that would get him to Vienna. But he was agitated, and I ended up shorting him, he only got—"

"Yes, yes," Totty replied, waving her hand in the air. "I just can't believe that I was struck."

"Neither can we," Frau Heider said. "I . . . something is wrong with that man. Totty. . . . He . . . Herr Bambridge . . . he took a pistol. From the glass case over there. I believe he has gone mad."

"If he hasn't yet, he will by the time I'm through with him," Totty said darkly. Then, turning to the proprietor, "You. Fetch me ink and paper. And a drink. When I'm done with George Bambridge, he won't know what hit *him*."

Twenty-four

Wherein our duo's search ends dramatically,
and—curiously—in a church.

THE problems associated with identifying the nunnery, convent, or abbey that had sheltered Maria F. some three hundred years ago were manifold. First, they had to identify the sisterhoods that, some three hundred years ago, would attend services at St. Stephen's on holy days. This was no easy feat. Luckily, Sir Geoffrey spoke a few well-placed words in a few influential ears, and Winn and Jason were able to hold an audience with the parish priest of St. Stephen's. Unluckily, the kind and cooperative priest was unable to help, being as he was not alive three hundred years ago, and the records that were kept were fairly general and not studied in their detail. He was, however, able to provide a list of those abbeys that attended services on All Saints' Day, Christmas, and other feast days, as long as he had been in tenure.

Unfortunately, this list had at least fifty items on it.

"What are we supposed to do?" Jason asked. "Do we just visit every church on this list and cross them off after we spend a few days rummaging around in their belongings?"

"Heavens no," Winn replied practically as they left St. Stephen's Cathedral in the center of Vienna and made their way down Stephensplatz. "It's going to be so much more difficult than that."

"More difficult?" Jason asked, still reeling from the length of the list.

"Yes. Happily, we can eliminate any church or abbey that wasn't active in 1500. But then again, there are likely some convents that existed then that don't anymore. Possibly they were destroyed outright in the Turkish sieges, possibly they were absorbed by larger institutions—either way, we have to track down their remains and add them in." Winn smiled at him cheerfully. "Also, there's nothing to say that our Maria F. wasn't a member of a convent outside of Vienna, and the trip to St. Stephen's was part of a special pilgrimage or visitation. For all we know, we already passed where she lived, in Linz or Melk or—"

"I get the idea," Jason said, beleaguered, pinching the bridge of his nose. Then he opened one eye, glancing at Winn's excited countenance. "Wait a moment. How can you possibly be enjoying this?"

"Because this is how it happens, Jason." She grinned at him. "There is a tiny piece of information, to be found somewhere, and this is how we find it. We explore, we dig, we look until our eyes are crossed and we can't look anymore. All in the hope of a moment of discovery. I'm enjoying it because *this* is the fun part."

Jason held this happy, shining person's gaze and simply shook his head. He was not going to be able to convince her to stroll through the streets of the city this time, taking in the local sights and people. He was not going to be able to purchase her a little trinket as souvenir in Vienna. No, now that the goal was in sight, the bit was between her teeth, and she would not let go. This was the person Winn was meant to be. And it was a glorious thing to behold.

"Where do we start?" He sighed and gave his arm to her as she directed him briskly to the first church on the list.

As they faded into the distance, they were each too focused on the quest or, alternately, the person behind it, to feel the eyes that were on them. Eyes that had chanced upon them as they had headed into St. Stephen's Cathedral, and then shocked by the luck, waited patiently for them to emerge. Eyes that followed them now, at a safe distance. Because he would be damned if Winnifred Crane would be let out of his sight ever again.

When one reads books about Vienna, they comment on the gracefulness of the city, the only real choice to be the capital of the Austrian Empire. They talk about the Danube and its meandering beauty. They talk about the music of the city, the opera house, the palaces . . . but rarely do they mention the churches.

Rather, Winn—picking at the edge of a lavender ruffle on her borrowed dress—thought grimly, they do not pontificate adequately on the number of churches, and how they are simply wedged into the city's corners and alleys, making them hard to locate on a map and even harder to find in person.

Her enthusiasm for the quest had not dwindled, oh no—if anything the past two days of visiting every church on the list provided by the St. Stephen's priest had whetted her appetite for the moment of truth. But when, oh when, would it come?

This is what you get, gambling your whole life on one instant, she told herself, exhausted after yet another church— their third today, and it was not yet tea. Luckily, Sir Geoffrey's influence had not only elicited the list of potential orders from the priest at St. Stephen's, but also a general letter of introduction to those they would need to speak to at various churches, abbeys, nunneries, and convents.

And speak to, they had.

Just that morning, they had visited the Ursulinenkirche, found in a quiet corner of the Innere Stadt, or first district, and were able to reject it almost immediately, as the first thing they learned was it had been built in the 1660s, far too late to house Maria F.

The Dorotheakirche was interesting in that it had converted from Catholicism to Protestantism during the Reformation and stunningly enough, *not* been converted back by the Hapsburgs during the Counter-Reformation. But alas, after several hours in the church's library with their chaplain yielded no hint that Maria F. had ever been there, in the name of efficiency, they had to move on.

The third church, the one they had just left, was little more than a monastic chapel, and undoubtedly the most disappointing.

"How on earth did that little place end up on the parish priest's list?" Winn asked aloud, utterly frustrated.

"It wasn't so bad," Jason replied. "Except for the decided lack of nuns."

"Well, one more church," Winn said, glancing at the list, "and then I am going to desperately need a pint of ale."

Jason laughed heartily and plucked the list from her hands. "Agreed, but I get to pick the next."

And Jason picked well. For it was at the next church they visited that they had their first bit of luck.

A small, baroque-style chapel within the Innere Stadt of Vienna, Franziskanerkirche was the Church of the Franciscan Order. They spoke for some hours with the Reverend Mother of the Order of St. Clare at the church, who had tried her best to help them but ultimately could not. At least not there.

"We have a sister abbey, in Döbling, just outside the city," the straight-mouthed Reverend Mother told them. "It is where our school for young ladies is." She looked pointedly at Winn, as if perhaps, she would have done well with some Franciscan schooling. "It has been there since the fourteenth century. And I do believe there was a sister from around that time, who had some claim in the world of art . . ."

Winn would be remiss if she did not note the effect that sentence had on the beleaguered spirits of both travelers.

"You have?" Jason asked, sitting up in his chair.

"You do?" Winn asked at the same time, her eyes suddenly very bright.

The Reverend Mother wrote down the information for the abbey in Döbling, and first thing the next morning, off they were. Again.

But this time . . . this time felt different.

"I don't know how, but I have a good feeling about this place," Winn said to Jason as they rumbled along in Sir Geoffrey's carriage. He had generously lent it to them that day . . . on the condition that Gail, Evangeline, and Mr. Ellis be allowed to join them. Gail and Evangeline, because as Sir Geoffrey said, he wanted the girls to "look around the school, see if there was anything to be learned there that they couldn't manage at home," and Mr. Ellis because . . . well, simply because.

"Why do you say that, Miss Crane?" Mr. Ellis asked.

Winn simply shook her head. "Because no other place had yielded so much as a rumor or a whiff of hope. And to have this one place out of a thousand, pointed out by the Reverend Mother of the Poor Clares . . . it simply feels right. Like how it felt when Herr Heider first wrote me about the letters in his collection."

"That's called instinct, Miss Crane," Mr. Ellis smiled. "A necessity for any explorer, or seeker of truth."

"And she has it in spades," Jason replied.

Winn looked up at Jason and her breath caught. If only they were alone in the carriage! She would have taken his hand. But here, now, she was unable to hold it, as they were in the presence of good people, unable to express . . . something. Gratitude? Friendship?

But Winn knew that Jason had just complimented her—in front of others, no less—for the same reason that over the course of the last few days (when they had not been under the close inspection of two young girls, their father, or a respected historian) Winn had perhaps grasped Jason's hand tighter than she used to, perhaps took his arm with more enthusiasm.

But she had to stop doing so. Because as the carriage rumbled into the little town of Döbling, they were coming to the end.

And so, she tucked her hands in her lap and bit the inside of her cheek to keep from making any pert comments back to him, and instead focused on what was in front of her. What she was so close to achieving.

The sisters of the Order of St. Clare, sometimes referred to as "Poor Clares" (as their patron was a follower of St. Francis of Assisi and gave all of her money and belongings away), were as accommodating as their namesake. The Döbling school, convent (the dormitory that served as housing for the nuns and the girls who boarded), and church were separate buildings, none of them auspicious in their scale or architecture, but original to the medieval time they were built—with more modern additions here and there to accommodate the growth of the school. Therefore, it had the look of a small castle keep on a hill, with the occasional baroque-style window or late gothic wall. There was a low wall that surrounded their grounds, keeping the nuns removed from the town and godly in their pursuits. There was some scaffolding in and around the modest church, but the visitors were told not to worry—the roof had merely caved in.

"Since we are outside of the city, we were not targeted during the Turkish raids," the Mother Superior—who went by the name Mother Agnes—told them kindly as she guided them through the school buildings, toward the convent and chapel. She spoke German, naturally, but this time Winn did not have to rely solely on Jason for translation: Miss Gail Alton proved her German to be incredibly accurate. It also seemed that the Alton girls were in charge of their own education and eager to pursue it—Gail fluidly asked all sorts of questions about the school and the curriculum, and translated the answers back to her less linguistically gifted sister, going on about whether they prized the sciences and mathematics, whether or not they taught all dialects of German here along with Latin . . . eventually, Winn, for the sake of expediency, had to interject.

"Mother Agnes—we are looking for the possible author of these letters . . ." Winn began, her speech so rushed and her heart beating so fast with possibilities that Mother Agnes held up her hand with the authority of one who had spent her life teaching overeager girls.

"I have been informed of your quest, my child," she said kindly. "Interrupting will not get you any closer to your destination."

Winn felt herself blushing, properly scolded.

"Perhaps, though, it is best if we divide our group?" Mother Agnes asked, and turned to a young novitiate. "Please take the Fräuleins Alton to see the school." The novitiate, young and deferential, nodded and lead the girls down a different hallway in the school.

Freeing the adults of the party to follow Mother Agnes at her smooth gesture.

"I know of your quest because I have received word from my sister at the Franziskanerkirche. But I am afraid that you will find little help from us here."

"Why is that?" Jason asked as they crossed the small courtyard from the school to the convent, passing a line of schoolgirls as they did so.

"Because we are the Order of St. Clare—we believe quite strictly in the lack of personal possessions, to a degree some other orders find extreme."

"That actually makes sense with our case—for you see, the author of these letters gave her paintings away," Winn said, pulling the letters—which had since been carefully wrapped in the vellum and then kidskin leather Mr. Ellis procured for them—out of a portfolio she held tightly in her hands.

Mother Agnes glanced at the letters but declined with a simple wave to read them. "Our beliefs make it highly unlikely that any correspondence your author kept would have survived even her lifetime, never mind beyond it."

At Winn's silence and Jason's quizzical looks, Mr. Ellis jumped into the fray.

"But you do have a library, do you not?" Mr. Ellis asked. "Important papers, ecclesiastical texts, perhaps a registry of the members of your order?"

"We do, and you are welcome to look," Mother Superior said, leading them into the convent and down the hall to a modest room, with little more than a neat desk, a number of locked cabinets, and an unadorned window for light.

"This is my office. All the information you seek would be in these cabinets," Mother Agnes said, pulling out a key from the depths of her scapular and unlocking them with smooth, measured movements. She revealed a number of books and ledgers, all neatly delineated, in progressive states of age.

"Please be kind with the older documents," Mother Agnes said, and then with a discreet bow of her head, "I leave you to your searching."

"Mother Agnes—forgive me," Winn said, stopping the woman at the door of the spartan room. "We came here—that is, we were told a rumor that there once *was* a sister of some artistic repute."

"I was told the same rumor as a novitiate," Mother Agnes replied with a smile. "Only then it wasn't an artist who painted with Dürer, but an astronomer who studied with Galileo. I'm sorry, my dear. Every place has its own mythologies."

Winn could feel all of her senses, all of the instinct that Mr. Ellis had ascribed to her, sitting up and shrieking against what Mother Agnes had just said. Because if it was true . . . then they would be back to square one. Back to the list. A list that had more than half the items checked off it already. To have hopes brought up and then doubted . . .

But she kept it to herself. She kept it to herself, set her shoulders, and turned to her friends.

Friends. How terribly funny to think of them as such. And how completely right.

"Well, gentlemen," she said with a smile. "No time like the present."

They each chose a cabinet and began. The light moved across
the floor, the sun shifting places in the sky as morning became
afternoon. They heard the church bells every hour, on the hour.
Heard the girls move from their classes. If Winn had brought
her head up from the books at all, she might have wondered
where Gail and Evangeline had gotten to . . . a question that
Mr. Ellis answered when he asked the novitiate, who brought
them a small repast of bread and cheese around two and told
them that the young fräuleins had elected to sit in on a few of
the classes at the school.

Mr. Ellis proved to be as good as his reputation. He was
meticulous, respectful, and thorough in his searching. Jason,
too, had by now, after all that time in Nuremberg and then
the proceeding time at various book rooms and libraries of
churches all over the Innere Stadt, worked up a surprisingly
good tolerance for the quieter, dustier aspects of study. She
found herself glancing at him more than once, his eyes straining on obscure German handwriting, and . . . well, it was silly,
but she was proud of him.

Silly, because . . . he had always been this way. At least
with her. He had always been steadfast, he'd always tried so
very hard. There was no need for pride, and yet there it was
anyway, shining and precious.

He glanced up and caught her gaze. Smiled. She glanced
down immediately. She had to stop doing that. With their adventure ending, seeking his eyes was a habit she had to break.
She had to maintain her distance.

But—those few kind glances aside—as diligent as they
were, as tirelessly thorough, they needn't have been.

Within the first hour, she knew they weren't going to find
anything.

No second half of correspondence, no record of a sister of
the Order of St. Clare from around 1500 . . . no other leads.

It must have been past six when she closed the last book in

the last cabinet. The light from the west was coming in bright yellow and orange, illuminating the dust that floated on the air like a dancing summer snow.

No one said anything for some minutes. Just allowed their eyes to adjust back to seeing distance, stretched their backs.

And again, her gaze unerringly found Jason's.

"Well . . . I think I shall go examine the chapel before we lose the light," Mr. Ellis said, backing out of the small office. "I'm terribly interested to see how they intend to repair the roof." They heard rather than saw him almost bump into the little candled prayer altar down the hall. "Oof! Here's hoping there hasn't been further damage caused to the works inside!" he cried, and was gone.

"Mr. Ellis is nothing if not the epitome of tact," Jason drawled, smiling that half smile at her.

But she couldn't smile back at him.

"I'm never going to find her, am I?" she said, leaning against Mother Agnes's desk.

"Of course you are," Jason replied, leaning against the desk next to her, crossing his arms over his chest, mimicking her exhausted posture. Perhaps he wasn't mimicking. Perhaps he was truly as exhausted as she. "How could you possibly even think it? There's half a list of Viennese nunneries yet to go through."

"I know." Winn shook her head. "Of course tomorrow is going to be another search of other churches, until another rumor is tracked down and another possibility opens up. But I felt so damned sure that this was the place. I had my hopes up. It's so hard to have them let down again." She chanced it, chanced connection, and reached out and patted his shoulder. "I'm simply indulging in a moment of self-pity. It will pass soon enough."

He looked for a moment as though he wanted to say something—a kind of anticipation crossed over his features. But then it fled, and he shrugged in his nonchalant manner.

"Self-pity?" Jason grinned. "How is it possible that you made it this far into the journey without indulging in self-pity?"

"I don't know." She smiled at him. "But I do think I would have succumbed to self-pity much sooner if you hadn't been with me every step of the way. Making sure I didn't fall into too bad of trouble. I would have been robbed, or taken for a ride all around the Germany, or ended up in a Turkish harem. I do thank you for that."

He looked at her then, his lazy half smile taking on a look of reluctant honesty.

"Actually," he said, his voice barely more than a gruff whisper, "I think you would have managed fine without me. I don't know how, but . . . you would have found your way."

Winn felt the tears sting at her eyes. She did her best to blink them back, but . . .

"Oh for God's sake, what did I do now?" Jason asked, worriedly coming off the desk . . . as if tears from a woman were an indicator of disease. Luckily, his reaction had her laughing.

"No, no . . . nothing terrible." She giggled back her tears. "That is simply the nicest thing you've ever said to me."

"Oh," Jason replied, relievedly settling back down against the table. "Well, it's true. You would have been fine, Winn. Not that I've minded coming along with you, of course."

She threw her head back in laughter at that one. "Oh, you minded. You minded several times in several different ways."

Jason sputtered in protest, before he finally shook his head in acknowledgement. "Yes, all right . . . I did mind. Some. Not all."

"Not all?" she asked, looking into his face, and finding it raw and honest.

"I want you to know—this is the best adventure I've ever had," he breathed.

"It's the only adventure I've ever had," she replied.

They held still there, the dust from all of their efforts settling around them, the golden sun casting him a reddish halo that threatened to unsettle her as much as this conversation. But as unsettling as it was . . . she was loath to have this moment end.

"I want you to know something else," he said, and her breath caught. What did he need her to know? She had no idea. What if . . . what if it was something she couldn't bear to hear?

"1 have forty-eight stable workers in my employ, at four different estates. That number fluctuates by five or so as I have local boys hired on when I visit my hunting box." He grinned. "I also tend to vote for conservative fiscal measures in the House of Lords, but strangely turn Tory when it comes to social matters. Drives my secretaries and fellow Whig party members absolutely mad. And I know the salary of my valet, and I know that I am going to have to have the fields of Crow Castle—that's my family seat—dredged within the year else the crops will suffer."

Winn's jaw dropped; she could only gape.

"Stop looking at me like a fish," Jason mumbled, blushing.

"Forty-eight stable workers?" she finally asked.

"Give or take five," he replied.

"But we spoke of that ages ago."

He shrugged. "It's been bothering me."

She let out a great breath. It was relief, she told herself, this feeling in her belly, that Jason's confession had been one of responsibility rather than . . . anything else.

But, not willing to reflect any longer, Winn wiped her eyes, squared her shoulders, and came off the edge of the desk.

"Shall we find the others?" she asked with a smile as Jason followed her lead. She took his arm, and they stepped out of the office and into the hall. "Tomorrow is another day of scouting churches. For I have to find some evidence of Maria F., because I will not be returning to England as George Bambridge's bride."

She continued to walk, but Jason became still. He caught her hand, forcing her to stop and turn around in the tiny hallway of the convent dormitory.

"There's a third option," he said seriously.

"What?" she asked.

"Other than finding Maria F. or marrying Bambridge. Winn—there is a third option."

And then . . . panic rose in her chest. Her hand remained firmly in his, and she fought to keep it there . . . to not pull away and run . . .

"There is no third option, Jason," she said, her voice weaker than she would have liked.

"Yes, there is," he countered. "I know you think you owe him a debt of honor, but if you were already mar—"

"No, Jason, there is no third option," she repeated, forcefully this time, with conviction. "Because there is no second option." She pulled her hand out of his grasp and watched his face go from open and hopeful to hard, aristocratic lines. "I will not marry George because I will not fail at this," she said. "I cannot. I have to find my evidence—the life I want is within my grasp."

"The life you want is a good one, but there are other lives to be had," he argued. "Why are you so afraid?"

"I'm not afraid!" she practically yelled. Then, more calmly, "But you cannot save me from this, Jason. I've told you that I have to have my voice, my independence . . . I will not be forced to rely on anyone or have anyone need me, ever again. It's all I've ever wanted. And if I . . . *give up*, I will hate myself forever. And anyone that asked me to." She looked down at her toes then, unable to hold his eye any longer as her answer to his unasked question made impact upon his features. "Please tell me you understand," she whispered.

When Jason's voice finally came, it came out harshly. "I do," he said. "So this is your choice, then?"

She flicked her gaze up at him, uncertain. He was pale, awed, refusing to look at her directly. Instead, he focused beyond her, down the short corridor.

"I will work my way through all the convents and monasteries in Vienna, in Europe, if I have to, to earn my own life," she vowed.

He nodded, and took in a deep ragged breath. "Then turn around."

Turn around? She blinked in confusion. His eyes fell to hers quickly, and he nodded, his face still giving nothing away. So she turned at his command and followed his line of sight to the end of the short corridor, where it turned to the left. In the corner of the hall was the small prayer altar, set with votive candles that Mr. Ellis had nearly tripped over. Or perhaps he had nearly tripped over one of the few chairs that were situated next to it. But that was not what had caught Jason's attention—and now hers.

On top of the prayer altar was a small triptych painting, set in thick pine, so it stood up of its own volition. The center panel rose in an arch and was no more than a foot and a half tall, a foot wide. Its two side panels were set on hinges, and each were half of the center panel's width, so they could be closed like church doors.

And while the center panel featured a Renaissance-era depiction of Jesus on the cross, the two side panels were far more interesting. There was one of Adam and one of Eve, with the Tree of Knowledge divided between the two.

And they were exact copies of the Adam and Eve from the disputed painting. Down to the snake winding around Adam's ankle.

"Oh my God," she breathed, taking measured steps toward the altar—she did not fully trust her legs now. She reached the triptych—were her eyes playing tricks on her? No . . . no, they were correct. Completely and utterly correct.

". . . the First of Man and Woman. That's what Maria F. called the painting in her letters," Winn intoned, her breath coming in little hitches. "But it wasn't a title . . . it was a first draft! This must be her finished work!" Her eyes focused unblinkingly on a lower corner.

"It's . . . oh my God. Jason . . . oh my God, is that, is that a signature?"

She peered closely, and then gingerly, ever so gingerly, lifted it up and used a votive candle's light to peer at the bottom right corner of the main panel.

"Well, it's certainly not Dürer's mark," Jason commented, his nose as close to canvas as her own.

"This is it, Jason," she replied, standing upright but still clutching the triptych. "This, plus the letters? This is incontrovertible proof. And to think, it's been sitting in this little abbey in Döbling for the past three hundred years. Forgotten." She looked up at him with shining eyes. "And you found it. Jason—you made the discovery of a lifetime."

He opened his mouth to answer, to say something . . . anything . . . about the discovery, about what she told him mere seconds before it . . . but it was not to be.

Because someone else answered for him.

"The discovery of a lifetime, Your Grace?" George Bambridge's voice came out of the shadows from down the left corridor. "My congratulations. A pity your life is going to be far too short."

Twenty-five

Wherein the dramatics conclude.

GEORGE emerged from the darkness of the long corridor, lead by the shine of a pistol in his hand.

"Good heavens, George, where did you get that?" Winn asked, surprised a little at her own tone.

"Linz," George replied conversationally. Then, with his spare hand, he dug into his pocket. "You left something there, Your Grace." He held up the ducal signet ring, its gold crest sparkling in the low light. Tossed it to Jason, who caught it and slipped it back onto his finger.

"My thanks, Bambridge," Jason said, his tone far more wary than Winn's had been. Slowly, Jason shuffled himself so that his body stood in front of Winn, protecting her.

"Ah, ah, ah," George said, seeing Jason's intentions. "That's quite far enough, Your Grace."

"Now, George, be reasonable. We have just had a moment of true academic discovery. This is important," Winn began.

"No! You do not order me about any longer. Your independence was fostered by your father and should never have been encouraged. You women, trying to tell me what is important and what is good," George spat, advancing toward them. "I'm tired of it. Now, you're going to listen to me."

It was at that point that Winn realized two things: First of all, it was eerily quiet in the convent dormitory. There was no one there but them. Where was Totty? Where were the sisters, the novitiate who had come to check on them periodically throughout the day? Where was Mr. Ellis? The silence told her that there was no one coming to save them.

The second thing she realized, as the first was sending a chill down her spine, was that George Bambridge had, over the last few weeks, gone past the point of reason.

Although, in fairness, the last was a point she should have realized as soon as she saw the pistol in his hand.

It was obviously a point that Jason had taken note of, as he held up his hands in a gesture of surrender. "All right Bambridge, you win." Gently, he took the triptych out of Winn's hands, closing the side panels over the main one so only the wooden sides faced out. Its hinges, obviously long held in the same position, creaked with the effort of use, shaking Winn to the core.

"This is what you want, correct? This is the proof that Winn was right all along. Take it." Jason held out the triptych to George, at arm's length. George glanced down at it, uncertain. Then, stepping carefully, he approached. He reached out his left hand, and in so doing, the pistol in his right fell by an inch.

That's when Jason tossed the triptych in the air. And suddenly, everything happened at once.

George reached for the triptych, dropping his pistol to the ground, luckily without discharge. But before the triptych even touched George's outstretched fingers, Jason had launched himself at George, tackling him. As George hit the ground, so did the painting, and Winn's strangled cry rent the air. She was about to dive for it, but as George and Jason wrestled on the floor, George's leg kicked out and knocked over the small altar of votive candles.

That was when things got truly interesting.

The altar itself was old, and little more than tinder. It went up quickly, with Winn on one side, and Jason, George, and the triptych on the other.

For one of the few times in her life, Winn did not know what to do.

"Jason!" she cried as George rolled on top of him and began pummeling his ribs.

"Go! Get help!" Jason said in strangled tones.

"I'm not leaving you!" she cried. Oh heavens, the fire was spreading to the chair. How long before the ceiling beams caught?

"Oh for God's sake . . ." Jason grumbled, and then, with a lucky kick to George's male parts, managed to turn the tables and get the advantage. He stood quickly and picked up the triptych, tossing it over the fire, startling Winn into reaching out her hands and catching it.

"Go get help!"

"Jase—"

"The fire is spreading. Go now!"

She ran. Winn ran down the corridor, out into the orange gaze of the setting sun. She looked around wildly, but could see no one. "Help!" she yelled, again and again. But no one came. All the sisters and students must be in the school, for prayers before supper, as the church was still being repaired.

The church. It was the closest.

"Mr. Ellis!" she cried, taking off for the doors to the little chapel that served as the convent's place of worship. It was a perfectly serviceable place, with rows of wooden pews on either side of a main aisle, leading up to an altar. It would not have stood out of place from any other church, except for the scaffolding and lack of roof. She burst through the doors, setting some nesting pigeons into flight, the flap of their wings echoing across the empty space. "Mr. Ellis! Mr. Ellis!" she called again, and thankfully, finally, Mr. Ellis appeared at the little podium at the altar.

"Oh thank goodness . . . Mr. Ellis, take this." Winn practi-

cally tossed the triptych at him. "It's terribly important. And
you have to go get help, there's a fire in the dormitory!"

"What on earth, child . . . ?" Mr. Ellis said, his eyes running over the triptych in his hands.

"Mr. Ellis. Fire! Dormitory!"

That was all that needed to be said. Using the door on the
side, he took the triptych and ran out to the school.

Winn headed back up the aisle to the main doors, the ones
she had come through, that lead back to the dormitory. She
had to get to Jason . . . She had to get him out . . .

And then she heard it.

The birds that had settled back into their nests, rustling, the
beginnings of flight.

She dove down in between pews just as the main doors
burst open, and George roared into the little church.

She held as still as she could, barely breathing, wedged between the kneeling stools and the seats. She was on her hands
and knees, as low and she could get. Watching the aisle . . .
listening to footsteps.

"Winnifred . . . come out now, I know you're in here.
I must say you chose your champion poorly. You missed it
when I knocked him down in two blows to the head." Footsteps crept closer.

"Funny, isn't it? I never liked boxing." He laughed then, a
hollow, wild sound that Winn had never heard before. It sent
pricks of fear to her scalp. "I seem to have a talent for it."

She couldn't hide here forever. He would find her, catch
her . . . She shuffled as far back in the row as she could, as
quietly as possible, sliding on her knees. But alas, she wasn't
silent enough.

"There you are." George appeared at her row, leaning casually on the pew. He was a mess—she hadn't noticed it before,
her focus had been mainly on the pistol (that he luckily no
longer carried), but his coat was worn, his face scruffed with
beard. His shirt and trousers were smattered with ashes. Normally, George was finicky about his appearance, to the point

of irritation. But now, his gaze and his voice were utterly, disturbingly calm.

"Might as well stand, you know," George drawled, his voice becoming harder and harder with every word he enunciated. "Are you going to make me come get you? Make me chase you more? I've been chasing you for fifteen years. One would think that's enough."

It was his anger that kept his eyes calm, Winn realized. His anger that he normally stomped out had now been ingested, and permeated his very soul. She didn't have to glance behind her to know that there was no means of easy escape. There was very little choice but to stand and meet him.

"Where is Jason?" she asked.

"Where I left him."

"And where is Totty?" She swallowed, taking a slow, small step behind her.

"Where I left her." George grinned. "Never fear, His Grace's injuries are far more severe than hers. At least I hope so."

Winn took another cautious step back. She was almost fully into the far aisle now, the full pew separating them. But George didn't move, didn't advance. Didn't need to.

"Do you mean, that you . . . hurt Totty, as you hurt Jason?" she said cautiously.

"I didn't mean to," George reasoned, desperation creeping into his voice. "But I had to. She was keeping me from finding you. I . . . just want things to go back to normal, Winnifred. You and me, in Oxford. Please understand . . . It was the only way . . . Winnifred, it was the only way. Totty just would not shut up. Her and her friends . . ."

Winn felt something hot burn her ears. Some deep-seated anger finally finding its way to the forefront of her mind, and she no longer saw her old friend George on the edge of madness. Instead she saw her jailer, her oppressor, and one who caused injury to her friends.

"For someone who seems so beset by women's voices, you

never listen to them." Winn breathed deeply, her gaze constantly on him. "I have tried in the past to tell you this, but you brushed it off. So hear me now: I will never marry you. I am done with this farce."

As George's eyes narrowed and the anger that drove him finally showed on his face, Winn knew in that fraction of a second before he dove for her, that at last, he had heard her.

"A farce, is it?" George growled as he dove into the row, stomping toward her. While George had size and strength, Winn had a surprising amount of speed, and she darted out of his grasp.

"You call the life I planned for us a farce?"

But there was very little in the way of places to go. George had the center aisle, he would get to the main doors before her . . .

"The love I've borne for you all these years is a farce?"

The door Mr. Ellis had escaped through was on the other side of the church . . .

"Even when my friends told me to look elsewhere, that you were a frigid headache, I always came back to you."

She could feel the hot swipe of his hand as he grabbed for her, just fractions of an inch out of his grasp. She ran for her life, ran in circles, barely keeping herself out of his grasp until she ran out of places to run. And then, there was nowhere to go but up.

"I endured the humiliation of your education, of those Marks papers, of your silly pursuits, and now *you* reject *me*?"

She clasped the rungs of the scaffolding, propelling her body up the rickety works, each board straining audibly with her slight weight. Quickly she moved . . . up . . . up some more. . . . She was almost to the large gaping hole in the roof when she felt the scaffolding shake violently, bow and creak. She chanced a look behind her and saw that George had begun his own assent after her. She doubled her pace. Reaching the top, she used every muscle in her arms, arms that were in general used for lifting little more than a quill, to hold her body at the hole in the roof. And then, with one solid kick, knocked the rickety scaffolding to one side.

It creaked and cried and buckled under the pressure of being thrown so far to one side. The twine binding the hinges snapped, and the whole thing went down in a great crash of sticks, wood, and dust.

And George went down with it.

She could hear his cry through the crash, as Winn used the last of her strength to pull her hanging legs up over the edge of the hole. She rolled onto the slate shingles of the roof, which slid loosely beneath her, her breath coming in heavy gulps. Seconds ticked by as she regained her strength and mind. Then, she scrambled to her feet, trying to keep steady on the slope of the unstable roof. (For the first time in her life, she was thankful for her shortness, thereby providing a low center of gravity.) She glanced down into the hole, into the depth of the church. She could see nothing beyond the cloud of dust that had been kicked up, but she could tell there was no movement on the ground.

Funny, but that cloud of dust . . . it smelled of . . . Was it smoke?

Her head whipped up. No, the smoke was on the air. She scrambled on unsteady legs up to the ridgepole of the roof, desperate for a better view. There she saw the dormitory, smoke blowing out two windows. The fire had spread. The place was being beset by organized nuns and schoolgirls, forming a line from the well to the fire, buckets being run up the line. She spotted Mr. Ellis with the Alton girls, the triptych still in his hands. But nowhere did she see Jason.

She walked along the ridgepole, almost losing her balance in her haste, to the bell tower at the end closest to the madness. She squinted into the setting sun, still unable to see Jason anywhere. Oh God . . .

"He's still inside," she breathed in horror. She had to get down, had to get to the dormitory . . . She had to find him . . .

How was she to get down?

She looked about her wildly, her eyes halting at the large iron bell in the tower and the long rope affixed to the top, dangling down to the floor below. Gingerly, she hauled herself over the ledge of the bell tower and, as gently as she could, took hold of the rope and slid off the ledge.

For all her intelligence, this, perhaps, was not Winn's best idea.

BONG!

The world vibrated as her weight rang the bell, shaking her vision, forcing her up and down as the bell rang back and forth.

BONG!

She struggled to keep her hands gripped tight around the rope as the bell steadied itself.

BONG!

Slowly, she put one hand beneath the other, her arms burning with the effort of lowering her body. Hand over hand, she went down, down . . .

BONG!!!

The rope started whipping violently back and forth.

"Need some help getting down, Winnifred?" George's malicious voice came from below her. She chanced a look down and saw that George, covered in dust, had the bottom of the bell pull in his thick hands, whipping it back and forth, shaking her down like an apple from a tree.

"No!" she cried, holding on for dear life as she was rattled in midair, halfway down the rope. "Stop! Please!"

But he kept shaking the rope, his entire face red with the effort and his temper. She had to hold on . . . She just had to hold on . . .

And suddenly the doors of the church burst open, and there was a great roar . . .

And she wasn't being whipped about anymore.

Winn chanced another look down.

A figure of smoke and flame had tackled George to the ground, was wrestling him with the fury of a beast from hell.

But it wasn't fire, the flame that she spied. It was red hair, shining through the dust and soot.

"Jason!" she cried, working her way down the rope. But if he heard her, his attention was elsewhere. George had inches and a stone as advantage, and was using it, fighting tooth and nail.

"You don't get to have her!" George growled, scratching and kicking against Jason, and quickly gaining the upper hand.

Winn quickly worked her way down the rest of the rope, her feet happy to be on the ground. But the happiness was not to be reflected on, for at that moment, George managed to grab hold of one of the beams of scattered scaffolding, fallen to the ground. He hoisted it high over his head and was about to bring it down when Winn ran with all her might and jumped on George's back.

And, well . . . she didn't really know what inspired her.

She bit down. On his ear.

"Argghhhh!" was the astonished cry of the ogre she rode. He reared back, came off Jason, dropping the wooden weapon, and throwing Winn to the ground. She landed on her back in the center aisle, banging her head against a pew.

The world, already gone mad, suddenly swum in colors.

But that moment of distraction, that bite, was all that was needed. Winn saw the vague black figure of George reaching down for her, about to grab, when Jason—dusty, sweaty, bloody Jason—rose behind him.

With that discarded piece of scaffolding in his hand, swinging down with a mighty fury.

George fell in one great lump to Winn's side.

And then, it was Jason alone staring down at her.

"Are you all right?" Jason asked, breathing hard.

"I think so," she replied, her whisper echoing off the walls of the church.

"Try to sit up," he said, kneeling before her, helping her. The world spun before it righted itself, but she was steady enough with his hand at her back, and another around her shoulder. Her eyes met his, and suddenly she couldn't breathe.

Because everything was there.

Every feeling she'd ever thought to avoid, she saw buried in his eyes. Of course, he kept a straight face, a stern countenance, as he gruffly helped her to her feet. He would give nothing away.

Except to those that knew how to look for it.

But then, *everyone* was there.

The main doors of the church, which had been flung open by Jason, were filled with Altons, Mr. Ellis, and a good deal of nuns.

"We put the fire out!" Gail Alton cried.

"It wasn't very much of a fire, just some chairs and things," Evangeline told them.

"Who the devil is this beast?" Mother Agnes asked sternly, her vulgarity gaining more than a few gasps and self-crosses from those holy present. George moaned on the floor.

"Miss Crane, what is this remarkable thing you have found?" Mr. Ellis elbowed his way in, the triptych still held delicately but securely in his hands.

"It's not fair . . . She's mine . . . She's always been mine," George whined deliriously.

"No she's not," Jason spat. And then, he took the triptych from Mr. Ellis's hands.

And looking into her eyes, handed it to Winn.

"She never belonged to anyone but herself."

As the Alton girls enveloped her with questions, as the nuns surrounded George in a black cage, as the world became a cacophony of emotion and explanation, Winn, the world still swimming slightly, sought the comfort of Jason's hand.

And did not find it.

For in the madness, he had allowed the crowd to swallow her up, and moved out the doors.

And slipped away.

Twenty-six

Wherein six months have passed,
and new adventures begin.

January 1823

THIRTY-ONE is an excellent age for a man to marry. An age at which adventure is abandoned and responsibility embraced. It is an age for proper dignity, neither too old nor too young, but more important, no longer thought of as young whatsoever. For Lord Jason Cummings in particular, it was the age at which he could finally and completely consider himself grown-up. And that adulthood was cause for the celebration tonight.

And it was a beautiful night for a party. The snow was just beginning to fall, lightly dancing to the ground. The first snowfall of the winter season, coming just after the New Year's dawn, as everyone returned to town from their sojourns at their country homesteads.

It had been over Christmas that Jason had finally proposed.

It seemed silly, really, to delay any longer. After all, they had spent every minute of the past months in each other's pockets. And Jane had told Jason if she had to stay in London and act as chaperone any longer, she was going to send Byrne

after him, with a gun and a special license, to be used at his
discretion. And so, while visiting at her home over Christmas,
Jason had gotten down on one knee, as was customary, and
ask for Miss Sarah Forrester's hand in marriage.

She gave it.

Naturally, her parents were ecstatic. Lady Forrester nearly
crying—now that she had the first of her three daughters practically settled (to a Duke, no less!), she could move her worry
onto the next. Lord Forrester gruffly took Jason's hand and
shook it, beaming, as he declared himself grateful that his
daughter had chosen a Historical Society man.

Jane was ecstatic, too—but her joy looked suspiciously
like relief. Her mind may have been tuned to Byrne's, who,
after six months in London, was chaffing himself raw to get
back to the little town of Reston and the Cottage in the Lake
District, and therefore shook Jason's hand vivaciously before
calling for their trunks to be packed . . . this of course, before
Jane told him they couldn't leave before the wedding.

"The north roads are likely unsurpassable right now," Jane
reasoned to her moping husband. "Might as well stay until
spring."

Byrne grumbled, and shot Jason a look of utter contempt.
As if snow in winter were his fault.

Indeed, most everyone was pleased for the happy couple.
Phillippa Worth, however, was livid. Oh, not at Jason and
Sarah and their joy, but because she had been denied the
chance to throw the engagement ball.

"But they were introduced at my garden party!" Phillippa
argued under her breath.

"Yes, but the engagement ball duties fall rightfully to the
bride's family. Would you deny Lady Forrester the pleasure of
planning her own daughter's ball?" Jane replied, hiding the roll
of her eyes by taking a sip of punch from the cut-glass cup.

Phillippa looked around the ballroom of the Forrester mansion, the dancing couples, the happy conversation. To any
other eye, it would have been a resplendent affair. However,

Phillippa could only grumble. "If I had been able to put my hand in, this would have been the affair of the Little Season. But instead we are stuck with off-white table linens and too many stuffy Historical Society members than one can reasonably keep track of."

"Jason is a member of the stuffy Historical Society," Jane reminded her friend.

"Which made it terribly difficult for me to find him a bride," Phillippa concluded.

"For *you* to find him a bride?" Jane nearly dropped her punch glass. "Are you rewriting history now?"

"I beg your pardon, but *you* are the one who asked *me* to throw a garden party, because *you* were incapable . . ."

At this moment, Jason decided it was prudent to step away from his sister and Phillippa, and get some air.

As he crossed the ballroom, Jason was congratulated by every person he passed, more than one trying to pull him into conversation. About their plans for the wedding, the procurement of St. Paul's Cathedral for the ceremony (of which Jason had to admit he knew nothing—he intended to simply be told where to go when and then show up). About his recent endowment of a search for a new professor of the history of art at Oxford—being as they were lacking a suitable candidate since George Bambridge had been discharged in disgrace. About the latest Historical Society gossip, involving one of their newest members and a book she was rumored to be writing.

That last one reminded him of his desperate need for air.

Somewhere in all this, Jason had lost track of his intended bride. He'd had her by his side most of the evening, but before he went to talk to Jane, Sarah was pulled away by her mother for some little emergency, likely involving centerpieces or cutlery. However, she should have been back by now. He scanned the crowd, relievedly finding her surrounded by a gaggle of young females talking and laughing and admiring his mother's emerald ring, which he'd placed on her finger no more than a fortnight ago.

A sense of calm washed over him as he caught her eye. That was why he had finally decided to ask her to marry him. That feeling, that sense of contentment. Sarah was everything the Duke of Rayne needed in a Duchess. She was lovely, well-bred, kind, and intelligent. As a bonus, she had a cunning sense of humor and was generally a pleasant person to be around. He wanted that in his life.

Her gaze lit with joy when she saw him from across the room. But she was caught in her group of girls and could do nothing but roll her eyes, indicating that her friends had her in their clutches.

Jason smiled at her. He pointed to the door to the terrace, waving his hand in front of his face, shorthand for *I'm hot, I need air.*

She waved her hand in front of hers. *Heavens, yes. Me, too.*

He motioned for her to come to him. *Well, come on, then.*

She held up five fingers. *I'll meet you in five minutes. Go.*

He nodded, holding up a comparable five fingers. *Five minutes.*

And then she turned back to her conversation, leaving Jason with nothing to do but slip through the terrace doors and out into the crisp winter air.

And directly into the outstretched hand of one Miss Winnifred Crane.

It was as if the world stopped, and time with it. She had been reaching for the door handle, turned away, looking behind her. She didn't hit his face this time, thankfully, her hand landing instead somewhere in the vicinity of his midsection.

A punch to the gut. And when he met her eyes, huge with shock, that accidental punch spread throughout his body, down his spine, rooting his feet to the ground even as it made his knees shake with the effort to keep his body upright.

"I'm sorry," she finally managed. "I . . . I didn't see you."

"It's all right," Jason said vaguely, unable to come up with anything more. He'd thought about this moment for the last six months, and suddenly he was robbed of speech.

Six months. That was the last time he had seen her. Clutching her triptych in the nave of the little convent church in Döbling. He'd handed her the triptych, handed her her freedom, and walked out of the church.

He did not look back. He'd relied on Mr. Ellis to lend him funds to put up at a hotel, then for passage home. While Winn had stayed with the Altons, where Totty joined her.

He hadn't seen her since.

Oh, he'd stayed in Vienna for the next few days, making certain that George Bambridge was made to pay for what charges were brought against him—including destruction of church property, when he set the altar and chairs on fire. However, those chairs proved to be nearly four hundred years old and therefore, quite precious.

It took all of George Bambridge's savings to pay for them.

That left him, unfortunately, with no money to buy off the proprietor of a trinket shop in Linz, from whom he stole a ring and a pistol and broke a vase. And as such George had to spend a few months in an unpleasant German prison.

However, destruction of church property and lifting a few trinkets abroad would not rank as much more than an amusing anecdote in England. Why Winnifred and Mrs. Tottendale did not have charges of assault or attempted murder filed against George, Jason did not to know for certain. He could have easily done it himself and was more than ready to, but Sir Geoffery Alton (whose own connections would have assisted mightily) told him that the ladies requested they do not. George was family, after all. He would not be forgiven, but nor would it go down in legal books that one member of a family filed charges against another. Instead, Jason was told, "women have better ways than men to exact vengeance."

And they already had. When Totty had regained consciousness in Linz, she immediately wrote a letter to Phillippa Worth of George's perfidy toward her, and Phillippa made certain that *that* information was known all over town, so when the time came for George to return to England, he had learned that if he did so, none would receive him. It was rumored he was in Ireland now, looking to teach at Trinity College. As if the Irish were any more forgiving than the English. George would have to go to America to find a school that would have him. Perhaps further.

And if Jason made damn certain—via hired men—that George Bambridge so much as never raised his voice to a woman again, well . . . who was to know?

But George Bambridge didn't warrant a thought anymore. Jason's brain could handle little more than comprehending that Winnifred Crane was there, standing in front of him. After six months.

Six months. She looked . . . she looked like Winn. His Winn. Oh, her hair was up and she was wearing a gown of fine silk, but she still looked like that small woman who had curled into a ball beneath the covers while he slept above. The Winn who had hunched over Herr Heider's collection of papers and paintings for days, thumbing through with white gloves on, hoping for some small trace of evidence that her hunch about the Adam and Eve painting was correct. The Winn who had laughed herself crying when they saw the bottle of Burgundy '93. The Winn who tugged at the heart-shaped locket around her neck whenever she was working something through her mind.

The heart-shaped locket, currently resting in the valley of her breasts, which had sparkled against her naked skin in the moonlight in Wurtzer's loft.

"Jason?" she said, drawing his attention back to her words.

"What did you say?" he asked dully.

"I asked how you are," she replied, her eyes never straying from his face.

"I'm fine. I'm . . . ah, I'm getting married." He indicated the party in the room beyond, the party that, in defiance of the stoppage of time, went on with light and laughter.

"I know," she replied. "Actually, I didn't know—I was invited by Lord Forrester to his daughter's engagement ball. They didn't mention the groom."

"Grooms are fairly incidental in these things, I'm told," Jason said, laughing weakly at his own pale joke.

What would she have done if she had known, he wanted to ask. Would she have come anyway? Defying any feelings that she might have for him, or acknowledging their lack?

"Congratulations," she said softly.

"Thank you," was the only response to be made.

They stood there, in the cold winter air, their breath visible in the light cast by the glow of the party beyond the glass doors. At some point, the door had closed, but Jason did not remember it. Nor did he remember taking the few steps away from the doors, to a more shadowed alcove, but they had. Maybe it was the wine, he thought briefly, robbing him of any other thought but the woman in front of him. But of course, it wasn't. It was foolish to hope that.

"I've been in France," Winn said suddenly.

"Have you?" Jason asked. "We've all been wondering. The Historical Society, that is."

"Yes, well." She blushed, looking to her toes for a moment, then to the side for anything for her attention to land on, skittish like the sparrow she was. "We stayed in Vienna, on the goodwill of the Altons—but when I received word that I had been awarded my inheritance, I didn't want to wait anymore to see the world."

"Did you?" he could not help but ask. "See the world, that is."

"Not all of it." She smiled. "Not even most of it. Yet. But I did see the Mediterranean. You were right. About the blue."

And suddenly Jason felt something in his heart drop. Foolish though it was, especially given what they were celebrating at this ball, but he'd held out hope in his traitorous heart that he would get to witness that moment. The moment her eyes fell on the blue of the Mediterranean Sea. He'd wanted to be there. And now . . . he never would be.

So, this is loss, Jason thought. Mourning moments you don't get to have, because they've passed you by.

"I've been here," Jason said as a void threatened to overcome the conversation. "In London."

Yes, he'd been here. And the moment he'd stepped back on English shores, his sister Jane was there to light into him for abandoning his responsibilities.

"What was so important that you simply had to go gallivanting around Europe for a few weeks?" Jane had said after she hugged him and smacked him upside the head in turns.

He'd wanted to tell her. He'd wanted to tell her that he was doing something important for someone. That he was helping a friend, and that in the process, he'd fallen madly in love with a woman who didn't want him. But she would never believe it.

Sir Geoffrey was as good as his word—he had made no mention to anyone of his presence in Vienna. (Mr. Ellis arrived some weeks later in England, and all it took was one visit to that good gentleman to have him keep his counsel.) And Jason knew that he was not mentioned in Totty's letter to Phillippa (as at the time, she was not able to confirm the identity of Winn's companion) . . . As far as the Ton knew, he'd dropped off Winn Crane in Dover and that was that. And since the last thing he'd said to Bones was "This little adventure may take longer than anticipated," when he didn't return in a goodly amount of time, all assumed that he'd boarded a boat for distant shores. Why fight the reputation he'd fostered for so long?

"I was there in Dover, and I thought it had been a while since I'd been to Paris." He'd shrugged nonchalantly. "Really, Jane, it was nothing more than a bit of fun—ow! Stop hitting me!"

"The next time you decide to leave the country, abandoning your sister and the lady you told me you intend to marry, *tell someone*!" Jane finished in a huff.

Luckily for him, Sarah was far more forgiving than his sister.

And if, while he begged for forgiveness from his sister and Sarah, he happened to make certain that a certain set of paintings were given back to their rightful owner, putting the full weight of his title to bear on his alma mater, who was to blink an eye? After all, he was simply doing what was right for the newest candidate to the Historical Society for Art and Architecture, a body that was headed by his hopefully soon-to-be father-in-law.

And if, he also made certain—through anonymous sources, of course—that those paintings went for a ridiculous sum at auction and then were donated by the new, nameless owner to Oxford, putting them full circle back where they were at home, who was there to know or care?

But Winn didn't reply to his inane statement that he'd been in London all this time. Instead, she met his eyes and asked the one question that no one in all the huge transition of his life had ever thought to ask—because they assumed they knew the answer.

"And are you happy?"

Was he happy? He'd thought so. Until three minutes ago.

But he couldn't reply to that, couldn't joke it away, nor answer with any seriousness—any reply would break the wall that needed to hold.

"You're shivering," he commented, his mind falling to anything other than her question.

"It's cold out here. And I do get cold easily."

"Right." Then, "I hear you are writing a book," Jason said suddenly, changing the subject.

She nodded.

"About your adventures in finding the letters, and the Adam and Eve painting."

She nodded again. "I wanted to fictionalize it, but my publishers said it was too good a story to not be told as true."

"Am I in it?" he asked tersely.

She regarded him quietly for a moment.

"Not if you don't want to be," she replied.

"Not if I don't want to be," he repeated, uncomprehending.

"No one knows you—that is, you never told anyone you were with me. And I understand . . . it would alter your life if you did. Your marriage to Miss Forrester, your standing in good society." She looked down at her toes again, her hand going to the locket at her neck, but she stopped herself.

"I would never do that to you," she said, straightening, looking him dead in the eye. "So, I can . . . write you out the story. Pretend I went on my journey alone. If you want."

He nodded, dully, comprehending her reasoning, if not agreeing with it.

"Well that's settled, then," she said, sighing and straightening her shoulders. "I should likely go," she said finally, with a smile too bright to be real. She dipped to a curtsy.

"I wish you every happiness, Your Grace." And she stepped neatly around him, quickly to the doors to the ballroom.

"Winn, wait—" he called out, but she had already slipped through, back into the real world.

And slipped past Sarah, on her way out to meet him.

"Oh, excuse me," Sarah said to Winn's retreating form. Then turning to Jason, met his with a look of surprised delight. "Was that Winnifred Crane?" she asked.

Jason nodded mutely—the only response he could muster.

"Where is she going? I so wanted to meet her. My father told me he wanted to invite her, but didn't think she'd attend, as she's been traveling through Europe—"

"You knew?" Jason interrupted suddenly. "You knew she would be here?"

"Yes," Sarah replied cautiously. Then, after a moment, "I did not realize you were acquainted with her, however."

"Only a little," Jason stuttered finally, remembering his lines. "Her father was one of my professors at school . . . and then when she wanted to get into the Historical Society, I was there and . . ."

"Oh, I remember now!" Sarah cried with a relieved smile. "You helped her get inside Somerset House and to her audience with my father. I hear she's writing a book, you know. All about her misadventures, trying to gain admittance to the Society." Sarah's eyes lit up like candles. "Do you think you'll be in it? You did play an instrumental part getting her through the door—"

"No!" Jason cried, crossing his arms over his chest and beginning to pace furiously. "That's just it! She's writing me out of it. How can . . . how can someone do that? Literally write someone out of their lives?"

If Jason had been paying closer attention, he would have seen all the joy, all the color, drain out of Sarah's face at his fevered, hurt words. But he was too much in his own head. Too much drawn into his own past with Winn, to properly see the woman with whom he intended to make a future. But he heard it, the painful realization in Sarah's voice, when she finally spoke.

"Jason . . . I, uh . . . how well do you know Miss Crane?"

"I told you, when I was a student . . ." he tried, but she shook her head.

"No, I think you know her better than that," Sarah replied astutely.

Jason held silent, his eyes finally coming to Sarah's pale face, her huge eyes. "Yes, I do," he whispered.

"I think I would like to sit down," Sarah breathed. Jason rushed immediately to her side, took her arm, and guided her to a nearby stone bench, further out into the dark. What she had to ask—and what Jason had to say—well, it would be difficult to say in the light.

"When?" she asked, once she was settled in her seat.

"When?" he replied, uncomprehending.

"When did you come to know Miss Crane. Was it at school?"

"After," he replied.

"Before we met?" she asked, hope in her words. Hope he would have to crush.

"No . . . this summer, when I went to the Continent for a few weeks."

"Oh," was the small distressed reply.

"Sarah, I am going to marry you. Don't worry. And

we'll . . . we'll be happy," Jason said in a rush. "What she and I have . . . *had*—it was a matter of circumstance. It's over between us."

"No, it's not," Sarah replied, her eyes directed outward, looking back at the party—their engagement party—beyond the glass doors. "I have made a study of you, these past months. You have been my favorite subject. And you have been many things with me—jovial, joking, pleased, content . . . but never happy. Not . . . not truly. Nor have I ever seen you as stirred up as you are after a mere few minutes in the presence of Miss Crane."

He shook his head. "That doesn't mean you and I won't—"

"Jason, look at me." He did, his frightened gaze finding her as controlled and clear-eyed as befit her upbringing. "If you are going to break my heart, do it now. Not three months from now, after we've made vows. Not even tomorrow. Do it now. Have the strength to say what you want. And to go after it."

Jason rose abruptly, unable to keep still. But he didn't walk away, he didn't pace. He merely looked out at the party beyond the doors. All of those laughing, happy, good people. And the only one he wanted to see . . . she wasn't there anymore.

He turned, looked down into the face of his fiancée. The strength she had was beginning to wear thin, the shine in her eyes threatening to spill down her cheeks, a small shiver her only concession to the cold. She was so good. So very good, that he said the only thing he could to her.

"I'm sorry," he whispered.

And that was it. The finality of breaking a woman's heart echoed across the night air, and there was nothing else that needed a voice.

Sarah nodded, her breath leaving her body, bowing her posture down with acceptance. Seconds ticked between them before Sarah had enough composure to smile at Jason with forgiveness.

"What time is it?" Jason asked, coming out of his breath-held reverie.

"About midnight," Sarah answered matter-of-factly. "Any minute now, my father is going to make his toast."

"I should go speak with him, then," Jason said, setting his jaw.

"No." Sarah put her small hand on his arm, stilling him before he could move. "Let me do it. I'll stop the formal toasting and the like. But let them have their party. For now."

"What will you tell them?" he asked.

"That you went home with a headache," she replied. "I'll tell them the truth tomorrow."

He reached down, took her hand, kissed it. Reverently, and for the last time.

"You should go," she whispered, her face painted by a sad smile.

Jason turned to leave, to make his exit discreetly through the garden, but he stopped himself. "Sarah," he said, his heart in his voice, "please believe, I know I would have been terribly happy with you. If only . . ."

"If only," she agreed.

If only.

The words echoed through his brain as he stalked through Grosvenor, across Berkeley Square, the snow coming down faster now, harder. But he didn't see it. Couldn't see beyond his own thoughts.

If only.

How was it that with something so simple as a minute's worth of conversation, Winn Crane managed to wreak havoc on his life?

If only she hadn't shown up tonight.

If only he hadn't followed her onto that ship in Dover.

If only he hadn't run into her in the courtyard of Somerset House. A mere second earlier or later and his life would be different, he would be contented with Sarah Forrester as his bride, he would have gone through the motions of this sum-

mer without any insane schemes to foster their way across the
greater part of Germany, he would have never had his heart
full to bursting and then laid low by a woman of *ambition*.

Yes, his life would have been different. But would it have
been better?

That thought made him stop in his tracks, the darkened
night enveloping him in its cold embrace. He looked up to the
heavens, let the white flakes fall down around him, turning to
nothing as they hit his fevered cheeks.

No, his life would not have been better. It would have been
easier, true . . . but then again, Jason suspected he'd always
had it rather too easy.

Because if he had never met Winn Crane . . . he would not
have known what it was to truly love someone. That three-
parts love: the caretaking of parental love combined with the
respect of friendship combined with the passion of lust, mix-
ing together to make something . . . more. It was there for
him. And he knew, in his gut, that it was there for Winn, too.

So the idea that she could *deny* not only what she felt but
also that they had even spent those weeks together—the most
arduous, terrible, adventurous, very best weeks of his life—
that spurred his blood more than anything, and had him kicking the cobblestones in anger as he stalked down the street.

What had she said? That she would not include him in the
pages of her story, if he didn't want to be. Why on earth would
she think he didn't want to be? Just because he hadn't wished
to go on the voyage in the first place? He'd continued it, hadn't
he? Because perhaps he'd simply tagged along, never saying
that he wanted to be included on her adventure?

Jason stopped moving. Stopped breathing. Just stood under the snow and stars, his entire body held with one single
thought.

Oh holy shit.

He'd never said he wanted to be in her life. She put him
off so deftly, on the road after their night in Wurtzer's loft,
telling him that she didn't wish to trap him or be trapped her-

self, that it was simply an experience. And so he let her go, let her find her path. But he'd never told her he wished for that entrapment.

They both simply assumed that their paths would veer. That the life of a Duke in England would never cross with the life of someone who wished to see the world. But sometimes, paths have to be forced together. He didn't know how, but he knew it would be done. However, it would not be easy. The proverbs were wrong: Love would not be patient. Nor kind.

It was going to be hard work.

But for once in his life, Jason was eager to tackle it.

Where was he, he thought blindly, looking around. He had managed, in his haze of fury and quiet thought, to walk east across the shops of Oxford and Bond Street, ending up near Russell Square. He was only a few blocks from Mrs. Tottendale's residence in Bloomsbury Street. He knew this because he had, when he first came back to London, found Totty's direction, and had his driver rumble past once or twice, in the masochistic hope that the little house would be open.

On his last pass, some months ago, he had left the little wooden doll on the doorstep.

His feet must have followed the object of his thoughts, his feet carrying him to where he knew she would be.

Now he moved those feet with purpose, his direction known, his objective clear.

Jason had no idea what he would say, or what he would do.

He knew only that he had to see her.

Winn arrived at Totty's house nearly an hour after she left the celebration of Sarah Forrester's engagement to the Duke of Rayne. Oh, she had made it out the door of Lord Forrester's house quick enough, that was true. But Totty's carriage driver, usually adequately nimble, was stalled in his progress by the madness of St. James's traffic, combined with the new falling snow, making everyone on the road more cautious. Winn couldn't blame them—she could only wish she herself had shown more such caution.

The carriage ride home itself was a torture chamber—she had no company, as Totty had stayed home, and therefore had only herself and her thoughts. By the time she walked through Totty's door, she was emotionally, physically, completely exhausted. She barely acknowledged Leighton as he took her cloak, barely registered more than the single, all-consuming thought that had quieted to a low hum in her mind.

Jason was getting married. Jason belonged to someone else.

As Leighton moved away, Winn leaned her back against the front door, breathing deeply. What a silly way to feel about the situation. It was not as if Jason had ever belonged to her in the first place—therefore, it was only natural to assume that someday, he would belong to someone else.

But never in her heart's mind did she imagine that she would be a witness to it!

She put her hands over her tired eyes, rubbed deep. She'd always thought the news would come to her after the fact—months, perhaps even years. Someone would visit her in the little space she had rented in Paris, or they would write a letter with all the London gossip and mention that the Duke of Rayne had just had another baby with his wife. And she would take the news with a little sadness, but ultimately, her grieving at the fait accompli would be brief, and in private.

"There you go again!" she whispered to herself. "You cannot grieve what you have no claim to."

"What's that, dear?" Totty called out as she came down the steps, glass of sherry in hand.

"Nothing, Totty," Winn said, taking her hands off her eyes and looking up with what she hoped was an expressionless face.

"How was the party?" Totty asked.

"Fine," Winn replied as nonchalantly as she could manage.

"Did you see Phillippa Worth? I hope you mentioned to her

how sorry I was to not attend, but these headaches—they are becoming less frequent but still overly annoying." Totty took an easy sip of her self-medication. "Sherry is really the only thing that helps."

"No, I'm sorry," Winn murmured. "I hadn't the opportunity." She'd arrived late. And when she had discovered who the groom was, she found herself requiring air and stepped out onto the terrace, and . . .

"Ah well." Totty shrugged. "When Phillippa wrote me about the party, I had the impression she would be the one to throw it, so at least I didn't miss one of her events."

Winn, who had been fixing her eyes at an innocuous point on the stairs, suddenly shifted her stare to Totty.

"When *Phillippa* wrote you about the party?" she asked.

Totty, for all her blithe abilities at social manipulation, looked like a child caught at mischief, turning red and averting her gaze.

"You knew!" Winn accused, coming off the door, taking the few steps to the base of the stairs.

"Knew what, dear?" Totty tried, but failed, to sound innocent.

"I hadn't wanted to leave France—who would want to leave France for England in the winter?" Winn exclaimed. "But then Lord Forrester's letter came, inviting me to his daughter's engagement ball, and since you said you wanted to go to London for a few days after the New Year, take care of some business, you *claimed*—"

"And we have taken care of some business," Totty replied defensively. "We had to meet with your publisher, show him your first two chapters, I had to instruct Leighton on the proper way to pack up things I would like to have, because if he did it himself—"

"Totty." Winn sighed. "You knew about Jason."

"Well, of course I did," she admitted guilelessly.

"You did. And you told me I should attend the party anyway. That I should 'renew my personal contact' with the Historical Society."

"Well, you did disprove that one of their most valuable paintings was created by whom they thought, they had every right to be mad with you, and yet they accept you as a candidate. That kind of goodwill has to be acknowledged. Besides"— Totty advanced down the steps slowly, purposefully—"what does it matter that the Duke of Rayne happened to be Miss Forrester's fiancée?"

What does it matter, indeed. She had never told Totty the full extent of her involvement with Jason. She had said only that Jason had, through chance and circumstance, become her traveling companion. Nothing more. She assumed the older, wiser woman assumed certain things, but she knew better than to try and talk about it with Winn.

And Jason had never told anyone of it, either.

Winn had the life she had chosen, that she had fought for. She should be happy. *Was* happy.

Besides, that involvement was six months ago. It hadn't been mentioned since. How did Totty know . . . ?

"Did you see him?" Totty asked as Winn had lapsed into silence.

Winn nodded mutely.

"Well?" Totty prompted.

Winn looked up at her friend then, her face resolute, strong. Betraying nothing.

"He's going to be very happy. Miss Forrester is all things lovely. There was no need to trick me into going."

Sadness crept into Totty expression even as she nodded resolutely. "It's better this way, don't you think? Now . . . now you'll never have to wonder."

"Wonder about what?" Winn replied, shaking her head. "Jason and I . . . we would have made each other miserable. I have the life I want, and it doesn't include another person. I have work to occupy my thoughts and the entire world to keep me company. I'm going to have another adventure. And then another one, and another. So don't you dare feel sorry for me."

Winn was not entirely certain Totty believed her bravado—

Winn knew she did not believe it herself. But whatever Totty's reaction would have been—be it to embrace her young friend or tweak her nose or pour her some sherry—it was not to be revealed. Because at that moment, all conversation was cut short by a loud rapping from outside. And a voice.

"Winn! Winnifred Crane, you come out here right now!" Jason's commanding voice resonated through the hard oak of Totty's front door.

Winn's head whipped to the door, but every other part of her froze, a bird caught in the moment before flight.

"He should know better than to call you that," Totty said sardonically—but her attention, too, was breathlessly caught by what lay beyond the door.

"He does," Winn murmured.

"I know you're home," Jason called out. "Totty's carriage driver told me he just dropped you off. Winn, open the door, please."

Another long pause, as Winn was unable to move, unable to give any answer.

"If you are not going to see me . . . then . . . then listen to me," Jason's voice commanded.

"What do I do?" she breathed, only to receive a wide-eyed blinking from Totty.

"Listen to him," Totty replied.

"You are an absolute idiot," Jason said to the door, his breath coming in great gulps from walking briskly through the streets, even at times breaking into a run—and from the unexpected task of yelling through a door. But it was glorious. His blood running through his body, certain for the first time in six months of his actions.

Except . . . he still was entirely uncertain of what he was to say.

And so . . . he decided, right before his fist hit the door, to simply say everything.

"That's right, I called you an idiot. For all your ability to analyze paintings, and write treatises about your thoughts, and convince innkeepers to let us have a cut of the profits to put on a show, you are an absolute idiot." Jason paced, swiveling back and forth on Totty's small stoop. "You're an idiot for thinking you could write someone out of your story. That you could write me out of your memory. I'm always going to be there, whether you admit it or not. And you are always going to think of your time in Nuremberg and Vienna, and it is entangled with mine. Those are my cities, their memory belongs to me.

"But the brilliant thing is, I'm an absolute idiot, too—in thinking I could come back to England and forget you. You and I made the same mistake, thinking we could put each other in the past. I thought time would put you there, but then I saw you tonight . . . and you are not in my past. And I know I am not in yours. Do you want to know how I know?" Jason smirked. "Because you made one mistake. You slipped up, Winn. You said you would not include me in your book, *if I didn't want to be*. Now, you said it was because it would wreak havoc on my life if you did, but you never mentioned your life. It would cause absolute madness in your life, destroy your reputation. But if I had said I wanted to be included, you would do it. You would have let the madness come. Because you want me there.

"Yes, you do want me in your life. All your protestations of an independent nature are for naught. But what's more, you *need* me in your life. You need someone who knows just how seriously you take your work. You need someone who will remind you to come to bed, and carry you there when you fall asleep over your papers. You need someone to think you're beautiful when you have pencils sticking out of your hair. You need someone who will travel with you to the ends of the earth, but also give you a place to call home. You need someone to tease you and show you how to give it back, because you have about thirty years of catching up to do in that department."

In the periphery of his vision, Jason could see lights being lit in all the little houses along Bloomsbury Street, the curiosity of the neighbors winning over their desire to sleep. Everyone watching the Duke of Rayne declare his heart to the door of Mrs. Tottendale's house. The snow fell harder now, Jason's breath coming out white, a slight shiver threatening to overcome him. But his body was too full of everything—of hope, fear, wine, dread, exhilaration—to pay it much mind.

"And . . . and I need you. I need you to make my life . . . unpredictable. It's remarkably predictable being a Duke. I need you to remind me of my responsibilities, but once that's done, be willing to follow my lead into mischief. Or I'll follow yours. I need your passion. I needed to see the look on your face when you saw the Mediterranean, and I missed it. I wanted it so badly. And I need you to smile at me at least once a day. When you smile you look like you know everything in the world, do you realize that?"

Jason came to a standstill, facing the door head on. He opened his arms wide, everything inside of him wholly exposed and vulnerable.

"So, I'm calling your bluff, Winn. I want to be included in your story. I want to be in your life. And the madness that will come with it," Jason said. "I am here, and if you couldn't tell, I love you. All three parts of it. I know you're afraid. But if you feel the same . . . hell, if you feel a fraction of what I do, then . . . then all you have to do is open the door and let me in. Please, Winn. Just . . . just open the door."

Jason grew silent, his speech made, and now . . . now, all he had to do was wait for the answer.

On the other side of the door, Winn had not moved. Had not even dared to draw breath. Every word, every syllable Jason uttered had pierced her skin like an arrow. And now she stood there, bleeding, somehow lost in Totty's small foyer, her hand gripping the pedestal of the staircase to keep her from falling.

The voice from the outside had stopped, but she could tell he hadn't moved from his position. He was waiting for an answer.

"I don't know what do," she breathed. Finally moving some small part of her body, she reached her hand out and grabbed on to Totty's, holding on with all of her might. Totty squeezed back.

"What do you wish to do?" she asked gently.

"I . . . I worked so hard. To gain my independence. And I *just* received it. It is all I ever wanted."

"Do you still want it?" Totty questioned.

"Yes!" Winn cried, the emotions she had bottled up ever since walking through the door of Lord Forrester's earlier that evening finally spilling over her cheeks. "But . . . I *missed* him. More than I thought possible."

And she had. She had missed him when she found the little apartment she rented in Paris. She wanted to turn to him and exclaim how it was barely the size of Wurtzer's loft, but it would be home. When she saw a painting of Adam and Eve in the Louvre, she wanted to ask him if he thought it was better or worse than the one by Sister Maria that had carried them across the Continent. And that moment, when she saw the Mediterranean for the first time . . .

"He is right about one thing." Totty shook her head. "You are an idiot."

Winn looked to her then, confused.

"Independence does not mean being alone. Independence means you have the right to make your own choices." Totty smiled. "And you seem to have a choice before you."

Winn breathed in, for the first time in minutes. Her gaze betraying her as it found its way back to the door. *All you have to do is open the door* . . . he had said. *If you feel a fraction of what I do* . . .

"What would you do?" Winn asked finally, her resolve crumbling.

"It's not my decision to make." Totty shrugged. "But I

would ask . . . do you love him?" Totty let go of Winn's hand, patting it, and turning up the steps. "Answer that, and the rest will come easily."

Seconds ticked by on the freezing stoop of Totty's little house on Bloomsbury Street. Jason waited still, out of arguments, the cold forcing him to flip the collar of his evening coat up, forcing his hands into his pockets. But his eyes never strayed from the door.

Minutes. Minutes had passed, Jason waiting breathlessly. Minutes, and the door had not opened. And as more time passed, a feeling fell through him, down past the pit of his stomach, past his knees and the soles of his feet, bleeding out onto quiet, rapt Bloomsbury Street.

She wasn't coming.

Jason had no illusions that she hadn't heard him. The entire street had.

So, this was the end of it all, he thought. His soul laid bare to a wooden door, only to receive no answer. He tried to laugh, but his body would not allow it. Could not move, frozen, numb. In fact, the only part of him that could move was his feet. And so, he looked to his boots, let them turn away and take the first step down to the street.

That was the moment he heard it.

The tumbling of a lock. The creak of a hinge. And a wedge of light from behind him fell onto his path.

Because that was the moment that, in the quiet of a winter night, on a little street in the middle of London, a breath was taken, and a choice was made.

Winn opened the door.

And let him inside.

Dear Reader,

Writing historical fiction is a balancing act. One always wants to be as true to life as possible while respecting that certain things cannot be altered. I couldn't have a story where Buckingham Palace was on the moon, for instance (well, I could, but that's a whole other genre). Therefore, what one ends up with is an amalgam of historical fact and, when research fails to yield what the story needs, plausible fiction.

The Society of Historical Art and Architecture of the Known World is my fictitious version of one of England's learned societies, such as the Royal Society, founded 1660 (which focuses on the sciences) and the Society of Antiquaries of London, founded 1717 (which focuses on art and artifacts). Both societies were housed in the early nineteenth century at Somerset House, London, so I decided the Historical Society should have its rooms there as well. Both the Royal and the Society of Antiquaries exist today, although they are now housed at Carlton House Terrace, London, and Burlington House, Piccadilly, respectively.

Like both the Royal and the Society of Antiquaries, the Historical Society's fellows had to be elected by existing members to join. However, my fictitious Historical Society outpaced its factual cousins in one respect: The London Society of Antiquaries did not allow for the admittance of women as members until 1921, and the Royal Society did not admit women until 1945.

Albrecht Dürer (1471–1528) is considered one of the preeminent masters of the Northern Renaissance. His paintings, engravings, printworks and woodcuttings grace the walls of museums worldwide, including the Louvre. In his early twenties, Dürer travelled to Basel, Switzerland, to study woodcutting and perfect his technique. While he travelled extensively across Europe in his life—to Italy, where he did some of the first watercolor landscapes in art history, and to Brussels, where he painted the portrait of King Christian II—he lived most of his life in Nuremberg.

Albrecht Dürer has always been a popular artist, but in the early nineteenth century, his popularity was reaching new heights. In 1828, the city of Nuremberg held a Dürer Jubilee on the three-hundreth anniversary of his death. Obtaining a painting ascribed to Dürer would have been a coup for an organization such as the Historical Society.

To my knowledge, there is no correspondence in existence between Dürer and a nun named Maria F. She, and her Adam and Eve painting, are of my own invention.

Albrecht Dürer's house in Nuremberg still stands. Today it is a museum and a testament to his life's work, and the life of a German Renaissance artist. It was purchased by the city of Nuremberg in 1825 (some sources site the date of purchase as 1828). Previous to that, it was privately owned and had fallen into disrepair. In Follow My Lead, Herr Heider, a Dürer enthusiast, has purchased the house and is attempting to rehabilitate it. Herr and Frau Heider are of my own invention, as is Herr Heider's collection of Dürer letters and papers.

While these histories, and several others (including the history of Oxford University, the topography of southern Germany, and the presence of the Franciscan Order of the Poor Clares in Austria) have influenced and helped shape the story of Miss Winnifred Crane and the Duke of Rayne's mad journey across Europe, in the end, it really is Winn and Jason's story. And I certainly hope you enjoyed reading about this mismatched pair as much as I did writing about them.

Sincerely,
Kate Noble

**Keep reading for a preview of the
next historical romance from Kate Noble**

IF I FALL

Coming soon from Berkley Sensation!

"BLOODY hell," Whigby breathed as their rented hack pulled up to the address that had been written on Lady Forrester's note. "Are you sure this is it?"

The town house on Upper Grosvenor Street was much the same as the others that surrounded it—pristine white, three stories, with columns that lined the doorway and supported the upper level balconies. Wrought iron fencing lined the property along the more public sidewalk, protecting the pansies and tulips that sprung up in wide Grecian urns that sat as centurions guarding the steps up to the heavy front door.

The main difference between this town house and the others that surrounded it was the half dozen gentlemen in their best black coats that bickered with the butler for entrance.

"It's number sixteen," Jack said, his eyes flicking automatically to the letter in his hand, checking once again.

"Maybe it was written ill?" Whigby asked, but Jack shook his head. No, there was no mistake, this was the house.

"Maybe someone died and they're paying respects!" Whigby cried.

Jack shot his friend a look.

"Of course, that would be terrible," Whigby was quick to amend.

"Well, I suppose we best find out what's going on," Jackson said, opening the door to the hack and letting himself down, while the coachman disembarked from his seat and helped unload Jackson's trunk. Whigby alighted as well.

"Do you want me come with you?" Whigby asked. "You know . . . to pay my respects?"

"No one has died, Mr. Whigby," Jackson assured his friend (at least, he hoped no one had died). "Go on to your uncle's. I'll be fine."

"You have my direction if you need it." Whigby extended his hand, and Jack shook it.

Then Whigby, in a show of emotion not uncommon to that larger fellow, pulled Jack into a fairly rib-crushing hug. "I'm so sorry for your loss."

"Whigby . . ." Jack wheezed. "It's not a funeral . . . And you're crushing me."

"That's right!" Whigby replied, releasing Jack so quickly that the air rushed back into his lungs. "Keep hope!"

And then, Whigby turned to reenter the hack to convey him to his uncle's, a few spare blocks away. But perhaps he should not have been so free with his condolences, because the hack had already started to rumble down the block, with Whigby's trunk still up on the back.

"Oy!" Whigby yelled after the coachman, taking to a run. "Wait for me!"

Jack, shaking his head, turned to front door of number sixteen. And the men there that blocked his path.

They were a variety of ages, from just out of university to those with white hair. But all the men wore their money: Jackson saw at least three gold cravat stick pins and seven watch fobs. They eyed his rumpled Naval uniform with severe distaste.

Jackson narrowed his eyes and stepped into the gauntlet.

"They come fresh off the boats now?" one man murmured to a friend. "I'm amazed they get the gossip sheets out at sea."

"What's amazing is that he thinks he stands a chance," his friend replied, sniggering.

Jackson kept his eyes straight ahead, ignoring these men. Their talk made no sense to him, but their manners did. They didn't think much of him. Well, the feeling was mutual.

Jackson reached the butler, who stood guard at the door with a hulking figure of a footman. Normally, the door would be opened with the butler standing inside, but here, they had gone so far as to stand outside the door, keeping it barred.

"I'm sorry, sir, but the Forresters are not receiving today," the supercilious man said, his nose in the air.

"Then why is everyone else here?" Jackson asked before he could think better of it.

He was met by chuckles from the peanut gallery behind him.

"We are staking our place in line!" one of the younger ones cried.

"Making sure people see us here," one of the others drawled.

"Besides, they have to come home sometime," another— the sniggering one—said, clamping his hand on Jack's shoulder, trying to pull him back.

One look from Jack had that man removing his hand forthwith.

"I have an invitation," Jack said, directing himself only to the butler.

But that sentence elicited raucous laughter from the men behind him.

"Of course he does!"

"And I've a recommendation from Prinny himself!"

"We all do!"

Jackson reached into his pocket and produced the letter from Lady Forrester—as he did, the men behind him grew uncommonly quiet.

The butler perused the letter with an unseemly amount of leisure. (Jack felt certain that the old servant took no small amount of pleasure in the power he wielded.) Then, with a curt nod to the burly footman beside him, he handed the missive back.

"If you'll follow me, sir," the butler said as the door behind him opened with silent efficiency.

Cries of outrage came from the assembly.

"What?"

"You can't mean to admit him! I'm a viscount!"

"I'm with him! We came together!"

But of course, these were ignored, and shortly silenced by one flex of the footman's muscles, as he took up the central position, and Jackson, hauling his own trunk, followed the butler inside.

"Wait here," the butler intoned, leaving him to go seek out his mistress, Jackson assumed.

Jackson removed his tricorn, shaking out his sandy hair into something resembling neatness. He pulled at his cuffs, straightened his coat, like the nervous schoolboy he used to be.

Alone in the foyer of the Forresters' London home, he was immediately struck by a sense of déjà vu. He had never been in this house before, but he had been in this position before, long ago.

There is little more frightening to a thirteen-year-old boy than being removed from all you know, he thought, letting himself drift into memory. Even the horrific, tantalizing prospect of thirteen-year-old girls compares little to no longer being in the daily presence of your parents, the paths you know to the village where everyone knows you. Even when one begs their father to let him go to sea, those faces fading away makes a thirteen-year-old boy feel like nothing so much as a thirteen-year-old man, but without any means by which to handle the transition.

Luckily, Jack's father knew something of being young and alone, and wrote a friend for help.

❧

He tugged nervously his cuffs. They were already beginning to come up short, even though his mother had sewn his Naval College uniform not three months ago. He was already a tall boy, as a first year cadet towering over most of the second years and even some of the thirds . . . and in a career where he was constantly told to stand up straight, he could do little to hide it.

When Jack crossed the entrance of Crawley Manor, the Forresters' country residence not five miles from Portsmouth, he had been expecting an inspection. Therefore, for the whole week leading up to this moment, he had been very careful with him uniform. His white pantaloons were spotless—a feat in and of itself for any thirteen-year-old boy, let alone one who had grown so increasingly nervous over the course of the week that he had spilled his food not once but twice at mealtimes. But somehow he had managed to keep everything from the top of his hat to the heel of his shoes in good order. Which was of the utmost importance, as he was to meet his possible future patron today.

Jack did not know what a future patron might want to know of him. He only knew that when he finally convinced his parents to allow him to attend the Royal Naval College, Jackson's father had written to his old school friend Lord Forrester and asked him to look in on the boy every once in a while, as he was unable to do so in Lincolnshire. As Jackson's father was always writing to great men asking for patronage for anyone of his and Mrs. Fletcher's charitable causes (for Mr. Fletcher refused to yield to expectation of being a retiring country vicar, instead choosing to involve himself vigorously in the cause of war orphans and widows), Jack thought nothing of it.

He'd expected, at most, a letter from Lord Forrester. Instead, he had received an invitation.

As he was admitted to the hall, he tried very hard not to be awed by the grandeur of the house. But how could he not be? Marble and oak lined the massive room, making even the smallest sound, from his footsteps to a gasp he hadn't managed to contain, echo across the space. When the butler went to fetch his master, Jackson couldn't help but poke his head around the corner and peer into an even larger room! Why this one room must have been bigger than his entire house! After a few moments, Jack decided it must be the sitting room for receiving callers. And there were plenty of places to sit, he thought, making sure to keep his mouth from hanging open in a gape. The dozens of sofas and chairs and things looked so fine they would surely break if he touched them. He briefly glanced at the ceiling, two stories above. How did the ceiling stay up in so massive a space? Churches have flying buttresses and the like, reinforced pylons, but this place just seemed to soar high above.

He wondered for the umpteenth time that week just what on earth was expected of him. Surely, people that lived in a house this intimidating would look down at him as nothing more than a . . . charitable annoyance.

He had edged his foot into the sitting room, when he heard it. It sounded like a fork striking a glass, but somehow . . . human. It must have been the echo, he thought, but it almost sounded like a giggle. He immediately straightened to attention. But when no one emerged, his curiosity won out again, and his gaze returned to the sitting room. Where, if he was not mistaken, one of the heavy velvet drapes was twitching.

Unsure if his mind was playing tricks on him, Jackson thought it best to ignore the twitching curtain, and instead remain at attention. Surely, that's what a man like Lord Forrester would want out of a cadet he sponsored. Someone who obeyed the rules, and stayed where he was told, and . . .

And there was that giggle again!

Finally, he couldn't help it any longer. Perhaps some ruffian had snuck in and was hiding until he could thieve everything out of this room in the dark of night. Which Jack could not allow.

And so, he went over to the window, and drew back the curtain dramatically, his hand going automatically to his side, where his sword rested . . . which of course was not there, as he had no sword.

Instead of a thief however, Jack found two girls. One far littler than the other.

"Hide-and-seek!" cried the littlest, who could not have been more than three, with dimples and curly blonde hair that bounced when she shrieked with laughter.

"Not yet, Mandy!" the elder girl said in a hushed voice. She looked about nine or ten, and whereas her hair matched the youngster's in shade, it was straight and plaited down her back. She looked up at Jack with the biggest green eyes, twinkling with mischief. "We're hiding, don't tell," she whispered to Jack.

"Hiding from what?" he asked.

"Will you be quiet?" came a hushed whisper from the other side of the room—a brown, curly head popped up, freckles gone mad upon her nose and cheeks. "Papa will find us without any trouble when he hears you talking. And Mandy, you're supposed to hide somewhere by yourself!"

But little Mandy just shook her head and inched closer to her sister.

"She couldn't find any place to hide," the elder girl whispered back.

"Of course she can, Sarah. You just baby her. Mandy, you're small enough to fit in the cabinet, go over there."

But Mandy simply shook her head and burrowed farther.

"Wait, are you playing some sort of game?" Jackson asked, utterly bewildered.

The eldest—Sarah—blinked back in surprise. "Of course we are. Haven't you ever played hide-and-seek?"

"Well, I . . ." Before Jack could appropriately answer that question, which would have been embarrassingly in the negative (his mother, while a kind woman, did not approve of games where nothing was learned or made useful), footsteps were heard in the hallway beyond.

All three girls went rigid with excitement and popped back into their hiding places.

Just then, a barrel of a man came thudding through the hall, his posture that of an ogre about to attack.

"*I know you're in here!*" *he cried, a stern expression on his brow. When he saw Jack however, his expression cleared and he straightened.*

"*Oh! You must be Dickey's boy!*" *he cried, his face no longer that of an ogre, but an easy smile on his face. "Forrester. Very pleased to have you in my home.*"

"*Er . . . yes, sir,*" *Jackson said—straightening to attention and bowing at the same time, which ended up as merely awkward. "My father is Richard Fletcher. I am Jackson Fletcher, and . . . they told me to wait in the hall, but I—*"

"*Happy to have you! How is the Naval College treating you?*"

"*Good,*" *Jack said, unable to keep his voice from breaking embarrassingly. And then, when Lord Forrester made no reply . . . Jack couldn't keep himself from rambling. "It's different than I expected: I wanted to go to sea first, but my father didn't want me on the ocean with no training and two wars going on—and it seems we would not have been able to obtain a King's Letter in any case. But my years at the college count toward my required six as a midshipman, so it's not lost time . . .*"

But Jack saw that Lord Forrester's attention had wandered from himself to just over his shoulder.

And the curtain that twitched ever so slightly there.

And suddenly, Jack found himself playing the game too.

"*Ah, Lord Forrester,*" *he said, inching himself ever so slightly to block the view of the curtain. "I am so terribly honored that you have invited me to dine. Indeed, I did not expect such kindness . . .*"

"*You didn't?*" *Lord Forrester asked, his surprised attention back to Jack. "Nonsense, my boy. Your father was one of my good friends at school. And how is the good reverend? We were all shocked that he went into the Church instead of the law . . . all the way up in Lincolnshire, of all places! He would have made an excellent politician."*

"Yes, well, my father always says he would much rather be doing than telling everyone else what to do," Jackson quipped, and turned red in the face before he could stop himself. After all, Lord Forrester sat in Parliament! He was one of the tellers, not the doers! He had just insulted his possible future patron!

Luckily, Lord Forrester just leaned his head back and gave a hearty laugh.

"That sounds like old Dickey. And it goes without saying that I would see his son properly fed for at least one Sunday dinner." Lord Forrester nonchalantly sidestepped Jackson, so he was not standing next to the curtain. "And I think you'll be pleased with the menu. We will be serving that rarest of all delicacies . . ." He reached his hand back behind the curtain. "Little Girl!"

Lord Forrester whipped the curtain back, revealing Sarah and Mandy, who began to shriek and run. While Sarah ran with direction and aplomb, little Mandy could do barely more than run on short legs in a circle.

Lord Forrester trotted after her, making sure to not catch her in good time. Because as she shrieked, she giggled, and Lord Forrester kept saying, "I'm going to get you and serve you up!" and she simply shrieked more. Then Mandy ran behind the couch, and the other brown-haired girl had to get up and run, lest she be discovered, too. Soon the entire room was filled with running girls, chasing fathers, and hysterical laughter.

No, he had not been expecting this at all.

Jack shook his head ruefully. Had he ever been that young and frightened? Waiting in a hall and surprised to learn that young ladies of rank played hide-and-seek with their fathers.

Although the pit that existed in his stomach when he had been thirteen and waiting in a Forrester foyer was uncannily similar to the one that rested there now.

He scuffed his toe on the marbled floor, the squeaky sound echoing off the marble tiles. Given the clamor of well-dressed gentlemen—"holding their place in line"—that existed just outside the front door, it was alarmingly quiet in the Forresters' town house, with only the tick of a grandfather clock to keep him company. He did not expect a reception by any means. He hadn't written a reply to Lady Forrester's letter, as they had docked in London before any such note would have arrived. But as that damned grandfather clock ticked on, he did begin to wonder if the supercilious butler had forgotten him.

"Perhaps he stuck his nose too high in the air and it got caught on a cobweb," Jack mumbled aloud, mollified by the echo that followed.

Jack was just about to try one or the other of the heavy doors that stood on opposite sides of the main hall, when the thudding of adolescent footsteps broke the silence and a gasp floated down from the top of the stairs.

"Jack!"

And before he could formulate a thought, Jackson found himself practically tackled by the young lady as she ran down the stairs and threw herself into his arms.

"Sarah?" he asked, disbelieving. The last time he had seen Sarah Forrester, she had been twelve, and just beginning to gain in height and womanly virtues. But this young lady that wrapped her arms—tightly—around his waist . . .

"La! Do be serious, Jackson! It's me! Amanda!"

"*Amanda?*" he couldn't help but cry. Jackson immediately pulled away, and stared down into her face. "But Amanda's the youngest!"

She laughed at that, which was followed by a decidedly unladylike snort. She covered her mouth quickly.

"My governess keeps telling me I have to *not* laugh if I'm

going to laugh like that—but it's too funny, you thinking I'm Sarah!"

Once given the benefit of a longer look, Jackson recognized the blonde curls down the back and slightly shorter dress style that exemplified youth. And he recognized the dimples that had been ever present on the child Amanda shining forth on the cheeks of the young lady in front of him.

"Well, you'll have to forgive me, Miss Amanda," he teased as he gave a smart bow. "The last time I saw you, you barely reached my waist. I didn't expect anyone quite so tall."

Amanda immediately hunched her shoulders, trying to make herself smaller. "I can't help it," she said mournfully. "Mother is afraid I'll be taller than any gentleman who might wish to dance with me. Miss Pritchett—my governess, you know—has recommended they restrict my food so I stop growing."

Jack refrained from shaking his head. Talking to females—especially fifteen-year-old ones—was always trickier than one expected.

"Well, I still have some inches on you, so I suspect you should feel safe to keep eating for a few weeks or so."

Amanda giggled and slowly her shoulders came back up to her full (remarkable) height.

"What brings you to visit?" Amanda asked, as she waved at the butler, who had magically reappeared and seemed to be eyeing Jack's trunk with distaste. "Take that to one of the guest rooms, please, Dalton," she instructed before a quizzical look crossed her brow. "Whichever one my mother would say. You are staying, aren't you?" She turned her gaze to Jackson.

"Your mother wrote me, and asked me to do so," Jackson replied.

"She did?" she replied, then shook her head, making her curls bounce. "I wonder that she didn't tell me—but then again, no one tells me anything anymore."

"Anymore?" he replied as he offered Amanda his arm,

which she took with girlish joy. They moved with absolutely no purpose whatsoever to the drawing room.

The first and indeed only thing that he noticed in the drawing room was the overwhelming amount of flower bouquets, of every variety, on every surface.

If Amanda had been wearing mourning clothes, he would have thought Whigby was right and there had been a funeral.

"Ever since *the Event*, everyone gets very quiet when I come into the room. I saw my mother elbow my father in the stomach when they thought I *finally* started talking about something interesting!"

The Event. The importance with which Amanda imbued those words made Jackson pause. Perhaps it was the disappointment Lady Forrester gave vague reference to in her letter.

"And then, when we came to town again," Amanda continued blithely, "or, more accurately, after everything changed, everyone's been too busy to think of telling me what on earth is going on!"

Jackson followed Amanda's conversation as best he could. Again, he could hear the emphasis she gave the words "everything changed." Talking to teenagers was like learning a new language, and Jack had to be careful to pick up on the cues. Finally, he asked, "So you don't know why there are a half dozen gentlemen loitering on your doorstep?"

"Oh, them." Amanda rolled her eyes. "They're *always* there. You would think they would take the hint, but panting after Sarah is something of a badge of honor, I gather."

"Panting after Sarah?"

"Mama likes to think I don't know of course, but Bridget constantly grumbles about how Sarah's swains have made it so she can't even get in our front door, and they should be shot as trespassers. But then Mama says 'what a thing to say!' and Lady Phillippa says 'it would certainly make the papers,' but she says it like making the papers is a *good* thing." Amanda paused long enough to ring for tea, frown quickly, and then smile again. "But maybe it is a good thing, because Bridget has *never* been mentioned, and I don't think she likes it. But enough about all that, I want to hear about you! You're so tan—were you in the West Indies? The East Indies?" She practically tore his arm off she clutched him so tightly in her excitement. "Did you meet with any pirates?!"

Before Jack could answer—or even realize that Amanda had stopped her monologue and begun asking questions—a commotion could be heard in the hall they had just vacated for the comfort of the drawing room.

It was the sound of a half dozen lovesick swains making their unhappiness known as feminine voices uttered sweet regrets . . . followed by a quick slam of the door.

"I'm telling you, we should shoot them." An acidic young lady's voice pierced the drawing room door.

"Oh, Bridget, it's sweet," came another voice, this one lighter, more relaxed.

"Besides, Viscount Threshing is out there. Terribly bad form to shoot a viscount," came another female voice, this one soft and yet authoritative.

"Well, I cannot help but be glad that the afternoon is over—driving in the park is meant to be relaxing!" This voice he knew, Jack thought with a smile. It was undeniably Lady Forrester's. He and Amanda made a move to the door, edging it open wider, to peer out into the hall.

There he was met with the sight of four colorful peacocks, doffing hats and gloves and spencers and packages to a number of mute ladies maids, in a mad whirl of movement and color that blinded the audience to little else.

But as the layers were shed, and four ladies emerged, their conversation did not stop, and Jack found his eye drawn automatically to the form of the golden blonde in a light blue dress.

She was stunning, elegant . . . but cool. Frighteningly so, as if the world were on her string and she hadn't decided yet whether or not to cut it.

"That's Lady Phillippa Worth," Amanda whispered in his

ear. "Everyone says she's the queen of society, but I don't think the actual queen would like to hear them say that."

Ah, that must mean that the grumbling brunette in green was Bridget (indeed, he would have recognized Bridget's freckles anywhere—as he did her dark curls, which matched Amanda's lighter ones), and the tall blonde in the smart violet was Sarah.

Even though they stood in full view at the drawing room door, they had yet to be noticed. The women were too invested in their own conversation. It allowed Jackson the opportunity to observe his fill.

He paid particular attention to the one in violet. Her face had turned out very angular, and she was quite polished. Funny, he never thought of Sarah as city polished. Strangely, Sarah didn't seem to be suffering from an extreme disappointment. Stranger still, she was the only one who did not remove her spencer and hat—in fact, she waved the footman away when he came to take them from her.

Surely he would have contemplated further—surely he would have figured it out . . . but at that moment, the lady in blue turned and Jackson saw her full face. And he lost his breath. She had a face made for whimsy, for mischief. But it had been schooled—or perhaps tricked, with rouge or powder or other women's secrets—into an expression of haughty superiority.

But . . . there was something familiar about those green eyes . . .

"Really, Bridget," the one in blue—Lady Phillippa—said, as she turned to admire herself in one of the foyer's mirrors, "you shoot one of those gentlemen, you could very well be shooting your future husband, and then where would you be?"

That face full of freckles came up, a hot anger burning across her cheeks.

"I'll never marry a man who mooned after you, thank you very much."

A pretty pout crossed the taller girl's reflection. "You may not have that choice," she said sweetly. Too sweetly. Jackson couldn't help but feel a little for Bridget as she huffed past the other women and stomped up the stairs.

But then . . . why would Bridget be so rude to a guest? And why would Lady Phillippa retaliate so?

"Well, I should be going!" said the lady in violet—obviously not Sarah, if she was leaving—as she took a few of the parcels out of the pile that had amassed in the hall. Hers, presumably. "I will be seeing you at the Langstons' card party this evening, yes?"

"Will Sir Langston let us play Vinght-Un, not just boring old whist?" the blue-clad Lady Phillippa asked to her reflection in the mirror.

"It is the only reason we shall deign to attend," the violet one responded with air kisses, followed by prolonged good-byes.

"Amanda, who is the woman in the purple?" Jackson asked in a low whisper, trying not to attract attention.

"I told you, that's Lady Phillippa Worth!" Amanda explained. "Look, she's almost as tall as me. Isn't her gown exquisite? When I'm of age, I'm going to wear a gown in just that color."

But Jackson didn't hear anything else. He was dumbstruck, because if the lady in purple was Lady Phillippa, the queen of society, that meant the one in blue, with the face made for mischief but schooled into snobbishness, who was so absorbed in her reflection she didn't notice the way she wielded power—or more likely, didn't care—

"Sarah, you should be kinder in how you speak to your sister," Lady Forrester chided.

The one with the familiar green eyes . . .

"I'm sorry, Mother," the one in blue replied, "but I was merely stating the truth. If she is determined to be unhappy with life, then nothing I say or do will change that." Then she smiled brightly and turned from the mirror, her reflection having finally met with approval. "Now, we simply have to find a dress in my wardrobe to go with this reticule we purchased—I insist on using it this evening for my Vinght-Un winnings!"

Thus Lady Forrester was successfully diverted, and took her daughter's arm to begin a chatty stroll up the stairs to prepare for the evening's festivities.

"See?" Amanda said, a little sadly, as they watched their retreating forms. "I told you they don't realize I'm in the room sometimes."

Jack could only nod. His mind was too consumed by one topic: that even though he was proven wrong, there was no way that beautiful, snobbish, mean creature was the Miss Sarah Forrester that he had known.

Or, at least, that he'd thought he'd known.